HEART BREAK HERO

JACKIE WALKER

Editor: Mindy Root
Proofreading by: VB Proofreads
Cover Design: Kim Bailey of Bailey Cover Boutique
Photographer: Wander Aguiar
Cover Model: Dane D.

For content/trigger warnings, please visit
www.authorjackiewalker.com
or scan this QR Code:

Dedication

This book is dedicated to my son and his delightfully beautiful mind. You're a constant inspiration for me. I hope you'll find someone who loves you *for* your quirks, not despite them.

When you're older.

Much older.

This book is also dedicated to all the awkward gals out there, and all the neuro-divergent people who don't fit into society's definition of normal. Be you. Be perfectly imperfect.

Prologue

Sue

Braless and holding warm poop.

That's me right now. I'm also wearing zero makeup, and a rat's nest resides where my hair should be.

Yep. Keeping it classy, as always.

My nips poke through the thin fabric of my tank top like they're trying to wave down passing cars. My eldest brother's dog just did her morning business, and like the obedient dog sitter I am, I scoop it up with a plastic bag, then struggle to keep hold of her leash as I twist a knot into the top of it. All while trying to keep from spilling my coffee and avoid looking like a total fool in front of this insanely handsome stranger — who incidentally looks like he jumped out of a *Sons of Anarchy* episode.

Oh, did I forget to mention that a burly hunk of a man is watching me with the intensity of a forensic examiner at a crime scene? Because that's totally happening right now.

Perfect time for me to be wearing jammies, resembling the crypt keeper, and probably not smelling much better considering what I'm holding.

I didn't expect anyone to be outside this early, especially since I don't live in a heavily populated area. It's just a simple rental home off the beaten path.

Yet, for some reason, I have an audience of one this morning.

He's sitting in a black SUV at the edge of my property. I can tell how fiercely he's studying me despite how he keeps nonchalantly glancing away. Not exactly sure why he tries for nonchalance when there is nowhere to hide, and it's obvious he's watching me.

But why is he here?

Here I am, in all my nipped-out glory, with the hair of a madwoman and a bag of dog shite dangling from my hand. Not exactly the best time to meet new people; not that there's ever a good time for... *people-ing*.

It's just another day in the life of Sue O'Malley — the world's most awkward gal.

The only thing that would worsen the situation is if the dog decided to dart away and drag me through her fecal matter. Thankfully, that'll never happen because this dog is the fecking *best*.

I absolutely love looking after her, and fortunately, it's been happening more often lately since my brother has been staying over at his girlfriend's house so much. Ahsoka is the best dog in the free world, hands down. And as you can tell by her name, Nick's a huge fan of Star Wars. Despite being an Australian Shepherd — typically a high-energy breed — she's quite calm. And so very well-behaved. I guess that stands to reason, given my brother is a dog trainer. He's also my boss, but that's not important right now.

What *is* important?

Figuring out why I'm being watched so closely by the sexy bearded-wonder over there.

Oh crap, crap, *crap* — and I'm not referring to the bag of dung in my hand — he's getting out of his car and coming this way.

Oh hell!

What should I do? Do I run? Try to make it back inside before he gets too close?

He's already so close, barely ten feet away, and I'm not all that fast. I'm wearing flip-flops, not cross-trainers. I'd probably trip and fall flat on my face if I tried to make a break for it.

Maybe it's because I have Ahsoka beside me, or it could be the intelligent portion of my brain — the part that tells me how to handle dangerous situations — hasn't woken up yet, but something tells me to just stay put. So, I do.

His boots crunch on the acorns in my driveway with each step. Ahsoka tugs slightly on the leash as she takes a step in his direction, but her body positioning is somewhat defensive, like she's protecting me. Such a sweet baby.

"It's okay, girl," I tell her softly.

Crunch. Crunch.

The handsome stranger inches closer, now only a few feet from me.

2

Jaysus, Joseph, and Mary! This guy is as tall and wide as a linebacker, and he's got to be the most ridiculously striking man I've ever seen in person.

Virility is practically wafting off him. My nipples sharpen impossibly harder as he comes to a stop, reminding me I'm without my customary boob armor. Instinctively, one arm comes up to shield my nips from his view. I try to make it look like a natural pose, but the fact that I'm holding coffee with this hand has made accomplishing this feat infinitely more difficult. It probably looks like I'm trying to give the invisible friend beside me a sip of my morning brew.

Feck it to heck! Why do I have to be so awkward?

He slides his sunglasses off his face, and a lump forms in my throat, which I force down with a tight swallow. Blood rushes, heating my cheeks.

Remember when I said he was handsome? Yeah, don't listen to me because I was wrong. He is *beyond* handsome.

He's handsome on steroids.

Greek god-level handsome — or some type of god — he's certainly reminiscent of *some* deity. He's also got a real bad-boy vibe happening with the tattoos peeking out of his dress shirt. His eyes have sparkly flecks in them that reflect the sun so much you'd think they were photo-shopped. Despite the full beard, I can see the sharp lines of his jaw, and oh my heavens, I want to run my fingertips over it.

Shaking these strange thoughts off, I find my voice. "What are you doing here?"

His face softens into a lopsided grin. "My name is Leo." He bends his large head down a little in what I recognize as an old-fashioned show of courtesy.

I narrow my eyes at him because he didn't answer my question. "Okay, *Leo,* why are you watching me? It's rude to stare at people," I tell him curtly. Under my breath, I add, "Especially early in the morning when ladies might be out and about without their proper undergarments on."

He laughs. It's a deep, rich sound.

What is happening to my stomach? It's clenching, but not like when I've had too many tacos. I don't think it's ever done this before.

"Sorry, Sue. Didn't mean to be rude. If you want to go inside to change, that's fine. I'll be here when you're done."

Well, this is odd — even for me.

Tilting my head to one side, I ask, "How do you know my name?"

That little part of my brain responsible for self-preservation wakes up, and I take a step back.

His palms non-threateningly raise out in front of him. "Don't worry. I'm not going to hurt you. I was sent here to look after you. But I just thought you might want to get changed since you're concerned about your... um... modesty." He looks away while motioning at my chest area.

I take the opportunity to study him once more, noticing the redness of his cheeks and how his eyes are searching around the front yard, studiously avoiding my all-you-can-see stiff nipple buffet.

"Seems pointless to change now, doesn't it? I mean, you've already seen me looking like an ugly bridge troll."

He scoffs and meets my gaze. "You look nothing like a bridge troll. You look... nice." He seems to bite back his words, and his cheeks redden even darker.

His blue eyes are staring directly into mine, and damn if that doesn't make my head spin. I break away from his locked gaze quickly because, as a general rule, intense eye contact and I aren't on good terms.

And this guy is kind of intense.

For whatever reason, I find myself looking back at him a moment later, craving another shot of his sparkling eyes. This time, I see something else hidden behind them — gentleness.

Okay, now it's not *just* my stomach clenching. It's happening in a slightly lower part of my anatomy. And I'm quite certain *that's* never happened before. I make a note to look up potential causes of vaginal clenching later, although I suspect I'm looking directly into the face of the reason.

"Who sent you to look after me? And why?" I raise my chin, trying to infuse some confidence into my shaky words.

"I'm with Redleg Security, and I was sent here by Ms. Amos and your brother Nick."

"Nick sent you?" That's strange. Why would my brother send a security guard to my house early in the morning? I know he thinks I'm a child, but this is absurd.

"Well, in a roundabout way. I'm not sure what else I'm permitted to say, so maybe you should contact him."

Well, that's entirely unhelpful. "Very well. I'll just go and do that, then."

Before I can walk away, he asks, "Has anyone approached you in the last few days? Any sketchy characters following you? Have you seen anything unusual?"

"You mean besides you?"

Although I wasn't trying to be funny, he laughs again. Shit, what is happening to my stomach? Every time he smiles or laughs, it feels like it's flipping around. My hand pulls close to my mid-section in an attempt to calm the rising storm inside, but when the bag of poop brushes against my abdomen, I cringe in disgust and push it back out in front of me.

"Yes, besides me," he finally replies.

His eye contact is unnerving, so I glance at my feet. Unsurprisingly, my toes are lifting in my flip-flops, and I'm nervously rocking on my heels.

Breathe, Sue. Just breathe.

Nick sent this man here for me, and he would never do anything to endanger me. Of all my siblings, Nick is the most protective. However, like all my siblings, he can be a bit of a trickster.

Ah, maybe that's it!

"Is this a practical joke? Because Nick knows I don't usually understand the humor in those. You might as well just tell me now if that's the case."

"Not a joke, ma'am. Just go call your brother or Ms. Amos."

"Fine. I will. But I'll be watching you, Leo." I remove my arm from my breastages and lift two fingers from the edge of my coffee cup, carefully point them at my eyes, and then flip them outward to his. I've seen my brothers do this movement before — minus the coffee cup — and they always get a laugh. And I'd love to make this big hunk laugh one more time before I take my mobile freak show back inside, where I'll happily stay for the entirety of the day, save for a few times when Ahsoka needs exercising.

Fortunately, my attempt at physical humor is rewarded, and a deep rumble comes from his chest, followed by the briefest flash of a smile revealing brilliant white teeth.

My knees quiver, and my nipples pebble again, so I wrap my arm back across my chest to shield them from his view.

I search my memory banks to determine an appropriate method for ending this interaction but come up empty. I don't think I've ever been told or shown how to handle this type of situation. I'm going to have to wing it.

Shit.

I hate winging it because I always make it so fecking awkward. Although, I'm not sure how things could get more awkward than they are right now, given my bridge troll appearance and all.

A handshake. That's probably a safe way to move on. Yes. I'll shake his hand and go.

"It was a pleasure to meet you, Leo. My name is Sue, but you already know that." I reach my right hand out, but since it's holding a coffee cup, I quickly switch to my non-dominant hand and jut it brusquely instead.

And that's when things go from bad to worse.

Apparently, I never finished tying off the bag of Ahsoka's waste when I was staring at Leo — who was also staring at me. The damn bag decides now is the perfect time to unravel and fling droplets of its contents in the same direction and force that my hand was moving.

So, to recap, actual dog shit is flung directly into Leo's chest.

I just threw dog shit on this handsome man's immaculately clean dress shirt.

What the fuck is wrong with me?

"Oh my God! I'm so sorry! I didn't mean to... I'm such a... Oh gosh." My eyes move frantically from his freshly splattered chest to his beautiful eyes and back down at least seventeen times. Possibly eighteen.

"Oh, well, *shit*!" he deadpans, then meets my eyes.

And when he does, we both laugh.

Together.

Doubled over in my driveway. I laugh. He laughs. We both just laugh and laugh.

And that's how I met Leo Mason.

Chapter One

Here's looking at you, kid

A few weeks later

Leo

With a tight fist, I close the door behind me. My chest expands as I force a deep inhale, then blow it out as if I'm trying to expel all my feelings at the same time.

The job is over, and there is nothing left for me here.

I don't belong in this house.

Damn sure don't belong with her.

She's safe now. I did my job and did it well. I should be relieved to move on. After all, no one got hurt, and the bad guy is where he belongs... behind bars. Mission accomplished. That's our goal with every single client. And that's exactly what she is.

A client.

Nothing more, nothing less. And that's all she can ever be to me — a job.

One that was completed successfully. Now, her life can return to normal. It's time to move on to my next assignment. Someone else needs my protection. Another douchebag is probably somewhere out there wreaking havoc. And it's my job to stop them.

Everything is squared away, as it should be.

So why does it feel like an invisible hand is wrapped around my throat, squeezing my windpipe?

A moment ago, when I told her goodbye, it took all the strength I had to deny her request to *call her later*. Such a simple request, yet granting it would lead her on. And I've already done too much of that over the last few weeks — all those longing glances and lingering touches. They were liberties I shouldn't have taken, but I was too weak to resist. Not anymore, though.

Yeah, it's best to make a clean break now before either of us gets attached.

I was only here to protect her. Not to be her friend — and certainly not anything more.

I choke out another breath as I attempt to quell the stabbing pain that's threatening to break my resolve, and I focus all my energy on squashing the instinct to turn right back around, pull her into my arms, and never let her go. To kiss those full lips as I hold her soft, lush frame firmly against my body. To keep her warm and safe. To shield her from all that haunts her — all the demons hidden behind her azure eyes.

"Leo, wait," her melodic voice calls out, halting me in my tracks not even two steps away from the front porch.

My spine stiffens as I turn slowly and pray I don't see the pain written on her angelic face. But those prayers will go unanswered because it's not only pain I see there — it's anguish and longing.

The same feelings are reflected in my own soul.

Seeing her delicate face in such distress is crushing me but from the inside out.

"What?" I ask.

My clipped tone knocks her back a step. I'm usually so soft-spoken with her, but I can't do that now. I need to be firm. Hard. Channel my resolve.

She juts her chin defiantly. "That's it? That's all you're going to say?"

She thinks she's weak, but she's so brave, and in moments like this, it really shows.

I grit my teeth. "What else do you want me to say, kid? I need to be at my next detail across town in thirty minutes. I just stopped by to say goodbye in person." My voice sounds cold and unyielding — almost foreign to my own ears.

Her face is screwed up tight in confusion. "I guess I just thought..." She trails off, biting her lip.

Uncharacteristically, her eye contact is unwavering, piercing straight to my soul. It makes what I'm about to say even harder.

Fuck. I don't want to do this. I wish I didn't have to.

With my voice mocking and dismissive, I tsk, "You thought what? That I'd ask you out on a date? I'd come pick you up and take you out to dinner or maybe to a movie where we'd share popcorn and hold hands? We could do another family meal at your folks' house, but this time, I wouldn't be there because I was being paid to protect you?"

Narrowing my eyes, I tilt my head to one side and cut her a glance so cold it could freeze lava.

Her gaze falls to the pavement as she sucks in a deep breath, then releases a shaky exhale.

Reminding her that I've been contracted to be at her side these few weeks is a low blow, given how close we've become during our time together.

Clearly, my harsh words have the intended effect on her, but each mocking word I speak flays another layer of my battered heart. The thought of hurting her is abhorrent to me, but it must be done.

Sue O'Malley is more than just a job to me. Hell, I would have been by her side around the clock to make sure she was safe even if I wasn't on the payroll. But now that the danger is gone, I need to go.

She finally glances back up at me, and her face is wrought with insecurity. My eyes both beg and challenge her to drop it and let me go. If she fights me, I'm not sure I'll be strong enough to walk away. I'm already wavering. And I have to leave her behind today. I need to end this... whatever *this* is.

I fucking feel like I'm breaking up with her, even though we were never together as a couple. It's been some sort of whirlwind, with a connection stronger than I've ever felt.

"Never mind. I see it doesn't matter what I thought," she responds, her voice laced with sadness, and I can see her physically withdrawing back into her shell of safety as her shoulders hunch and her chin drops.

Fuck. A knot forms in my stomach.

Rubbing the back of my neck, I remind myself it's better to hurt her a little now than drag her any further into my orbit. If she were mine — not just my client, but *my woman* — she'd be miserable for so many reasons. I can't let that happen.

Scratch that.

I won't.

She's too fragile. Too pure. And so damn young.

Her whole life is ahead of her; a world of possibilities awaits. The worst thing I could do is taint her future with the stains of my past.

My boots are rooted to the driveway. I know I should go now. Walk away. Yet the thought of her in pain puts a sickening taste in my mouth. Maybe I can soften the blow enough to leave on better terms.

"Listen," I start, my voice softer this time. "It's nothing personal, but there's no future for us, kid."

Her eyes narrow at me, chin tilting upward again like a stubborn teenager about to throw a tantrum. It reminds me how much younger than me she is. That's why I always call her *kid*. Despite how enticing she is, that nickname serves to remind me of our ten-year difference. A repeated warning to keep my hands to myself — something I needed more as the days went by, and her proximity made my cravings for her intensify to the point of pain. I've never felt a pull like that before. I doubt I will ever again.

She places her hands on her hips, holding my gaze. "A *kid*? Is that how you see me?"

I glance at my watch, then back at her, unsure of how to answer. Truthfully, I sure as hell don't see her that way.

She's all woman — from the swell of her breasts to her decadent curvy hips, thick thighs, and plump ass that's always begging for my hands. She might not be everyone's idea of beauty, but Sue is *my* definition of feminine perfection. When you add in her outwardly quiet demeanor, which serves to hide her wicked sense of humor, quick wit, loyal heart, and sharp tongue, you've got the total package. She might as well have been made for me. All the traits I crave — physically, intellectually, and emotionally — wrapped up in one irresistible woman.

But if I tell her that, it will only lead her on.

"Well, you *are* quite a bit younger than me." I shrug and hope she accepts this evasive answer.

Judging by the narrow slits of her eyes, she isn't buying my bullshit one bit. Just my fucking luck. I should've known better than to think she'd be pacified with those words.

I know it's too much to ask, but I wish I could leave here today without her hating me.

Approaching me slowly, she quirks a brow while holding my gaze and placing the flat of her palm against my chest. She's never maintained this much eye contact with me before, and fuck if that doesn't make me want her even more.

I inhale sharply as she invades my space, surrounding me with her sweet scent. And I let her because I'm greedy for her. It's a delicious torture to let her get this close while knowing I can't have her the way I want — naked and splayed out before me.

I always was a bit of a masochist, though.

She licks her lips before softly replying, "You don't look at me the way someone looks at a child."

Nail meet head.

To make matters worse, she's still looking me dead in the eyes. Fuck, I want her desperately. The longing settles in my balls, and they become so heavy I have to shift my stance.

"Sue, don't," I warn her, but my voice is lacking the harshness I used earlier.

She's breaking me down, bit by bit. How the hell does she do this to me? As a former Army Ranger, I've been taught to withstand torture — actual torture — without breaking. But this innocent woman can make me fold with a simple glance.

She tries for playful. "But you promised me a ride on your motorcycle. I never took you for a liar."

I can tell by the way she's trailing her fingertips across my pecs that she knows her effect on me... well, she suspects it. And this is a test. Sue always did like her little experiments in human interaction, as she called it.

I squeeze my eyes shut and try to shove away the memory of how the pink tints her cheeks when she looks at me — *really* looks at me. It's like she sees me, and I sure as fuck see her.

For a moment, with my eyes still closed, I imagine what it would be like to let myself give in and finally kiss her. To feel her breasts pressed up against my chest. To ease my hand around her neck and command her mouth. The way she'd taste. What her soft moans would sound like.

As my dick starts to stiffen, I immediately lock those forbidden thoughts away in a vault in the back of my mind — never letting them see the light of day again. No good can come from thinking like that because Sue and I aren't meant to be.

"Susie, I know I said I would take you for a ride, but I no longer think it's a good idea, I just —"

She cuts me off. "I might not know a lot about people, Leo, but I know when I'm being lied to." Despite the strong words she's using, her confidence starts to waver, and her eyes drift away from mine, glancing at my lips briefly before falling to the ground. I notice her throat bob as she swallows.

Softer this time, she says, "I know you feel something for me, but I don't understand why you're fighting it."

Seeing she is far more insightful than I'd hoped she'd be, I grit my teeth as I go in for the kill. I'm going to have to make this sting a little.

I hate myself right now.

Hate my past.

Hate that it follows me.

Hate that I can't be the man she thinks I am.

It's for her own good, I remind myself, but the thought does very little to ease the deep ache in the empty cavern of my chest.

Drawing this out any further is making us both needlessly suffer.

"It's adorable you think so, kid. You're sweet, but we'd never work. Just look at the two of us for a minute. It's not like you've got anything special that I *can't* get elsewhere." I punctuate my dig with a condescending wink before doing an about-face. I can't stick around and see what those words will do to her. Even the bravest of heroes have cowardly moments, and this is mine.

The sound of her sharp gasp reaches my ears over the chirp of birds, the crunch of acorns under my boots, and the whiz of a passing car. I try to block out everything but the din of the neighborhood as I get in my company-issued SUV and start the engine. My pulse thrums loudly, and I force down a knot in my throat.

I came here to say goodbye, and I did that.

It's time to move on.

Without looking in the rearview mirror, I shift into gear and pull out of her driveway. And I leave Sue standing alone in her front yard, where she can remain *safely* out of my life.

Forever.

Chapter Two

Quick, where's the eye bleach?

Six Months Later

Sue

My eyes. My poor, sweet, innocent eyes.

They'll never be the same.

Hell! Forget my eyes; *I'll* never be the same after witnessing that hideousness.

Where's the eye bleach?

"Why do you look like that?" Nick asks, narrowing his eyes at me.

I set my purse down on the table, along with my venti caramel frappuccino — my Saturday morning indulgence — and shake my hands out in front of me like I'm frantically trying to dry wet nail polish.

Of course, I'm not, since my nails are plain and boring, like always.

I'm just trying to shake off the image that will forever be branded in my mind.

The *horror*.

After exhaling dramatically and dropping my hands, I face my brother and briefly hold eye contact for two point three seconds. It's the perfect amount of eye contact not to be considered rude or creepy.

With the requisite eye contact out of the way, I calmly reply, "Peach leggings."

I emphasize the statement by raising my shoulders to my ears and making a gagging motion with a pointed index finger into my open mouth.

"Peach leggings?" he parrots, clearly confused by either my vague statement or by my entire state of being. Or maybe by both.

Not that I can blame him. I'm often confusing to people.

"Yes! Why are they not illegal?" I stick my arms out to my sides, palms facing the ceiling.

I'm still idly wondering why eye bleach isn't a thing. If it is a thing, why haven't I heard of it? A product like that could come in handy in so many cringey situations.

Nick's eyes travel from one side of the room to the other, likely looking for some supporting details to help him unravel the mystery I've presented to him. "I have no answer for you, Susie Q. In fact, I have no idea what you're talking about. Is this some new internet trend thing? Are you filming me for a Tic Tac video?" He squints one eye and wrinkles his nose while trying to hold in a laugh.

My freaking brother thinks he's hilarious, and he knows it's TikTok. He's always teasing me about being part of the internet-raised generation. But that's what I get for being the youngest of seven kids.

And yes, you heard me right. I'm one of *seven* kids.

My parents didn't care much for birth control, I suppose. Irish Catholics *do be breeding*, as they say.

Nick and I are separated by twenty years, with him being the oldest at forty-six to my twenty-six. For all intents and purposes, he's a lot like my second father.

"No, ya sack of gobshite! This isn't a trend thing; it's a common courtesy thing. What is wrong with our city council and state legislature? This crime against nature needs to be addressed promptly. Think of the innocent children who might be subjected to the atrocity of which I personally suffered this morning," I heave, letting my muddled Irish accent slip out a bit.

I'm not as smooth with the accent as my brothers. We were all raised here in Florida, but our parents speak with the full brogue of our ancestral homeland.

My brothers can deftly whip out their accents at a moment's notice and make it sound like freshly churned butter melting on hot toast, but when I try to sound charming, it comes out more like a frozen tub of generic margarine falling off the counter and shattering the tile floor. In other words, not graceful at all.

But I digress. Let's focus on one troubling thought at a time, shall we?

And this moment's focus is peach leggings. *Shudder.*

Using my peripheral vision, I see Nick turn fully away from his laptop, giving me his complete attention. Good manners dictate I return his gaze, but I hate doing that.

Even for people I love — in other words, my family, since who else will I ever love?

When I have to hold eye contact, my mind starts running through a million scenarios, and I get a little twitchy. Thoughts start jumbling like...

Is this long enough? Do I have something on my face? Why are eyebrows a thing? What purpose do they serve? Which part of the eye should I focus on? The pupil? The eyelid? The iris? Should I look at the right or left eye? Side note: it's impossible to look at both — believe me, I've tried. Are they looking at my pupil or iris? Did I turn off the stove this morning? Okay, that's got to be enough eye contact for one lifetime, right? Right?

Nick breaks my train of thought by asking, "Sue, did you see someone in peach leggings this morning?"

I go about unpacking my laptop and setting up my temporary workstation on Nick's dining room table while I try to convey the seriousness of the matter.

"Yes! It was horrible, Nicky. My eyes will never recover. I was at Starbucks waiting for my drink when I saw something troubling out of the corner of my eye." A heavy breath escapes as the memory hurdles across the mental barrier I tried to erect to keep it at bay.

I continue my rambling at a brisk pace, "I couldn't be sure, but it appeared to be a woman who was naked from the waist down. Although I kept my vision trained on the counter in front of me, I could see long, dark hair, a colorful blouse, and shoes — but then just legs between her blouse and shoes! *Legs*, Nicky! Covered with skin instead of some type of pant-based fabric. And here she was, just breezing in to get some coffee like it was no big deal that she forgot to finish dressing before she decided to get her caffeine fix." I raise my index finger and continue, "Or so I thought."

My brother's mouth quirks into a grin, and he purses his lips like he's about to speak, but I'm not done.

I wave him off and press on with my story. "I had an internal debate about whether I should look. At first, I was like, maybe I should respect her privacy and not look. Then I thought, if she gives two shites about her modesty, why on earth is she half-naked in public? And since she doesn't care, then why should I? But I don't want to see a naked lady. Not my kink. So I did the logical thing and ran through statistical probabilities of her actually being naked or a simple trick of lighting — like an optical illusion. Once I determined the odds of her forgetting to don pants were well below 3 percent, I decided I needed to look — you know, for science."

"And lo and behold, she was in peach leggings," he finishes for me, clearly amused by my ramblings, as evidenced by the shaking of his shoulders and the laughter hidden in his tone.

"Yes! Peach leggings. *Peach*! Nick, it's the color of flesh for many people — including her! And peach leggings hide nothing. *Nothing*, Nicky. I saw everything. She might as well have been nude."

"Was she hot?"

My shoulders fall as my eyes search the ceiling for strength. "Gross, man. Ew! And *no*, she was not hot. She was easily in her fifties, and the years had not been kind to her. I could see every ripple, dimple, and divot — of which there were plenty. Now, to be fair, it's not like I've got the best body, and by no means am I fat-shaming. That'd be like the pot calling the kettle black. But there are certain things you do *not* do — regardless of your size. And peach leggings are at the top of that list. The very top. No! No! No! Just no! Argh! My eyes!"

I rub my eyes again as if I could scrub the image from my retinas. Nick is now full-on laughing at my dramatics.

Through chuckles, he asks, "Is it safe to assume you'll be driving the long way from now on to hit the Starbucks with a drive-thru?"

"That's a duh, Nicky. I'm never going back there again. I might avoid the street altogether."

I catch my breath as we both stop laughing, then I cut my eyes over at him and add, "And why the hell are you asking if she was hot? Don't make me tell Millie on you!"

Millie is his new wife. They've been married for about a month. She's a take-no-shit kind of gal, and I don't think she'd appreciate her husband scoping out other ladies.

"She wouldn't care. In fact, when we go out, she points out hot chicks for me to look at. Of course, I don't look, but she wouldn't care if I did. Just part of her charm."

I feel my nose wrinkle at that little glimpse into their relationship. People are so perplexing.

Intrigued, I ask, "Do you point out hot guys to her?"

"Sometimes."

"And does she look?"

He chuckles. "Yes, she always looks and then comments on their hotness factor."

I quirk my head to the side as I study him carefully. "And that doesn't bother you or worry you?"

"Nope. Not at all."

"Why not? I mean..." I trail off, completely flabbergasted at this development. Why are they admiring other potential sexual partners when they're committed to each other? This isn't logical.

He stalls, taking a sip of his water. "Because she usually comments about their body or appearance in relation to mine. And she always makes it known how much hotter she thinks I am."

Oh, I think I see now.

"Is this sort of like a flirting game? You point out other guys to get her to compliment you. To make her focus on you in the end."

With his eyes to the ceiling, he wiggles his jaw and tilts his head from shoulder to shoulder a few times as if he's chewing over my assessment of his behavior. "Yes and no. I guess you could call it flirting, but I don't do it to get her to compare them to me." He pauses for a moment, then adds, "At least, I don't think so. Maybe it's subconscious." He shrugs as if it doesn't matter.

"Well, why would this be flirting if the purpose is to make her focus on other guys? I always thought it was meant to inspire lust in oneself, not in others."

"Honestly? I have no fecking idea. It's just something we started doing, and it makes us laugh. I think it's a way for us to acknowledge there are others out there, but then reaffirm our attraction and devotion to each other."

He takes another swig of water. "Why are we overanalyzing this again?"

Fair question.

"I don't know." My mind sorts through potential motivations, but I come up empty. "Just curious, I suppose."

"Let's get to work. We have a lot to do today, kid."

Ouch.

Did he have to call me *that* nickname? It reminds me of...

Nope. Forget it. He's gone and *never* coming back. There's no need to so much as think of his name.

And Nick's right; we do have a lot of work to do today. We've yet to review our financials for the month, and I have several new training requests to discuss with him.

Ever since Nick got married, he spends less time with me, and the administrative side of his dog training business tends to get pushed aside. I do quite a bit independently without his oversight, but we still need to sit down regularly so I can verify we're meeting his strategic goals.

It's his business, after all.

As his only employee, I do everything I can to ensure the success of Naughty Dogs Obedience Training, apart from actually training dogs. I leave that to my brother. However, Nick's determined to change that, much to my chagrin.

Clicking through my note tracking software, I pull up the pending requests I need to discuss with Nick.

"Okay, Pete Jenkinson from Clearwater Police Department is requesting some help with a new K9 they got a month ago. He said the dog is having some challenges they can't overcome with their usual methods. Interested?"

"Did he say what type of challenges?"

"Nope. It was an online request. Want me to get more details before you decide?"

"Nah. It's fine. I'll take it. Pete's a good guy. I've worked with him before. Set it up."

"Perfect." I make a note to schedule a consultation, then move through the list.

After a few minutes, we switch to reviewing the accounting details. When I ask about his recent business expenses, he hands me a stack of wadded-up receipts.

"Ask, and ye shall receive," he says with a shit-eating grin, embellishing his accent.

Fucker.

Not sure what I'm madder about — the stack of wrinkled paper he handed me or how he can wield the accent so much better than I can.

Probably a little of both.

"Gee, thanks," I say sarcastically as I take the garbled tree remains from him. At least I can dish sarcasm, even if I don't always catch it when it's thrown at me. I'm getting better at it, though.

Time to move to the next topic on the agenda. One I'm not looking forward to because I know what he's going to want me to do. It's not something I want to do.

And before you ask, *yes, I'm the type of girl who prepares an agenda for a simple meeting like this with my brother slash boss.*

I need my lists to keep us both on task, but it's mostly for me. I like lists in general, but especially when I'm with Nicky. It's too easy for us to get sidetracked with immature jokes or useless nonsense — usually started by an errant thought that pops into my ADHD-riddled brain. Nick always takes the bait, and the next thing you know, we're creating memes to send to our brothers and sister.

Lists are good.

Lists are our friends.

Lists mean order, and I like things orderly.

And did you see what just happened? I just took you down a rabbit hole, and you followed willingly. You're worse than Nick.

"Let's go over the thirty-day outlook together. It's really looking hectic," I tell him.

"I've noticed," he says while we both look at my screen where I've got the next month of appointments displayed.

"And depending on how much extra time Pete needs for the K9, this could get messy. I think you need to hire a part-time trainer, or else Millie is going to feel like a *single* newlywed."

"The evenings are the worst since that's when everyone wants to meet. I wish I could squeeze more hours in the day," he laments, his finger running over the screen.

"And don't forget. Winter is coming," I add in an ominous tone.

"Settle down, Jon Snow," he replies with a wink and a chuckle.

I smile, pleased he got my somewhat outdated reference. "Joke aside. The sunset will come earlier, and you'll lose an hour of evening training unless we can find a safe park with good lighting to hold sessions after dusk."

"I guess I can do more in-home stuff in the evening. That worked fairly well last winter."

"Okay, I'll start scheduling that way whenever practical. Might mean I have to switch in-home clients to the later slots. I can work on it. But still... you need more help."

He sits back and crosses his arms over his chest. I can feel the heat of his glare hit the side of my face. But I bite my lip and keep facing the screen, steadfastly ignoring him.

Please don't say it, Nick. Don't say it.

"It's time, Susie Q."

Shit. He said it.

"I'm sure I don't know what you're referring to," I lie, maintaining my gaze on the screen.

He keeps saying I'm ready to take on some of the easier clients, but I beg to differ. Doing so would lead to far too much human interaction. I mean, working with the dogs would be fine, and I agree I could handle that part. But if I had my own training clients, I'd have to speak with the humans.

In person.

Like... to their faces. *Ew.*

I don't mind talking to clients over the phone since there are still those dinosaurs who insist on speaking with someone instead of simply filling out our online request form. I've learned to handle talking on the phone without it bothering me. *Much*. But I'd much rather avoid dealing with people face-to-face if at all possible. Behind the scenes is much more my speed — less chance of me making things awkward on the phone.

"How about if you take Scooter Johnson, Puffy Rodriguez, and Louie Pierson? You can schedule them at the same time and location where I'm working with other dogs. If you have issues, I'm there to help. All three are following basic obedience programs, and they're already doing well. It's mostly maintenance and reinforcement at this point, with a few exceptions. What do you say?"

"How about I draft up a job posting and get it on Indeed by the end of the day?" I offer him a solution and a tight-lipped smile.

His silence sits heavy in the room until my eyes wander in his direction. When my gaze hits his, it looks like he's pitying me and comforting me at the same time. Shit. I hate it when he does that.

"Nick, I don't know. I..."

After a deep inhale, he softly says, "You can do this. I know you can, and I'll be right there with you. I know how much you love training the dogs. Don't let the human aspect hold you back. You've got this. I believe in you."

I feel my shoulders fall as my head rolls back. I've been preparing for this moment for a while, which is good because preparation is important. Without it, I often overreact and panic.

I just need to make my final decision.

"Can I have a day to decide?"

He smiles triumphantly like he thinks he's won.

"Yes! Let's revisit it tomorrow. But promise you won't let your self-doubt take over. Okay?"

"I promise. I'll give it some good thought. Maybe make a list of pros and cons."

Now his grin turns sad, his lips pinching in one corner of his mouth. He nods but adds, "I don't think you need to pro-con this one out. It's only three clients. Yes, it would help me tremendously, but more importantly, it would really be good for you. You shouldn't be alone so much."

I nod but remain silent, staring at the screen like it holds the answers.

Thankfully, Nick drops the topic, and we're able to meander through the rest of the list. He teases me a little here and there, and I do the same in return, lifting the mood. When all our business is done, he turns to read his email while I dig into mine.

My mind keeps wandering, though.

After a while, I notice I haven't been able to stop my toes from tapping inside my shoes. I think I've been doing it for the last hour. I usually start with my pinky toes and work my way toward my big toe and out again.

I was doing the same with my fingertips under the table by slowly tapping each one against my thumb from smallest to biggest, then back out again. These are what my psychologist refers to as self-soothing behaviors, and they're supposed to be helpful for my anxiety. I've been doing them for so long that when I get anxious, I just do them — often without realizing it, much like today.

But now that I'm aware of the motion, I'm consciously aware of my anxiety.

Why am I feeling anxious? It started before he brought up me taking Louie, Scooter, and Puffy — those are dog names, by the way. It's not like our clients are a bunch of cartoon characters.

I'm supposed to track down potential triggers to talk about with my therapist.

I didn't realize the peach leggings were bothersome enough to cause so much discomfort that I'd need to self-soothe. Mostly, I was just being silly. Although, it was somewhat horrifying and something I won't soon forget. But once I realized she was wearing pants, the entire encounter became humorous, and I wanted to make my brother laugh too. He's always worried about me and trying to cheer me up lately, so when I can make him laugh for a change, it feels good. *Normal.*

If there is such a thing.

There probably is a normal for other people, but not for me. Not anymore. Isn't it odd that the only time in my life I felt *right* or normal was when my life was in danger? That's how you know you're fucked up. The aforementioned ADHD is just the beginning of my issues.

The thought pushes me out of my denial at what is causing my toes and fingers to tap. It's because of him.

Leo.

I thought of him again. If I'm being honest with myself, that's when these anxious feelings started.

Reaching into my purse, I pull out my ratty spiral-bound notepad. When Nick referred to me by that cursed nickname, I felt my heart start racing like it was going to pound out of my chest. My breath became strained, and it occasionally felt like I was being sacked in my gut with a muted fist.

That's when the tapping began. I diligently flip to the right page and write down my entry.

Saturday, August 6 — Nick called me "kid," and I saw a woman in peach leggings. Noticed toe and finger tapping for at least an hour afterward. He also wants me to start training dogs, which I will say yes to.

It hasn't always been like this... the anxiety... not always this bad. After I graduated from college and started going to therapy regularly, it improved. Then my mental health tanked again after he... after Leo left me. But it was getting better again. *Finally*, the pain was lessening to the point I barely noticed it anymore.

Until I saw him again at Nick and Millie's wedding about a month ago.

He came with the rest of his Redleg Security friends who were assigned to our case. Twenty minutes of him sitting on the other side of the aisle a few rows back — and that's all it took to send me reeling backward.

And there Leo was, towering over most of them, making it even harder for me to pretend I didn't see him. Of course, he didn't talk to me or even wave in my direction. I knew he wouldn't — and that made it monumentally worse.

Yet, I know he was looking at me during the ceremony. I could sense his eyes burning my skin.

I could feel him in my soul or something.

Thankfully, he didn't stay for the reception. That would have been agony, and I don't think I would have made it to see my brother dance with his new bride or cut the cake.

As it was, seeing Leo at the ceremony, just from my peripheral vision, caused enough damage. It brought me right back to that day when he said goodbye and left me feeling like such a fool. The embarrassment I felt for practically throwing myself at him lives in my head rent-free.

On a stupid loop.

How could I have been so foolish?

As if someone like him could ever want someone like me. *Pathetic, Sue.*

It was nothing more than me misinterpreting body language and misreading what I thought were signs of attraction. At the end of the day, I was merely a job to him.

When the job was done, he left — taking that newfound sense of *normal* with him.

And now I'm alone again.

Well, as alone as one can be in a large Irish American family who all live in the same town. That includes working with my oldest brother, who treats me like I'm made of glass.

Speaking of... I guess Nick noticed me writing in my journal because he's stopped typing. He's watching me over the top of his screen.

Smiling, he asks, "Everything okay, Susie Q?" His voice is calm and warm.

"Yep. Just making a note of something I need to tell my therapist."

I used to conceal my therapy details from him, but he's not exactly one who likes to be left in the dark about things. It's best to answer him flatly, avoiding the inquisition.

"Want to talk about it? Anything I can help with?"

I think I'll try a joke to keep the mood light. "Did you figure out time travel yet so I can go back and stop past-Sue from embarrassing herself at every possible opportunity?"

Specifically, I'd like to travel to about six months ago when I made a humiliating pass at my former bodyguard.

He snaps and dips his hand. "Ah, shucks. Not yet. Still haven't cracked the design. Something is wrong with my flux capacitor, I think."

I wrinkle my nose and squint my eyes at him. "Your flux what now?"

He shakes his head in what appears to be disgust. "Did they teach you nothing at that fancy college?"

"I didn't take astrophysics, Nick. It was an art degree."

"I was kidding," he says, sounding put out. "The flux capacitor was from *Back to the Future*, the movie."

Huh. Well, that's a perplexing title.

"How can you go *back* to the future? Wouldn't you go forward to the future? I mean, it wouldn't be the future if it wasn't ahead of you, right? If it were in the back, then it'd be your past. That's a terrible title and an even worse premise for a film."

Nick shuts his laptop and heaves a weary sigh. "Forget it. I don't know why I try to talk to people of your generation. You have no culture."

"And the movies from your generation were dumb, old man." I cross my arms across my chest and add, "There. I said it. Someone had to."

He playfully tosses a wadded-up receipt at me. A smile tugs at my lips until a guffaw takes its place.

We laugh together, but soon he rises and places a kiss on my head. "Gotta go train a pooch, Susie Q. Stay as long as you like, but lock up when you go if Millie isn't back from her sister's house yet."

"You got it." I look up at him and smirk. "In fact, I think I'll enjoy your couch when I'm done working and hang out with your dogs for a little while. Maybe I'll even stay until Millie gets home, and we'll drink liquor and watch cheesy movies or a true crime docuseries while you're out making the bacon."

His lower lip rolls out. "Are you trying to make me jealous? Because it's totally working. I want to stay, have drinks, and hang out with my two favorite girls and my two favorite dogs."

I get up and playfully shove him toward the door. He really does need to leave, or he's going to be late. "Sorry. You have clients to see, dogs to train. It's a very busy and glamorous life."

As I shove him out the door, I notice a gray van parked down the street. Not sure why, but it looks familiar. It sort of sticks out in this neighborhood. Rusted with a mismatched back door. Not quite a work van, but not something you'd see in an upper middle-class area like this, either.

That's probably why I noticed it.

It's different — like me.

I shrug it off and close the door, locking it behind me.

Now, it's just me, my work, Ahsoka and Jekyll — two well-trained dogs — and all my scattered thoughts.

Chapter Three

Another day, another diva

Leo

"Here's the particulars. You sure you're up to leading the team?"

Big Al plops a folder on the conference room table in front of me, then puts his hands on his hips and stares me down, awaiting my answer.

I flip open the manila folder embossed with the Redleg Security logo on the cover and scan the contents.

Looks like the usual info we get on a new client. Name, age, address, occupation, known associates and immediate family members, tentative itinerary, photos, social media profiles, risk assessment basics, and details of any active threats or anticipated danger.

On my cursory scan of the details, this job seems straightforward. It's basically a quick cash grab for the company, carrying low risk and offering zero excitement. A week-long gig protecting a vacationing celebrity — some pop musician from Italy I've never heard of before — who has no active threats.

She'll be soaking up the Florida sunshine on the world-class beaches here in Clearwater. An entourage will be traveling with the pop princess, and they've planned an itinerary of debauchery and pampering.

Just the typical shit.

These celebrity protection gigs are the bread and butter of Redleg — a security company formed by my Army buddy Alan, or Big Al as he likes to be called, but we often just call him Boss. I've known him for over a decade, and he's saved my life more times than I can count. He's easily the person I respect most in this world, and I'm proud to call him my friend as well as my boss.

Biting the inside of my cheek, I twirl the tip of my short beard and feign interest in the dossier in front of me.

I nod in response to his question and meet his scrutinizing gaze. "Can I pick my team?"

He crosses his arms over his barrel chest as a grin lights his age-weathered face. "Three max. And no overtime unless a verified threat presents."

"Boss, come on." I crook my head to the side and hold my hands in front of me. "I need at least four on my team if this is going to be twenty-four-hour protection for seven straight days without overtime. For three, we can't do round-the-clock."

I can do it with three plus me, but I like to fuck with him. He expects it from me, and I don't want him thinking I'm getting soft.

He's already been taking it easy on me these last few months.

"Three and a half." I don't know why, but Big Al likes to make everything into a negotiation. He's been that way since I met him.

I make a show out of scrubbing my face and narrowing my eyes at him before caving. "Three and a half, twenty-four hours, and no overtime without a new threat. Deal."

"One other thing," he says with a raised eyebrow and pointed index finger.

This will either be good or a shit show — no in-between.

I can tell by the twinkle in this asshole's eye — and I call him that with the utmost respect. He lives for fucking with me. Hell, we both do. As we used to say in the Rangers, *WETSU — we eat this shit up.*

"I'm almost scared to ask, but what?"

"The new kid is part of your team, and you watch her closely to make sure she's ready to go. You need to be on her like white on rice. I want you to test her — really push her limits — and, hopefully, you can vouch for her readiness for solo work by the end of the week."

I'd rather shit in my hand and clap.

"Boss, seriously? That's the last thing I need. Anyone but her —"

"Are you questioning my orders with a valid argument or just crying to your mama?" he snaps, interrupting my whining.

I'm not usually one to question orders, and since he was my squad leader in the Rangers, objecting like this feels wrong deep down in my core.

But I *do not* want the new kid on my team.

Even if this is a cake mission, she's a hothead who's cocky as hell and fresh out of the sandbox. She thinks her shit smells like roses.

My chest caves inwardly as I stare him down and grit out, "Sorry, sir."

Although I've been out for seven years, the response is automatic. When a superior barks at you like that, you show some damn respect.

"Don't call me that. I work for a living, remember? Plus, we're not in the Rangers anymore. You can speak freely but can that whining bullshit."

"Roger that." I respond and force a steadying breath.

"Now, is there an actual reason you don't want Kri on your team? I never took you for a sexist pig."

"That's not it, Boss. You know me better than that."

We've got several female guards at Redleg — all of them former military, like the rest of us. Some were marines or sailors, and the rest were soldiers.

Working with females isn't a problem for me. I hold everyone to the same high standards, and the women hired by Big Al are the best of the best.

"Good, because she's damn qualified. Do you know how hard it is to get assigned to work with the fucking Deltas?"

"Yeah, I remember. And I'm sure she's competent, but it's just..." I trail off, not sure what my real problem is other than her attitude. That alone is not a reason to have her barred from my team.

He leans forward, all his commanding posture gone. Now he's just my friend and mentor instead of a hard ass. "Then what is it, Lionheart? Is this about —"

Flicking my palm up in his direction, I cut him off with my widened eyes and sharp inhale. Despite his playful use of my old Army nickname, *Leo the Lionheart*, I don't want to talk about her.

I can't.

The pain is still too fresh.

The wound, which was pulling itself closed one stitch at a time, was ripped wide open a few weeks ago at that damn wedding.

He sits back in his chair and props a leg over his knee.

"Talk to me," he commands softly. "You've seemed... *off* for a while now. It's like you're not yourself. Ever since the Amos stalker job."

His expression turns knowing.

He's leading me somewhere I'm not sure I want to go. I can't think about her without feeling a compulsive need to check her location on my phone. In fact, my hand is twitching to reach into my pocket to pull it out to make sure she's somewhere safe.

I'm ashamed to admit it, but I'm still monitoring Sue via the tracker I installed on her phone and the GPS I put on her car when I was assigned as her guard.

For six fucking months, I've checked in on her a few times a day.

Every day. Without fail.

I *need* to know she's okay.

Even though I can't have her, the need to protect her is equally strong as if she were mine. I keep waiting for it to dissipate, for the urge to pass.

But it hasn't yet.

I'm beginning to wonder if it ever will.

My hand fiddles with the edge of the manila folder while I contemplate my answer.

Without a response from me, Big Al continues with his speculation, trying to draw a reaction from me. "If it's not her, then is this about your sister? I know Kri resembles Samantha. Is it that?"

My jaw ticks at the mention of Sammy, and I twirl my pinky ring unconsciously. "No, that's not it, Boss."

Although Kri does look a little like my baby sister with her short blond hair and pixie nose, that's not what bothers me. In fact, I don't have a good reason.

"It's fine. I'll make it work. Kri's just a bit rough around the edges, and my patience for her type of hotdogging is lacking at the moment. It's my problem, though, not hers. I'll make do."

"Good. That's why you're my best guy."

He pauses and taps his fingers on the table.

"But are you sure you don't want to talk about..."

He raises his salt and pepper brows at me once more in a comforting gesture. "We've all been there, bud. My heart is no stranger to unrequited love. I'm here if you need to talk."

"It's fine. I've got it under control," I lie through my teeth, hating myself for being a coward and not being able to fess up to my internal struggle.

Unrequited love was not the problem, but it's funny that he thinks that to be the case. In a way, it proves my point that Sue deserves better than me.

Even Big Al knows she wouldn't be with someone who would bring her down the way I surely would.

"If you've got it under control, then do you want to explain why the equipment inventory shows our missing GPS tracker blipping a few times a day, often over on Brookside Avenue? Last I checked, it was assigned to you, and Sue O'Malley resides on Brookside."

Busted.

I feel my Adam's apple bob as I resign myself to the guilt and shame of being exposed.

"I won't make you stop tracking her because I assume you have an honorable reason for doing so. But I need to know if your head is focused on the people you're supposed to be protecting," he says, making this far too easy on me.

I deserve worse than what he's dishing out.

I wish he'd yell and rage at me. Maybe that would shake me out of this loop I'm stuck in — where I obsess over her safety and replay our every moment together in my mind to draw the tiniest bits of comfort. At least I'm able to say that for a time, Sue was mine.

Well, not really.

Not mine like I wanted her to be.

But at least I was responsible for her safety and able to exist in her world. It was close enough. Looking after her and spending hours talking about everything and nothing. Watching her paint and getting lost in the mesmerizing way she carried herself when she was engrossed in creating her art. Making up fake words that had us rolling with laughter. And treating her like the cherished prize she is.

Being with Sue felt... *right.*

Each day, I remind myself of those feelings. I cling to the fact that she's safe, and I consider myself lucky to have known her for the time I did.

That's all I can have.

I can't hold Big Al's perceptive eye contact, so I look away and stare at my hands, wringing them needlessly.

"I'm not stalking her, if that's what you think. I just need to know she's okay. I *need* her safe. And I occasionally check to make sure."

With his normally gruff voice coming across as soft and compassionate, he asks, "Why do you feel that need? Who is she to you?"

Isn't that the fucking question to end all questions?

She's everything to me, but she can never truly be anything to me.

"Something happened those weeks when I guarded her, Boss. She became..." I pause as I struggle to form the words. "*Important.* For some reason, I can't get her out of my head, and I feel responsible for her. It's like she's my girl, but I know she can't be mine. No matter how much I want her to be."

I put my head down. Regret and shame fill my soul in equal measure, and a morose chuckle shakes my chest. "Damn, that sounds pathetic. I can't explain it. We're connected somehow."

Reluctantly, I meet his eyes. He doesn't wear a mask of judgment — only one of stoic thoughtfulness.

"Leo, why don't you —"

I cut him off because I can't talk about this any more without breaking down. "Don't worry. When I'm on duty, I'm completely focused. The thing with Sue is under control."

She deserves better than me.

No matter how much I want her to be mine, I can't let that happen. Being with me would snuff out her light.

"I'll trust you with this. For now."

I glance up, and this time, I see compassion laced with pity reflecting in his intelligent eyes. He gives a slight nod, which I return in kind.

After a pregnant pause, he adds, "You've got to tell me if you need a break, okay? I appreciate all your long shifts and dedication to the safety of our clients — you know I do. But I also know you've had a rough few years. Don't hesitate for a second to tell me if you start to slip. If you can't concentrate on the client's safety, above all else, I need you to tell me. I'll give you the time off to handle whatever you need to handle, with no questions asked. Got it?"

"Copy that," I reply, then more softly add, "Thanks, Boss."

"No problem."

He leans his chair back and folds his hands behind his head. "Now, who the hell do you want on the team for Trixie Valentine's detail?"

Pop stars have the stupidest fucking names.

"I'll take Sawyer, obviously, and I've got Kri, per your request." I heave a sigh and pucker my lips at him, drawing one of those deep Big-Al trademark chuckles. "Shep can be my third full-time guy, and I guess I'll take Jonesy for part-time backup."

Big Al taps through a few screens on his tablet. "Schedule looks good for everybody but Jonesy. He's got vacation time for the end of the week. I'd rather not ask him to change it."

"Can I have him for the beginning of the week at least, and he can cover a few days off during the front half of the week for the rest of the team?"

"That I can do. I'll let them know they're with you this week. You can pull your team together this afternoon for a briefing. That'll give you time to review everything in the file and develop a coverage schedule. Sound good?"

"Works for me, Boss."

As soon as he gets up to take his leave, I pull out the phone and toggle to the tracking app with a slight tremble in my hand. Once the red dot reveals Sue is safely at her house, a feeling of lightness surrounds me. My shoulders sag, and a relieved breath escapes.

Looking at my watch, I send a quick text to my mother since she should be awake by now.

Me: Good morning, Ma. Everything okay today?

While waiting for her response, Big Al's words keep running through my mind: *Why do you feel that need? Who is she to you?*

Like it often does when I'm alone, my head pulls me back to those weeks when I was with Sue, and a memory comes to mind that perfectly answers Big Al's questions.

It was the moment everything changed for me.

"What are you painting today, kid?"

With all her painting supplies laid out on the table beside her, she stares at a blank canvas, tapping the end of her paintbrush against her lips.

Like most mornings, I join her in her in-home art studio because I like watching her work. I feel like a bit of a voyeur, but she doesn't mind.

In fact, she's told me her creativity improves when I'm watching. I'll try not to read too much into that.

I get the feeling Sue is alone a lot, and I don't think she likes it as much as she lets on. Despite the danger that brought me to her door a few weeks ago, I'm enjoying getting to know her, and the feeling seems to be mutual.

Tucking my dog-eared paperback in my lap, I set my full coffee cup on the desk beside my chair.

She looks over at me with a curious expression on her face. It's almost as if I can see her wheels turning with the mischievous sparkle in her eyes.

Damn. She's so cute.

I wish she weren't so young. And a client.

Her chin tucks to her chest as she pinches one eye shut. "What do you think about being my model?"

"Me?"

"Yes, you. I want to paint you, Leo, the giant bodyguard." A beaming smile lights her face, and something in my chest squeezes.

Before now, she's mostly done landscapes and a few household objects. There was also that abstract she did, combining all my favorite colors into streaks — blues, greens, and yellows. But I've never seen her paint a person before.

"Clothed?" I tease because I'm itching to see her reaction.

Honestly, I'm not sure if the attraction I feel is one-sided.

Sue's different from other girls, but not in a bad way.

To be frank, she's different in all the right ways. There's no artifice with her. What you see is what you get.

Something about the way she guards her emotions. There's depth behind those blue eyes, but she's also hesitant to let it show.

She fascinates me.

Her cheeks redden to an adorable shade of deep pink while she chews her bottom lip — one I'd very much like to taste. But I can't let myself do that.

She's a client, and I need to keep my damn mouth and hands to myself.

With a slight shrug, she finally responds, "Yes. With clothes on. I only want to paint your face."

Drawing my hand across my scruff, I ask, "This ugly mug? Why the hell would you want to do that?"

"It's a nice face. Good lines."

Her hand lifts to cup my cheek as she studies my face, and her fingertips graze the outside corner of my mouth.

Fuck. She's trying to kill me.

My cock is immediately on notice, but I close my eyes and will it to stand down.

"Uh-huh," I mutter, unable to hide my eye roll, but it makes her chuckle.

I like her laugh. Her smile. Her body. Her eyes when they twinkle.

Damn. I like a lot about this girl.

I put the paperback on the desk beside my coffee cup and rise.

"Fine. Where do you want me and my good lines?"

She claps her hands twice in front of her chest, and I cut my eyes in another direction. Thankfully, she's wearing her baggy coveralls, which hide some of her curves.

With that shy smile in full effect, she puts a stool in front of her canvas a few feet away.

"Here is fine." She taps the stool twice.

I take my seat and follow her instructions as she directs me into the perfect pose. I try not to lean in to her touch as she angles my chin with her hands.

Her skin is soft and warm. Damn, I want to feel more of it. Is it smooth and silky like that everywhere? Her thighs? Her stomach? Her neck?

Client, client, client, I remind myself.

Heaving a deep sigh, I wait patiently while she creates. Three songs advance on the portable speaker she's set in the corner — it's probably been about ten minutes.

Whether that time has been torture or heaven is yet to be determined. Probably a bit of both.

Fortunately — or maybe unfortunately — she's positioned me so I can watch the area behind the easel where she stands. She pokes her head out every few seconds, and our eyes meet each time. My heart speeds up with each moment of eye contact like a lovesick schoolboy with his first crush.

This isn't a crush, though. It's an intimate moment between two lost souls.

Intimacy isn't always sexual — there's nothing sexual about this moment. But I feel like she's looking into my soul as she studies each line of my body. Even fully clothed, I'm exposed to her and entirely vulnerable.

Likewise, I'm studying her every move. The light in her eyes. The outline of her lips. The angles of her neck. The way she gets lost in her art. The intelligence behind her gaze.

All of it.

It's scary, but I don't want to stop. I want... more.

More time with her. More vulnerability with her.

More everything with her.

As the moments pass, the feeling that this is nothing but a mere crush dissipates. It's replaced with something else. Something strong and terrifying.

Something bordering on love.

Sue's not just a quirky young gal with a hot body. She's more.

My feelings for her grow stronger each day — approaching dangerous territory.

Client, client, client, I remind myself yet again.

Then I tell my heart to shut the hell up. I should know better than to let my thoughts head down this path. I can't follow through on my desires for so many reasons.

Sorry, heart. This one isn't meant to be.

As if it knew the moment I decided to lock it up, my heart clenches in my chest.

Prior to that exact moment, she was only a woman I was attracted to. I knew I liked her, but I had no idea how much.

Once I realized the depth of my feelings, all my fears and worries came rushing in. Loving me comes with a set of risks I won't ask her to accept. I had to lock up my heart before it got more invested.

But it was too late.

Shaking myself from the intrusive memory, I peruse the file to prepare for my new client, making notes in the margin for things to mention at my team briefing later. Another breath of relief is released when my mother's reply pings through.

Mom: All good here, son. Hope you enjoy your day. I love you, big guy.

Me: I love you too. I'll check in again tonight. Call me if you need anything.

Mom: And I thought it was the mother who was supposed to be the worrywart.

Me: Worrying about you is my job. It's also my pleasure. Be safe today.

Mom: Yes, sir! <smiley face emoji> <kiss emoji>

I consider sending a text to check on my brother, Andrew. But he won't reply, making my worries worse.

He's told me to stop hovering, and I'm trying to respect his wishes. Although, I don't see what's so hard about responding to a simple text so your loved ones know you're okay. We're family, and we need to stick together. We always said we'd be there for each other after everything we've been through, and I just wish he'd let me be there for him like I used to when we were kids.

Oh well. I can't fix that today, so I might as well focus on what is within my control. And that's preparing for what's probably going to be a nightmare of a week with a pampered Italian pop star.

I've been in private security long enough to know that these types of stars are usually the personification of the shitty comic sans font.

I'm not looking forward to what lies ahead, but at least it will provide a welcome distraction from the rest of my mundane existence.

Chapter Four

"Art is therapeutic" my fat white ass!

Sue

I nibble on my lower lip as my tiny round-tip brush slides over the canvas to complete the stroke. It's frustrating that I can't get the right shade for this part. My memory is fuzzy, but I know it should be somewhere between a rich caramel and gingerbread brown. And this is close, but it's not right.

"I need it to be right," I whine. Although, there's no one to hear me since I'm in my painting studio — a spare room I converted into a happy space where I dabble in various art mediums.

It's dawn, but I couldn't sleep, so I thought some art therapy would be a nice way to start the day.

Alone.

Just like always.

"I think I'll add a bit more orange to brighten the tone. Maybe with a touch of yellow too," I tell the empty room, thinking again maybe the time has come for me to get a pet so I can at least pretend it's not entirely odd to be speaking out loud when I'm alone.

And I'm always alone.

I used to crave being alone, but sometime in the last year, the silence and solitude lost their luster.

Impulsively deciding on an approach, I set the brush down flat on a paper towel to grab the orange and yellow tubes of acrylic paint and unscrew the caps. I go about mixing and blending until I get what I hope is the perfect shade.

The portable speaker is playing my favorite melancholy album — *Doves & Ravens*. It only has four songs, so it repeats often. I find the repetition comforting. Dermot Kennedy provides the perfect soundtrack to set the mood of my recent painting sessions. I love his gritty voice coupled with his Irish accent occasionally slipping through. It reminds me of my family. Dermot's music is raw and honest, if not slightly dark. It fits my recent emotions, really getting my creative juices flowing.

Well, usually it does.

But this morning isn't turning out to be an overflowing fountain of creativity like I'd hoped. Everything on the canvas looks awful, and I'm not enjoying myself in the least. It's like I've broken my ability to paint for pleasure. It's starting to feel like a fruitless search or a quest. Yet I don't even know what I'm trying to achieve once I have the brush in my hand. No matter what I do, it feels like I'm failing.

If painting doesn't fill my *joy well* anymore, what else is there to look forward to?

I shake off the morbid thought and curl my hand fiercely around the brush handle as I stare at the newly blended brown shade I've dabbed onto the canvas. I bite down too hard on my lip and am suddenly assaulted with a twinge of pain. My tongue dabs out to soothe the sting but almost immediately recoils from the disgusting metallic taste.

Dammit! Why can't I get this shade right?

Out of nowhere, I'm experiencing the physical sensation of running despite standing still — my chest tightens, and my muscles twitch while my heart runs away from me faster than my brain.

Okay, it's time to use my calming techniques.

I can do this. Need to think soothing thoughts.

I open my mouth to suck in air, close my eyes, and force myself to think of soothing thoughts so the tension releases in my jaw. Whenever I get hyper-focused on painting, my jaw gets impossibly tight to the point of pain. Add in today's failure to get the right shade of caramel gingerbread on top of how my panic is setting in, and the jaw is the least of my concerns. If I don't calm down soon, I'll be in the fetal position rocking in the corner in no time.

Wouldn't be the first time.

I'll start by picturing myself at the beach at sunrise so I can focus each of my senses better.

Here I go. Breathe in. Breathe out. And visualize the beach.

The wind blows through my hair.

I feel my toes sink and dig into the white sand.

I hear the squawk of the seagulls overhead.

I smell the salt in the air.

And...

Shit! That's only four things. I need a fifth.

My therapist says I should think of five things to ground me. Five things.

Five.

Even if it's a terribly unbalanced number, I need a fifth beach thing. Those are the rules she gave me.

Sometimes — like now — the sheer panic I feel trying to come up with the fifth thing is enough to launch me into an even deeper state of alarm. It's always the fifth thing that's the hardest to think up.

Stay calm, Sue. Breathe in. Breathe out. Just picture yourself at the beach. You can do this. You only need one more thing. You've got this. Don't be a spaz. Calm down. Stop freaking out all the time.

Let's see, I did the wind, my toes in the sand, seagulls, and salt. What else is there? What else? What else? Wind, toes, seagulls, and salt. What else?

Ah! Got it.

The figurative me hanging out in my mind's peaceful vision can see the sun's rays shimmering off the water.

Perfect. I did it.

Five things.

Now, I just need to repeat them.

Wind, toes, seagulls, salt, and sun. Wind, toes, seagulls, salt, and sun.

For the next several minutes, I keep my eyes closed and run through the five sensations. Again and again. I even manage to block out the hypnotic music coming from my speaker. When I open my eyes again, I'm much calmer. A smooth breath leaves through my rounded lips. I can feel my shoulders shift back into a more relaxed state, and my hand loosens its death grip on the paintbrush. Ah, that's better.

Until I look at my painting.

Instantly, I'm brought back to my earlier state of panic, or is that... rage? Because I can't get the *fecking* shade of brown right. I can't do it. I can't do anything. I can't get it right.

It's been weeks... or longer. Maybe even months since I've gotten the shade right. It's there somewhere in the recess of my mind, but it's also gone. I'll never get it back. Gone, gone, gone. Because I'm not good enough. I'm too much of a mess to get it back.

And the worst part is, I don't even know why I keep trying to create this same portrait. Why is it so important?

I don't know, but I keep trying.

Over and over again.

It's pointless, but I do it all the same. I'm not able to stop. And not able to get it right.

Because I'm broken.

In my frustration, I take the large tube of base white paint and angrily squeeze a sloppy stream directly onto the canvas, then run my hand down the middle of the figure, smudging my pasty fingerprints all over the rough, woven texture, ruining the painting entirely.

Ruined.

Just like me.

Warmth stings the back of my eyes, and salty tears overflow, running down my cheeks in streams. Sobs rack my chest as I stare at the mess of white and brown paint on my hand.

The brown that's *still* not the right shade.

I grab the canvas from the beechwood easel my sister bought me and throw it against the wall, where it smacks solidly before tumbling to the ground.

And I scream.

Jonesing for the java juice

After having a good, long cry early this morning during my failed painting session, I decide I need my Saturday morning pick-me-up. Even though it's Tuesday, I'm making a latte run.

Screw my rules! Rules are stupid.

What good have they ever gotten me? Does always taking my medication really help? Does limiting caffeine make a difference? Does going to therapy help?

Nope. I'm still a mess.

A freak who can't do anything right.

Ugh. Enough with the self-pity, Sue. Don't listen to that voice. That voice is wrong. Therapy and medication do help. The other stuff? Well, maybe not so much.

Not bothering to change out of my paint-stained coveralls, I jump in my car. It's not like it's fancy — just a used sedan over a decade old. A little paint on the seat is the least of the car's issues. It's paid off, though — a hand-me-down from my brother Connor.

One of the many *little things* my family does for me. They say they're *little things,* but I know better.

I'm not stupid.

Giving someone a car isn't a little thing, even if it is on the older side.

To some extent, each of my six siblings feels the need to look after me — the baby of the family. Whether that manifests as gifting me a car, helping me find an affordable place to live, making sure I have groceries, or giving me a job. They all like to coddle their little Susie Q.

Poor little Susie Q needs our help.

Poor little Susie Q doesn't have any friends.

Poor little Susie Q can't hold a job.

Poor little Susie Q will be alone forever.

I'm not whining — I'm truly grateful for their help and love. But it's a tad exhausting feeling like the family charity case. The screw-up who can't take care of herself.

The freak.

Dammit! I'm doing it again. Stop it, Sue. Get your shit together before you lose it again.

I need to watch my negative self-talk or it will start to pile up on me, dragging me down into a heavy depression.

I'll look forward to my mid-morning caffeine-fueled escape instead of listening to all the ways I'm fucked up as they sprint through my head. But trying to quiet my thoughts is like trying to bail the ocean with a bucket.

And the bucket has a hole in the bottom.

But I'm committed to trying today. I even brought my e-reader and earbuds so I can enjoy the outdoor seating facing the beach and try to decompress a little. I'll sip my coffee while I read and listen to music with the sea breeze pressing against my skin and Vitamin D soaking into my pores. For real this time, not some imagined scenario designed to keep me from succumbing to crippling anxiety.

And I'm not going to feel bad about ditching work to escape for a while. Nick won't care, and it's not like anyone will die if I don't return phone calls or emails about dog training today. Plus, I deserve a little treat after pulling myself from the fog of that breakdown as quickly as I did.

Boy, I was a mess this morning.

I haven't had an episode like that in a while... well, not one *that* bad. I live each day riddled with anxiety, but full-on meltdowns are not that often. Maybe once or twice a month. This was a rough one, though.

Perhaps it was the lack of sleep that triggered it.

My therapist told me once that sometimes my emotions are bigger than my capacity for containing them.

Seems like a plausible explanation. Logical.

I haven't figured out whether my emotions are too big or my ability to handle them is too small.

The answer to that riddle probably wouldn't matter to other people, but it's an important distinction for someone like me. I *need* to understand things down to their roots. It makes me twitchy when I can't rationalize something.

I don't like feeling twitchy.

It leads to anxiety, which leads to meltdowns, which leads to depression. It's a slippery slope, but if I can at least understand causes and rationalize them, it helps.

After pulling into a curbside spot at the beachside coffee shop, I quickly jump out and toss my bag over my shoulder. There's a pep in my step at the mere idea of the beverage-based nirvana I'm about to experience.

While I'm waiting for my order, I'm certain to only face the beverage pickup window — just in case there is anyone else brave or sick enough to wear peach leggings today.

You can never be too careful.

A few minutes later, my hand finally wraps around a cup of liquid gold, and I find a table. Before I dive into a novel and attempt to find my Zen, I pull out my journal to make notes about what could have triggered this morning's episode.

Tuesday, August 9 — Didn't sleep well. Had the dream again. Painted with acrylics but couldn't get the right shade of brown. Tried beach visualization to ground myself. Destroyed the painting because of the fucking brown!!!!

While tapping my pen on the table, I stare at the page and consider what else I need to write down. Before I close the notebook, I underline the last two words in my entry repeatedly, nearly ripping a hole in the paper. Forcing myself to pick up the pen from the page, I inhale the coffee-scented sea air before writing another line.

I can't remember the specific brown hue anymore. It makes me feel broken since my memory is normally so strong.

I press the journal closed, toss it in my bag, and pull out my e-reader. While I'm waiting for it to power on, I scan the street. Just as I start to look back down, I see a wash of gray zoom past from the corner of my eye.

A *familiar* shade of gray.

The same gray as the van I saw outside Nick and Millie's house the other day. Instantly, my shoulder blades pinch together, and my pulse quickens.

I stare as the van drives away, watching the road until I can no longer see it. I blink a few times, wondering if it was my imagination. What are the odds it was the same van? Clearwater Beach is busy this time of year, so it's not exactly *small-town USA*.

But it looked like the same van, rust around the back bumper and all.

Paranoia starts to prick at my senses as a chill creeps down my spine. My head swivels around the Starbucks patio so I can study the faces of everyone around me, looking for any ill intent and hopefully avoiding any peach leggings. I swipe my tongue at my suddenly dry lips, then force my shoulders to roll in small, soothing circles before taking a sip of my latte. My eyes continue to search the patio for a sense of danger, but I find none.

So much for finding Zen.

After three failed attempts to escape the real world with the words on my Kindle, I give up and shuffle everything back into my bag.

As I drive away, my eyes dart from the road to the rearview mirror so often I'm beginning to think I'm a hazard to other drivers. I didn't get my license until I was twenty-two because I was afraid of having a panic attack while on the road, killing myself or others. What's happening right now is the exact reason I hate driving and put it off as long as I did.

I quickly pull off the road into the nearest parking area. Making a spur-of-the-moment decision, I shove a few things in my pockets and head to the beach to make my calming beach vision into a reality. Perhaps the real thing will have a better effect than the imaginary one.

Or at least make it last longer.

It's still early enough that the beach isn't crowded with tourists, so I won't feel like I'm being watched, have to deal with someone trying to talk to me, or worse.

What could be worse, you ask? That's simple. Someone might ask me to take their picture.

Shudder.

People are *ew*.

A few moments later, my toes are blissfully sinking into the warm sand. I breathe in the salty air and focus on the sounds around me.

It seems to be doing the trick as rational thought starts to return. At this point, I'm pretty sure I imagined the gray van. Or if I did see it, it doesn't mean anything. It's not that big of a town — like Tampa proper or Orlando. Seeing the same vehicle here is entirely possible, and certainly doesn't mean I'm being followed.

My therapist would probably tell me it's just my anxiety-fueled morning causing the paranoia. Especially given that I had the dream last night.

I sit down in the sand beside my discarded shoes, thankful I'm still in my painting coveralls since they'll keep out most of the sand. Although, inevitably, I'll still end up with some down in my *national treasure trove.*

After soaking in the peaceful scenery for a few minutes, I pull my rolled up, ratty sketchpad out of my pocket along with my charcoal sketching pencils. Since it's a black and white medium, I won't have to worry about the stupid shade of brown. *Look at me — problem-solving and shit.*

I flip to the first blank page and begin sketching. Not sure how worried I should be that I feel the need to continuously create this same image. It's beyond obsessive at this point. Then again, my therapist told me it's okay to seek comfort in repetition.

As the tip of the pencil slides over the page and the image begins to take form, its familiarity comforts me — a feeling I gratefully soak in after such a stressful morning. And thanks to the charcoal pencil, this one won't end up a ruined mess on my floor.

Fecking brown.

Chapter Five

It's all coming back to me now

Sue

As I sketch, my pencil seems to work on autopilot — which makes sense given the vast number of times I've drawn this.

I love the repetition — it's soothing for me.

Like always, my mind starts to wander and dance around in my past. It's almost like a movie reel. A film made just for me.

Today, it starts the same as always, with bits and pieces of my childhood. The first scene is from when I was about five years old. Mom and Dad were working late that night, I think. My eldest brothers — Nick, Callum, and Shane — weren't home. They were probably working too, or off with their girlfriends. Fiona was in charge, making dinner for Connor, Finn, and me. Macaroni and cheese.

"Come on up, sweetie," Fiona says.

She pushes a chair in front of the stove, and I climb up. "I'll pour, and you stir."

I grab the long wooden spoon from her, wrapping my pudgy fingers around the handle. Instead of stirring, I tap the spoon against the back of the chair while I bounce along to the beat. The rhythm of the tapping seems to put me in a trance, and I keep doing it. I don't want to stop.

Tap, tap, tap, tappity, tap.

Tap, tap, tap, tappity, tap.

Tap, tap, tap, tappity, tap.

"Stop it! You're giving me a headache," Finn yells from the other side of the room.

He's poured milk for each of us and put the pink strawberry powder I like in mine. He stirs it for me and then sets the cups on the kitchen table.

I frown. "Pink cup!" I yell at him, feeling my chest tighten when I see he's put a white cup at my place.

That's my spot.

Only I sit there.

I don't have many words — not like they do. But I know what I know. And I know I need the pink cup when I have strawberry milk. Not the white. White is for white milk. Pink is for pink milk.

"It's dirty. You have to use the white one," he says.

No. No. No. I want the pink cup. The pink cup is for pink milk — only the pink one. My breathing increases as those uncomfortable feelings fill up my stomach. I don't like these feelings.

Tap, tap, tap, tappity, tap.

Tap, tap, tap, tappity, tap.

"Pink cup!" I yell at him again.

Tap, tap, tap, tappity, tap.

The tapping isn't helping calm me down. He's not getting my pink cup. Why won't he just get the pink cup?

I need it.

I throw the spoon at him and wail at the top of my lungs. I'm so mad. I need the pink cup. Why doesn't he understand?

Fiona grabs me under my arms roughly. She's mad. I don't want her to be mad at me. I just need my pink cup.

And now I can't make the tapping sound.

"You can't throw things at people. That's bad," Fiona says as she marches me down the long hallway.

I'm crying now. My cheeks are red, and my nose is snotty.

I don't want to go to my room. They always put me in my room alone when I'm crying like this. I wouldn't be crying if they'd give me the pink cup.

"Pink cup!" I cry again and again.

My hands are waving around, but I can't stop them. I must get the feelings out, and they seem to come out of my hands sometimes when I get upset like this.

Shake, shake, shake, shakity, shake.

But it's not the same as the wooden spoon.

"Shh! Don't cry. Just don't throw things." Fiona tries to get me to stop crying, but I can't.

I still need my pink cup.

My fists ball up and shake, shake, shake, shakity, shake.

She sets me down on my bed — it sits low to the floor because Mommy says I roll around a lot when I sleep. She was afraid I'd get a boo-boo if I had a high-up bed like everyone else.

I'm different from everyone else.

I'm different.

Fiona closes the door, leaving me alone in my room.

I'm all alone.

I wish Nicky was here. He doesn't put me in my room alone. He sits with me when I cry and roll around like this. Mommy does too. I wish Mommy or Nicky were here. They'd give me the pink cup.

But they're not here. And so I'm alone.

Fiona is mad at me. Finn is mad at me. I hope I didn't hurt him with the spoon. I don't want him hurt. I just want the pink cup.

But I'm alone.

I'm different and alone.

I don't know why my broken brain always brings up that memory first. I wish it wouldn't — it's far from a pleasant memory.

I've talked about it with my therapist, Jaynie. She thinks it's because it might be when I first realized I wasn't like the rest of my family. Until I come to accept my differences as strengths instead of weaknesses, my subconscious will keep showing me where my thoughts began to break down and become flawed.

Maybe she's right.

I didn't do things the same way my siblings did. I didn't even learn to talk until I was around three, and even then, it was very few words — or so my mom tells me.

I wasn't interested in sports or group activities; I wanted nothing to do with other kids. I didn't even enjoy art until high school when I used it to help my brain calm down. It took all my focus, so my mind didn't have time to run amuck.

Yet now that I've become so accustomed to creating this picture in my mind, I'm no longer able to shut out some of my troubling thoughts.

That's why they keep flashing through my mind as my pencil makes several long strokes down the page, from top to bottom, over and over, to show the streaks and weathered surface.

Am I a disappointment to my family because I'm different?

Do they still want me to change like they did when we were kids?

Maybe I should train some damn dogs like Nick wants me to. I know I can do it. I've prepared enough, practiced plenty. Nick's been so patient with me — teaching me everything he knows. Nick's love is unconditional, and I know I'm not trying to buy his love by agreeing to train dogs.

But I do feel some guilt pushing me to make this decision. After all, I've let my family down all my life — it'd be nice to please them for a change.

With another down stroke on the page, my mind's movie projector flashes to the next scene. It's from when I was going into middle school.

"There are so many kids," I tell my mom quietly, tugging the sleeve of her soft pink sweater.

"Yeah, darlin', there are loads more kids here. That means yer gonna have even more chances to make friends."

Her accent is so pretty. I wish I sounded like her.

I also wish I shared her optimism about making new friends. The reality is, the more kids I interact with, the more relentlessly I'll be teased.

We're walking side by side, heading into the cafeteria of my new school for orientation. I'm supposed to get my schedule tonight. I wish they'd have given it to us sooner.

School starts in a few days, and I haven't had enough time to prepare.

My pulse pounds wildly in my throat at the thought. I lick my lips four times, then force a deep breath.

It's always four times.

Mom's high heels make a nice clicking sound as we march along. It's hard to hear it, though. Too many kids talking all at once — loudly. I wish they'd shut up. Some of them know each other and are hugging. Probably haven't seen each other all summer.

I don't have anyone who'll be happy to see me.

But that's fine.

I don't need anyone.

I have a loving family. My parents always tell me that having a large family is better than having lots of friends.

I'm not so sure about that. In fact, I think they're just telling me that to make me feel better for always being alone.

I clench my hands into fists and force myself to shut out everything except the sound of her clicking shoes.

As we walk, I focus on the pattern of the tiles on the floor — careful not to step in two of the same color tiles in a row. I need to alternate between the gray and beige squares.

It feels wrong if I don't.

It should be equal.

Mom pulls me along, then points us down a row toward some empty chairs. "Let's sit here, yeah?"

"When will I get my schedule?" I ask her as soon as we take our seats.

"Susie, look at me."

I'm glad she's finally using my new nickname. I'm so sick of being teased for my real name. I have enough other things to be teased for — I don't need to add to the list. My middle name is better.

My eyes are still studying the tiles on the floor even though we've sat. I've got one foot in a gray square and the other in a beige square.

It feels balanced that way.

Reluctantly, I look up at her and focus on her nose. She has a pretty nose, thin and feminine.

"Calm down now, lass. Yeah?"

"I am calm," I lie right through my braces.

"Yer countin' under yer breath. I can hear ya."

I didn't realize I was counting again. Dang it.

"Sorry, Ma." My head drops back down to study the tiles.

No wonder kids make fun of me at school. I'm always doing things I don't even know I do.

Weird things.

I wouldn't like me either.

In fact, I don't like myself at all.

A tear falls to my chest, then another. I didn't realize I was crying. *Shit.* I'm a mess.

I don't have anything to wipe my face with, so I unzip my coveralls and use a sleeve to dab at my eyes and nose. When I'm done, I let the sleeves fall to my waist. They rest in the sand. I'll wash them when I get home. That's the difference between people and possessions. You can't wash away the stained parts of yourself — the less-than-perfect parts.

And I have many, many imperfect parts.

No wonder Leo didn't want me.

I'm a stone-cold disaster.

As I go back to sketching and relax once more, my mind starts to bring up another scene, but I stop it this time. We *will not* relive that nightmare from high school when the popular kid asked me to meet him after school because he wanted to kiss me.

Nope.

Not going there. Hard pass.

I do *not* want another sad, pathetic memory. I want a good memory — a happy one.

Reminding myself that I'm the director of this movie montage, I clear my mind, letting some uplifting options run through my mind's eye. Happy times with the family — playing games, going to a movie, and having a dinner that didn't end in tears.

Ah... family dinner. That sparks something.

A smile lifts my cheeks as the perfect scene jumps up, waving at me like it's saying: *Pick me! Pick me!*

It's a memory from earlier this year when Leo was my assigned protector because of a threat involving Nick and Millie that spilled over to me.

My pencil begins to flesh out the grass and shrubbery at the bottom of the picture. Light swipes of my pencil add the right amount of texture. And the little director in my mind yells, "Action!"

"We can either go in together, or I'll sit on the front porch the entire time," Leo says to me as if the decision has already been made.

His blue eyes are calm, even if his voice sounds irritated.

"Or, option three, you stay in the car." I run my hands across the dashboard like I'd pet a dog, trying to emphasize what a nice option the car is for him. It's a monster luxury SUV. He'll be fine here while I go inside and get my familial duty over with.

"Maybe you're not hearing me, kid. I can go in with you — posing as your friend — or I'll wait on the porch. There is no option three."

I scoff and laugh. "A friend? Yeah, that's believable."

"Why isn't it believable?" He genuinely doesn't seem to see it.

I make a show of looking at him — from head to toe — then looking down at myself and raising my shoulders and hands. We couldn't be more different.

He frowns, mashing his lips together.

Oh, how I want to run my tongue along those lips.

I don't have a lot of kisses in my past to draw upon, but something tells me kissing Leo would be substantially better than any other kiss I've had.

And I really want to test my theory.

My thighs press together, heat suddenly pooling in my core.

When he doesn't answer, I offer another choice. Anything to get him out of being the first person I've ever brought home to meet my family. He's too kind to be subjected to such hellish torture.

The O'Malleys can be a bit much.

"How about a fourth option, then? We just go back home," I offer. "I don't even like family dinners all that much."

He closes his eyes, squeezing the bridge of his nose with those thick fingers. It's embarrassing how much I dream about those fingers touching me.

Stroking me.

Diving inside me.

My nipples pebble under my blouse, and the press of the tight fabric of my bra causes painful friction.

"You already told your parents you were coming for dinner. And I think your brother needs you. He's had a rough few days. You should be there for him."

"Which one?" I ask, idly wondering how he knows what's going on with my brothers.

"Nick," he says exasperatedly, shaking his head at me like I'm daft. His eyes flicker with mirth.

Fair point. That's my mistake.

I promise, I'm aware Nick and Millie broke up, so he's obviously the one who needs me. I just can't seem to think straight around Leo. And his muscles. Damn, he has so many muscles. Rippling muscles. Bulging muscles. Veiny and throbby muscles. Corded muscles. Lean muscles. Tattooed muscles. Beefy muscles.

Leo Mason has all the muscles.

I'm having some type of brain malfunction induced by those inky biceps. Then again, my brain often goes wonky each time I notice the sexy tick of his chin when I'm frustrating him — like I am now.

It's the same way I feel when he tries to hide his grins from me behind his fist and when I see the twinkle in his eyes when I make him laugh — really laugh.

He has a sexy laugh.

Quite possibly, his laugh is the hottest thing about him — which says a lot, considering how utterly sexy he is from head to toe.

And when he flashes me that mischievous smirk? I go weak in the knees. That smirk comes out most often when we're passing time coming up with outlandish words.

Words like frugleminder — *which is someone who thinks about being budget-conscious but can't follow through and still spends frivolously. Hence, it only being in their mind. That one was mine.*

Leo came up with laughternoon — *which is, as it sounds, an afternoon filled with laughter. I've only known Leo for a few days now, but I think we've had three or four laughternoons so far.*

But anyway, I'm not able to think clearly around him. Especially when he looks at me like he is right this second, in the confined space of this SUV, where his clean, masculine scent overpowers my senses.

His eyelids look heavy, and his lower lip hangs down so his mouth is barely open. Just enough for me to get a peek at his red tongue, which is moving behind his teeth like it's dancing to a song I can't hear.

Leo likes me.

Even if he doesn't want to admit it, I'm pretty sure he likes me.

Well, let's say 60 percent — which is pretty good, as far as odds go for me when human interactions are being wagered on.

He taps his finger on the steering wheel, and the glint of his pinky ring catches my eye. We're parked just down the street from my parents' house. He pulled off the side of the road to get our story straight before we got there.

Apparently, Leo thinks I'm going to be in big danger around the dinner table.

Perhaps a stray dinner roll to the head will take me out.

"Listen, Leo. I appreciate how much you want to keep me safe. I really do. But this is an O'Malley family dinner, not a gunfight at the O. K. Corral. It's not like I'm in danger tonight. Except the danger of overeating because my mom is a far better cook than me."

"Are you going to deny me your mom's allegedly fantastic cooking while bragging about it at the same time? I didn't take you for a cold-blooded tease, Sue."

My eyes narrow to slits. "Leo, are you trying to manipulate me into letting you come inside to dinner?"

He leans across the center console, moving closer to me. In response, I find myself moving in his direction like we're magnets. Our bare forearms brush against each other, and my skin pebbles with gooseflesh.

"That depends," he says huskily. "Is it working?"

I swallow — my mouth is suddenly very wet. Also, my panties — those are feeling very wet too. I hope I still have some clean pairs left in my old bedroom. Mom might have finally done that spring cleaning she's been threatening where all the things we've left in her home are put on the curb.

"It might be working. But only a little," I answer, trying for playful and hoping I pull it off. I've never quite mastered flirting, but I'm trying.

He reaches up and takes a lock of my hair, swirling it around his finger until it curls. His eyes flit from it back to my eyes.

"So soft," he mutters. "Feel it."

I immediately obey, reaching up to take the curl from his grasp. As he passes my hair back to me, our hands touch, but I don't pull away. I let my hand linger there, and he does the same.

His eyes are glued to where our knuckles are touching, just barely grazing against each other's.

That pull he has over me seemingly intensifies, and I find myself inching forward.

Closer.

Closer.

The stupid leather seat makes a squeaking sound as the exposed skin of my thighs moves across it in my desperate quest to get closer to the man in the driver's seat.

His gaze moves from our hands down to the source of the distracting sound. I suddenly feel embarrassed by the wide expanse of my thighs and wish I'd opted for jeans instead of shorts. It's just so damn hot out.

His eyes widen, and his tongue comes out to dab his lips.

Those lips.

I want to lick them even more than I did before.

We're mere centimeters away from each other now. I can feel his warm breath on my neck as his eyes travel up my body slowly, landing on my face. I shock myself by holding the intense eye contact he's giving me. It's like I'm trying to absorb his presence through his hypnotic gaze.

"Sue..." He doesn't finish his sentence as he leans forward and licks his lips once more.

Oh my gosh.

He's going to kiss me.

I want that, don't I? Yes. No. I don't know.

The terrifying thought shakes me from the spell he has me under, and I push backward. My body stiffly pivots, and I shift toward the other side of the car. I can't meet his eyes, so I face the windshield instead.

"Um, I think it's fine if you want to come inside to dinner. We can pretend to be friends. They won't believe it, but whatever."

I tug my shorts down in a pathetic attempt to cover my skin. I feel like he's watching me there — everywhere — and it makes me so warm.

His eyes on me are too much to take. Once the shorts aren't riding up so high, I brush my palms down my thighs four times.

Four is good, balanced.

He's silent, but from the corner of my eye, I can see him shifting back to his side of the car.

Somehow, I manage to calm my racing pulse enough to say, "Let's go."

I should have let him kiss me that day.

The memory of how his lips felt could have comforted me after he left. He was destined to leave me either way; at least I'd have known what it's like to kiss a man — a *real* man, not a boy. Instead, I'm stuck with this disappointed lady boner when I think about how close we came.

But I chickened out.

Bawk, bawk, bawk, my conscience mocks me.

Maybe Leo would have been a terrible kisser.

Yeah, let's go with that. Lying to myself seems like an excellent way to deal with my past failures.

A sorrowful smile comes to my face as I finish the last strokes with my pencil and stare at the finished piece. This one is a little better than the last time. Somehow, the distortion I saw before is less noticeable.

Maybe it's because I controlled my mental movie reel this time and recalled a more pleasant memory.

After folding the pencil in my sketchbook, I stand and stretch. I tie my sleeves around my waist and stare into the surf for a few more minutes before I head back home.

For another night alone.

Chapter Six

Beachside Creeping

Leo

I sign the note the same way I always do, right down to the small *x* under my name.

After rolling the paper up good and tight, I slip it inside the empty wine bottle. I fish the cork out of my jeans pocket and push it in deep, sealing the note safely inside. Once I place a kiss on the side of the bottle, I tuck my arm back behind my head, then shift my weight as I propel the bottle forward, chucking it a good forty feet into the surf.

As I watch it jump across the top of the ocean's surface a few times before drifting out of sight, I feel the same sense of longing settle in my gut. My arms hang to my sides, my hands empty.

Empty, just like me.

I shove my hands in my back pockets as I stare into the small morning waves. The sharpness of the pain has lessened over time. I no longer feel queasy or faint when I think of her and all she went through, but the dull ache deep in the pit of my chest will probably never go away.

And that's okay.

The hurt reminds me how I let her down so I never make the same mistakes again. I think that might be why I come here each week. It's a place where I can allow the thoughts of her to surface — where I can't hide from the vividness of my memories — the fear, the pain, the bruises, and the scars.

This place won't let me forget, which is good because I don't deserve such mercy.

She always loved the ocean and sailing. It was her special place, so it became mine after I lost her. Especially considering the way I lost her. And here I don't have to hold the tears back if they choose to come.

I can just... *be.*

There are no tears today, though. Probably because I'm still frustrated over the last two days' events. Dealing with Trixie Valentine has been a clusterfuck from the word go. I had a bad feeling about this gig, and I hate that my hunch was right. Just once, it'd be nice to be wrong. Is that too much to ask?

My phone buzzes at the same time as the alarm I set on my watch. Time to head to work so I can relieve the overnight shift. The pop princess will be rising soon, and I need to get there before Kri so I can make sure the hand-off between shifts goes smoothly. I still don't trust the new kid on her own.

Kid.

That reminds me of Sue.

As I walk back toward my motorcycle, I pull out my phone, happy to see Mom already responded to my last check-in text — everything's fine today, as usual. Out of habit, I toggle over to check Sue's location for the first time in a few hours.

Wait, what?

This can't be right.

My head cricks to the right as I zoom in on the red dot and make sure the tracker is set to reveal her location and not mine. Sure enough, it's Sue's car pinging less than a hundred feet away. My eyes search over the edge of the dunes and golden haze of sea oats toward the parking lot, but the tourists are starting to arrive, and the lot is substantially fuller than it was when I got here. Pausing at the end of the path connecting the lot to the beach, I tap a few times to view the location of Sue's phone.

It pings on the same spot.

She's here.

My heart skips a beat as I scan the sea of cars, my boots shuffling along the gravel parking lot at an almost run. I'm not sure why I'm moving so quickly, but I haven't let myself catch even a glimpse of her in weeks. I just want to see her — if only for a moment.

I feel like a former smoker who hangs around the smoking section, desperate for a whiff of the familiar scent of burning nicotine. I need a little fix.

Maybe I can even talk to her... just for a minute to see how she's doing.

I've kept myself away, needing that physical distance to keep myself in check. But knowing she's so close makes the need to connect with her again so much stronger. It's a pull I don't want to resist anymore. A quick check-in shouldn't hurt anything. That wouldn't be wrong, would it?

I finally spot her old beater at the edge of the lot — parked under the nonexistent shade of a palm tree. My feet grind to a halt a few cars away, and I glance over my shoulder to see if I'm being followed. Old habits die hard.

Returning my gaze to Sue's car, I notice it's empty. I take a few steps closer and pause when I see her driver's window is down.

Dammit, Sue, you can't do that, I chastise her in my head. Someone could plant anything in her car or even get in the back to hide, waiting for her return. My jaw clicks from the force of my grinding teeth. The thought of someone lying in wait so they can choke her from behind sends tremors of unease up my spine, and a knot forms in my stomach.

I wonder if she still remembers the technique I showed her to break free from a choke hold.

Peering inside her car, I spot her purse on the floorboard. It seems like she tried to shove it under the passenger seat but didn't try hard enough because the strap is visible to anyone who cares to look.

How can she be so brilliant about certain things yet so careless about others?

She probably has tons of identifying information in her purse that anyone could find. Next thing you know, she'll have her own stalker or become a victim of identity theft or a dozen other crimes. Doesn't she care about her safety? My hands twist into tight fists as I force down my worries.

This.

This is why I'm still checking up on her, I reassure myself, attempting to ease the guilt I feel for being a creeper.

My phone rings with an incoming call, distracting me only slightly from concerns about Sue's safety.

It's Sawyer from my team — my best guy and closest friend; he's probably calling with an issue on the Trixie Valentine job.

Shit.

I press answer while I quickly head to a nearby picnic table to talk to him without standing in the middle of the parking lot. It's not entirely a coincidence that the table I select will provide an out-of-the-way place where I can keep an eye on Sue's car to make sure no one attempts anything. If Sue comes back to her car, I'll have to come up with an excuse for being here. I can't tell her the real reason.

"What's up, Sawyer?" I answer in a clipped tone.

He replies without preamble, "We're moving. *Again.*" The annoyance is heavy in his tone.

"What the fuck for this time?"

The pop princess moved out of her initial rental villa because the pool was too small for swimming laps. I pointed out the enormous ocean just a few feet away, but she wasn't having it.

At Ms. Valentine's insistence, we relocated yesterday to another villa. But in order to do that, we had to run a rushed security check on the new property, reinstall cameras, and find out who was living or staying in the surrounding properties — we have to make sure there are no paparazzi or criminal concerns in the neighborhood. The last thing we need is for one of our clients to be staying next to a local mob boss who'd use her presence to his advantage or worse, another celebrity — a bigger one who'd draw even more attention. That's entirely possible given the swanky neighborhoods she wants to stay in. Usually, the upscale homes come with fewer risks than the big hotels, but that's not always the case, and we don't take chances with shit like that at Redleg.

Sawyer clears his throat before replying, "Ms. Valentine doesn't like the color of the walls in the main bedroom. She says it's not good for her creative energy or some bullshit."

"You've got to be fucking kidding me. She's only here for five more days." They'll probably be the five longest days in history if the first two were anything to go by.

"Not kidding. You know I tell much better jokes than that," he replies. "In fact, here's one now. How do you make a pool table laugh?"

"Sawyer, come on, be serio —"

He cuts me off. "You tickle its balls."

His laugh is so annoying it's funny, and I end up laughing with him.

"How much coffee did you drink overnight?"

"The usual. Fuggedaboudit."

Even though I can't see him, I'm sure he's shrugging his shoulders and scrunching up his lips in that funny Donnie Brasco impersonation of his.

"Two pots then." I shake my head, not that he can see me. He's going to overdose on caffeine one of these days.

"You say that like it's a bad thing, Lionheart. But I see it as a way to ensure I'm alert enough to fend off Ms. Touchy Valentine." He says the fake name with a terrible Italian accent, garnering another chuckle from me.

56

"Look, I'll be there in about twenty minutes. Did she find a new place yet?"

"She wants *us* to do it."

"Fuck that."

"Can I quote you on that? She was a little handsy last night, so I'd really love your permission to tell her to fuck right off."

"No, I'll tell her when I get there. I don't want to subject you to any more inappropriate touch on the job. Next thing I know, you'll be telling Big Al I contributed to your toxic work environment."

He laughs. "I'll tell her to have her manager find another place. I can handle it. I'm just bustin' your balls."

"I thought we talked about that before. Please be gentle with my boys. They're sensitive," I tell him, feigning seriousness.

"See you in twenty, asshole," he says before tacking on, "Be careful on that hog with your gentle balls."

"Fuck off," I say, then hang up. The customary way we end our calls. Sawyer's like a brother to me.

I decide to give Sue another five minutes to show up before I leave her to her own devices, as much as it bothers me to go while she's potentially in danger — even if the threat is minor.

As the clock ticks down, my knee bobs up and down, and I begin twirling my pinky ring, cursing under my breath.

Maybe I should take Big Al up on his offer for some time off. I could visit my old Army buddy West for a few weeks. He's been asking me to spend time with him since he moved back home. That would probably be good for us both.

I need to clear my head and get my priorities straight. If I wasn't obsessively checking on Sue's location, I never would have known she was here today, wouldn't have noticed the open window on her car, and damn sure wouldn't be making myself late for a shift because of a foolish need to protect her... from herself.

After all, she doesn't have any enemies — no one could ever hate her. Plus, the man who was causing trouble for her and her brother earlier this year is safely behind bars, as far as I know.

With that thought, I fire off a text to Tomer back at Redleg headquarters. He's the guy you go to if you need anything. Whatever it is — he gets it for you. Information, equipment, classified documents, video footage — anything. He's essentially our *guy in the chair*.

Me: T, I need two things. 1: Ms. Valentine wants to move villas again, so we will likely need you to help with protocol later. I'll give you an update in about thirty minutes on that. And 2: I haven't had you check the FDLE database in a while to see if Alec Davies is still in prison. Can you check for me?

Tomer: For 1: Fuck! For 2: you got it. Give me five, unless it's urgent. I'm in the middle of the stew right now for another client.

Me: Five minutes is fine.

I recheck my watch. It's officially time to shit or get off the pot.

I take a few steps in the direction of the beach, determined to catch a glimpse of my girl before I leave. Just one look to make sure she's all right.

She's not your girl, Leo, my conscience tries to remind me, but I shoot it the bird.

Before I get too far from the picnic table, I see her cresting the hill as she passes over the top of the dunes and starts her descent down the pathway to the parking area.

My heart stops.

Well, metaphorically, at least — not like this is my ghost talking to you now.

My training takes over, and without thinking, I quickly dodge out of sight, squatting down between a parked car and a pickup truck.

I'd planned to talk to her, but my conscience tells me I should leave and let her move on with her life.

No matter what my heart wants.

No good can come from me bothering her.

I'll just stay out of sight while making sure she leaves safely, and then I'll go.

Holding my breath and peeking over the hood, I watch her walk to her car. She seems to be in her own world, her normally expressive eyes hidden behind dark sunglasses.

What I wouldn't give for a closer look at her heart-shaped face and a glimpse into those haunting blue eyes. I'm sure my memory doesn't do them justice.

Looks like she's been painting since she's still wearing her coveralls. She has the top unbuttoned and the sleeves wrapped around her waist like a belt, leaving her in only a tank top from the waist up. My mouth waters as I take her in from head to toe... still so fucking unconventionally beautiful.

She's just... effortlessly perfect.

She probably didn't even brush her hair today or put on a drop of makeup, not that she needs it.

I shift around the back of the truck I'm using for cover as she makes her way closer to me. Once she's safely in her car, I heave a sigh of relief and feel some of the tension leave my shoulders. I feel like a grade A creeper as I watch her start the car from about ten feet away.

She's almost close enough to touch. The thought renews the longing feeling I had when I threw my bottled-up apology note into the ocean earlier, although that longing was for an entirely different reason.

While her car is warming up, she bends over to reach toward the floorboard — I assume to get her *not-so-well-hidden* purse. Her sunglasses must fall off with the movement because I can see her entire face when she rises. Her skin is splattered with flecks of white paint, which normally would make me smile. I always loved watching her paint.

But it's her eyes that gut me... they're so damn sad.

I rub at my sternum to ease the quickly forming ache. All the light that was once in those eyes is gone, leaving her looking like a tormented ghost of her former self. Her cheeks have hollowed like she's lost weight or become ill. A sinking sensation mixes with queasiness in my stomach when I take in the red rims of her eyelids and pink on the button of her nose.

Before I even have time to talk myself out of it, I've risen to my full height and started moving toward her car. I *need* to comfort her — the urge overpowers my every thought.

Suddenly, my phone buzzes, shaking some much needed sense into me.

I stop immediately, pulling back beside the truck where I'm hidden from her view. A few seconds later, she drives away without seeing me.

A bitter smile lifts the corner of my mouth. It's for the best I didn't talk to her. She doesn't need me. I'll only make whatever is going on with her worse.

She's better off without me.

I glance at my phone to read the alert that saved me from making another mistake while cursing my stupidity and reckless behavior.

Tomer: Davies is still locked up. No changes to his case since the last time you had me check.

Me: Thanks, T.

Twenty-two minutes later, I'm pulling into the driveway of the villa to guard an Italian nightmare with more money than sense. But my heart drove off in the other direction in a beat-up yellow Hyundai.

Chapter Seven

Why am I craving oatmeal?

Sue

"Thanks for seeing me on such short notice. I know it's not our normal day." I sit down on the plush blue couch and tug on the hem of my blouse to pull it down.

"Absolutely, Sue. I'm glad I could get you in so quickly. On the phone, you said you had a bad day. That was yesterday, right?"

I meet the kind eyes of my therapist, then look away after two seconds — I don't want to be rude to the person who taught me how long to hold eye contact. Jaynie's an older woman with gray hair, tightly wound in curls.

I wonder if they're naturally curly or if she gets perms like my mom used to until my sister Fiona talked her out of it... *thankfully*.

"Yes," I respond while running the flats of my palms up and down the front of my shorts.

I should have worn pants — I don't like how exposed my legs feel when I sit. But it's stifling outside, so the cutoff shorts seemed fine. Regretting that decision now.

I've noticed the more stressed I am, the worse I feel about my *larger-than-most* body type. I wonder why that is. Perhaps I should ask Jaynie about that one day.

But not today.

My eyes flit up to hers again, but only for a split second this time.

"And are you doing any better today? Are you jumpy? You seem tense." She pats her hair, feeling for her pencil, eventually finding it tucked away behind her ear. Perhaps she uses hot rollers to get those curls.

"I'm only a little better today. I *am* jumpy. Yes, I'm also tense," I answer her questions, being careful to respond in the same order she asked them, then force a cleansing breath before she tells me to do it.

"Take all the time you need to get settled, dear. I'm in no hurry to begin. You're my last patient of the day. We have all the time in the world."

Wonderful. I'm all that's standing between her and going home. Why does that make me feel worse? She probably intended to make me feel better by saying that, but nope. Not me.

Sigh.

Jaynie leans back in her recliner and pulls the lever on the side to extend the legs. I used to think it was so odd my therapist sat in a living room-style reclining chair during our sessions. I asked her about it once, and she said it's because she has a bad back. Jaynie used to pace around during our sessions, but she noticed it made me agitated. When she asked me if I preferred her to sit, I instantly replied, *"Yes, please."* She stopped walking around after that.

When I found out about her bad back, I felt guilt for a solid year over not letting her walk during my past sessions. I still feel awful when I think about it.

Annnd now I'm thinking about it.

Crap on a cracker. I can't wait until I try to fall asleep tonight when the thought of the pain I caused her for all that time will play on repeat along with a slideshow of all the other unintentionally rude or awkward shit I've done lately.

Fecking hell.

"Sue, what did you have for breakfast this morning?"

The silence must have been too much for her to take.

"Um, oatmeal with pecans and brown sugar. No coffee today."

"Do you make it with milk or water?"

"Almond milk. Regular milk upsets my tummy. Water is too bland."

"Oh, I use that too. Small world. Do you eat your oatmeal hot or cold? I see lots of people talking about eating cold oats. What do they call that?"

"Do you mean overnight oats?"

"Yes. That's it. I tried those once. Is that what you're eating over the summer? Not that it ever gets cold enough for hot oats around here."

I see what she's doing. Trying to get me talking about mundane gobshite so I'll relax.

Nice trick, Jaynie.

But this is more than oatmeal-level anxiety we're dealing with today. We might need to discuss soufflé recipes or detailed plots to each of the Harry Potter books before I'm ready to unpack all this garbage floating around my head.

"... apple with cinnamon is my favorite," she rambles.

I must have tuned her out, but it sounds like she's still trying to draft her Tinder profile in hopes of matching with Wilford Brimley — may he rest in peace — or Mr. Quaker himself.

"I can start now," I say as soon as she takes a breath.

If she had started talking about grits next, I would've had to walk out on principle alone. Clearwater isn't *that part* of the south.

Despite my interruption of her fascinating breakfast speech, her face is gracious and encouraging.

"Go on, then." She nods at me, her smile spreading wider.

Dammit.

Now I feel guilty for my internal fit about her oatmeal commentary. She's so patient with me and kinder than I deserve.

With a shaky voice, I blurt, "I think I'm being followed, but I'm not sure if I really am or if I just want to be."

"Followed? You mean like a stalker?"

"Yes."

She scribbles something on her yellow legal notepad. "Why would you *want* to be stalked?"

"I don't. Well, not really. It's just... I... well, if..." I stumble over my words, unsure about how to say this without sounding like that *special* level of pathetic.

"If you were being stalked, then what?" she leads, tilting her head.

After opening and closing my fists four times because it's a good number — balanced — I look down and answer, "If I had a stalker, then maybe he'd come back and keep me safe again. It could be like it was before."

Shame, meet guilt. Guilt, this is shame. I'm sure you two will become best friends.

"He... as in Leo, I assume?"

"Well, yeah. Who else?"

I roll my eyes at her, then instantly feel bad for being bratty. I amend, "Yes. Leo."

"I'm hearing you say you're not sure if you're really being stalked or if you're simply being paranoid. And if you were being stalked, then maybe Leo would come back to protect you... like when Nick and his wife had a stalker."

She's looking at me like I should respond, but she didn't ask a question. I hold still and wait patiently for her to either ask me something or give me some good advice. That's what I'm paying for, after all.

Lay it on me.

Still waiting.

She leans her head toward me and raises her brows.

Any minute now, she's gonna hit me with all that sweet, sweet psychologist wisdom.

Mimicking her expression, I lean my head toward her, raising my brows in response. I guess this is a thing we're doing now.

Getting awkward. And you know it's awkward if I notice the awkward since I'm usually the one causing the awkward, thus completely unaware of awkward's existence.

"Did I get it all?" she finally asks, breaking our eyebrow-raising competition.

Thank St. Paddy that's over. I was almost fearful she was having a stroke.

"Yes, that's correct."

"And what about the dream?"

"I've had it twice since our last visit." I put my head down once more, hiding my eyes. Not sure why I'm feeling ashamed. It's not like I can control my dreams.

"Woke you up each time?"

"Yes."

"Was it the cabin?" Her voice is drenched with sympathy.

"Yes. It never changes... always the same."

I grab a tissue from the box on the coffee table between us because I can already feel the tears building as the sting reaches my sinuses.

"We'll circle back to the dream in a moment. First, why do you think you're being followed?"

"I've seen this gray van — like an old, dirty, rusty van — four times since Saturday."

Normally, I'd be okay with something happening four times — since it's a good, balanced number — but this time, it's not a good sign.

"Do you mean when you're driving, you see it behind you?"

She starts writing again as soon as I answer.

"Not really. The first time was Saturday outside Nick and Millie's house. It was parked down the street. The next time was yesterday outside a Starbucks — I saw it drive by while I was sitting on the patio drinking my coffee. I blew it off as a coincidence and went to the beach to do some sketching and relax — sort of like a real-life grounding. But when I left the beach, I saw it at the gas station on the corner of the street I live on. And then it was there again this afternoon — saw it on my way here. Same gas station. Same van."

She pauses her frantic note-taking to ask, "How far away is the gas station from your house?"

"About a half-mile."

"Not directly in front of your house?"

"Well, no," I start, feeling the need to defend myself. "Jaynie, keep in mind I live on a remote road, so it would be impossible for anyone to be in front of my house without it being obvious they were there to watch or interact with me in some fashion. The closest house is at least 2,500 feet away, and my road is very sparse. If I were the one stalking me... I'd probably park at that gas station where I could watch for when I come and go."

"Logical." She smiles, and it seems like she's proud of me for the way I've come to this conclusion.

Sometimes, it's like she hasn't ever met me. All I know how to make are logical arguments. Since my instincts are virtually non-existent, it's logic all the way for me.

Seeing I have nothing else to add, she continues the conversation. "I can't say for sure if they're following you, but I want to remind you that if you feel like you're in danger at any time, you need to call 911 right away."

I laugh, and it's not a small giggle. It's a punchy, braying donkey type of laugh.

She twists up her face in confusion at my unusual outburst, especially given the seriousness of the topic.

I school my features immediately. "I'm sorry. That was probably rude. I don't mean to mock you, but if I called 911 every time I felt like I was in danger, I'd be in a mental institution by now. My brothers would have me locked up. Or at the very least, they'd make me move back in with my parents."

Narrowing her eyes at me, she asks, "Are you being sarcastic? I can't tell."

Not understanding sarcasm? That's *my* job, lady.

"I'm only being partially sarcastic, Jaynie. If my family knew how often I was scared, they'd most definitely insist I move back home."

She puts the footrest down and leans forward, placing her folded hands on the legal pad in her lap.

Quietly, she asks, "Have you told them about your diagnosis yet, Sue?"

I stick out my chin like a petulant child. "No. And I'm not sure if I'm going to." Next thing you know, I'll be crossing my arms over my chest and stomping my feet.

"Why not?"

I pause, trying to identify precisely why I don't want them to know.

After nibbling on the inside of my cheek for a second, I reply, "Well, for one, they might feel guilty for not catching the signs sooner. But mostly, I don't want them to see me as any more broken than they already do."

"Sue, we've talked about this. You are *not* broken. Why do you think you are?"

"I didn't say I saw myself as broken."

Although, sometimes I do.

Okay, most of the time I do.

"But *they* would see me that way. They already handle me like I'm fragile. If I tell them this, they'll probably wrap me in bubble wrap and throw pillows down all over the floor."

"Your sarcasm game is really improving." She grins and winks at me.

"Thank you." I nod my head in response.

Smiling, she says, "What if you just told one person? Is there a friend you could tell? Someone you could swear to secrecy?"

Friends? Ha. She's hilarious today.

"No one comes to mind."

"What about your brother's new wife? You've spoken fondly of her quite often. Could you tell her?"

Millie.

Yeah, I probably could. And to be honest, she'd probably be a great person to talk to about it because she never makes me feel broken. She doesn't treat me like I'm defective. She's the only one to ever do that... except Leo.

With Leo, I felt *normal*.

Brave, smart, and capable.

He never talked down to me or shot me pitying glances.

Except for the day he walked away and made me feel like an idiot for thinking I was special to him. Like I meant something to him.

Nothing about that day makes any sense. It's utterly contradictory to everything he ever made me feel. Everything he ever told me. It's like something switched when the job was over.

I suppose there's my answer. I was only a job to him.

Those tears that were threatening to appear earlier finally make their grand debut.

"Why are you crying right now? Was she cruel to you?"

"Who?"

"Your brother's wife."

"No. Never. She'd never. No, Millie is awesome to me."

"Then why are you suddenly crying at the mention of her?"

"I was just thinking about how Millie never makes me feel different. And the only other person who ever treated me like that... like I'm normal... was Leo."

"And you miss him," she surmises astutely.

"Yes. Very much. But then I feel insane or pathetic for still missing him like this so many months later." Cradling my head in my hands, I rub at my pounding temples and wish for the millionth time I could get over my incredibly pitiful crush on Leo Mason.

"I'm so sorry, Sue. I know how much it can hurt. It was a long time ago for me, but I can still feel the pain of my first heartbreak. That's the thing with your first love. No matter how it ends, the feelings you had never fully leave. Even several decades later, I can still feel tightness in my chest when something reminds me of our parting. But the good thing is, I can still feel the love too. The pain does lessen. It will get easier for you."

I scoff, dabbing at my nose and grabbing another tissue. "It wasn't love, though. And I certainly don't have all these grandiose, romantic memories to look back on. It's just me being pathetic and lonely again." I jab my index finger into my chest. "I was the only one with feelings. It was all in my head. He didn't care about me like I cared for him."

"Is that what you believe... that he didn't really care for you?"

"Ye..." I start to answer yes, but the truth is... I don't believe it, so I bite off the word.

That *cannot* be true.

"I don't know anymore. I *thought* he felt it too. That connection. It was like there was a string between us."

I press my fist into my sternum. "It attached here, and sort of pulled me to him. I certainly had never experienced that kind of draw to anyone before. In fact, I always thought people who described such a connection were full of crap, or it was just a romantic notion — not grounded in reality. I'd certainly never felt the need to be close to someone like I did with him. And when he looked at me, *my gosh*."

I suck in a deep breath, then drop my head backward as a whoosh leaves my chest.

"Jaynie, I could've sworn he felt it too. When he spoke to me, he was so gentle and kind, but not patronizing or pitying like my family tends to be. Leo was just... he was everything I never knew existed. Never knew I needed someone like that in my life. He was entirely perfect for me right up until the day he left."

I pinch my lips in a hard line to stop from blabbering any more about my stupid crush on my former bodyguard.

Pathetic, Sue.

With narrow slits in her eyes, Jaynie asks, "You know what I think?"

"That I'm making up for not having schoolgirl crushes when I was actually in school?"

I joke, but I do think this might be the case.

I suspect most girls go through this type of dramatic thing in high school, where they have all these big feelings for some guy who blows them off, and then they're devastated.

Thoughtfully, I continue, "When I was in high school, I overheard so many girls talking about this type of thing — being lovesick. I never felt the same way back then, and it's not like I had any friends to discuss it with in-depth, but I suspect it's very similar to what I'm feeling for Leo now."

Unrequited crush syndrome.

Not sure that's a thing, so maybe don't look it up. *But if you do look it up, let me know what you find out. K? Thanks.*

"Well, it's quite possible, yes, that this is a one-sided crush. But you're far more observant than you give yourself credit for, Sue. If you think he felt strongly for you, then he probably did. There may be another reason he left the way he did."

"Well, I guess we'll never know."

"Did you ever think about calling him up and talking to him?"

And cue the donkey braying laugh again. Boy, this woman should start her own stand-up comedy routine. She's on fire today.

She sits up straighter. "I'm serious, Sue. You could call him. Nothing is stopping you."

"Yes, there is. Crippling fear of spontaneous death by embarrassment is stopping me."

I really wish I could snap a picture of my therapist right now because her face is totally meme-worthy.

I'd caption it: *Your therapist is not amused.*

"Well, I can tell we're not getting anywhere on that topic today. We can talk about this more on your next visit. Let's move on. Did you bring your journal? We need to talk about your triggers to see if we can figure out what's going on before we circle back to your dream."

I pull my notebook out of my bag, flip to my recent triggers, and read them aloud.

When we're done talking about my triggers and dissecting the dream a little, our session comes to a close. I feel a touch better for talking out my issues, and she did give me permission to only come up with four things to ground me if I can't come up with five. Four is a better number, anyhow.

Jaysus, what a relief. But if I start getting stuck on three things, I'm going to conclude the whole concept is bullshit.

"One more thing, Sue." She stops me before I leave her office, placing her hand on my arm.

"Yes?" I turn, giving her my full attention, which includes more than two seconds of eye contact because it just feels right after a productive therapy session like this.

"Promise me you'll do two things."

"What?" I ask with more than a dash of trepidation.

"One, if you feel scared, call for help right away. Don't take this potential stalker thing lightly. I doubt it's in your head. Paranoia isn't really something you've exhibited before, and it doesn't seem to be the case now."

"Okay. And two?"

"Think more about telling Millie or someone else in your family about your diagnosis. Please."

"Did anyone ever tell you that you're a lot like a cat pushing things off a ledge?"

"What am I pushing?"

"Your luck." I wink and leave, feeling lighter than I have in a few days.

Chapter Eight

Good girl, Sue

Sue

"You're going to be reinforcing sit and stay, building up to staying with distractions, and then start training for walking in heel position."

"Okay. I know those really well," I tell Nick.

My boss-brother was pleased when I told him I'd take on one client — not three — this week to see how it goes. Scratch that. He was more than pleased. He was as happy as Larry.

And no, I don't know who Larry is. No one really does. It's just something we Irish say when someone is especially joyous. I grew up hearing my parents say this, and it stuck.

But I digress.

Back to dog training.

I made no promises about additional dogs beyond this one. As far as I'm concerned, it's on a trial basis. I opted to work with Louie, a one-year-old yellow Labrador.

"Sue, are you still with me?" Nick asks, waving his hand in front of my face and snapping me back into reality.

"Oh, my bad."

"I've noticed you zoning out lately. You look tense too."

Inflecting fake sincerity into my voice, I sass, "Thanks! It's the anxiety and depression."

When my attempted humor falls flat, I sulk a little, letting myself feel the tiniest bit of self-pity. Not because of the failed joke, but for the anxiety.

He looks at me with his lips turned downward on both sides. Does that pouting shit work on his wife? It's not going to work on me.

Oh, who am I kidding?

It's totally going to work on me. It's a solid pout. Five stars.

I shrug, then say, "Yeah, it has been happening a lot lately. Not entirely sure why, but I keep spacing out."

His lips press into a straight line before he says, "It might be time to consider changing up the ADHD meds like your psychiatrist was suggesting."

"Ugh." I run my hand through my hair. "I don't think I want to change my medications again, Nicky. I understand the value it may provide, but I'm really nervous about changing things up right now. All the risks of new side effects, the dosage changes, the danger of things getting worse. I just don't think I can go through that right now."

He cricks his head to the side, raising one eyebrow. I can do that too. I bet it's genetic.

Hmm. I wonder if eyebrow motions are genetic like tongue rolling is. That's something I *cannot* do.

Annnd I'm mentally off topic again.

My mind seems to be on a mission to prove my brother's point today about needing more medications.

He makes it worse when he says, "On the other hand, wouldn't it be nice to be able to follow a conversation without looking like you've suddenly started buffering?"

I cover my giggle with my hand, then nod a few times as the laugh wains. "Nice one, Nicky. Solid attempt at relating to my generation. Four stars."

He takes a mock bow.

I roll my eyes and ask, "Anyway, what were you saying?"

"Oh, let's see. You'd just told me you were good with the training plan for Louie, and I was telling you how proud I am."

"Of course you are," I reply with seriousness.

He laughs and wraps me in a great, big, smothering hug.

Too much. *Too much.*

"Stop. Ew. Gross. Enough with the hugging," I joke, pushing him away after the hug lingers a tad too long for my comfort level.

Shaking out my shoulders, I resume mental preparations for today's training session — which is what I was doing before Nick decided this was a good time to go over the plan. Again. Like I'm an idiot.

That's probably why I spaced out. Not the ADHD as much as the need to fill my brain with interesting thoughts in lieu of hearing my brother lecture me.

"Well, since you're all set, I'm going to go for a quick run. I can get in at least three miles before we leave. We're riding to the park together, right?"

"Yes. I'll be ready to go when you are." I hold up my Kindle, shaking it at him. "I can easily kill time until it's time to head out. I'm finished with all my Naughty Dogs work for the day. And I've gone over my training plan twelve times. It's memorized." I tap at my temple twice.

And I'm not exaggerating.

I've reviewed it twelve times. It's a nice number.

"Sounds good. Back shortly, then."

He finishes tying his shoes and heads to the kitchen to grab a bottle of water. A few minutes later, he's out the front door. And I'm alone.

Just like always.

Chapter Nine

Pretty sure it's not medicinal

Leo

The crack of my knuckles echoes loudly in the empty foyer, as does the scuff of my boots pacing on the polished marble floors.

I can hear feminine laughter and *something else* coming from the back of the house. *Is that supposed to be singing?* I don't understand the words since she's "singing" in Italian.

Very loudly.

And badly. Damn, that's freaking terrible.

It sounds like a feral cat giving birth to a tank.

That's why I'm up here at the front of the house. Well, aside from the crude gestures Trixie and her friends keep throwing in my direction. However, it was impressive what the redhead could do with that banana. Not at all interested, though.

If this screeching continues, I'm going to strongly consider placing Flex Seal over my ears or her mouth.

How is this chick a successful enough pop singer to hire Redleg for security? They must have auto-tuned the shit out of her voice in order to capitalize on her pop star appearance.

I'm going to assume she's only this bad because she's drunk. She and her friends have been doing lemon drop shots and chasing them with Fireball.

At the thought, I rub my chest, imagining the heartburn drinking that combination would cause.

I check the cameras surrounding the property perimeter, even though I didn't get an alert to notify me of any activity. But an uneasy feeling has settled in my bones, and I don't think it's because of the squawking coming from the back patio.

At least she's singing in English now, but too bad it's *Nickelback*. The night's going from bad to worse.

Nothing looks amiss on the camera feeds, so I walk around the outside of the house, doing a perimeter check. When I get to the back, the pungent skunky aroma of marijuana assaults my senses.

Shit.

Florida hasn't legalized cannabis for recreational use yet, and I saw nothing about medical issues in Ms. Valentine's dossier.

I pull my phone back out of my pocket and fire a text to Big Al to cover my ass. I'm required to inform him when anything illegal takes place on a job. I'm pretty sure he's going to tell me it's fine to let her continue, but it's best to let him make that call since it's his company on the line if shit ever goes sideways.

Me: FYI Trixie Valentine — signals 2 and 18

Boss: 18 Type?

Me: 420

Boss: At the residence?

Me: Yes.

Boss: As long as she's being safe, let it ride.

Me: 10-4.

Using the 420 code to refer to marijuana and the signal codes for things like drug use and being intoxicated is something we adopted from our law enforcement brethren and modified to suit our needs at Redleg, and it helps expedite our conversations. The boss often has his hands full, so it's best to make our conversations as brief as possible.

If the boss says to let it ride, then I shall let it ride.

Anything that can get our clients thrown in jail must be avoided at all costs. Fortunately, it's just pot and not anything more extreme. That's happened before, and our clients get pretty pissed off when we try to impede their drug use. But can you imagine if one of our clients overdosed on our watch? Or was arrested?

Fuck that.

It's in their contract with Redleg that they'll avoid illegal activity — including drug use — but celebrities sometimes think rules don't apply to them.

Continuing my perimeter walk, I approach the back patio cautiously, trying to stay in the shadows as I make my way to the other side of the property. I just want to get to the other side without having to engage with an intoxicated drama queen.

"Hey, handsome. Care to join us?" The slurred-sounding feminine voice causes my fists to clench.

I'm practically counting down the hours until she's on a flight back to Europe.

"No, thanks. I'm on duty."

"Oh, come on, Leooo." She drags out my name like that's going to change my mind.

I glance at her with my brows furrowed and see her lips scrunch up, pouting like a fish.

"There have been no photographers chasing us, so I think you should take the evening off and have some fun with us," she pleads, batting her eyelashes at me.

"I'm being paid to ensure your safety and nothing else."

"But we need some manly company, and you're sooo handsome, Leooo. Come and be our big, strong American hero," one of the other girls says — her Italian accent much more distinct. She presses her arms together, drawing my attention to her ample cleavage.

It does absolutely nothing for me.

Once upon a time, I would have been tempted — I'd never act, of course. But lately, it feels like my libido is entirely dried up. The only exception is when I think about Sue's thick thighs or her full lips.

I can get hard just imagining.

I abruptly halt that train of thought before the ladies on the back porch get the wrong idea.

"I'm flattered but not interested. If you want company, you'll need to handle that on your own. Now, if you'll excuse me, I'm going to finish my check of the property."

I walk away without waiting for a response, but I can hear the groans of disappointment despite the crashing of the waves in the distance.

"We should do that," one of them says as I walk away. She then smoothly shifts into Italian, and they all start speaking rapidly. Their voices become more and more animated, and I say a silent prayer they aren't concocting some trouble I'll have to deal with. Before I turn the corner at the edge of the property, I hear one of them say — in English this time — "I want some American dicks!"

Shit.

Since I turned them down, I'm guessing it's about to turn into a house party.

I check my watch. Kri should be here any minute to start her shift. So far this week, she's been doing an adequate job — not that there have been any challenges to deal with.

It's been beach days and shopping trips, with dinner either catered in or fine dining at expensive restaurants. Nothing too risky or daunting. But she's been respectful and followed all orders without question.

For tonight, I split her shift — she's got half her shift with me and the second half with Sawyer. He'll report back to me with her progress.

As I reach the front of the property, incoming headlights temporarily blind me. My hand raises to shield my eyes so I can see who's arrived. It's Kri — right on time. That's another good sign. I don't often have to eat my words, but she's proving to be much less of a handful than I expected.

"Sup Lionheart?" she asks, a cocky grin splayed across her face.

She's wearing a basic white V-neck shirt that's tucked into dark pants with a tactical belt worn snugly around her slim waist. When she gets closer, I can see she has on a touch of makeup, but nothing over the top. She looks professional and well-rested. All good signs showing she's taking the job seriously.

I nod as she approaches and stops in front of me. "Evening, Kri."

Together, we head up the front steps and enter the villa.

"What's the princess up to this evening?" she asks.

"Smoking dope and drinking like a fucking fish. A fish without taste buds."

Kri's head pulls back. "You're going to have to explain that."

"They're drinking lemon drop shots and Fireball."

"Shit. That's harsh." She cringes, scrunching up her shoulders and wrinkling her nose and lips. "Are they pledging a fraternity? Or are they training to join the Corps? That's how the jarheads drink."

"Nah, they're not eating crayons or drinking MD 20/20," I joke, enjoying this side of Kri and our camaraderie.

Since we're both Army vets, we enjoy poking fun at the Marines.

"You mean not yet."

"Yeah, I heard them talking about wanting some 'American dicks' tonight." I put up air quotes around the ridiculous phrase I overheard. "Don't be surprised if we get a request for a trip out to the clubs or they start ordering male escorts. There's no telling what tonight will bring."

"Is it wrong that I want it to be male strippers?"

"I'd be a hypocrite if I gave you shit about that. I can remember a job or two when female strippers showed up, and it wasn't exactly a hardship to stand guard on those occasions."

Although, those nights did start to feel disgusting when I saw how some of my fellow males would talk about and sometimes treat the strippers.

The incessant beeping of the door alarm sounds as we enter. I tap in the code to silence it. Kri sets her bag down and looks around, peeking her head around the corner toward the living area.

"They out on the patio again?"

"Yeah."

"I don't know how they stand the humidity."

"Pretty sure the alcohol took away their ability to care."

"That bad?"

Nodding, I respond, "She was singing acapella again too."

Kri hisses while shaking her head. "Are we sure Tomer accurately verified her parental lineage? That bitch sounds like Roseanne Barr had a baby with Bobcat Goldthwait."

I let out a deep guffaw at the image that provokes. "Aren't you a bit young to know who they are?"

I nudge her shoulder. Despite my substantial size and girth, she doesn't waver a bit.

Impressive.

She scoffs, "Deltas know all kinds of shit they shouldn't."

"I'm fairly certain late eighties pop trivia isn't on the ASVAB," I tell her, jokingly referring to the military's placement test.

It doesn't escape my notice how she's often referring to her time with the Deltas in conversation. Although not officially a Delta, she worked enough undercover operations with them to consider herself one. If she wasn't a woman, she would have easily made Delta Force.

"You know, you don't need to do that," I say with a softer, more serious tone.

"Do what?" She swallows a lump down her throat, and a tightness sets in her jaw.

"Throw your resume at me every chance you get."

She looks away, putting her hands in the back pockets of her black cargo pants. "You don't know what it's like for someone like me."

"Tell me," I prod gently.

"To be a woman in the military is one thing — it's a daily struggle. But when you're a woman trying to become one of the elite, it's a whole other level of fucked up."

She shakes her head softly, eyes still scanning the room — a sign she's still monitoring her surroundings for threats. I know because I'm doing the same.

"I can imagine it being difficult, Kri. We didn't have any female rangers when I was enlisted, although we did have some go on ops with us. It couldn't have been easy, but —"

She cuts me off with a scoff. "Easy? No one wants you there. The only way you get any respect is to be better than them. But when you do, it gets even worse. They still resent you. Instead of seeing me as an ally, they're threatened. It's as if my being good enough takes something away from their own abilities. Nothing makes a man more insecure than a strong woman."

"You're not in anymore, Kri. It's different here."

"It takes a while to downshift from that type of competitive environment."

Just as I'm about to respond with some pearls of wisdom — talking out of my ass, really — I'm rescued from the heavy topic with the buzzing of my phone.

When I see what's just been sent to me, my heart squeezes painfully in my chest, and my knees go weak.

With one hand squeezing the phone tightly, a shaky finger swipes through the photos. Five of them... taken over what looks like several days, judging by the variety of clothing and locations.

No!

No, no, no, no, no, no.

This *cannot* be happening. Not again.

"Leo?" Kri's worried tone catches my attention, only briefly shaking me from what I'm seeing.

My deepest fear is realized as I read the words accompanying the pictures.

Sweat begins beading along my brow, and my muscles twinge as the adrenaline roars through my body, priming me for action. My free hand forks through my hair, tugging at the short strands as I struggle to breathe.

"Lionheart, what is it?" she asks again.

My response is one word, so pained that my voice cracks.

"Sue."

Chapter Ten

Fuck my life

Leo

Because you've taken away something important to me, I think I'll do the same with something important to you.

I read the words to myself again, trying to figure out what the fuck to do first to mitigate the fallout.

"Leo, talk to me! Now!" Kri demands, attempting to yank me from my panicked state.

My eyes meet hers, and I notice the soft lines crinkled around the corners. She grabs me by the upper arms and shakes when I don't respond.

It's like I've been struck catatonic. I'm here, but I'm not here. My mind is running through a million thoughts at Mach speed.

Who sent that text?

Where is Sue?

I need to get Tomer to track down the sender.

What do they think I've taken?

How fast can I get to Sue?
What if I'm already too late?
Did I miss any signs?
I can't fail again.
Who should I call first?
I need to stop this.
I will stop this.

My feet start moving before my mouth does, hefting me to the back porch where my client is sitting and enjoying the quiet night air with her friends. She *should* be my priority, but she's not.

Sue's my priority.

Always has been.

Ever since I first laid eyes on her that morning last spring, I felt something shift inside me, irrevocably connecting me to her.

I was afraid of something like this happening — something from my past coming back to bite me in the ass — and that's why I refused to act on the attraction. It gutted me, but I left.

So why the hell is she still being sucked into a mess like this? It makes no sense.

As I storm through the house, I pull up the tracking app on my phone and verify Sue's current location based on her vehicle and phone. A breath of relief leaves me when the red dot shows her at home — hopefully safe for the time being.

I halt to a stop when my feet hit the wood deck of the back patio.

Without a preamble, I announce, "Something urgent has come up, and I'm leaving immediately. Kri is here. Don't do anything stupid."

Judging by the offended look on Trixie's face, I might get in trouble for speaking to a client like that, but right now, I officially give less than zero fucks.

Kri trails me through the house as I grab my motorcycle helmet and bark orders at her.

"Call Sawyer as soon as I leave and tell him I said he needs to report in early. If he can't do it, call someone else — Big Al should be your last resort. I don't want you alone, especially if she's partying and talking about having other people come over. Don't fucking let her leave unless Sawyer goes with you. I want you to do a visual sweep of the perimeter every half hour and check on Trixie every ten minutes at a minimum, at least from a distance. Keep your ears open for the alarms and check the tablet for any equipment notifications."

I toss the tablet — our mobile command center device — at her as she nods along with my rapid-fire instructions.

"Is Sue a codeword for a tango? Is Trixie being targeted?"

She doesn't know anything about Sue and my... *connection* with her.

The Amos stalker job happened before Kri came to work with Redleg.

"No. There's no tango — no threat to Trixie. The text was about Sue. She's a former client."

And the owner of my heart.

"No threat to Trixie?"

"No," I answer flatly as I rush out the front door with Kri still nipping at my heels.

The urge to bodily shrug her off is so strong because every second she delays me is one more second Sue is in danger.

I can't let anything happen to my angel.

When we get to the spot where my bike is parked, I notice Kri cross her arms across herself in a defensive posture out of the corner of my eye.

"I don't need Sawyer to babysit me. He can come at his usual time. If there is nothing new threatening Trixie, I'll be fine. I can handle it." She sticks her chin up and out in defiance.

Fuck my life.

I don't have time for a pissing contest right now.

I throw a leg over my bike and cram my helmet on my head with no finesse. After I flip open the visor, I tell her, "You have your orders. It's not up for discussion." I lower the visor back down, effectively ending the conversation.

My Harley roars to life, and I feel the rumble beneath me. As I pull out of the driveway, I tap the button on the side of my helmet to activate the voice assistant. It runs through my phone via Bluetooth, connecting to a microphone and earpiece built into my helmet.

"Call Sue O'Malley," I say after the tone notifies me the system is ready for my command.

Three painstakingly long rings later, the call goes to voicemail. My heart bottoms out. I hope I'm not too late.

Hanging up without leaving a message, I decide to try her brother. "Call Nick O'Malley."

It's a few rings before he answers, "Leo?" He sounds pleasantly surprised to hear from me.

"Yeah, it's me. Lis —"

He interrupts with exuberance at my unexpected call. "Good to hear from you, my man. It's been too —"

"No time to chat right now. Is Sue with you? She's not answering."

"I dropped her off at home about two hours ago after we trained some dogs at the park. She did her first solo lesson tonight. Why? Is something wrong?"

It took him a minute, but I think he finally realizes this isn't a social call.

"Not sure yet. I'm en route to her place now. How far away are you from her?"

"We can be there in ten or fifteen minutes." I hear some shuffling in the background. "We'll leave right now."

Racing almost as fast as the wheels of my bike, my mind concludes it's not a good idea to get anyone else involved until I can further assess the threat. Never bring in more people who could be placed in harm.

Always minimize the risk.

"No. Don't. I'll be there by then. And until I know what's happening, I don't want to risk getting anyone else involved."

"Leo, dude! You're scaring me. What the hell is going on?"

"It might be nothing. Just got a text that worried me."

"Is that Leo Mason?" a feminine voice in the background calls out — sounds like his wife and my former client, Millie Amos. Well, she's Millie Amos-O'Malley now.

"Don't worry your wife about this. I'm sure it's probably just a false alarm."

I fucking hope it is.

"Nick, I'll check on Sue and call you back in a few minutes. I'm five minutes away."

"Okay, we'll try to call her."

"Good. If you get her on the line, tell her to stay inside and lock all the doors until I get there."

"Got it."

"Talk soon."

I disconnect the call, freeing him up to call his sister. She might have sent my call to voicemail — probably still pissed at how harshly I treated her the last time we spoke — but maybe she'll answer his call. He'll have her wait for me safely inside her house.

Yeah, *everything will be fine,* I reassure myself while whipping between cars to get to Sue as fast as two wheels can take me.

I must get to her before they do.

Then I'll find out who the fuck *they* are and what they want.

And I will end them.

It's just a jump to the left…
and then a step to the right

As I dive past cars waiting in traffic, I mentally flip myself the bird more times than I can count. I abhor people who drive motorcycles like this — endangering themselves and others by thinking they're entitled to weave in and out of cars like a dog on an agility course.

A dog.

Huh.

The thought spurs to life a sequence of memories starring the woman I'm on my way to save.

When I was guarding her before, she was taking care of her brother's dog Ahsoka most of the time. Most nights, we'd take the dog for walks together after dinner — often going to a well-lit park for safety. Then we'd go inside and cuddle up on the couch. The dog would sit between us like she knew I wanted to be close to Sue but also knew it was a bad idea.

Despite being a four-legged cockblocker, she was a good girl.

Good girl.

Another memory hits me.

"You can hit harder than that. You're not going to hurt me," I tell Sue.

"That's all I've got," she says flatly but won't meet my eyes.

"Sue, you're a shitty liar. Now, hit harder. Pretend I'm the bad guy."

She sighs and presses her lips together in a flat line as she stares at the target I've given her.

I've got my hands up in front of me, palms facing her, and I'm trying to teach her how to throw a punch. It's not as instinctive as you'd think, and I've noticed Sue isn't all that coordinated. But I have a feeling with a little practice, she'll be better able to protect herself should she need it — heaven forbid.

She drops her hands, no longer in fists, down to her sides. "But you're so nice," she finally says. "You could never be the bad guy."

Rubbing the scruff on my chin, I try to hide my smile behind my hand. After a moment, I put my hands back up as a target.

"Make a fist. Let me see it."

I've already shown her the proper way to make a fist, wrapping the thumb along the underside of your fingers, so it doesn't get broken by being in front of or behind your knuckles. And you certainly don't leave it sticking out to the side unless you want it dislocated.

She concentrates hard on putting both hands into the proper position as I requested.

Once she's ready, I tell her, "Okay, kid. Give it to me. First two knuckles on top of the fist. Push through on contact."

With her face a mask of concentration, she finally throws a decent punch — her wrist, forearm, and shoulder all in line.

"Nice one! Good girl. Again."

She makes contact, and I repeat, "Good girl. Again."

The grin that appears on her face as she improves is so radiant it could make a blind man see. She's proud of herself. I'm proud, too, even though I don't really have a right to be. I've got no claim of ownership on Sue — she's not my blood, my girl, or even my friend.

She's a client.

A client. A client.

I keep telling myself that, but it's not getting through anymore.

Guarding Sue these last weeks has been a test of willpower in more ways than one.

And now, I'm beaming at her like I have some right to be.

All I did was show her how to throw a punch. Hell, it wasn't even my idea. We were sitting around her place after she'd finished painting, and it was still too early for dinner. I'd checked the perimeter, and we were just killing time making up more ridiculous words — she always comes up with better ones than me. Out of the blue, she looked over at me and asked, "Can you teach me how to defend myself?"

And here we are.

Once she's mastered punching with her dominant and non-dominant hand, I ask, "What do you want to practice next? Breaking a chokehold? A bear hug from behind? Or deflecting punches?"

Her hand reaches up to her neck, and she tentatively asks, "A chokehold?"

"Yes, I can teach you if you want. You want to try?"

"I don't want you to really choke me. I don't think I'd enjoy that. I mean, I know some people like that, but it's not my kink."

Note to self: don't attempt asphyxiation play with Sue.

No! Dammit.

I'm not going to try anything like that with Sue.

Ever.

I'm no good for her... not like that. I can protect her and teach her how to fight back against an attacker, but that's it.

Focus on the mission.

"I won't actually choke you, but I can show you a few moves to help you get loose if someone tried to choke you. Is that all right? We don't have to do it if you don't want."

She eyes the floor for a few seconds, then nods, saying, "Okay. Let's do it. Teach me how to get out of a chokehold."

"Good girl. Come here."

She marches up to me so quickly that I need to tell my dick to stand down. My cock is throbbing its appreciation of her obedience and how willingly she came to me.

"Turn around," I instruct.

With her facing away from me, I bring my arm around her neck, resting my forearm across her throat. I'm not putting any real pressure on her. I don't want to scare her.

"Now, the first thing you want to do if someone grabs you from behind is —"

She cuts me off. "Calm down, right?"

I laugh. "No, that's terrible advice."

She cocks her head back so she's looking at me over her shoulder. Her brows furrow in confusion. "It is? Then why do people always say that?"

"Well, I guess in a perfect world, it would be ideal if you remained calm. But it's not likely going to happen. If someone is choking you, it's not normal to be calm, and your chances of forcing calm are next to none. So, rather than struggling to remain calm, I think you want to let your body's fight-or-flight response take over — the adrenaline will make you stronger. Plus, what are the odds you could actually calm yourself down?"

"I guess that makes sense. But I'm getting really good at calming myself down in times of stress."

My arm falls a little, grazing the top of her breasts behind her thin cotton shirt as we continue our conversation. I've almost forgotten about the impromptu self-defense lesson. It's so easy to talk to her, and I want to learn everything I can about her.

She fascinates me.

"Oh, really, Susie? Have you had much experience with high-stress life or death situations?"

Her eyes fall, but not in sadness. It's more like she's deep in thought.

Her voice is almost a whisper when she finally says, "When you're like me, every day you leave the house feels like it's high stress or life or death."

My arm falls the rest of the way. I move the three steps it takes to bring myself directly in front of her.

"What do you mean?" I whisper, mirroring her volume.

"Just that... I have all these extra feelings, and my senses aren't like most other people's. Noises are louder, lights are brighter, and emotions are sometimes more than I can handle. Everything feels overwhelming, especially when I don't take my medications... and sometimes, I admit, I forget to take them. I wish I didn't have to take them, but I know I do. I've had to learn how to deal with it — all the extra stimuli. It's very stressful."

She inhales a wobbly breath before adding, "I'm different."

My hand reaches out to lift her chin. "You think you're different?"

"I know I am."

"Well, then different is a good thing. I like you this way."

She squints at me, probably in disbelief, but it's hard to tell with her sometimes. "You don't even know me."

"I've been by your side non-stop for the last twelve days. We've spent that time talking, laughing, getting to know each other, and doing all kinds of everyday shit together. We've eaten almost every meal together and entertained each other from sunrise to sunset. I might not know you as well as your family — and it's only been twelve days — but I think I have a good grasp on who you are. I'm also damn observant, which goes with the job. And I think you're amazing. If that means you're different, then I like you different."

"I think I should make an appointment for you to meet my therapist," she says with a wide grin.

"I see what you're doing."

"What am I doing?"

"Shaking off the genuine compliment I gave you with humor."

"Maybe you don't need therapy. Maybe you already are a therapist."

"There it is again."

"Ugh... will you just choke me already?"

I can't hold back my laugh, and there is no sense in trying to hide it, so I let it fly. Sue joins me in laughter too. The lighthearted feeling once again between us reminds me of the day I met her, and we laughed for a solid five minutes after she flung shit at me.

Never thought I'd find that funny, but I sure as hell did that day.

"All right, let's get to choking," I tease and take my place behind her.

I pretend not to notice the swell of her ass and how it presses just below my groin. She's on the taller side for a girl, so I'm not completely towering over her — which is a nice change since I tower over most people.

I also actively tell myself I don't notice the strawberry smell of her shampoo when I move my forearm back under her neck.

However, my junk has made no such promise to avoid thinking of how delectable it is being this close to her. I force myself to think of her like a kid sister in an attempt to send blood flow away from my stiffening cock.

"Okay, kid. The first thing you want to do if someone grabs you like this is to tuck your chin down. Any time someone makes a move for your throat, try to cut off their access and reduce the amount of area they have to play with. Go ahead and jam your chin down."

She does as instructed, cramming her chin into the space between my upper forearm and her neck.

"Good girl. Next, grab my arm with both your hands. Just reach up and wrap your hands around my arm."

"Got it."

The feel of her hands grasping my arm does nothing to deflate my cock. Neither does the sound of her breath as it increases the more I tighten my hold on her.

I'm not even putting a fraction of the pressure on her that I would on someone I was trying to subdue, and I won't. I know my own strength and have mastered the ability to be a gentle giant, as I'm often called. And Sue needs only to grasp the concept of this lesson.

My breath is hitching the longer we stay like this. I think her breathing might be intensifying because of our closeness too.

At least that's what I think.

Then again, she's the one who pulled away from me last week when I almost kissed her in my SUV.

Fucking idiot that I am for even trying that.

I blame her pheromones for overpowering my wits in the small space. Or the way her thighs kept smashing together like she felt the lightning bouncing between us too.

"Now what?" *she asks, shaking me from my mental detour.*

"Take a step to the right."

"Like this?"

"Yes. Bend forward a little so you're pulling me downward with you."

When she does, I swear all the dirty images I've ever had of her leap in front of my mind in flashing neon. I move my hips back so she doesn't feel what she's doing to me. I need to get myself under control.

"That's far enough," *I tell her.* "Kick me in the knee with your left leg."

"But you're behind me."

"Raise your foot, bend your knee, and shove the flat of your foot backward toward my knee or shin. Slowly, since we're practicing."

She attempts the motion, going off balance.

"Any time you lift one leg in self-defense, make sure your other leg is ready to hold your weight. The last thing you want is to be off balance and fall over."

"Okay, sorry."

"That's okay. Try again."

She does, this time distributing her weight better.

"Good girl," *I tell her.* "Now, let's start again and see if you remember all the steps and can do them quickly."

And let's see if I can get through the bear hug practice we still need to do without busting my fucking zipper.

The haze of the memory clears from my mind as I glance at my watch, coming to a slow-roll of a stop at the stoplight on the corner on Sue's street. I made good time, less than seven minutes from start to finish.

I'm almost there.

She's going to be there when I arrive. I know she is. If they were going to take her right away, they would have just done it and then told me they had her. What's the point of telling me they could take her?

They want me here. Maybe they want to know if I'd really jump to protect her at the drop of a hat. They could be testing the hold she has over me. They could be drawing me out for some reason, but that's okay. I'll be ready for them when I get there. As long as she's okay, everything else will be fine.

She's going to be okay.

She fucking better be.

If she isn't... well, I'm not going to think about what I'll do to anyone who even dares to harm a hair on her head.

She's going to be okay.

It's all going to be fine.

Seeing her again, though? I have no idea how that's going to go. She's probably pissed at me. I bet she hates me — as she should.

But that doesn't matter now. Just her safety. Only her safety matters.

She's going to be okay.

I'm almost there. Almost there.

Chapter Eleven

They must be selling audacity in bulk these days

Sue

My paintbrush comes to an abrupt halt on the canvas with the first notes of the electronic melody coming from my cell.

For the second time in the last two minutes.

Sigh.

Why do people insist on using the phone to speak to others instead of just texting or accessing apps like Steve Jobs intended?

My pulse hasn't fully recovered from the first call. Fortunately, my instincts took over and sent him to voicemail in a fraction of a second. I've honed my ability to seamlessly send calls to voicemail in very much the same way an Olympian trains for their preferred sporting event — with years and years of dedication, practice, and sacrifice. And it was all worth it. Tonight was the moment I've been preparing for since I was first able to swipe.

Ha.

I find myself hilarious when I'm trying to avoid looking at whose name is showing on my cell's caller ID.

I can hear my therapist's voice in my head. *Avoidance is not a proper coping mechanism.*

Guess I need to face it.

If he's calling back, I'm going to lose my ever-loving shit. And then what? I don't know... answer it, I guess?

Can I do that?

Am I ready to talk to him?

Will I ever be ready?

I can't believe he had the gall to call me.

Leo.

After all this time — six months and not so much as a word, and then *bam!* A random phone call out of the blue. As much as I've daydreamed about him calling me, especially lately, I never expected to hear from him again. Oddly enough, the feeling I had at the sight of his name on my caller idea was not relief or joy, nor happiness like I would have anticipated. After the shock dissipated, one emotion was left.

And it was stone-cold anger.

Because he must have some fucking nerve to contact me after the way he treated me. Dismissing me like I was nothing but an annoyance and acting like he was happy to finally be free from me.

After everything that transpired between us.

All we talked about. The little moments and secrets we shared. The way he looked at me... touched me. Made me feel.

No. I'm not going down that road again. I refuse to follow the path where my good memories of him outweigh the sting of the rejection at his abrupt exit from my life.

That *fucker.*

Taking a reluctant step in the direction of the offending sound, I sneak a glance at the screen and see it's *not* Leo. It's Nick.

Relief and disappointment are battling for the distinction of being the prevailing emotion.

At least I won't be having my own personal crisis tonight due to being forced to finally deal with Leo Mason.

I tap the green button on the screen with my pinky finger — the only part of my hand not currently messy with paint.

"What's up, Nicky?" I infuse my voice with a cheerfulness I don't feel.

Putting the call on speaker, I return to my painting, gazing at the angles and shadows and trying to illustrate the image that's vividly imprinted in my mind after all this time. Except for that motherfecking shade of brown, but I'm not going to obsess over that right now.

My brother's voice practically leaps from the tin can-sounding speaker. "Oh, thank St. Paddy. Are you all right?" He seems out of breath. Is he running?

I shake my head at the absurdity of his question and stroke my paintbrush downward. "Um, yeah, Captain Random. Why wouldn't I be?"

He ignores my question, asking one of his own instead. "Are you inside?"

I feel my brows pinch as I lift my brush from the canvas.

Nick sounds... *scared.*

Perhaps something is wrong. At the thought, my spine lengthens, and my shoulders roll back.

"Yes, why?"

"I want you to make sure all the doors are locked. Immediately."

A shiver runs up my spine.

"Nick, stop freaking out. What's wrong?"

"Just fucking do it, dammit! Check the doors and windows. Now!"

The paintbrush falls from my hand and clatters to the ground as a whirlwind of emotion pelts me from all sides — panic and fear in equal measure with excitement and curiosity. My eyes pivot quickly around the room and glance out the windows, trying to find any potential source of danger. "Fine! I'm checking now. Just calm down."

I wipe the paint from my hands roughly on the lone clean patch of my coveralls so I can grab the phone to carry it with me throughout the house while I check the door and window locks. I narrate my activities to Nick as I proceed, hoping to calm him down.

"Front door is locked," I reassure him. "I'm going to check the kitchen door now."

"Good girl."

"Don't talk to me like that. I'm not one of your dogs, ass goblin," I joke, trying to gain a sense of normalcy. "Okay, all the doors are locked, and I haven't opened my windows all summer. Now that I can assure you of my safety, will you please tell me what the hell is going on?"

"Sue, I don't know what's wrong, but Leo Mason from Redleg just called me. You might be in some type of danger. He's on his way to you now..."

I might be mistaken, but I think Nick continues talking. However, I'm no longer able to listen and decipher his words. The part of my brain responsible for taking in auditory stimuli and converting them to information that I can process for comprehension has left the building.

It's exited hastily.

Gone the way of Kodak film.

Flown the coop.

Ceased to be.

No, the only thing present now is the rush of my pulse pounding through my arteries and echoing in my ears.

My mouth goes dry, and I feel my body sway on wobbly legs. I've heard precisely enough to know I'm utterly fucked. Cue the personal crisis.

Leo Mason is coming here.

Now.

Because I might be in *danger*.

The nervous excitement I felt when I was in danger all those months ago returns. The force is so intense that I almost fall to my knees.

Sure, the last few days with the gray van sightings were scary, but I thought I merely imagined danger where none existed. But now... it's becoming tangible. It's no longer just me and my imagination. This time, it's... real. It must be serious if Nick is acting like this and Leo is on his way.

"Sue! Are you with me?" My brother is shouting now, yanking me from my errant thoughts.

"Yeah, I'm here. Sorry. Calm down. Everything is fine."

Everything is most definitely *not* fine.

Nick rattles on in my ear about my safety and ends by asking if anything odd happened after he dropped me off this evening.

"Nope. Nothing unusual. I ate dinner, then started painting."

Shit.

Painting.

All my paintings. In my studio.

I *cannot* let Leo see that room. I wonder if he'll want to come in once he arrives. Of course he will! This is Leo. And unless he's changed his stance on personal protection over the last six months, he'll probably want to check every room from floor to ceiling and back down again.

I tuck my cell phone in the front pocket of my coveralls so Nick can continue his rant while I dart into my art studio with two free hands. As I scan across the room, I see it with fresh eyes and realize there is absolutely no freaking way I can cover all of this up before Leo gets here. Unless...

"How long until Leo gets here?" I ask, interrupting Nick from something... not sure what because now he and Millie are both on the line, yapping at me to stay put, get down and hide in a closet or some shit.

Jaysus! Yet I'm the one in therapy.

"He'll be there in less than five minutes," Nick answers.

"Fuck!"

The back of my hand presses into my forehead as I wonder how the hell I'm going to cover up *all* my insanity in five freaking minutes. It's inconceivable that I'd be able to pull off that feat.

"What's the matter?" Nick asks.

"Nothing... I uh... stubbed my toe," I lie as I go about bunching up some of my smaller pieces, bundling them in my arms and shoving them in the closet.

I don't have a clue what to do about the larger canvases. Not to mention the mural stretching across one entire wall... yeah, that's a problem. At least the mural is incomplete, and therefore, he might not be able to tell what it's supposed to be.

And other lies I can tell myself.

Shifting my attention to the corner, I see stacks upon stacks of black and white sketches and watercolor paintings littered across my desk. Without ruining them, I begin sweeping them into the drawer as quickly as I can. Once it's full, I slam it closed with the side of my thigh and turn around to see what I can cover up next.

The rumbling sound of a roaring motorcycle engine makes me freeze like a kid caught with their hand in the candy drawer.

"I think he's here," I whisper to Nick and Millie, who are still on the phone that's hanging out in my pocket. "I'll have to call you back."

"Sue, wait —"

Hanging up, I back out of the painting studio, turn off the light, and close the door behind me.

I must keep him out of here. It's my house, and he'll just need to respect my wishes.

Yeah. Sure. No sweat.

A second later, he's pounding at the front door and simultaneously ringing the doorbell over and over. I take a deep breath while my feet move me toward the door at a steady pace.

"Sue, open up. It's Leo. Let me in, please."

I open the door with a surprisingly steady hand, feeling secretly grateful my brother called to tip me off. If Leo had appeared without warning, I'd have probably tried to escape through the back door like the coward I am.

My eyes widen, and my throat threatens to close when I take in the boulder of a man on my front step. The gentle giant. Breathtakingly handsome, as always. But he looks more worried than I've ever seen him — red cheeks, wrinkled brow, disheveled hair, and lips pressed firmly together.

Without warning, he yanks the screen door open and barges in.

My feet shuffle backward, granting him entrance while I studiously watch his every move. Once he's inside, he turns and closes the door behind him, promptly locking and bolting it.

"Well, hello to you too. Make yourself at home," I say sarcastically, suddenly feeling perturbed at the way he forced his way into my house without even a word of greeting.

After *six* motherfucking months!

He spins around, finally meeting my eyes, and I feel my jaw drop. I study his handsome face, noting each line, crease, and shadow are the same as I remember. His beard looks freshly trimmed, and his eyes are still the most stunning shade of blue.

"Are you..." His hands rise and cup my cheeks, then fall to my shoulders before trailing down the outside of my arms. The comforting movement leaves a trail of tingles across my skin. He studies me from head to toe like he's inspecting me for injury, almost expecting something to be wrong with me, while his warm, rough palms keep stroking my arms. I can't help but soak up the feeling of his skin on mine.

Finally, he speaks again. "Are you okay? Safe?" His voice is raspy and utterly delicious, sending a surge of heat directly to my core.

I ache to smooth the tightly furrowed skin around his eyebrows. So much concern etched on his striking face — all the sharp lines and angles on the surface, even the imperfections, come together in a contrast of fierceness and gentleness. He effortlessly sucks me under his spell.

"I'm fine," I answer in a timid voice, dabbing my tongue at my dry lips.

I notice his gaze drops to my mouth. On reflex, my eyes drop to his lips too.

What I wouldn't give to kiss him.

And I could right now. His face is mere inches from mine. I could just lean in and...

Good heavens, the power this man has over me.

Still.

I shake my head, suddenly annoyed by the spell he puts me under and the sharp turn my thoughts have taken. I toss my arms out to the sides, brusquely removing myself from his grip.

"I'm *fine*," I state more emphatically this time and take a step away from him. Then another.

A flash of something crosses his features, but it's gone before I can identify it. "Are you alone? Has anyone been here?" He visually searches the space around me.

Is he jealous or something? Ha. Good one, Sue.

"Yes, I'm alone."

"And everything is locked up?"

"Yes."

"Thank fuck," he mutters under his breath.

Taking a step closer to me, he invades my space once more and turns all my senses into mashed potatoes. Before I can object, he brings me into a comforting hug.

I allow myself one second to feel his body against mine before I push away because I don't want to be comforted right now. I want answers.

When I shove away from him, I instantly miss the warmth of his skin. Schooling my features in an unaffected mask, I face him, determined to get some answers. First, Nick calls, totally freaked out, and now Leo Mason shows up on my front porch, shoving his way into my living room like he has a right to be here and demanding to know if I'm alone.

I'm the one who needs answers. "What are you doing here, Leo?"

He glances at his boots, his shoulders dropping slightly — like a child who's been scolded. I giggle at the image that appears in my mind unbidden of a young Leo getting called into the principal's office.

"What's so funny?" he asks.

Dammit.

I need to focus, but my emotions are coming at me faster than I can process them. So, of course, I'm going to make it awkward.

Sigh.

"Nothing. I just remembered a joke I heard earlier. Tell me why you're here."

He exhales, then begins, "I got a text tonight. I don't know who it's from or what it's about. But the sender threatened you."

"Me? Why?"

"I'm not entirely sure. But he had pictures of you."

A laugh bubbles up from deep inside me.

Pictures? Really? Again?

Between guffaws, I mock, "Oh no, not pictures! *Anything* but that!" I press my hand to my chest, feigning horror. "Pictures of me exist? Oh, then I *must* be in danger. Better rush right over and save me, Leo!"

Absurd.

So what if someone has pictures of me? It's ironic because that's how Leo ended up sent to protect me the last time. Millie's stalker sent her pictures of my brother and me, threatening us if she didn't comply with his demands. Last time, I was scared once I found out about it.

This time, though?

I'm over it.

Over being scared because of some stupid pictures. Who cares? As a millennial, I'm contractually obligated to be comfortable with thousands of people having pictures of me. Ever heard of social media? Pictures are life now. We live in a time where there are cameras everywhere — in everyone's pockets and on nearly every streetlight or building — and thousands upon thousands of pictures exist of us.

Probably millions.

A picture is not a threat. Anyone can get their hands on pictures of anyone. Big flipping deal!

I turn my back on him and head to the kitchen. When I was laughing with a hand to my chest a few seconds ago, I felt the smear of wet paint on my chest, reminding me that I had never cleaned up from earlier.

"This isn't a joke, Sue." His boots thump as he trails behind me.

"Leo, give me a break! Just because someone has pictures doesn't mean I'm in danger." I turn on the water and lather up my hands with soap.

"He said he would *take* you, Sue."

Okay, I can admit that sounds worse than just pictures showing up in a random text.

"Why would anyone take *me*, of all people? I'm no one. And what does that even have to do with you?"

Leo sighs loud enough that I can hear it over the sprinkling sound of the water running into the drain. He doesn't speak while I finish scrubbing under my fingernails and across the grooves of my knuckles. But he's inched so close that I can feel the heat coming off his body.

Once my hands are clean and dry, I face him. With his gaze firmly on mine and chin tucked to hide his throat, he softly and slowly says, "Sue, whoever he is, he thinks I took something important from him. He said he's going to take something important to me in return."

His gaze intensifies as he swallows, the movement in his throat catching my attention briefly. Taking both of my small hands inside his giant ones, he lovingly adds, "*You*. It's you, Sue."

He stares deeply into my eyes, and for once, I don't want to look away or care how long I maintain eye contact. I'm not counting the seconds — I'm just feeling the intensity of him... of Leo and his words.

Something important to him.

I'm important to him.

The words are trying to sink in, but they don't make sense. This new information directly conflicts with what I believed to be true.

Because I'm nothing to him. Otherwise, why would he have walked away the way he did?

I shake loose of his hands and close my eyes, squinting to break the moment. I can't think while looking at him or while I'm this close to him, so I take a few steps.

Mashing my teeth together, I struggle to figure out what he's trying to tell me. My mind sifts through years of interactions with others, examining the social cues and how I misinterpreted them. I apply those lessons to my memories of Leo, attempting to identify what I'm feeling. And more importantly, decipher what he's saying and if his words match his actions.

When I open my eyes, the expression he wears nearly rips my chest open. All that hurt and vulnerability — from the short breaths he's taking to the bowed head and sad wide eyes. For once, I'm certain of how he's feeling, and I can tell he means what he's saying.

He's telling me *I'm* important to him. And he truly means it.

The fuck?

Fire burns in my veins. My head cocks back, and my eyes widen in outrage. "Was audacity on sale, Leo? Because you're coming in here with *loads* of it. How dare you?"

"Susie —"

I cut him off with a sharp, "No! Don't do that. Don't try to calm me down or manage me."

His head falls, and his mountainous frame folds in on itself.

I take a deep breath and lay into him with six months of fury.

"You don't get to brush me aside and tell me I mean nothing to you, leaving me feeling like a pathetic fool. You can't treat me that way and disappear for six months without so much as a word *and then* barge back in, telling me I'm *important* to you. No! It doesn't work like that."

I storm off, heading toward the living room.

I need to get away from him.

My hands run through my hair, and my nails scratch my scalp as I try to calm the avalanche of thoughts and emotions crashing into me. It's too much to process all at once. I think my brain might be short-circuiting. My senses are overwhelmed, and if I don't ground myself, then I fear I'm headed for a meltdown.

What does he even mean? Okay, I'm *important* to him. Like a kid sister? Or something much more?

He silently watches me fume and pace from his position in the kitchen. I don't think I've ever been this angry, and certainly have never been this hurt. Not even when he callously walked away, leaving me embarrassed and confused.

And I'm even more *confused* now than I was then.

How could he do this to me?

He needs to leave.

I need to be alone with my thoughts and go through my psychologist-prescribed process to calm down... to avoid this looming freak-out — because the pounding in my head and chest tells me one is certainly coming. And it's going to be a doozy.

I can feel his presence like he's right beside me, even though he's on the other side of the room, and it's making everything more acute. All the feelings he stirs in me are clawing up from inside, trying to break free. While all the sensations on the outside of my body are shoving inward through all my senses.

"I think you should go," I say in a tone that, although shaky, should leave no room for argument.

I can hear the slight hysteria in my voice, and it makes my head spin. Well, *something* is making it spin. Might be Leo's pheromones — I'd forgotten how powerful they were.

My legs feel weak. Heaving a trembling breath, I collapse onto the couch, then shoot right back up because this is a new couch, and I'm covered in paint that's likely not dry yet. I might be approaching emotional disaster territory, but I'm not going to ruin the first quality item I've bought with my own hard-earned money.

My hands go to work on the zipper, tugging it down as my arms duck out of the sleeves. The top of the garment falls until it hangs on my wide hips. The cool air feels good on my fevered skin, and I revel in it for a second, taking a calming breath.

I start shoving the fabric down the rest of the way when Leo coughs, catching my attention. His eyes bulge and brows raise. With his mouth hanging open, his gaze sweeps down my body from my head to my hips.

And there it stays.

I look down at my body to see what's caught his eye. It's only then I realize I'm not wearing clothes under my coveralls tonight.

After getting home from my first training session, I was warm from being outside all evening. I stripped down to my bra and panties before putting on my coveralls. Now here I stand — mid-panic attack and half-naked in front of Leo Mason, also known as the man of my dreams.

Yet this isn't even close to how I pictured taking off my clothes for him all those times I touched myself with memories of him dancing through my mind.

Not even close to how I pictured it.

Shit.

Just another day in the life of Sue O'Malley — making things awkward since 1996.

Chapter Twelve

That's incredibly inconvenient

Leo

Those. Fucking. Thighs.

I'm spellbound by them. By her. Her body. Her voice. Her smell. Her eyes.

Her everything.

I need to turn around. Immediately. I shouldn't be looking at her like this.

She doesn't realize what she's doing because she's upset. Sue would never be so free with her body. She couldn't possibly have changed that much in six months. And I know after she told me to leave that she mentally entered that world her mind takes her to when panic overwhelms her. That place where nothing exists but her frantic, racing thoughts. I bet she doesn't even realize I'm still here.

But I'm mesmerized by her creamy skin and generous curves. Her body is calling to me.

Turn around, Leo.

I can't. I want to bury my head between those thick thighs and satisfy my hunger. I want her to scream my name as she climaxes again and again. I want her taste to linger on my lips and tongue. I want her soft body pressed so close to mine nothing could come between us and nothing ever will again.

Turn around this instant, Leo.

I want to hold her, calm her worries with my touch... like I did before. I know I could soothe her if I took her in my arms and whispered in her ear. I should do it right now — calm her down and bring her back to reality.

No. Don't let yourself get that close.

Maybe I was strong enough before, but I'm not anymore.

Seeing her again and finally confessing some of my feelings has altered something inside me — the restraint I worked so hard to put in place frays like an old, worn ship knot. The hold I have on the tattered rope is slipping, and the fibers are wearing thin.

Snap out of it. You can't have her. Nothing has changed. You're no good for her.

That last thought does it. I choke my desires down while clearing my throat to remind her of my presence.

Her eyes widen as realization dawns. With her mouth agape, she stares blankly at me. It's just as I thought. She'd forgotten I was here.

With rational thought back in place, I turn around to give her privacy. I hear the thick fabric of her coveralls ruffle behind me and footsteps. Sounds like she's heading to her bedroom.

"I'm not going anywhere, Sue. Not until I know for certain you're safe," I call out over my shoulder.

She offers only a sharp *harrumph* in response, bringing a rueful smile to my face.

This is my penance.

I'm being punished for the lives I took in service to my country. For the villages we annihilated and lives we destroyed. Being punished for failing my sister and not protecting my mother when I should have. Punished for hurting Sue six months ago when I made her feel like she didn't matter.

For all of it.

Sue's pissed — she has every right to be. But worse, she's in danger... perhaps *grave* danger. Yet she's pushing me away.

"I asked you to leave, Leo!" she yells as she retreats.

I calmly reply, "Well, that's too fucking bad. I'm not going anywhere."

"Why not?"

"I told you why."

"That's incredibly inconvenient."

I'm glad she can't see my grin and the shake of my shoulders because she'd think I was laughing at her. And I guess I am in a way, but only because she's so unexpected. I mean... who else would call getting death threats *incredibly inconvenient*? I freaking love how her mind works and her dry sense of humor.

But this situation is no laughing matter. I know I have dangerous enemies out there, and one of them somehow thinks I've taken something precious away from them — although I don't have a fucking clue what that could be, nor do I have any idea how they knew my feelings for Sue. Add it to the list of shit I need to figure out.

My gut twists.

The last hour has been a test of my fortitude — mentally and emotionally. The threat, the race to get to her side, seeing her, touching her, telling her what she means to me — well, sort of — and then her asking me to leave... it's been a roller coaster.

But all that pain doesn't hold a candle to the torture of watching her strip down to her bra and panties — and seeing those fucking luscious thighs and full breasts spilling from the white silk cups — but not being able to touch her. To watch her fall apart in panic and not be able to help her hold it all together. To be this close to her pillow-soft lips and not kiss them.

Fucking torture.

I hear the slamming of her bedroom door, and my feet are hauling me in that direction before I even realize it. The chances of someone waiting in her room to attack her are slim to none, especially given she was home alone before I got here — if someone were going to grab her, they would have done it by now. But the pull to be near her and make sure she's safe is as strong now as it's ever been.

"I'll be right here in the hallway, Sue." I plant myself firmly outside her door.

"Go away!" she hollers back.

I grin. "Not happening, kid. You know me better than that."

A few moments later, she snatches the door open. She's thrown on some black leggings but holds her shirt across her chest. The fair skin on her shoulders where her white bra straps are resting has a smattering of freckles. I want to run my tongue across them.

"Don't you dare call me that anymore," she bites out.

My gaze snaps from her exposed skin to her eyes, and I see the anger there.

Fuck.

She's *furious*.

I can see I've got my work cut out for me.

More penance.

"Sorry. Force of habit. Your objection to the nickname is noted." I nod my head slightly and offer a figurative tip of the hat.

She narrows her eyes at me while her cheeks puff up around tightly sealed lips. It looks like she's holding back her words.

Damn, I've missed her.

Her eyes dart around my face and body, ultimately landing on my chest. "We need to talk about... a lot of things. But I can't do that right now. Maybe not at all tonight. I need to... process what's happened before adding to it. This is all too much."

She's right. We do have a lot to talk about.

I can see she's flustered, so I tilt my head toward her and warmly respond, "That's fine. There's no rush to talk."

"But you won't leave." She's making a statement and asking the question at the same time.

Despite how I left her the last time, I think, deep down, Sue knows how much she means to me. She knows I won't leave her when she's in danger.

At least, I hope she does.

"I'm staying by your side to keep you safe."

"All night?"

"All night," I confirm. "And tomorrow too. Might as well start processing the fact that I'm going to be with you until I can neutralize the threat. That might take time because I have no idea who it is or what they want."

Dammit.

A jarring realization of how difficult it will be to protect her again hits me. I don't think I'm strong enough to be with her and resist the pull like I did before. I've missed her too damn much.

She nods a few times, her gaze dropping to the floor. The way she's nibbling her lower lip causes my cock to twitch behind my zipper. My left foot steps forward like it has a mind of its own, bringing me closer to her.

Don't do it, Leo.

"Go get dressed," I suggest in a feeble attempt to reduce my suffering.

If I have to look at her creamy skin for another second, I'm going to do something idiotic.

"I want to tell you something first." She tilts her head back up and finally looks at me — *genuinely* looks at me. "Let me say this before I lose the nerve."

I gulp. "All right."

"I'm mad at you, Leo. I mean it... positively livid." She sighs and shakes her head. "When you left, it was confusing and painful."

Nodding, I feel the hefty weight of guilt settle on my shoulders. I knew it hurt her when I left, but seeing how much is a jagged pill to swallow. I'll force it down because I deserve the discomfort and pain.

"Sue, I'm sorry for hurting you." My voice is barely a whisper, and my eyes are fixed on hers, even if she doesn't look directly back at me.

Her head tilts sharply to one side, and her eyes narrow to slits. "Not sure I'm ready to accept an apology yet. I'm still... confused."

"That's fair enough. You can be mad at me, and I'll keep apologizing."

Her soft blue eyes open again as she exhales deeply. "But I... I missed you. I *missed you, Leo*. So much." Sincerity shines through in the shimmering of tears in eyes that are once again locked on mine.

"I missed you too," I confess.

It's almost painful how quickly my restraint is breaking down. But it's also freeing.

Her feet launch her a step forward, like she's compelled to be closer to me — as I am to her. That pull between us is growing stronger by the second. It's becoming impossible to resist.

Tug, tug, tug.

Closer, closer, closer.

With her head tilted back to look up at me, she carefully searches my face. "You missed me?"

The quiver in her voice makes my breath catch.

"Every day. Every minute."

Finally allowing myself to be honest with her is a sweet relief, wiping away a layer of tar from my soul.

"Really?"

I bring my hand up to touch the soft skin of her cheek with my palm. My skin tingles when it touches her.

Tug, tug, tug. Closer, closer, closer.

"Yes. I know I said otherwise when I left, but you need to know I had my reasons."

She nods solemnly, leaning into my touch. "Things are going to be different now that you're back, aren't they?"

"I think they are."

Because I'm no longer strong enough to resist her.

"I think so too," she says softly.

A tear spills down her cheek as she sucks in both lips with a sharp inhale, like she's angry with me again. Her fist slowly presses into my chest a few times — as if she's letting out some of her anger with feather-light punches. Even though they don't hurt physically, those strikes add volume to the anguish I've felt over hurting her.

Her pain mimics my own.

I only hope I can figure out how to heal *our* pain now that I'm back in her life.

"I promise I'll never hurt you like that again," I tell her as she opens her fist and rests her palm on my chest.

The way she looks up at me — a mix of disbelief and acceptance on her delicate face — shreds the last of my resolve to keep my hands off her. That's it. Resistance is pointless. I simply cannot resist the pull one second longer.

Tug, tug, tug. Closer, closer, closer.

Her fingers curl into my shirt, bunching the fabric and guiding me closer toward her.

To hell with my fears.

I'll figure out a way to make sure she's safe and still keep her with me. It might be tough to keep her safe and in my life, but she's worth the effort.

She's worth everything I have and more.

I'll never stop trying to make myself worthy of her.

Because being *without her* is no longer an option. I need to touch her, kiss her, hold her against me, and soothe this ache we've both felt since the beginning.

Don't do it. Don't do it. My conscience tries one last time to stop me.

It's futile.

Fuck it.

I'm doing it.

My other hand reaches out to cup her cheek, and I allow my thumb to travel across the paint splatters on her skin. Bodies in unison, we both take that last step forward. With my head bowed and knees slightly bent, I move one arm around her waist and pull her flush against me.

The arm covering her chest lifts to my shoulders, leaving the dangling shirt pressed between us. Although I'm tempted to look down for another glimpse of her bra-clad chest, my eyes stay affixed to hers. Those captivating pools of shimmering light draw me the rest of the way in.

I'm committed now. No turning back.

Slowly, *painfully slowly*, she raises to her tiptoes as I dip my head and bring my lips to hers.

Finally.

She's so fucking soft. Everywhere.

We're both tentative with our movements at first as our lips simply fuse together. That string connecting us has never been tighter.

Delicately, I coax her mouth open and run my lips across hers. She responds eagerly, wrenching my body closer and whimpering the softest sigh.

Heaven.

Our mouths dance together gently, opening and closing around each other's as we explore the rightness of the kiss.

Our first kiss. After all this time.

It feels so right. *Perfection.*

I ache to move faster, kiss her harder and deeper, and claim her mouth completely. The need to devour her is warring with my desire to ensure her comfort by going slow. I remind myself of her innocence and tendency to overthink things or panic, and I'm able to hold back.

I don't want to overwhelm her.

I'm content soaking in the heavenly feel of having her in my arms and the soft brushes of her lips against mine. We don't have to go any further. I'll wait for her to be ready.

But I will have her one day.

She surprises me with an aggressive swipe of her tongue against mine. In response, a growl tears up from my chest as my hand travels from her cheek down to the side of her neck, squeezing gently. I savor her soft moans, and her warm breath flutters against my skin.

My tongue delves into her slightly parted lips and swirls with hers. The carnal urge to claim her rages to life inside me with such ferocity, I idly wonder if I'm turning feral.

This woman.

I've been under the assumption that Sue is somewhat inexperienced with physical intimacy, so I've been moving slowly and being overly gentle.

Cautious.

But right now, she's giving me all the signals that she's ready for more. With her desperate moans and gasps, greedy hands, exploring tongue, and needy lips, she's more passionate than I expected. There's fire in this woman. And I'm burning alive for her.

It doesn't take long before we're writhing against each other, passion overflowing between us.

This moment feels so right.

Her. Me. Us. Together.

It's like two pieces of a puzzle have finally popped into place.

My every move is slow and deliberate — giving her plenty of time to stop me if I cross any lines. Her hands travel over my shoulders to the back of my neck, where I feel a prick of pain when her nails scrape at the base of my skull. I trail my hands along her back until they settle on that haunting ass.

So thick and lush.

The velvety feeling of her leggings under my calloused palms is intoxicating. I've wanted my hands here since the first time I saw her walking the dog with those tiny sleep shorts on. I've dreamed of how it would feel to touch her for months. And now that it's finally happening, all my fantasies are rising back to the surface.

Damn, I want more, so much more.

I want to hold on to this ass while my cock plunges inside her from behind. I want to watch this ass shake and jiggle as she rides me. I want to squeeze this ass as she wraps her legs around my waist and I thrust into her with her back against a wall.

Touching her feels better than I imagined it would. I squeeze those supple globes, and she tilts her hips forward, thrusting her lower belly into my pulsing erection.

Fuck, that feels carnal.

I do it again, and she grinds against me once more.

And again.

So good.

I'm enraptured by the feel of our bodies moving together. Somehow, I force myself to stop. We're moving a bit too fast. I don't want her to panic. Plus, the friction is becoming painful behind my zipper. And if I keep pressing myself against her, I'm going to rip our clothes off and bury myself inside her.

I know she's not ready.

To remove some of the temptation, I lift my hands from her ass — scratch that, it's *my ass* now — and move them to her waist, where it narrows over the swell of her hips.

Our lips slowly pull apart, and her eyes flicker open. I reach up and trail my knuckles over her cheek, pressing our foreheads together.

"That was a long time coming," I say reverently, my lips still brushing against hers.

I release my hold on her frame and step back slowly. As we part — eyes locked on each other — the shirt wedged between us falls to the ground, leaving the skin of her upper body exposed again. I bite my lip and force my gaze away.

"Oh my," she squeaks, and I smile.

Bending down, she grabs the shirt, quickly spins around, and tugs it over her head. Once it's on, she takes a few seconds to catch her breath, running her hands down the fabric to smooth it out while facing the wall.

My fists tighten at my sides, and I'm suddenly fearful of what extra stress I may have put her through with tonight's developments. Not just showing up out of the blue and kissing her, but also the news that I'm back because she's in danger.

Danger.

Fuck. She's in danger.

The threat.

How could I forget?

I've been so distracted by her presence and my raging lust for her that I'm not being careful with her safety. I should be securing her house or moving her to a safer location. I should be making calls and finding out who sent that fucking text. Dammit.

I rub my hand over my face. When my hand gets to the wetness around my swollen lips, I stifle a groan of frustration. I can't let that happen again — can't let myself get distracted and compromise her safety.

No more getting lost in her body.

At least not until she's safe. Otherwise, it's a distraction from my mission. Keeping her safe is my priority. Winning her heart and making amends will have to wait until she's out of danger.

Sue must be using these few post-make-out seconds to do some thinking of her own because when she turns back around to face me, her expression has changed. She looks closed off — hardened — like she's angry again.

She should be.

I'm letting her down by thinking with my dick. It's not like me to be careless with safety, especially with an active threat.

Dammit all to hell.

I need to shift back into protector mode, so I break the stilted silence. "Sue, I'm sorry. I shouldn't have done that."

Her face falls, and she opens her mouth to speak.

"Let me finish, please," I say quickly. Her mouth closes again, and she gazes intently at me.

I continue, "I'm not sorry for kissing you — only for the timing. I should have done it months ago, not tonight when there is danger hanging over our heads."

She raises her shoulders and starts to respond, but I press a finger to her lips to silence her. "It's okay, my angel. We don't need to talk about it right now. In fact, it's probably best if we don't."

I drop my finger from her lips and graze her cheek with my knuckles. "You need time to process, and I need to deal with this text threat. I'm going to go into the other room to make some phone calls. Safety first. Us second. We'll talk later when I have a better grasp on whatever danger we're in and know whether it's safe to stay here. Right now, I'm not sure."

She angles her head, cutting a shrewd glance at me. "The danger *we* are in?"

"I'm with you, Sue. If you're in danger, then I am too."

"Why did you leave me?" she asks, almost out of the blue.

I press my lips into a flat line and shake my head. "That's not a short answer. We'll talk about it later. I promise. Just finish getting dressed and throw a bag together — anything you can't live without. I'm going to make some calls while you do that. Chop, chop."

"Okay." Her lips lift into a grin, probably at my sudden shift to business mode.

"Good girl."

She spins around with a huff and tosses her hands to the sides. "Why does everyone say that to me? Like I'm a damn dog?"

I grab her hand, halting her in her tracks, then pull her back to face me. "You're not a dog. I'm sorry if that sounded demeaning. You're my sweet angel. Is that better?"

"All right, now I'm not a dog or a kid, huh? We have an *amazing* kiss, and suddenly I'm some type of distressingly perfect, radiant, celestial being of light and purity?"

"I was actually thinking it was a play on your real name, but if you don't like it..." My brows raise in question.

"No, I think I like it." A shy smile plays at her lips.

My cheeks warm as I think about something else she just said.

"You thought it was an amazing kiss?" I ask with a teasing grin.

"No doy," she deadpans without any humor whatsoever.

I adore her.

She shakes her head, seeming annoyed. "People are so weird," she huffs, then turns to go again, shaking loose of my grip. "I'll pack a bag. Go do your overprotective thing."

As I leave the room, I feel myself grinning like I'm nuttier than squirrel shit.

But I quickly shake off the euphoria. It's time to focus on my angel's safety. I can finish falling in love with her after whoever means her harm is either behind bars or six feet under.

Chapter Thirteen

Ma'am, we'd like to ask you a few questions

Sue

Well, that was unexpected.

Not sure how much time I'm going to need to process whatever the feck just happened. Could be minutes, hours, or years. Or I might never be able to sort it all out. Probably need to call Jaynie and get on her schedule.

There's a lot to unpack.

One thing I already know for sure — Leo really cares about me and one hundred percent *not* the way you care about your kid sister. And I want to do that tongue stuff with him again. Well, I guess that means there are two things I know for sure.

My phone rings, bringing me back to the here and now. I set down the duffel bag I've been packing and grab my phone from the dresser.

It's Nick.

Oh shit balls! My brother. He's probably worried sick. I told him I'd call him back.

Shit, shite, gobshite!

I tap the screen and immediately go on the defense. "Hey, sorry for not calling you back like I said I would. Leo arrived, and everything is fine — no need to worry. I kissed him."

My voice cracks, but I continue without even breathing. "He's checking the house right now and making some calls to get to the bottom of the threat. It was a great kiss. Apparently, he got a text from someone who says Leo took something of his — something important. I really enjoyed kissing him and want to do it again. In the aforementioned text, the bad guy threatened to hurt *me* because I'm allegedly *important* to Leo — it's like an eye for an eye thing. He said something like, 'You took something from me, and I'm going to take something from you.' Godfather style. You know what I mean? But Leo's still trying to get more details — he's also making sure the house is safe. His lips are surprisingly soft. We might need to leave. Right now, I'm packing a ready-to-go bag like they do in the spy movies. So yeah..."

I finally heave a ragged breath. "That's everything I have to share."

Whoops.

Might have overshared a tad there. The brain is still not at full function.

A full five seconds of dead silence.

"Wow."

Nick's never a one-word response type of guy. Possibly, I broke my brother's brain by forcing him to keep up with the extensive amount of information I dropped on him at warp speed.

Great. We can both have broken brains and be the broken brain sibs. The Naughty Dogs business will probably tank since neither of us can function intellectually. Too bad Nick's got his entire future riding on the business's success. But on the bright side, he's got a wife who can help support him. He'll be fine.

Me? Not so much.

I'll probably have to start selling my plasma to get by.

Oh my gosh! Make it stop! Someone, shut my brain up!

"All right," Nick says slowly. "You shared a lot in fifteen seconds. I'm trying to piece it together." He sounds calm, and it's comforting.

"Fair enough," I reply.

"I'm going to ask follow-up questions one by one."

"Good plan."

"Leo is there, and you're safe for the moment. Right?"

"That is correct."

"Someone sent him a text — threatening you. Right?"

"Also correct."

"And in that text, there is some sort of eye-for-an-eye thing happening. Leo stole something, and now they want revenge. And that involves you somehow. Did I get that part right?"

I collapse on my bed, squeezing the phone tightly and pressing it to my ear so hard I'll likely have an imprint on the side of my face. It's possible I'm a little tense.

"As far as I know, yes. That's a good summary, Nick."

I'm glad he's breaking down the events of this evening for me because it's helping me wrap my knowlecules around it. Oh, those are what I sometimes call my knowledge brain cells — knowlecules.

But that's off topic again. Sorry.

"Leo doesn't seem the type to steal something. Did he have any guesses about what it could be?"

"I believe he implied he didn't have knowledge of the item or items which were allegedly taken."

"Maybe the person is mistaken, then. Hopefully, he'll clear it up so we can put this all behind us."

"That's one potential conclusion, I suppose."

"Okay, I think that's all my questions... except one."

Wait for it.

"I'll take it from here, Nick," Millie's cocky voice comes through the speaker, and a smile appears on my face. I adore this spunky fireball.

"Sue, what the fuck do you mean you and Leo kissed and you liked it and want to do it again? I need all the details. Immediately!"

"Exactly like you surmised. It was a lovely kiss, but it confused me. I'm currently in my room. And before you go there, I'm not hiding. I'm simply processing it — trying to make sense of everything that's transpired."

"Hang on for a second. We need to conference in Fiona for this conversation. She's going to flip her lid."

"Oh St. Paddy. Do we have to?" I ask, not really wanting to involve my sister. I mean, I love her and all... but her obsession with my lack of a love life has been exhausting. I'm not sure why, but she's been all up my ass — figuratively, of course — always saying how I need to put myself out there and find my unicorn man. Considering she's not all that happy in her marriage, it's baffling why she's this desperate for me to follow suit.

Ugh. People are illogical.

"Sorry. But I'm pretty sure she'd kill me if she knew we talked about you and Leo and didn't involve her. And Fiona is one of the dozen or so people on this planet I'd do anything for."

"Fine."

For the record, I'm only conceding because it's a fruitless endeavor to talk Millie out of something once she's already made up her mind.

"Hold, please," Millie says, sounding entirely too professional for the nature of this call.

Once again, I'd like to restate my case about how people make zero sense. Let's consider this exhibit one.

After a few seconds of silence, I hear Millie's voice once again. After verifying everyone is on the line, she gives Fiona a brief update, including a summary of the threat and the kiss.

"Oh my God! Oh my God! It's finally happened!" Fiona gleefully exclaims.

I pull the phone away from my ear slightly due to her volume.

"Sue, did he kiss you, or did you kiss him?" Fiona asks.

"Um," I start, then pause because I'm not sure. "My recollection is a tad foggy. Maybe it was mutual. Is mutual kiss instigation a thing?"

Millie answers, "Yes. Moving on. You like him, right?"

"Yes."

Fiona wastes no time nudging the conversation along. "And he obviously likes you, given how he rushed over and also that this shitwad is threatening Leo with something happening to *you*."

Millie jumps back in. "He finally admitted you're important to him. This is so awesome."

"Is there a question in any of that?" I ask.

"Not really. More of a statement. Next question... how did the kiss end?" Fiona again.

Jaysus, are they passing a microphone back and forth? Did they have this interrogation scripted in advance?

I don't know what she means, so I repeat her question, "How did it end?"

"Yeah."

"How do any kisses end? The lips stop touching and tongues return to their mouths of origin."

Millie laughs, then says, "Oh my God, Sue. I fucking love you so hard right now. What she means is... did you pull away or did he?"

"I think I did."

Back to Fiona. "And did you talk after the kiss?"

"Yes."

Sounding a tad exasperated, she says, "Gosh. When we say we need all the details, we need all the damn details, woman! What did you talk about? Were there regrets? Or was it more like... 'gee, I can't wait to do that again'?"

Millie piles on, adding, "I bet he said something like, 'I've always wanted to do that.' Did he say that, Sue?"

Nick cuts in, "Ladies, can we please focus on what really matters? For shit's sake, she got a damn threat on her life!"

Thanks, dear brother o' mine, for getting us back on track. I guess his brain isn't broken after all.

I hear Millie sigh heavily. "Babe, we already know Leo is there, so she's safe for the moment. I've waited a very long time for them to finally admit their feelings for each other. Let me fucking have this for a few seconds. I need to pelt her with questions!"

"Fine," he concedes.

I feel my eyes roll. Some help *he* is. Let's consider him exhibit two in my case against people.

"Thank you," Millie says with triumph in her voice. "Sue, what the hell did you say to each other after you kissed?"

"I don't remember it word for word. As I said, it's all a little foggy."

Because they won't shut up and let me process it!

"But..." she prods.

"I think it was a positive ending. He did say he should have kissed me long ago."

Fiona and Millie both squeal, then Fiona speaks. "Swoon! I'm fecking swooning over here. Was anything else said?"

"Um, I don't know. Let's just move on, okay? It was a great kiss. It's over now. I want to do it again. He says I'm important to him, and he's sorry for the timing. I'm possibly in some type of danger, but he's going to protect me. That's about it. Can I be left alone to process my feelings now?"

My sister is the first to reply, "Baby girl, I apologize for all the questions. We know you need time to think. This is just such wonderful news. We've all been speculating about you and Leo for a while, and we're happy you both pulled your heads out of your arses and realized how good you'd be together. Now that we've gotten that out of our systems, we can focus on your safety."

Priorities? They have none. Exhibit three.

Millie adds, "Yeah, sweetie. It's all going to be fine. Sorry for getting you wound up. We'll stop now. Do me a favor, though. When he comes back in, ask him if we should come over or not. We want to be there to help in any way we can. Or you're both welcome to come here. We can put you up in the guest room and blow up the air mattress in the office for Leo. You'll be safe here — you know I have the best security system in the free world. And two very well-trained guard dogs."

"Thanks, Millie. I'll ask him when he's done making his calls, and I'll text you to let you know where we're going or if we're staying here. He's figuring that out now."

Note I said *text* because this night has been exhausting with the phone calls. My gosh — talking on the phone makes me want to crawl into a hole and suck my thumb. And I quit thumb-sucking when I was ten. Yes, that's a bit late in life, but I was a special case.

Hence my recent diagnosis. *Cringe.*

"Text me too! In fact, text the entire family!" Fiona demands.

Oh shite. Anything but that.

That time I started a family text about Nick's love life is coming back to haunt me.

Nick clears his throat and says, "Susie Q, I want you to follow Leo's every instruction to the letter. *Stay safe.* Hopefully, it's all a misunderstanding, and we'll be laughing about it tomorrow. But don't take any chances or do anything foolish. I want you to do everything Leo says. Okay?"

He pauses, then quickly amends, "Unless it involves sexual acts, and in that case, I want you to stand up for yourself and only do things you're completely comfortable with."

"Easy, McOverprotectiveson," Millie chides him. "Leo is not going to do anything without Sue's consent. You've seen how he is with her. He's the ultimate gentle and consensual soul. Plus, Sue knows how to stand up for herself. You can relax and put your big brother cap away."

"Fine. I'm just glad she's okay, and I want her to remain that way. Always. And I guess I was wrong about her and Leo. I think it was denial."

"Let the record show I was right, and you were wrong. Again. And man, it was worth the wait! You're doing dishes for a month, Irish Spring!" Nick told me once that this is another one of the ways they flirt. Fighting is foreplay for them, which is incredibly bizarre behavior. Yet again, people are fecking weird.

"Who was that washing the dishes thing directed at?" I ask, adding, "I mean, we're all Irish." Millie has always been lovingly playful with jokes about our heritage. In return, Nick likes to tease her about her red hair and short stature. And yet, they're supposedly madly in love. Weird. Exhibit four... or is that five? *Oh feck it! The prosecution rests.*

"Sorry, Sue. That was most definitely directed at my husband. I made a bet with him back when we were still under Redleg's protection. I saw how Leo looked at you, and your doting eldest brother here refused to see what was right in front of his handsome face. The poor fool." She punctuates her statement by making a tsking sound.

I smile again, loving how my brother finally has someone who'll stand up to him. But given she's so short, it's comical when I can see it happening in person.

"All right, that's enough gloating," Nick says. "Sue, do you need anything from us before we let you go?"

Do I?

Nah. I only need to be alone with my thoughts.

"I don't think so."

"We're going to text you in a little while to check in," Fiona says.

"And make sure you let us know if anything changes," Nick adds.

"Don't forget to ask Leo if you should come here or if we should come there to offer you support," Millie chimes in.

Jaysus!

"Okay! Fine! Got it. Let me go now."

Nick sighs and says, "We love you, Susie Q."

"I love you too."

We end the call, and I fall back on the bed. With my phone resting on my chest, my thoughts swirl around in the vacuum of my mind. Instead of trying to calm them, like I normally would, I let them come.

I might be in danger again. Someone is mad enough at Leo to threaten him.

He's here.

Again.

After all this time.

And he wants me. I'm important to him. And he kisses like a tattooed angel... and now he's calling me his angel.

Sigh.

Bright colors flash behind my eyes when I relive that kiss. My hands go to my lips, fingertips tracing over skin still slightly puffy from the increased blood flow.

I've never been kissed like that before. Has anyone ever been kissed like that before? That was probably the greatest kiss of all time.

In fairness, I only have a very small number of kisses to compare that one to. And all were from one man. Well, he was more of a guy than a man.

But Leo is a *man*.

A mountain of a man. A mountain I want to climb — hike up to the summit and plant my flag on top, claiming it as mine. He's strong, confident, loving, kind, gentle, fierce, passionate, and protective.

And my feelings for him are so intense it scares and overwhelms me. I tend to flip out when I'm overwhelmed. But after that kiss... walking away from Leo or pushing him away to prevent being overwhelmed doesn't seem possible.

Of all the thoughts and emotions surrounding and consuming me, one stands out more than the others. I feel like my world has just been turned on its head. And it frightens me.

So *very* much.

I don't like change because it tends to throw routines and expectations into a blender. And Leo is hovering his huge finger over the puree button.

Life as I know it will never be the same.

I don't know if I can handle change of this magnitude.

But damn it all.

Leo makes me want to try.

Chapter Fourteen

Just like Thanos once said

Leo

"What's up, Lionheart? I heard you walked off the Valentine job tonight. You okay?" Tomer asks, his typically stoic voice holding a hint of concern.

I called him as soon as I left Sue safely in her bedroom for some much-needed alone time.

Actually, let me amend that.

I called him *after* waiting a few moments for my hard-on to subside. Something about talking to another man on the phone while I'm packing wood doesn't sit right with me. Not that I'm homophobic, it just makes me uncomfortable. Part of me fears they'll know I'm erect, and it would make the conversation awkward — for both of us.

I'm weird. I know.

"Yeah, that's why I'm calling, T. I need your help. Do you remember the Amos job from earlier this year?"

"How could I forget? That's how I got my nickname."

I can't hold back my chuckle as the memory jumps into the forefront of my mind. When Tomer was doing a protection shift covering Millie, she couldn't remember his name and kept calling him *Chuck...* which she embellished by adding *the no-fun fuck* to the end.

Priceless.

Once Sawyer found out about the nickname, he had a door sign made for Tomer's office reading: *Chuck Nofunfuck.* Every time Tomer takes it down and destroys it, another one shows up the next day.

Every time.

Without fail.

"Well, I got an alarming text this evening while I was on the job, so I had to leave Kri in charge of Trixie and her entourage, but I'm sure she'll be fine. Sawyer should be heading in early to back her up."

I pause to clear my throat as I refocus my wayward thoughts. "Anyway, I'm sending the text I received to you now. I need you to do your thing and find out everything you can about the sender."

I toggle over to my messaging app and forward it to him. My anger spikes once more at the sight of the damn message, sending my blood boiling.

"What kind of text?" he asks.

"You'll see in a minute."

I pause, impatiently waiting for the message to transmit. My toes tap frantically on one foot with the intermittent bursts of adrenaline.

"Got it." He pauses to read it before adding, "Oh shit."

"Yeah, exactly."

"Something *important* to you," he reads quietly. "Hey, isn't that O'Malley's little sister?"

I guess how I feel about Sue will soon be watercooler fodder at the office. Most of the guys have already figured it out — at least those who saw Sue and me interact when I was assigned to her detail in the spring.

I really don't give a shit about hiding it any longer.

Ever since I saw her open the door tonight, and now that I've tasted her sweet kisses, I'm not stopping until she's safe and mine.

In that order.

"Yeah, that's Sue O'Malley in the photos. As you can see, it looks like the tango was trailing her and wanted me to know they could get to her — a typical power play. Thankfully, I got to her first — I'm at her place now. She's under my protection until further notice. I'm just trying to figure out our next move."

"What did you take from him, man?"

"Not a goddamned thing. I don't even know who they are, for that matter. That's where you come in."

"I'll do my best, but more than likely, all I'll be able to get is a cell tower location of the last ping. The perp probably used a burner phone."

Unless he *wants* me to find him. Or her... but whatever.

"I'm assuming it's a burner too, but let's see what you can find out."

"I'll call you back when I have something. Did you call Boss yet?"

"Not yet. I'll call him in a few minutes. I'm also going to text this douchebag back and see if he responds with more details. It's in his best interest to tell me what he wants unless he's merely playing a fucking head game."

"Good idea. Be safe. I'll call you back in a few minutes."

"Thanks, Chuck."

"Fuck you, asshole."

Despite the heaviness of the situation, a grin creeps up my face. Redleg isn't just a job — we're a family. It's part of who we are.

And one thing is for damn sure. Even when we're busting balls, we've got each other's backs. Like a family should.

Internally, my stomach rolls at the unintentional memory of how I let my blood family down. But I push it aside because I have work to do. I can't dwell on the past.

Before I call Big Al, I decide to see if I can draw this asshole into a conversation. I need to figure out who they are and what they *think* I stole.

Me: I don't know who this is or what you think I took from you, but I won't let you hurt her. Why don't you just tell me what you want so we don't have to play these games?

I wait a few seconds as potential next steps run through my mind. While I have my texts on the screen, I send a quick message to Sue's brother to alleviate his worries. He's probably climbing the walls.

Me: I made it to Sue's place. She's safe, and I'll make sure she stays that way. We'll be in touch when I know more.

Nick: Thanks, man. We just got off the phone with Sue. She sounds good.

Nick: Also, Millie wants you and Sue to come over here for the night. You installed the security system, so you know it's good.

Me: It's the best. I'll let you know what we decide shortly. Thanks.

Nick's offer is a solid option. We shouldn't stay here much longer, and their house certainly has its appeal. Aside from camping out at Redleg headquarters, I can't think of many safer places to stay locally.

To help ease Millie's fears post-stalker, I ensured she had all the bells and whistles at her place. My only concern is making Nick and Millie potential targets.

Then again, if the tango knows about Sue, they probably already have her employer slash brother in their sights too. She spends all her time with Nick when she's not at home. And let's face it, we're sitting ducks here.

We need to leave.

Without any further hesitation, my feet launch me toward Sue's bedroom. No time to waste. I have a few more calls to make, but I don't want to stay here any longer. I'll make the rest from the road or when we get settled for the night.

Me: Tell Millie we'll be over in twenty minutes or less. If we aren't there by then, call Big Al and tell him what's going on.

Nick: Sounds good. Drive safely and watch your back.

Me: I'll protect her with my life.

Nick: I know you will. We trust you.

I knock on Sue's bedroom door and call out, "Sue?"

"Yeah?"

"Did you pack a bag yet? We need to get out of here ASAP. We'll stay at Nick and Millie's house tonight."

"Okay, sounds good. I'll be right out."

While I'm waiting in the hallway — pacing in front of her door — I send a text to Sawyer to make sure he's reporting for duty early and another to Big Al to let him know I'll be calling him tonight once we're settled. I need to get him up to speed. I'm going to need Redleg's help.

Sue opens the door and comes out with a bag slung over her shoulder. I gulp when I see her — it's like she gets more beautiful every time she enters a room.

Get it together, man. Focus on her safety.

"Um, Leo." Hearing my name come from her mouth makes me think of chocolate-dipped pretzels — my favorite food — so comforting and satisfying. "I need to grab some art supplies in case I get anxious. It helps me calm down. Is that okay, or do we need to leave this instant?"

119

"No, that's fine. We can quickly grab your art stuff. I want you to be able to relax. Is your studio still back here?"

I point at the spare room at the end of the hall and begin moving in that direction. It used to house her art studio, and I assume it still does.

With each step, memories start to pepper my mind — of the times we spent inside those four walls. I'd read while she painted or sketched on her easel. She'd blare music — an eclectic variety of songs from practically every genre in existence. I rarely paid attention to what I was reading because I kept getting lost in the hypnotic way she created her art. Occasionally, she'd catch me watching her and give me a side-long glance that made my dick twitch. I'd usually compliment her work and call her *kid* to remind myself to keep my hands to myself. And her answering smile always made me think she knew why I did it.

While I'm lost in sweet memories, she steps between me and the doorway so I can't advance any closer to her studio. "That's okay. I'll get them. Here, take this." She sticks out her duffel bag strap for me.

I eye her carefully as I slowly take the bag, noting her eyes are jumpy and her pulse is pounding visibly in her neck. After waiting for a beat, she pivots and speed walks away from me. I take two steps in her direction, only for her to turn and stick a hand out — effectively stopping me in my tracks.

"You can wait here. I'll be right out."

My head tilts to the side as I try to decode her behavior. She's hiding something. But what? And why?

"Everything okay?" I ask.

"Yes, everything is perfectly fine, Leo. It's just messy in there, and I don't want you to see it. It's embarrassing."

The right side of my mouth quirks. "Has anyone ever told you that you're a terrible liar?"

"Only you and everyone who's ever met me."

I lower my head and narrow my eyes at her. "Sue," I warn.

Her hip cocks out as she puts a fist on it. "Leo."

"Why are you lying to me?"

She worries her lip before meeting my eyes and truthfully saying, "I just don't want you to go in there, that's all. Now, wait here, and I'll be right back."

"Fine."

She disappears into the art studio, opening the door wide enough for her frame to slip in, then quickly closing it behind her.

Definitely hiding something.

I've seen her studio in disarray before. So why the secrecy now? I should respect her privacy, but I'm painfully curious to get a glimpse inside. So I keep my eyes trained on the door like a hawk.

My phone rings — it's probably Tomer calling me back. Without even glancing at the screen, I answer the call.

"Go for Leo," I say.

"Hey, bro! You finally answered. Must be my lucky day," an unexpected voice shoots from the receiver.

I glance at the screen, confirm what I already know, and cringe. "Hey, West. How are you, man?"

"I'm getting by. I was beginning to think you're too busy for your oldest Army buddy."

"No way, man. Never. But it's been a busy time. Sorry for not returning your calls."

"I suppose I can forgive you if you agree to come and hang with me this weekend. We can go to the lake. Like we used to."

Shit.

"West, I wish I could, but I'm going to be working every day for the foreseeable future."

"You're killing me, Leo. Come on! You're working your way into an early grave, bro. When are your next days off? I really need to see you." He pauses, sighing loudly.

Oh fuck. I know what that sound means.

"Things haven't been good for me lately. I need your help, man," he whispers. I can hear the pain in his voice.

He's spiraling again. It's likely either his bipolar disorder or his addiction getting to him.

I know it might make me sound like an asshole, but his issues are exhausting.

I've dropped everything more times than I can count to rush to his side — helping him through a detox or talking him off a metaphorical ledge. It's what he expects because I've never told him no. So much so that he acts entitled to my presence in his life at the drop of a hat.

He's told me numerous times I'm the only person he can count on. The guilt from knowing that — and knowing everything he's been through — always compels me to take care of him when he needs it.

The thing is — I'm all he has because he's driven everyone else away. It's a mess of his own making.

But right now, I've got my own fucking problems. And he's never supported me the same way I'm there for him. Not when I first got out of the service, and certainly not when shit went down with my sister a few years ago. He told me that being around my suffering would cause him to relapse. And while I can respect that and know how hard it is for him to stay clean, it results in an entirely one-fucking-sided friendship.

I clear my throat, trying to decide how to let him down gently. "Damn, man. I don't know when I'm going to be off again. Did you call your sponsor?"

"Man, fuck that guy."

He's supposed to work with his sponsor or see his therapist when he gets like this.

"So, that's a no, then. West, listen... you need to follow the program. It's the best way to deal with your —"

He cuts me off. "Shut the fuck up with that bullshit. And what do you mean you don't know when you're going to be off next? Are you going to be there for me or not?"

As much as I hate to tell him no, my mind is made up.

"It's not bullshit. I wouldn't lie to you, man. A threat came in on a high-priority client tonight, and I'm going to be providing twenty-four-hour security until further notice."

"It's gonna be like that, huh?"

"No, it's not *like* anything. I've just got competing priorities. You know I'd be there for you if I could, but you need to reach out to someone else this time. Call your therapist or your sponsor. Maybe you could reach out to one of the guys from the unit."

I pause and add, "I promise you'll be the first person I call as soon as I know when I'm going to have some time off. It's just not going to be right away. I'm sorry."

"You need to tell Big Al to suck a dick and give you some fucking time off."

"This one is on me, though. It's not his doing — it's mine. I can't leave this client high and dry."

"Ah, some *client* is more important than me? So much for loyalty."

"Man, don't do that shit. You know it's not like that."

"Yeah, whatever. Forget it. I see where I fucking stand," he seethes.

"West, wait."

He hangs up without uttering another word.

Fuck.

Maybe I should call him back and explain why this situation matters so much — open up and tell him about Sue. Then again, he probably won't even *try* to understand — he's never cared to listen to me before.

It's always about him.

All the explanations in the world won't matter. He'll still expect me to choose between him and Sue because he's that self-centered. And I don't have time to be sucked into his slow descent into madness. Sue needs me more than he does right now. And I won't let her down. I refuse. I'm not going to make the same mistake I made with my sister.

Never again.

Sue comes out hefting a backpack overflowing with small blank canvases, journals, notebooks, paints, brushes, and other art supplies.

The mere sight of her soulful eyes reaffirms my top priority — her. Always.

It should scare me how quickly my feelings have ramped up for Sue, but it doesn't. It only feels right... finally. After all this time, I feel like I'm exactly where I'm supposed to be. The only thing scaring me now is losing her — be it from whatever danger is lurking or my inability to be the man she deserves.

That is fucking terrifying.

I don't know how or why she came to mean so much to me, but things like this are often beyond our comprehension. Whether it's serendipity, some god pulling the strings like a cloud-dwelling puppet master, a mystical fate, or a preordained destiny, I'll never know.

The simple truth is some things are just meant to be. And judging by how my soul has felt more at peace in the last twenty minutes than it has at any time in the last six months, I'm beginning to believe I was made to be her man — not just her protector, although I'll do that gladly — but made to be her partner. Like soul mates, we're connected.

How the hell was I strong enough to stay away from her as long as I did? Was I bull-headed enough to think I'd be able to stay away?

Sue and I are inevitable.

Fuck. I'm not only waxing poetically, but now I'm mentally quoting Thanos.

What is happening?

I shake my head. "Are you ready?"

"Yeah, I just need to grab my purse on the way out. And my laptop in case I need to do some work for Naughty Dogs."

"You're handling this very well," I tell her as we start moving to the front door a few moments later.

"Well, maybe you and your tongue have a relaxing effect on me."

My cock swells by a degree. "Stop flirting with me, Sue." I wink at her, then immediately grow more serious. "We both need to be focused once we walk out this door."

In truth, I should have been better focused this entire time, but it's so damn hard to think when she looks at me like that. And when I smell her sweet scent and touch her soft skin? Forget it.

Toughen up, Ranger. Mission first.

"Yes, sir," she sasses and winks.

Sue never winks. At least, she never did before. I wonder what else has changed about her in the last few months.

I can't wait to find out.

As I study the volume of items she intends to bring, I regret not having the company SUV. I'll need to rectify that immediately. Thank fuck I didn't remove my *big ass rack* from the back of my bike and have lots of bungee straps in my saddlebags. I'm going to need them to secure all this shit to the back of my Harley.

I consider driving her car and leaving the bike here, but that clunker is unreliable at best, and getting stranded when the perp is likely following us would be far too dangerous. Taking separate vehicles is immediately out of the question. I won't give the asshole an opportunity like that.

She's not leaving my side until I can guarantee the threat is taken out.

"Angel, I want you to stay inside while I make a quick sweep of the property and load up the bike. I'll leave the bags here at first. When I come back around to the front of the house, you'll open the door and pass them to me. Then you'll close and lock it again until I call you to come out. Got it?"

"Yes. I understand." She swallows, revealing how nervous she is now that we're leaving the safety of her home.

"Watch me through the peephole, and only open for me, okay? If something happens, call 911 and then Big Al — in that order. You still have his number programmed in your phone?"

Her frightened eyes are wide but clear. "Yes."

"I'll be right back." I turn to leave but stop when she grabs my hand. My palm heats with her touch.

"Leo, wait." Her voice cracks.

When I turn, I see her chin is wobbling like she's holding back tears. "Hey, angel, it's going to be fine. Sorry to worry you. I'll be right back, okay?" My thumb rubs over her knuckles to offer reassurance.

"Yeah, yeah, yeah." She nods repeatedly and grips my hand tighter. "I'm just..."

"I know you're scared, but I've got you. I won't let anything happen to you. Ever."

"I'm worried about you, not me. Who will protect *you*?"

Without thinking, I bring her to my chest and wrap my arms around her. Comforting her is as natural as waking with the sunrise each morning. Even though I'm holding her to provide her with reassurance, it's soothing for me too.

I greedily soak up the feel of our embrace, inhale the sweet scent of her shampoo, and have a moment to reassure myself she's truly in my arms after all this time.

It's not a dream.

As her shoulders soften and the tension leaves her body, I run my open palms up and down the outside of her arms, then tilt her chin up for a quick kiss. Just one moment to press my lips to hers so I can feel closer to her — even if only in the simplest of ways. That cord connecting us is so tight it almost causes me pain to drag myself away from her.

Her eyes flicker open as I pull away and let my hand fall from the soft skin of her face. I reach for the doorknob and feel a jolt of adrenaline flash through my veins, sharpening my focus on what I need to do to protect her.

It's go time.

A quick trip around the house reveals nothing standing out. Is it possible they aren't watching right now? Why did they warn me if they didn't plan to make their move?

My feet move even faster as I reach the front steps. She opens the door as instructed, swiftly passing me the bags before closing and locking the door without missing a beat.

That's one thing about Sue — she has always been excellent at following step-by-step directions. She's surprisingly reliable about keeping her emotions at bay when I need her to.

I go to work fastening the bags to the rack on my bike while keeping my eyes peeled at the open spaces around me. The floodlights on the house provide adequate lighting to work by but also leave a sharp line where the darkness takes over at the end of their reach. I squint while scanning the yard, but I'm heavily relying on my ears to pick up anything my eyes miss.

So far, so good.

A few minutes later, as I help Sue onto the bike and secure my helmet to her head, she wraps her arms around my midsection and jokingly says, "At least I finally get to ride your motorcycle."

Somehow this woman manages to break my heart and make me smile with just one sentence — I did promise her I'd take her way back when. It was in one of those moments when I wasn't thinking clearly from being under her spell. I made a promise I shouldn't have, but now I have the chance to make it right.

"Should have been sooner. Sorry, angel. We'll go out again for a pleasure ride when all this is over."

I fire up the engine, feeling it rumble and purr beneath us.

"Oh my!" she gasps. "Wow. I think the pleasure part might be inevitable, judging by the feel of it so far."

Dammit. Riding with an erection is not comfortable.

But as she leans forward, pressing her front to my back with only the thin material of our T-shirts separating us, I think that, just like Sue and me, a boner is inevitable.

Chapter Fifteen

Peanut butter confessions

Sue

"Who was that?" I ask Leo after he hangs up his cell.

He's just come into the kitchen where I'm making myself a peanut butter and jelly sandwich — the breakfast of champion-slacker-hybrids.

"Sawyer. Works at Redleg. Do you remember him?"

I nod and slop another load of the delicious peanuty paste onto my bread. "Of course. I never forget people I've met. Nice guy. Short brown hair. Kind of jumpy."

After I glance at him to see if I'm right — even though I know I am — he nods and flashes that million-dollar smile at me.

Oh my ovaries.

"He's jumpy because he lives on caffeine."

I stop lusting over my sandwich long enough to put my hand over my heart and wistfully say, "Mm. I miss daily caffeine."

"You gave up coffee?" he asks, a look of disbelief on his face.

I shrug. "My therapist suggested I drastically cut back to see if it would help with my anxiety."

"It's been bad?" He walks closer to where I'm still drawing the knife back and forth across the bread, stopping to eye my handiwork.

"Yeah, I really miss daily coffee. I still have it — just less often."

His lips turn down at the sides. "I meant the anxiety. Has it been bad?"

"No worse than normal," I fib — a tiny white lie won't hurt him.

Telling him the truth, though? That would undoubtedly cause him pain. And I don't want to hurt him — even if he hurt me. Vengeance isn't in my character.

Honestly, I don't see the point in telling him how it's actually been. *Yes, Leo, my anxiety spiked after you blew me off for some mysterious reason you've yet to disclose. My therapist and I think it's because I began to doubt my ability to trust any of the instincts I'd been working on developing my entire life. Human interaction has always been a challenge, and I thought we had a connection. Then you left me like I was worthless to you. I didn't know what was up or down anymore. No big deal.*

"Was the sacrifice worth it?" he asks, leaning his hip against the counter and resting one of his tree-trunk arms on the cabinet door near my head. I try not to stare at the way his bicep flexes as he props himself up.

And I fail. *And, I mean, it's an immediate failure.*

Because those inked biceps are mesmerizing. Pretty sure they render all women useless piles of micro and macronutrients — just a big ol' pile of chemical elements laying on the floor. Hormones take over, and all signs of intelligent life vanish. *Poof!*

"Was it?" he asks again, prodding me.

After being caught staring, I shake my head and return to my sandwich, scooping on another glob of the good stuff and smearing it on the other piece of bread.

Putting peanut butter on only one side of the bread should be a crime in all fifty states, plus the District of Columbia. If Florida state law says you must pay the parking meter if you tie an elephant, goat, or an alligator to it — look it up — then they can certainly start arresting people for crimes against sandwiches.

"Um, I think it might be working. It's hard to say — there are still good days and bad days."

He stays silent, just staring at my sandwich like he's coveting a treasure. But this is my sandwich... *my precious.*

And yes, that line should be read in the voice of Gollum from the *Lord of the Rings.*

"Did you want me to make you a sandwich of your own?" This motherfecker might have those brain-goo-causing biceps, but he's not getting my damn sandwich.

He smiles his stupid ovary-bursting smile again. "No. I'm actually allergic to peanuts."

My head jerks back, and my jaw drops.

"Oh my gosh, Leo. I'm *so* sorry."

Of all the cruelties Mother Nature could bestow on a person. How could she be this vicious to someone as good and kind as Leo?

"No, it's fine. I can be around it. I just can't eat it. But I won't go into anaphylactic shock just from you having it or anything like that."

"I wasn't apologizing for that, although now that you mention it, I probably should be." He smiles, and I continue, "I said I'm sorry because I feel horrible for you — gutted even. Not being able to eat peanut butter is the saddest thing I've ever heard. Makes any Nicholas Sparks or Colleen Hoover book I've ever read pale in comparison."

He laughs, a warm, deep chuckle that, when added with his smile, makes my stomach clench in a weird way. But I like the feeling.

"I'm not kidding, Leo. I pity you. Peanut butter is life. In fact, peanut butter is the glue that holds my life together."

When he's done laughing, his smile fades away quickly. I notice him gulp before saying in a serious tone, "I think we should leave. This morning. As soon as you're ready to go. I want to take you away — hide you. I don't want to make things more dangerous for Nick and Millie than we already have."

Hide me away? What am I? Rapunzel?

Heh. Don't flatter yourself. You'd be more like Quasimodo.

Wow. That's harsh, conscience. Take it easy on a girl.

"Why do you think Nick and Millie are in danger?" I ask, keeping my bizarre inner thoughts hidden behind a stoic expression.

"The perp sent another text indicating such."

I cock my head to the side and raise one eyebrow at him — I might not have gotten the smooth Irish brogue thing like my siblings, but I did get the ability to raise one eyebrow. Score one for genetics. But ten million points are deducted for the rest of my mental health issues. Therefore, "genetics" is still operating at a severe loss.

"Indicating such, huh? How vague. Are you going to share the contents of said text?"

His arm comes down from the cabinet — such a shame — and he puts his thick paw on my shoulder, turning me in his direction. I don't usually like being distracted from making peanut butter perfection, but for him, I'll make an exception.

He eyes me with the intensity of Tom Hanks in the scene from *Saving Private Ryan* right before they hit the beaches of Normandy. I know it's an odd reference, but that's what jumped into my head. Apparently, it's not only his biceps that make me loopy but also his haunting dark eyes.

It's possible I didn't take my ADHD medicine yet. I like to have it with food, and I haven't eaten yet.

"I'm glad Nick and Millie are still sleeping because I need to talk to you. You have an important choice to make before we do anything else."

My lips stick out like a pufferfish. "I'm not going to get to eat my sandwich yet, am I?"

One cheek lifts in a half grin. He nods to the empty barstools at the counter. "Let's sit, and you can eat while we talk."

"Thank you for respecting my need to feed." I wink playfully as I take my seat.

"I like that you aren't afraid to eat in front of me."

"Are some women opposed to eating in front of you? That seems foolish. As a species, we need to eat to live."

"You'd be surprised how many women suppress their normal bodily functions when they're around a man."

"Hmm, well, obviously, I'm not like those women. I told you I was different."

"And I told you I like you different."

"Thank you," I answer with a shy smile, tucking my chin down toward my neck.

He smiles in return, and fireworks go off in my reproductive system. Maybe I'm not as terrible at flirting as I thought. I'm also thrilled Millie taught me how to wink appropriately that one night over wine spritzers.

Padding over to the fridge, he opens it and peeks inside. "Almond milk?"

He remembers what I drink with my sandwiches.

Swoony-faced emoji.

"Yes, please. If you don't mind." Then quieter, I mutter to myself, "Those damn biceps made me forget to get my own drink."

When he comes over with a glass of cold almond milk a few moments later, he's smiling like he might have heard my mention of his jacked arms. He squeezes his bicep in front of me after setting down the cup — much like a bodybuilder would — confirming my suspicion that he heard me.

I take two bites of my sandwich, then chase it with the almond milk while failing to ignore the way he's watching me.

He's the first to break the silence. "First things first, Sue, I'm not going to let anything happen to you. I swear it."

"I know," I respond truthfully.

After all, he's always shown he takes my safety very seriously. My heart is the only thing he wasn't careful with that one time.

"This guy thinks I have something of his — but he's not telling me what. I swear I didn't take anything from anyone, but you need to know I have enemies out there. My past is... well, it's complicated. Being an Army Ranger comes with its own set of risks. And working at Redleg, I've helped to put lots of bad guys behind bars. Plenty of people mean me harm. Somehow, I've gotten you wrapped up in something you didn't sign up for, and I'll never be able to express how sorry I am for that."

He clears his throat, and his shoulders lift with a deep breath. "I'd understand if you want someone else to protect you. I can get my boss to assign someone else while I go out and try to track down whoever is threatening us."

I glance down at his hands and notice his fists clenched tight, his knuckles bright white.

Curious.

"Most of the other guys at Redleg are former military — many of them special ops — correct?"

"Yes."

"And having worked at Redleg, they have likely put people in prison before. So most of your peers likely have a similar number of enemies as you. Correct?"

"Also, yes."

"Then help me understand how having someone else from Redleg protect me is going to be any safer or advantageous than you."

"Only because this particular threat is directed at me. This asshole has made it personal against me by threatening you. By continuing to be around me, I guess you're likely to be sucked further into this shit-storm."

"Well, I'm already in it, whether I like it or not."

"True. But I guess I just want you to make the choice with your eyes wide open."

His voice, already soft and gentle, dips even lower in volume. "Being with me... it's dangerous."

"Seems to me that being without you — at least at this current time — is also dangerous."

"When you put it like that, I guess so."

A long silence stretches between us, tension filling the air. Our gazes stay locked, but once again, the prolonged eye contact doesn't upset me.

It arouses me.

That's what I've been feeling low in my core — arousal. It's not a feeling I'm used to having, so it took me a while to figure it out. But there it is.

"I have another question, Leo."

"Go ahead," he says.

"If you continue protecting me, how will you track down the person responsible for this? Am I distracting you or keeping you from stopping them?"

"If I stay at your side, then I'd leave it to my Redleg team to track them down — while doing what I can from afar. Maybe we'd figure out a way to set a trap with a decoy target. At a minimum, I need to keep them talking and see what else they reveal. Either I watch you while Redleg helps me hunt them, or vice versa. Either way, my whole team is involved and on board."

"You guys are a really tight unit, huh?"

"A family," he affirms.

"Family, huh? Do you tease each other too?" My lips raise into a grin as his family reference reminds me of my own. Fiercely loyal but relentlessly teasing.

"Without mercy." He chuckles. "But we always have each other's backs. I spoke with Big Al last night, and he said he'll make available whatever resources he can to help stop this asshole."

"That's a kind thing for him to offer."

"He might owe me a favor or two, but mostly, he's just that type of man."

"All right, I'll think it over. I can't answer you right away."

"Fair. But I can't give you much time. We need to leave soon if we're going to go. I want to get to our destination before dark."

"Okay, I'll process fast."

"Thanks, angel."

Swoony-horny-faced emoji.

He gets up to make himself something to eat. Given that he spent a large amount of time here when he was guarding Millie, he knows his way around the kitchen. Last night, before everyone finally fell asleep around three a.m., Millie insisted we all make ourselves at home and do our best not to wake her this morning — she likes her beauty sleep. She said when she doesn't get enough rest, she gets scrappy and fights like a prison inmate.

She's hilarious.

And I don't want her to be in danger again, so it's probably for the best that we leave. She and Nick can take care to watch their backs for a while. Maybe Leo will send someone from Redleg to watch over them. Knowing him, he's probably already on top of that.

I finish my sandwich while my mind runs through various scenarios of Leo running around trying to find out who is targeting us versus him staying by my side at some mysterious hideout. I'm attempting to not think with my nipples, but they're hard — I mean, it's hard. My nips want him near me all the time — it's been like that since that first day I threw Ahsoka's shit at him. Spending the last twelve hours with him within twenty feet of me has brought it all back full force.

And okay, it's not just my nipples. My whole self wants his whole self nearby — at all times.

After licking my lips clean, I look at him and notice he's staring intently at my mouth. I probably have peanut butter smudges all over my face. If you put this much peanut butter on your sandwich, it's bound to get a little messy when you finally dive in. But I'm all about the peanut butter life, so I've accepted this as my fate.

Fortunately, he's done making himself breakfast and sits down next to me, granting the wish of my nipples and whole self.

"Tell me about this text. What did it say?"

He looks at his plate while twirling his pinky ring. "It said time was running out to return what I took. It also said that by running straight to protect you, I confirmed how valuable you are. He also said to give his best to the dogs."

"He knows we came here."

"Yep."

"Interesting. He's following us and watching us. If that's the case, why would leaving help? He'll just follow us again."

"Not if we give him the slip." A sly smile creeps from his mouth up to his eyes.

"Am I right in assuming you have a plan for this?"

"Yes, I do."

"I've never mentioned this before, but thanks for always directly answering my questions. You're very good at that. Most people talk in circles, and it makes it hard to follow. Just thought I'd tell you that."

"You're welcome."

I wipe at my face with my napkin, hoping it hides the smile I'm beaming. "See, you did it again. Responded directly without adding any superfluous fluff."

"I'm a simple man. No fluff here."

That word — fluff — puts a thought in my head, and before I can stop myself, it leaps from my mouth. "Huh. I guess you've never had a fluffer nutter sandwich, have you? With your peanut allergy and all."

"I don't recall ever eating that abomination. My mom found out about my allergy when I was very young."

Poor Leo.

"I'm heartbroken for you," I joke with the utmost of pity I can muster for him and his tragic ailment.

"I'm getting by."

After a few minutes of companionable silence and a few more scenarios leaping through my head, I ask my last question, "Anyway, if we were to leave, where would we go?"

"I have a place hidden away on a lake in the Ocala National Forest."

One of my eyebrows springs up again. "Oh, you want to dash me away to your little lakeside retreat?"

He puts his hands up in front of his chest. "I swear, it's not at all because I want to get you alone in the woods."

I look at him intently as if to telegraph I'm not buying his bologna.

He looks away briefly, then continues, "It's fairly off the grid, outfitted like a safety bunker, difficult to find, and it's not tied directly to Redleg or me. It would be nearly impossible for someone to figure out where we are. Only a handful of people have any idea it even exists — and those are people I trust with my life."

"And do you trust them with my life?" I ask.

He scoffs, looking away once more. "Damn, girl. You just put it out there, don't you?"

Oh shit. Did I cross a line?

"Was that inappropriate to ask?"

"It's perfectly appropriate to ask — it just shocked me. I wasn't expecting that. But to be honest, I'm not sure there are many people I'd trust with your life. Sawyer, Big Al, and Shep. That's probably it."

"Okay. Now, I have one more question before I decide," I say.

He nods, encouraging me to continue.

"Why do we need to hide because of this threat, but it was okay to stay local when Alec Davies was stalking Millie and threatening us back in the spring?"

He sits back in his chair and runs his hand down his face, scratching his beard. "Well, Sue... in the other case, Millie was determined to live her life as usual. The threats had been coming for months and months with very little escalation. And we were trying to draw him out, knowing we were well-positioned to pounce once he revealed himself."

"And this time?"

His forehead wrinkles as if he's in pain. My fingers twitch to run across the folds and soothe whatever fears or worries he's having.

After what seems like a lifetime of tense silence, he growls, "Because I'm not willing to let you be the bait."

Chapter Sixteen

Happy Vag Birthday!

Leo

"You sound tired, son. Make sure you get some rest. You can't help anyone if you're dead on your feet," my mother says with the sad tone she always has in her voice.

Instead of a check-in text this morning, I called her. Maybe having Sue in danger made me feel even more concerned for the other woman in my heart. I needed to hear her voice today.

"I'll be able to rest if you promise to be nice to Henderson when he gets there."

"Oh, pish-posh. You know I'll be well-behaved." She sighs before adding, "For someone under house arrest."

Even though the culprit didn't make specific threats involving my mother, I'm not taking any chances. He might get desperate when Sue and I give him the slip today — provided she agrees with the plan. After running through scenarios most of the night while everyone else was sleeping, I decided it's our best option. Sue's still thinking it over, though. Meanwhile, I'm making a few calls to get things in order. Once I'm done, I'll need to press her for a decision.

"Mom, you're not under house arrest. It's only one guard keeping an eye on you for a few days. Please try to understand my position. I can't be there to protect you, so I need to know you're safe while I'm gone."

"I do understand, and that's why I'm agreeing to it. And also, because I love you."

"Thank you."

"But it's not your job to protect me. It never was."

My chest heaves as dark thoughts from my past pepper the back of my mind. "Mom, we can't get into that today. Just promise me you'll be safe while there's some psycho out there threatening me. Henderson is good. His presence will ease my mind. I'm going to be out of pocket, but that doesn't mean I won't be worried about you."

She sighs, then clears her throat. "Leo, baby, I know you blame yourself for what happened, and now you have this overwhelming urge to make sure I'm safe at all times. I get it, son. And normally, I would humor you."

"Mom —"

"No, I need to say this, and you need to hear it." The line crackles with her deep breath. "It wasn't your fault. Not what your father did to us, and certainly not what happened to your sister. And you don't have to put me in a bubble to keep me safe. You need to free yourself from this guilt you're carrying. I love you and want you to be happy. But constantly worrying about me isn't good for you — it can't be healthy. I'm an old woman. I've lived my life, and when my time comes — so be it."

She'll never understand what it was like for me growing up. I don't fault her for that. After all, she was dealing with her own hell. The only one who came close to understanding was my sister, Sammy... but she's gone now, and it's all my fault. Mom might not think so, but I know the truth. I couldn't save her from herself. And my overprotective nature drove her to do it.

But now is not the time for that type of heart-to-heart with my mom. I only need her to agree to be under protection for a few days while I take care of Sue.

"Ma, we'll talk about it another time. And hey, you're only fifty-four — not an old lady by any stretch."

"Can you send that silver fox of a boss to watch me instead of Henderson?"

I'm glad I'm not on FaceTime right now because if my mom saw the way I was gagging, she likely wouldn't be amused. She might even stop making me her famous banana bread, and I love that stuff.

Then again, maybe she's trying to get a rise out of me.

"Big Al is busy running his business, Mom."

"Fine. I guess I'll have to hope Henderson's as nice to look at as Alan."

My mother is the only person allowed to call Big Al by his given name. Not even his family members call him that.

"I can't comment on Henderson's attractiveness."

"Can't or won't?" she teases, a playful lilt to her voice.

My lips curve upward. It looks like she *is* trying to get a rise out of me with this silver fox thing.

"Both, I suppose. Just behave. I need to run."

"Okay, I'll behave. Send over hopefully-handsome Henderson." She chuckles, clearly amused with herself.

"I'm going to leave my cell phone behind in case anyone is tracking it, and I won't be able to check in with you for a few days. Henderson knows how to get a hold of me if there's an emergency, though. Okay?"

"You're starting to scare me, son."

"Sorry. But it's necessary." I pause, heave a haggard sigh, then add, "I love you, Mom."

"Love you too, my gentle giant."

I swallow a lump down my throat as the line disconnects. For the millionth time, I wish I'd been a giant in my youth, because if I'd been even close to this size at age thirteen, my shitbag father wouldn't have been able to use my mother as a punching bag. I could have stopped him.

Footsteps distract me from my dark thoughts.

"Leo?" Millie asks.

She sticks her head inside the doorway to the office where I'm making my calls.

"Yes, Millie?"

She yawns while scratching her head, then sighs, "Want anything for breakfast?"

I grin at her disheveled appearance. "Nah, Sue and I already ate."

Bending her head forward, she drops her jaw. "Already?"

"We've been up for almost two hours," I answer with a smile.

"What? Why? Ew." She yawns again.

"I apologize for keeping you up late last night, and I really appreciate you making us comfortable."

"It's no problem. I don't have any meetings, so I took a personal day. Nick doesn't have any appointments until this afternoon. It's all good." She offers a sleepy smile.

"Thanks, but we'll be out of your hair soon, I hope."

Her brows raise, and she leans forward conspiratorially. "Did you get intel on the person behind this threat?"

"Nothing new. The brains at Redleg are trying to come up with a plan."

"Well, it's no bother. It's like old times with you hanging around. Stay as long as you like."

"I don't want to put you guys in any more danger than we already may have."

She crosses her arms over her bathrobe-clad chest and narrows her eyes at me, cutting me with that fierce sneer of hers. She's a badass. All five feet of her. "Sue is family. And if she's in danger, then we're going to be there for her. End of story."

I nod my head. No sense in arguing with family loyalty. I can relate.

Millie leans back into the hallway, peeking her head out of the door and looking both ways. She then steps closer to me and whispers, "So you finally vagged up?" She waggles her brows.

"Excuse me?" I lean in with my eyes wide as soccer balls. Did she just use vag as a verb?

"You finally kissed her, huh?"

I shift backward in the chair and roll my eyes. "Millie, I'm not talking about this with you."

She looks offended, chin jutted out and nose wrinkled. "Listen here, big guy. You might be this super badass military man who's twice my size in both width and height."

I cut her off by asking, "Might be?"

With a cocked head and a smirk, she flips me off. "Okay, you definitely are. But that doesn't mean I can't torture all the sordid juicy details out of you."

"Millie, you're no match for me." I raise my arms, flexing my biceps in a mocking gesture.

Shaking her head, she slowly backs out of the room with a displeased groan. "You just made the wrong enemy, buddy. Tittie twisters are coming when you least expect it." She raises her fingers up into a pinching position and taps them, looking like a sand crab.

I laugh at her dramatics, and she pauses her retreat, taking a large step into the room again. She leans in and says, "Seriously, though. I think you guys are the most perfect couple, and I'm so glad you finally grew a vag and kissed that girl. Happy vagina birthday to you, sir."

She offers her hand for a high five, but I leave her hanging.

"What the *what*?"

Her hand falls to her side. "You've been away from me for too long if you're not able to follow my train of thought. You poor man. We used to be on the same wavelength. I'm so glad you came back to me before it's too late."

Smiling, I say, "Never mind. I don't think I want to know what you were implying."

"Vaginas are tough, Leo. They can take a real pounding — and they even like it. Unlike nuts, which are soft and pathetic. So instead of saying you grew some balls or nutted up, I'm simply saying you grew a vag. You vagged up. It makes perfect sense when you think about it. And also, fuck the patriarchy."

"You're right, Mills. Makes perfect sense. Happy vagina birthday to me!"

"Aww, that's the spirit. Happy vagina birthday, Leo!"

She spins on her heel and walks away, laughing as she goes. I shake my head a few times, then run my hand down my beard. Grabbing my cell, I make another call. The long tones ring loudly as I wait for Sawyer to answer.

"Hey, Lionheart!" he says when the call connects. "Calling again? You must have missed me. I'm touched."

I shake my head and roll my eyes as I say, "Yeah, asshole. That's exactly why I'm calling. I missed you."

We both chuckle before I speak again. "Everything go okay overnight with Trixie?"

"Just as you suspected, it ended up being a night on the town prowling for male companionship. They were pretty trashed, but Kri and I handled it, never letting them out of our sights — bathroom hookups aside because I wasn't going in there. Listening at the door was bad enough."

I feel my nose wrinkle in disgust. I'll never understand why people think hooking up in a bar bathroom is a good idea, but you'd be amazed how often it happens.

Disgusting.

"Shep come on duty this morning without issue?"

"Yes, we've got this. You already went over everything with me last night when we spoke. Go take care of your girl. We'll finish out this job without you, bro. If I have any trouble, I'll get with Big Al. Oh, did you talk to him yet?"

"Yeah, after I got off the phone with you last night. He was sympathetic to my situation and offered any Redleg assistance I might need."

"Dope. I knew he would."

"Yeah, me too. Speaking of which, I do have something I need your help with before you go to sleep."

"Anything."

Coordinated chaos

Two hours later, my plan is in motion.

Sue's agreed to head to Ocala to hide out until the team can find some actionable intel or the perp reveals his cards — whichever happens first.

A lot of moving pieces need to come together to get us out of town without being followed.

Once Sue decided to go along with my plan, she quickly became overwhelmed by all the details. She took some time to sketch and process her thoughts in the spare bedroom while Nick, Millie, and I made calls to square things away.

I'm glad I could give her that quiet time to adjust. She seems much more comfortable with the situation now that she's rejoined us in the living room.

Sawyer arrived a few minutes ago via one of the Redleg SUVs, along with Deb — another female guard from Redleg. She's going to serve as Sue's decoy. Sawyer will have to puff up a little to pass for me, but I think we can pull it off if we stuff his riding jacket.

Three other guys from Redleg are here — Klein, Big Al, and Tomer. Additionally, some family members from both Nick and Millie's families are here.

All part of my master plan.

This room is *filled* to the brim with warm bodies. It's a good thing I'm not claustrophobic, or I'd be getting increasingly uncomfortable by the minute.

"Okay, explain how we're going to give this dude the slip." Sue says as she sits down on the couch beside Millie.

"Or dudette," Millie interjects. "Females are just as capable as males."

Everyone looks at her with their heads quirked in some visible version of a "what the fuck" gesture.

"What? I'm just saying. The bad guy might actually be a bad *girl;* you don't know. Or they might not even identify with any specific gender." She crosses her arms over her chest — a common gesture with her — and sinks back into the couch.

"Excuse me. I stand corrected," Sue says flatly to Millie before looking across the coffee table at me. "How are we giving the slip to the person of unknown gender who wishes us harm?"

My lips threaten to quirk upward, but I hide it behind my hand.

"Much better," Millie says under her breath.

A chorus of chuckles bounces around the room.

I catch Sue's gaze and answer, "You and I will be leaving via Sawyer's SUV — not mine, in case the perp knows the tag or put a tracker on it without our knowledge. I'll have you lie down in the back to stay out of sight so it looks like there's only one person in the vehicle. Deb and Sawyer will leave on my bike, going in the opposite direction. They'll be unrecognizable in riding clothes and dark helmets. We're hoping the bad *person*," I pause and look at Millie with my brows raised. She nods back quickly and grins. I continue, "follows them, assuming they're us. We should be able to drive undetected in the other direction."

"Nick and Millie's garage is full of crap, so we can't exactly pull the SUV in there to load up. Won't they be able to see which vehicle we get in?"

Callum, one of the O'Malley brothers, speaks up. "Easy, Susie Q. According to Nick, it's not crap. It's mostly old furniture from his bachelor pad he hasn't been able to part with yet. But given the condition of said furniture, I can see why you'd think it's crap."

Nick flips off his brother. In return, Callum blows him a kiss. My heart squeezes when I think about how Sammy, Drew, and I used to be close like that. Fuck, I miss my siblings at times like these.

Trying to regain control of this sinking ship of a conversation, I explain, "Sue, that's why we have so many people here — to create a distraction. The large number of SUVs, trucks, and even the ambulance — thanks for that, by the way, Callum — will obscure the view of the bike and my SUV while we load up. It will be extremely difficult for the perp to track what's going on in the driveway. The plan is for everyone to pull away simultaneously, splitting up the directions we head. It'll be confusing for the enemy, further lessening their chances of trailing us."

"We'll be using all the chaos to our advantage," Sue surmises.

I offer her an answering nod and grin.

"Never underestimate the power of a little chaos," says Millie's sister Cara.

She's sitting next to Millie with an adorable tiny baby boy in her lap. Millie keeps calling him a *baby Amos-hole*. When we were protecting Millie in the spring, we learned that Amos-hole was what they called themselves — the Amos siblings and their partners. Some sort of joke, I guess. Since Cara's off work on maternity leave, she came over with the baby to contribute to the driveway distraction.

"Does anyone have any questions?" I ask the group. My eyes flit to each of my teammates, making sure everyone knows their part.

Big Al lifts one hand to get my attention. He and Tomer are tasked with forming plans to draw out the culprit along with some of the other strategy guys at Redleg.

Boss speaks up. "We'll let you know what other intel we can dig up and any new tactics we come up with."

"Thanks, Boss," I say, nodding in his direction, then turn to the man on his left. "Tomer, you good?"

"Who's Tomer?" Millie asks with a shit-eating grin over the top of her coffee cup.

Sawyer chimes in, smiling over the top of his much larger coffee cup. "Yeah, Lionheart, who the hell is this Tomer you speak of? Time to get some new glasses, old man. You're looking at Chuck."

"My name is not Chuck, you monsters." Tomer flips off Sawyer first, and Millie second.

Dramatically, Millie puts her hand on her heart. To her sister, she says, "Cara, cover up little Jace's ears for a second." She then looks pointedly at Tomer and Callum. "So many fucks have taken flight on the wings of the fickle finger of fate today. My cup runneth over. Thank you both. From the bottom of my cold, black, motherfucking heart." She flips double bird fingers to the room at large while making *pew, pew* sounds in much the same way someone would shoot finger guns.

It's a lot like being back in the service — all the cussing, sarcasm, and joking.

Nick, who's standing behind his wife, leans down and kisses her while the rest of the room either *oohs* or *ahhs*. A few people just laugh.

However, Shane — another O'Malley sibling — stands stoically in the corner, wearing a disapproving expression. I've only met him once before today — at Nick and Millie's wedding. He was pretty quiet that day too.

Beside him is another one of the Amos-holes... Archer. He's a big dude with tat sleeves like mine and is also former Army. He and Shane have been very quiet this whole time. They both left a job site to come over and help create a distraction. Archer's big-ass work truck could probably hide us on its own, even without the ambulance and other SUVs in the yard.

"Moving on," I say loudly. "Klein, you good?"

With a nod, he replies, "I got you, buddy. I've already talked with the other guards. We're up to speed on our detail."

"Oh, honey, we're a *detail* again. Yay us!" Millie jokes sarcastically to her husband now that they've stopped upside down making out Spiderman style.

Klein and two other guards have been assigned to protect Nick and Millie for the next few days in rotating shifts. Until we get this shit contained, we're not taking any risks. Nick offered to pay, but Big Al nearly smacked the offer out of his mouth.

This is Redleg family business.

Once a few other questions are asked and answered, I throw one of her brother's ball caps over Sue's head and ask her to put on some sunglasses before we head out. I'll be doing the same, and I've borrowed one of Nick's dark jackets to cover up my arms so my tattoos aren't visible when I drive. It's tight, but I can make do until we get out of town.

I'd like to dwell on how utterly edible Sue looks in the ball cap and glasses, yet now is not the time for those types of thoughts.

But I noticed, and so did my balls.

My heavy fucking balls are aching for this woman. Being around her and not touching her is agony.

Even though she's still mad at me for how I left her before, she's putting her trust in me and not holding the heartbreak over both our heads. Her ability to forgive is another thing I adore about her.

Archer and Shane take our duffel bags and load them for us. The faster Sue and I get in the SUV, the better.

As everyone else takes their places, my phone buzzes, so I take a glance. It's a text from Henderson. He's already at my mom's side and wants me to know how delicious her banana bread is. That fucker.

I reply and tell him Big Al is taking possession of my cell phone for the time being, and I'll be contacting him for updates about my mom from a burner phone. Boss will also be monitoring for any incoming text threats or demands.

"Everyone ready?" I ask as I hand my phone to Big Al.

I'm met with nodding heads and affirmative mutters.

"Be safe, Lionheart," Big Al says to me with a handshake before pulling me in for a chest bump-type man hug. "Let me know if you need reinforcements, and I'll send a team up there."

"I think we're good for now," I tell him, hoping the confidence I'm placing in my safe house isn't foolhearted.

Klein hands me two burner phones outfitted with anti-location tracking software — one for me and one for Sue. "The team will contact you through these phones. No laptops or other devices except the Redleg iPads. And remember not to give out any details regarding your location over the phone, because even though *your phone* is secure, you never know who's listening on the other end," he says.

I nod and resist rolling my eyes. As a former Army Ranger, I fucking know how to stay off the grid.

"Call me as soon as you get there, Susie Q," Nick says as he gives her another goodbye hug. Pretty sure that's the third he's given her in the last five minutes. And I thought I used to smother my sister. Yikes.

"I will. I've got your phone number written down on my list," she tells him in response.

Earlier, I asked Sue to make a list of important phone numbers since she won't have access to the stored contacts on her phone. For all we know, her phone may have already been compromised, and we don't have time for Klein or Tomer to do their tech shit to safeguard it. Mine either — hence the burner phones.

I meet Nick and Millie's eyes over Sue's shoulder as the hug breaks. "I'll take care of her. I promise."

"Damn right you will," Millie interjects.

She's threatening me with titty twisters again with her crab-like pinching fingers snapping away in my direction.

"You better take care of her, or I'll sick Millie on you," Nick responds with a grin and a punch to my shoulder.

I don't even flinch.

"Dammit. Fecking giant boulder," he mutters under his breath while shaking out his hand.

Three seconds later, the front door opens, and the crowd starts pouring out into the driveway as we planned.

Archer and Shane go first, followed by Callum and Tomer.

Klein, Deb, and Sawyer exit in the next wave. Sawyer shields Deb with his arm — adding to the odds that the perp will assume Deb is Sue and track them instead of us.

A few seconds later, Big Al leads Sue outside, putting her in the back seat of the SUV and closing the door swiftly once she's inside.

He catches my eye over his shoulder and gives a quick nod before taking his place in the driver's seat of his own SUV.

Millie, Cara, and I file out next, with Nick picking up the rear.

Shane drove his motorcycle, so he fires that up. A few seconds later, Sawyer cranks my baby up — the roar familiar and soothing to my nerves.

Engines in all the SUVs, trucks, and cars roar to life over the next few seconds.

We alternate taking rights and lefts as we pull out of the driveway. Each motorcycle goes in separate directions, further adding some challenges for anyone watching for a bike leaving.

Just as planned, it's chaos for the observer but a coordinated ballet for the participants.

As I drive away, my eyes constantly check for any tails. I can only hope Cara was right, and the power of chaos will prove to be in our favor today.

Chapter Seventeen

Patent Pending

Sue

"You doing okay back there?" Leo's voice is soft and gentle, soothing my frayed nerves.

It's been a rough morning.

"Can I sit up yet?"

My neck hurts from how I've crammed myself into the back seat. I'm too tall to lie down fully across the seats. I had my knees bent for a while, but they started to ache, so I straightened them and tried to collapse my upper body instead.

I don't care what make or model it is... humans above five foot seven aren't meant to lie down flat in any vehicle. Especially when they've got a little extra meat on their bones like I do.

Okay, maybe more than just a *little* extra.

Regardless, this totally sucks. And not seeing where we're going is the worst. I'm sucking it up and trying not to be a whiny brat. Leo's been so good to me — so kind — the last thing he needs is me complaining about a sore neck. He's upended his entire life to protect me at a moment's notice. I can at least push through this half hour without crying.

Then again... he sort of owes me this much, doesn't he?

"Five more minutes, angel," Leo tells me with an apologetic tone. "I want to make about three more turns to double back to make sure we're not being followed before I get on the interstate. So far, so good. But I don't want to get careless. I need to be sure, since I'm transporting precious cargo."

A smile crests my lips despite the aches and pains. He keeps calling me *angel*. Given it's a play on my dreaded given name — Angelica — I should hate it. But the sound of it rolling off his lips makes my knees weak.

"Okay."

"You sound a little pouty. What's wrong?"

Damn. I was hoping I could hide my pain from him, but he's too observant.

"I'm fine."

"Terrible liar," he says under his breath.

I sigh with resignation. "I'm just getting a little achy from the way my neck is craned against the door. But I'll survive."

"I'm sorry it's not comfortable. I should have brought you a pillow. Just a few more minutes. I can't risk this asshat catching our tail."

"I understand."

From my vantage point, I can see his profile and notice a slight grin lifting at the corner of his mouth. His eyes continue bouncing from each of the side mirrors to the rearview. He's so focused. And protective. It's hot as hell.

"I know you do. You're a very understanding person."

"That just shows how little you know about me," I joke.

I've been told my rigid tendencies and preferences make me seem inflexible and self-centered.

A deep rumble comes from his chest that nearly resembles a laugh — it's a dark laugh, maybe. Like the laughter is marred with sadness. That's curious.

"Why that laugh?" I ask.

He shakes his head softly, letting out a quiet groan. "I'm feeling a little wistful, I think. There's a lot of regret tugging on my emotions."

He pauses as the car rolls to a stop and stares intently into the rearview for a few seconds before his eyes shift back to the road ahead, and he accelerates once more. I assume it was a stop sign.

Once we reach cruising speed, he continues, "I wish I would have done things differently. You're right — I don't know you as well as I should. As well as I want to. I regret the time we've wasted. I thought I was doing the right thing, but now I'm not so sure. I mean, you ended up in trouble, even though I left — which was one of the main reasons I left."

He puts his blinker on, and the soft ticking sound is comforting. All too soon, it's gone, leaving just the sound of our breathing and the SUV rolling down the highway. Leo was never one to have on music when driving — which struck me as odd.

I'm tempted to ask him to explain more about why he left me all those months ago if he's feeling all this regret now. But that topic feels too heavy while I'm hiding in the back seat.

Despite my deficit in social skills, I do sometimes get a sense of how certain conversations should be conducted. Right now, he's still got his hat on, covering part of his face. When he talks to me about why he left, I want to see his entire face.

He owes me that.

For some reason, seeing how upset he is about leaving makes it easier for me to forgive him. I can already feel my anger at him dissipating.

Not wanting to comment on the topic of wasted time, I change the subject. "Why don't you ever listen to music when you drive? Don't you like it?"

His head pops to one side, probably surprised by my random question. "When I'm driving my bike for a road trip, I listen to music. Rock and country mostly. In the SUV, though, I'm usually working. The music would be a distraction to my mission. I try to eliminate those as much as possible. I've already been distracted enough where you're concerned, and I don't want to make it worse. Is it okay if we keep it off?"

"It's fine by me. Whatever you need to do your job. I don't want to be a hindrance." I think about what else he shared and ask, "Why are you distracted around me? Am I doing something wrong?"

I tuck my hands under my head to add a little cushion to where my cheek is now resting on the solid armrest on the door and continue staring at Leo's handsome profile.

That jaw — Jaysus — what it does to me.

I'm enjoying staring at him this entire time without feeling awkward since he's focused on the road and constantly checking the mirrors to make sure we're not being followed — so he probably doesn't know I'm watching him like a creeper. It's made the last thirty minutes much more enjoyable. I can channel my inner Joe Goldberg and watch my fill — minus the homicide, of course.

His tongue sneaks out of his mouth to swipe his lips before he replies, "Angel, you're not doing anything wrong. I'm distracted around you because I want you so much. That's not your fault."

"I want you too," I confess before I can stop myself. To make it worse, my stupid mouth adds, "All the time." My voice is breathy, as if I've been exercising. "I've never wanted anyone the way I want you. It's like an ache that starts in my chest and settles in my stomach." I have to bite my lip to stop talking.

Oops. Bit of an overshare again.

I think my brain is still broken from that kiss last night, and I hope my filter isn't permanently damaged.

Leo inhales sharply. From the side of his face, I can see under his sunglasses and notice his eyes closing for the briefest of seconds before they seem to fix back on the road.

"Listen, angel, when we get to the safe house, I'll need to focus on keeping you safe. So, I need you to refrain from saying things like that."

Then flipping stop calling me angel, I want to scream at him but don't. Guess my filter is working a little. It's probably just set too low. Need to crank that sucker up to max when we get to the safe house. If I don't censor myself, I'm liable to jump him.

If that happened, maybe then I'd know if every sexual encounter would be like my last was. Ugh. I still cringe when I think about how disastrous and uneventful that night was.

I'd much rather think about how hot it could be with Leo — a man who probably knows how to handle a woman and bring her pleasure. I wonder if he's big *everywhere*. If the legend of foot and hand sizes correlating to penis length is true, then he's probably got an enormous cock.

Would it hurt or feel good?

Fiona once told me that size is important, but a man who knows what he's doing is what really determines pleasure. At the time, she was venting about how unsatisfying her sex life with her husband was — he's small and doesn't know what he's doing.

A double whammy.

Poor Fiona.

I shared with her about the only time I've had sex, and we bonded like never before that day. I told her how porn makes sex look so exciting, but when I finally tried it — I wasn't impressed. Although I do enjoy my vibrator.

She said her first time was terrible too and encouraged me to try again. Preferably with someone I actually felt a spark with. But I'd never felt a spark before, so I wasn't sure what she meant.

Then I met Leo.

And it's not just a spark with him.

Oh no.

My attraction to Leo can only be described as fireworks and the Big Bang theory getting together with the Manhattan Project and then having an orgy with the CO_2 machine that makes sodas fizzy.

Utterly explosive.

Is it hot in here? The temperature in the SUV must have increased by about twenty degrees. My thighs squeeze together as my hips rock slightly. The ache between my legs is starting to get uncomfortable. I wonder if I could sneak my hand down without him noticing. Just for a second.

We drive in silence for a few more minutes with only the sound of my erratic breathing and his slow, steady breaths filling the space around us. Occasionally, he taps his pinky ring against the wheel, and it makes me wonder how it would feel if he tapped his hand against my core, running his thick fingers through my slit.

My hand starts to snake down my stomach like it has a mind of its own.

He finally breaks the silence. "I think we're good. I can't see anyone following us. At this point, we've been the last vehicle through enough stop lights that I can't fathom anyone maintaining visual on us. Do you want me to pull over so you can get in the front now?"

With his words, my hand halts before it hits the target.

"No, I don't want you to stop the car. I can crawl up," I reply.

I don't want him to stop driving until we get wherever we're going — barring any unavoidable bathroom breaks. The thought of getting out of the vehicle frightens me. The fear of potential danger lurking is messing with me. Logically, I know I should trust Leo when he says we weren't followed. But sometimes, hysterical paranoia takes up residence and makes itself at home in my psyche.

"Come on up, then," he says softly.

I rise to a seated position, stretch my neck, roll my shoulders, and arch my back to get the kinks out. I throw the ball cap and sunglasses back on since I'm upright again — it seems logical to continue to hide as much as possible. At least it can't hurt to do so.

The leather scrunches beneath me as I move up toward the front. Once my upper body has made it through the valley between the seats and my hands brace myself on the dashboard, I realize I may have underestimated the size of my hips in relation to the open space between the driver and passenger seats. So I have to contort my body a little to get my hips clear and end up shoving my ass into Leo's face in the process.

Keep it awkward, Sue. Great job.

"Sorry for the gratuitous butt shot," I tease as I keep working my way forward.

His soft chuckle reaches my ears, bringing a smile to my previously cringing face.

"Angel, I'm never going to complain about your sweet ass in my face. That's a promise."

I don't know how to respond, so I remain quiet, aside from an occasional grunt or sigh, while bringing the rest of my body through. Turns out cramming my fat ass into the front was more exercise than I've done in the entire last year combined.

Why didn't I just let him pull over so I could get in the front?

When I finally make it into the seat, I heave a big exhale before buckling the seatbelt. Trying to break the awkward silence after Leo mentioning my *sweet ass* — his words, not mine — I try for a joke.

"Well?"

"Well, what?" he asks.

"A round of applause would be nice. Do you know how much effort that took?" I mask my features to feign outrage, but I probably look more like a confused panda who smells burnt toast for the first time.

Leo laughs with me before sticking out his fist like he's holding a microphone. "I can't take both hands off the wheel," he adds.

Feeling confused, I lean forward, put my mouth near his fake microphone hand, and say, "Hello? Testing one, two, three. Is this thing on?" I finish by tapping it twice with my open palm.

He drops his fist to the console and laughs uncontrollably.

Well, I guess I'm really killing it with my jokes today. My siblings would be so proud of me.

Through heaving breaths, he gasps, "I was trying to give you a fist bump." He resumes laughing, his cheeks morphing from rosy pink to bright red.

Oh, for fuck's sake. Kill me now. This is just another example of how I'm unqualified to be around other people. Classic Sue O'Malley.

As embarrassed as I am, I can't help chuckling along with him. His laugh is infectious, and it sucks me into the hilarity of my gaff.

If I didn't know how to laugh at myself, then I'd have lived a very miserable existence. Seeing the humor in my own mistakes is the best thing I have ever learned in my life. It's come in handy on so many occasions — many of which have happened around this handsome man who seems to like my brand of awkward.

After the moment passes, I rest my elbow against the window, pull the cap down lower on my head — ridding myself of the remaining giggles — then cradle my cheek in my palm and rest it against the cool glass. "That's it. I'm going to have to file a patent so I can trademark being awkward."

Chapter Eighteen

People probably grapple in the grocery store all the time

Leo

"Your turn, angel."

"Again? Wasn't it just my turn?"

"No, I went last. It's your turn again."

My cheeks hurt from laughing, but she's so good at these. I can't wait to hear more of what comes out of her beautiful mind... and mouth.

She rubs her palms across her thighs as she thinks, and I try not to imagine how it would feel to touch her there. It's fucking killing me to keep my hands to myself the longer this drive goes on.

"Oh, okay. I've got one." She claps and rubs her palms together. "Collateral laughage."

After rechecking the mirrors, I grin and crick my head to the side. "I think I might know where you're going with this one, but go ahead and explain it."

"It's when you're trying to do something that isn't funny, but it ends up being funny. Or if you're trying to make one person laugh, but a different person laughs instead of the target. They're collateral laughage."

"This sounds like something you have a lot of experience with," I tease.

"Oh, I'm an expert at this. Case in point — the microphone fist bump."

We chuckle together. I love how she's able to laugh at herself. I'm like that too — I own my fuckups, and it's hot that she doesn't take herself too seriously. Then again... what is there about Sue that I don't find hot? Probably nothing.

After the car grows silent again, she keeps our game going. "Your turn."

"Okay, I've got one I've been sitting on for a while. I think it'll remind you of someone we both know."

She bends her left leg and tucks it under her as she turns to face me. "Oh, I'm intrigued. Please do tell."

"Ambitchous," I announce proudly.

"Ambitchous?" she parrots. "You mean like a play on ambitious?"

I nod and add, "But like someone who strives to be the biggest and best bitch."

"Millie," she responds without missing a beat.

"Yes, Millie. One hundred percent."

She leans back in her seat, holding her stomach as she laughs — that deep belly laugh.

Fuck, I want to see her happy like this all the time.

The laughter continues, each of our guffaws spurring the other on into deeper fits.

"No more! No more! I can't take anymore," she gasps.

"Fine. We can stop playing for a while. As long as you concede defeat."

"As long as I live, I'll never be able to create a word better than ambitchous." She giggles and covers her mouth with her hand.

"We're getting close to the cabin anyhow. I'm thinking we can get off the interstate at the next exit to grab some groceries."

"You sure it's safe to stop?" She spins her head to look behind the SUV, worry marring her beautiful face.

"No one is following us, angel."

She bites on her lower lip, eyes still fixed behind us. "You're sure?"

"Positive."

"How can you be so sure?"

I know she trusts me, but I also know she needs to understand things from a logical standpoint. I don't mind explaining each step I took to make sure we weren't being followed. Anything to ease her mind.

After putting on my blinker, I move into the exit lane and slow down. She keeps her eyes locked behind us, whereas mine only glance at the rearview a few times. No one is following us — the exit ramp remains clear behind us.

"Sue, while you were lying in the back seat, I made a mental list of the colors and makes of all the cars behind us and kept repeating them in my mind until I memorized it. Each time we turned, I did it again. The list got shorter and shorter. I turned and circled so many roads it would have been nearly impossible for anyone to follow. Especially considering all the instances when I timed it so I was the last car through a yellow light. We're fine. I promise."

She slowly turns her head back to the road ahead of us, nodding a few times. My eyes catch a glimpse of her tapping her fingertips against her thumbs in a rhythmic pattern. She's nervous — she only does that when she's really upset.

We come to a stop at the traffic signal at the end of the exit ramp. Unable to resist comforting her, I grab one hand and lace my fingers with hers. "It's fine, angel. Trust me."

Her big eyes look up at mine. "I do trust you. I'm just..."

"You're worried, and that's okay."

"You don't think I'm being a baby?"

I feel my brows pinch together. "Not at all. It's natural to be worried in a situation like this."

"Then how come you aren't?"

"I am worried. I'm just used to this kind of stress. So it doesn't show as much."

"That makes sense, I guess."

Picking up our joined hands, I draw them to my mouth and place a kiss on the back of hers. Her skin is soft and warm, so I let my lips linger there for a second or two longer than necessary. Her eyes sparkle as she studies my face, zeroing in on where my lips meet her flesh. I notice her pupils dilate, and my cock twitches its response.

A horn blares from behind me. Damn. The light turned green while I was lost in Sue's blue eyes. Letting loose of her hand, I wave an apology to the car behind us, then accelerate through the intersection.

A few moments later, we're walking into a grocery store with our hats and glasses on.

While we shop, she stays tucked in close to my side, and I do my best not to let her proximity go straight to my cock.

It's a constant battle.

I know I've *never* wanted a woman like I want her. And each time I remember how her ass grazed against my shoulder when she climbed into the front seat, a raging need to press myself up against her roars to life in me. But I tamp it down by remembering the texts threatening her.

Damn, I still need to figure out who this asshole is. The two-hour drive from Clearwater didn't provide me with any more clarity on who could be behind this insanity. I hope my team at Redleg can find something from the digital trail, but I'm not optimistic. It's going to fall on my shoulders to figure out who this fuckface is.

"You said you have condiments there, right?" she asks.

"Yeah, and some canned goods. Just nothing perishable."

It's only been a few weeks since I've been at the cabin, so it should be pretty well stocked. It's my little hideout where I can get away and clear my mind. I've found myself needing that more often than usual over the last few months. And I know why.

We load our cart with fresh produce, meats, frozen foods, and canned goods before grabbing some bread and lunch meat for sandwiches. When we get to the peanut butter, she grabs a jar and looks at me over her shoulder, making the most kissable face I've ever seen. It's like she's offering me pity and lust at the same time with her lidded eyes and pouty lips.

My fists hold tight to the shopping cart as I struggle not to slam my mouth against hers, right here in aisle nine.

"Get enough to satisfy your cravings," I tell her.

Not sure why I made peanut butter sound sexual. This woman does something primal to me.

"I'm never fully satisfied," she answers, setting two jars in the cart without breaking eye contact — impressive.

And is that a challenge?

Oh, I'll rise to that challenge, baby girl. One day soon.

After the threat is removed, then you're all mine.

As the cashier scans our groceries, I check my phone. With nothing new from the team, I send messages letting them know we're almost to the cabin. I ask Klein for a report on Millie and Nick, ask Big Al for an update on our strategy, and Henderson for a report on my mom. I slide my phone away before any replies have a chance to come through because Sue is pulling out her purse like she's going to pay.

Oh, hell no.

"No, I got this, angel," I tell her.

Her eyes pinch as her gaze flicks up to me. "Why?"

"Because I'm buying. Put your money away." I grab the hand wrapped around her wallet and push it back into her purse before elbowing in front of her slightly so she can't get at the card reader.

"Half of it is for me. At least let me pay for half."

Although she makes a logical argument, it's not gonna fly with the guilt I feel for sucking her into my mess.

"You wouldn't even have to be leaving home if it weren't for me. It's my fault. So, I've got it."

"That's gobshite! You don't know if it's your fault or not," she objects in a hushed whisper and tries to shove back in front of me.

I puff up to keep her off to the side, starting to enjoy seeing this side of her.

"Consider it a date, and I'm buying."

Why did I say that? This is not a date. We're going into hiding, not off on a romantic weekend getaway. Is my cock making all the decisions now? Is this what's happening to me at age thirty-five — ruled by my junk like a puberty-riddled youth?

She makes a scoffing sound of disgust. "Who takes a girl on a date to Ocala? What the hell kind of shit is that? No thanks," she huffs and gets a laugh out of me.

Without warning, she rears back and slams her hip into mine, knocking me off balance enough that I wobble. She takes advantage of my momentary stumble to place herself directly in front of the card reader.

Next thing you know, we're essentially tussling in the grocery store line — complete with hip checks and elbow throwing. All the while, we're laughing and cursing under our breath at each other. I can't remember having so much fun.

At one point, she has her hands bracing herself by holding the checkout station with locked arms. From behind, I reach my arms around and secure her in a bear hug. I'm about to lift her up so I can deposit her next to me when, without warning, she drops her weight down and stomps my toe with the heel of her foot — just like I taught her all those months ago.

"Dammit!" I holler in shock and pain.

And sure, it hurts like hell, but I'm so fucking proud of her for remembering that move and for executing it like a pro.

She looks back over her shoulder with a triumphant smile. I'm about to rush back to her side to take her down when the cashier clears her throat. It's then I realize we're causing quite the scene.

Shit. We're in a grocery store.

This woman has a way of making everything disappear except us. Everything else just slips away.

"I can split it if that would help," the cashier says, looking moderately amused, judging by the quirk of her lip.

I open my mouth to agree to pay half — as it seems the quickest way to end our quarrel — when a manager rushes over to Sue's side. "Do you need help, ma'am? Should I call the police?"

Sue's eyes widen in surprise, her mouth pops open, and she takes a step closer to my side, throwing a nervous glance up at me.

"Oh, my goodness. I'm so sorry. No, I'm fine," she stammers, eyes shifting to the ground.

At the same time, I say, "Apologies. We were just messing around." I straighten my hat.

Not only are my hormones ruling my body, but I'm also acting like a child. And I'm not all that mad about it.

"Are you sure you're okay?" the manager asks Sue.

She gets tenser the closer he gets to her.

Now he's pissing me off.

She said she was fine — move along, man.

In response to his nearing approach and outstretched hand, Sue takes a step closer to my side. The manager's eyes widen, and he cuts an accusing glare at me.

Now I see what's going on.

From what I remember of being with Sue in public, she doesn't feel comfortable interacting with new people, which explains why she's acting like this. The way she's deferring to me probably makes it look like I'm a controlling, abusive asshole or something. I know what he's thinking as his eyes dart between the both of us — especially given my large stature. But I'd rather die than ever lay a hand on Sue in anger.

I'd never.

We need to get out of here already. I hand my credit card out toward the cashier. "Please use this," I say in my gentlest voice. But then I catch myself and yank the card back. "Actually, I'll pay cash."

Almost made a rookie mistake. Without knowing who the bad guy is or his capabilities, he could be tracking our bank accounts to find us. We can't risk leaving a digital footprint.

Once again, I'm forced to admit how much being with Sue is detrimental to my focus. I've got to get myself under control.

The manager is still hanging around while I fish out the cash from my wallet, looking at us with a suspicious glare. The cashier looks at him and finally says, "I'm sure she's fine. They were just arguing over who was going to pay. It was playful."

I notice Sue nodding in agreement from the corner of my eye. My heart aches for her. I wish she felt more confident in herself. Then again, maybe it's not confidence in herself, but a lack of trust in others. Whatever it is, I wish I could help her fix it.

That thought makes me wince. Nothing is wrong with her that needs to be *fixed*. She just is the way she is... she's not broken. I need to stop trying to fix everything. It's just like Mom is always trying to get me to understand. *I'm not responsible for making sure everyone is safe and happy.*

But still... the urge to make whatever might be bothering Sue go away is compelling.

Satisfied with the cashier's explanation, the manager leaves. He throws a glance or two over his shoulder as he goes. I take our change and apologize once more for causing a scene with our roughhousing.

Sue's quiet the rest of the drive to the cabin. Her eyes grow wider as she takes in the expanse of forest and the winding streets leading to my little lakeside getaway. I keep my eyes fastened to the road except for the glances to check the mirrors, looking for any tails — there are none.

As we get closer to our destination, I keep reminding myself to stop fixating on her so much and allowing those distracting thoughts. I need to remember my mission. I can't keep slipping up and getting wrapped up in the draw of her enticing personality.

If only it weren't so easy to get swept away by my feelings for her. The more I'm around her, the stronger that tug is pulling us together. That connection of ours puts blinders on — blocking out everything else around us.

But I'm a soldier — a Ranger.

I've been through far worse.

As good as it may feel to let my guard down and fall into Sue's world, I know I need to resist. I have to put her safety above all else.

I have to.

Losing is not an option — I won't let anything happen to her.

Period.

Happy to be back at the lake, I've got a grin on my face when we pull into the gravel driveway, and I shift into park. Until I look over at Sue and see she's as pale as a ghost.

Her eyes are wide, her jaw is slack, and her face is completely ashen.

She's pointing at the windshield with an absolute look of horror on her face.

"Sue, what's wrong?" I ask, my head deftly whipping around to see if I can spot the danger I see reflected in her eyes.

But I only see my place.

"It's. The. Cabin." Her voice is a soft, shaky whisper.

After a sharp intake of breath, she covers her mouth with trembling hands as tears start to pool in her eyes.

What the fuck?

Chapter Nineteen

The cabin in the woods

Sue

How is this possible? Is this whole thing another dream? Am I about to wake up screaming and covered in sweat? Is Leo even here with me, or is he part of my dream now?

This can't be real.

It's not possible.

It's. Not. Possible.

"Sue, what do you mean by *the* cabin? What's wrong? Talk to me," Leo commands. His voice has shifted into the deep, dominant tone of a military operative.

"It's the cabin," I repeat.

My throat tightens, and my hand raises to cup my neck.

"You said that already, angel. Yes, it's a cabin — it's *my* cabin. Why is that scary? I don't understand what's happening."

My head swivels around the car so I can look out all the windows, surveying the entire scene. I see no danger present, but the fear inside me grows all the same. The only part of the view surrounding me that's familiar is the front of the cabin and the greenery surrounding the structure — it's more overgrown than I remember, but it's definitely the same. I've never been more certain of anything.

And that's absolutely terrifying.

Because rationally, I know I've never been here before, and yet I know exactly what atrocious things happen inside. *This* is the place.

"I've seen this cabin before. My nightmares." A choked sobbed steals the rest of my words.

I must look and sound insane to him. My emotions are making it impossible to talk. To think. To breathe.

Although I'm lost in my fear, I'm faintly aware that Leo removes his seatbelt and gets out of the car. In what seems like the blink of an eye, he's opening the passenger door and pulling me out.

He wraps me in his strong arms and whispers soothing words in my ear while running his hands over my hair, shoulders, and back. I can feel the warmth of his breath on my cheek. The heat and scent of his body begin to overwhelm the rest of my senses, calming them.

"It's okay, Sue. I've got you. You're safe," he whispers.

I can feel the wetness from my cheek seeping into Leo's shirt.

Wait — I'm crying?

Through shuddered breaths, I force myself to focus on the feel of my feet as my shoes sink into the sugar sand beneath them. To feel Leo's big hands running over my body. To hear the birds chirp and sing overhead. To feel the smooth skin of his bicep press onto my lips from the way he's wrapped himself around me. To smell the grass and woodsy scent of the forest. To hear the ducks squawking on the lake nearby.

I force myself to be present in this moment, trusting it's real and believing with my whole sense of being that if there is danger, Leo will protect me.

As pathetic as I feel for being a damsel in distress, I know I'm out of my league with whatever is happening. I'm just an average girl who's found herself in a situation she can't control or explain. And for me, that out-of-control feeling is the *worst* possible thing.

Call me a control freak if you want. But with my condition, routines and expectations are critical to my mental health. And I'm going to allow myself to lose it for a minute. I'll pull it back together as soon as I can.

For now... I'm with Leo. He's in control, and that's good enough.

After who knows how much time has passed, I pull my head off his chest and look up to face him, scared of what I might see there.

But I should have known better than to expect any harsh judgment from Leo. I see nothing resembling pity or disgust — I only see concern.

"You okay?" he asks, drawing his knuckles across my cheekbone.

I nod.

"Can you talk yet? Explain to me what's going on inside your mind?"

"I need another minute."

He brushes a few locks of my hair out of my face and places a kiss on my forehead.

"Take your time... just know we're safe here. I promise."

Forcing away the desire to object to his promise — because I already know what's going to happen here — I just place my cheek back against his chest and soak in his comfort.

Sure, it's nice, but look at the location

After I finally calmed down, Leo locked me in the SUV so he could do a quick walk of the house and turn on all the alarms and sensors. He said he wanted me to feel 100 percent safe about going inside.

Nice try, buddy. Not likely.

While I wait, I decide to make a quick call to Jaynie. I reach for my phone, only to realize I had to leave it behind. So I dig out my list of important numbers from my back pocket and dial my therapist using the burner phone Leo gave me when we left. I have to talk through this new discovery. Thankfully, she answers after a few brief rings.

"Hello?"

"Sorry for bothering you, but I —"

"Sue?"

Oh, yeah... no caller ID on this burner phone.

"Yes, it's me... Sue O'Malley. I'm on a different phone. Sorry. I know I'm supposed to call the office —"

"It's okay," she interjects. "How many times have I told you that this phone will always be on for emergencies? Now, are you all right? I assume you're not if you're calling my cell."

"I'm not sure. I... I..." I exhale the breath I've been holding. "Honestly, I don't even know how to begin. You're never going to believe this."

"Well, you've caught me between patients, so I have about ten minutes. If we need more time, I'll have to call you back after six."

Maybe I can unload this bombshell and get her thoughts in ten minutes — that seems possible. Plus, Leo should be done getting the cabin ready by then.

"You remember the cabin?" I ask.

"Of course."

"Well, it's Leo's cabin. I'm there now."

The line is silent, and I pull the phone away to ensure the call didn't drop. "Are you there?"

"Yes. I'm just... confused. You're saying you're at Leo's cabin, and it's *the cabin*... from your dreams? And all the —"

"Yes! That's exactly what I'm saying." My voice creeps up hysterically, but I pinch my eyes and lips shut in a feeble attempt to inject some control into the chaos I'm drowning in.

"Well, first — how did you end up *with* Leo? Did you call him like I suggested?"

"No, it's actually a long story. He showed up out of the blue last night. There was a threat made on my life — to him, about me — and so he came over to protect me."

"Oh my! A threat on your life? Is this about the gray van?"

Oh shit biscuits. I never told Leo about the gray van. How could I forget that? Had I really blocked it out as paranoia?

It's probably related to this bizarre threat. At a minimum, it's a clue... a lead that might help us solve the mystery of who is behind this nightmare. I need to tell him as soon as he comes back.

"I don't know if it's the same person from the van. All I know is Leo got a text threatening me, and then he came over to guard me. We stayed at Nick and Millie's last night because they have a fancy security system. This morning, Leo and I drove to his cabin in Ocala to hide out. And it's *the* cabin."

"Are you sure?"

"One hundred percent. I could send you a picture."

"No, I believe you. But now that you're there, are you sure you've never been there before?"

"I'm absolutely certain I've never been here until now."

"How is that possible?"

"That's what I want to know, Jaynie! Does clairvoyance come with my diagnosis? Precognition? I haven't read anything about that in the literature you gave me, but you never know. How else could I have never been here before today and yet know it the way I do? Am I going to end up like..."

I pause, gasping for air. I can't even say it. What happens in my dreams is horrible.

"Oh my gosh, Jaynie! Help me! What's happening to me?" I'm aware my volume is steadily increasing, but I'm somehow unable to stop it from happening. I'm essentially yelling by the time I ask, "Are my dreams coming true? And not in the Cinderella fairy tale way, but in the worst way imaginable? Is that a thing, Jaynie? Can you dream something before it happens? What's happening to me? How do I stop it?"

I stop yell-rambling long enough to let her speak. My heart is racing, and I can feel my pulse thrumming away wildly behind my eyelids and in my neck.

"First, we need to calm down, Sue," she cautions. "I can hear you getting worked up. Remember your grounding techniques. Let's go through them together."

"Okay, I am. I am."

I force a cleansing breath, then another, and close my eyes to envision the Clearwater coast.

"I'm feeling the sand in my toes and imagining the wind whipping through my hair." My volume starts to lower.

"That's a good start. Picture yourself there. What else do you see and feel?"

I wince as my beach grounding visual turns into a scene straight out of my recurring nightmare. "I can't focus on the beach, Jaynie. Each time I try, I see myself taped up. My mouth and wrists are bound behind my back on the cabin floor. Blood is streaming down from my temple. But unlike in my dreams, I see it like I'm watching it happen from above — not like I'm experiencing it myself — like a movie."

"Okay, I'll walk you through it. First — are you safe where you're at, right now? Where are you? In the cabin?"

"No, in the car outside the cabin."

"Is Leo with you?"

"No, he calmed me down and then went to check the inside and outside of the cabin, turn on all the security features. I'm safely locked in the SUV. He'll be right back."

"All right, that's good. You're safe. And Leo will be right back."

"Yes."

"And do you feel safe with him?"

"Very safe." I nod, even though she can't see me.

"Excellent. You're safe in the car, with Leo nearby, and now you can just focus on the sound of my voice."

"Okay. I'm focusing on your voice."

"Good. I want you to take a deep breath — inhale for three long counts, and exhale for three long counts. Inhale. One, two, three. And exhale. One, two, three."

She walks me through deep breathing for a minute or so. Then she lists things for me to see and feel — taking my typical beach scene and adding even more soothing descriptors. Jaynie's better at describing the beach than I am.

"Feel a little better?" she asks once we've been through the process twice — it took quite a bit of visualization to ground me, but I feel better now. I'm so glad I thought to call her.

"Yes. I do."

"I'll need to do a little research to find out about precognitive abilities, but my initial thought is that it's highly unlikely. There's probably another reason, especially since it's related to Leo. As I told you before, I've always suspected the dream had to do with him — I just thought it was your brain manifesting and processing your fears from your past stalker danger along with your desire to have Leo back in your life. The cabin was just a space for all that fear and desire to unfold... but this changes my theory a little. Maybe there is some type of mental block about the cabin from your past."

"You'll check, though? About the psychic thing?"

"Yes. I'll call you if I find anything that may help — but don't expect there to be much that's reliable or scientific on the topic. I will try my best, though. Until then, I think you should stay close to Leo. Do as he says and trust that he'll keep you safe. You've told me before what an outstanding protector he is, so you're probably exactly where you're supposed to be."

She's got a good point — I'm probably with the best person to keep me safe in the entire world. "He is very good at what he does." He's good at calming me down too. Always has been.

"Good. And if you start to panic, remember your grounding techniques. If they don't work, call me. Give Leo my name and number too. I keep my phone with me at all times."

"All right. And Jaynie..." I pause, thoughts still jumbled in my mind. "I'm very sorry for bothering you."

"That's quite all right. It's not a bother at all. I care about you, Sue. You're like a daughter to me."

"Really?" My voice cracks a little.

"I do. I probably shouldn't say that — I should keep things more professional. But you've been my patient for a long time, and you've come so far in your treatment. I feel such a connection with you. And... I'm proud of you. You've always been very special to me."

"I don't know what to say," I admit.

That's one of the nicest things anyone has ever said to me.

"You don't have to say anything. I'm only telling you this so you don't feel the least bit guilty for reaching out to me — anytime day or night. All right?"

"Yes."

"While we're on the subject, let me say this. Sue, you should be proud of yourself too, and I mean that wholeheartedly."

My eyes blur with unshed tears.

"You're a totally different person from the girl who walked into my office six years ago. She was out of touch with her feelings and virtually unable to relate to others. Life was just a ball of worry for *that* Sue. Do you remember her?"

It's odd how she's talking about the old me as if I'm a different person, but life was incredibly hard back then. It's still challenging, but I really have come a long way.

"Yes. I remember. You've helped me a lot."

She continues, "See — you just did it again. Even in this conversation, you're doing great engaging with me and staying focused on things other than what's immediately going on in your mind. You've come so far. Be proud, Sue."

"Thank you." My throat nearly swells shut with emotion.

"I'll research your question. Be safe in the meantime."

"I appreciate it."

"We'll talk soon. Goodbye."

The call disconnects as my thoughts wander. I feel better after having told Jaynie some of what's happening. I couldn't get into the complicated feelings I've got for Leo and that I'm *important* to him. That'll have to wait for our next appointment.

As if my thoughts conjured him into being, Leo walks onto the front porch, then down the steps, heading straight for me. His head pivots from left to right so he can scan the forest for anything dangerous.

He opens the door and offers his hand, a smile softening the hard planes of his face. "Shall we?"

I swing my legs out while taking his hand. He gives it a gentle squeeze to reassure me. As I rise, he studies me closely — I can feel the weight of his gaze bearing down on my skin.

Despite the support and encouragement he exudes, I'm still shaken to my core. My chin wobbles as I move closer to the cabin. With each step, my heart rate increases, and fear compounds.

Once I get inside, if the interior layout is the same as it is in my dreams, I'll ask him if we can find a nearby hotel.

That's the logical thing to do, and as insane as this situation seems to be, I can still make a logical-sounding argument. For the time being, he believes us to be safe here, and I have no reason to doubt him — aside from my dreams. But my dreams are damn convincing.

Chapter Twenty

Just livin' the dream

Leo

Each step closer to the cabin seems like it's causing her physical pain, judging by her winces and frequent swallowing.

I still don't know what's happening, so I'm taking it one slow step at a time.

Literally.

We're moving slower than a procession of senior citizen inchworms using walkers and canes.

Kidding.

"You okay?" I ask while leading her in through the front door.

Without answering, she looks around the cabin with wide, unblinking eyes. I see a hint of fear mixed with her stubbornness to be strong reflecting in those blue orbs.

As much as she puts herself down for being weak, I think she's quite the opposite. Being brave isn't an absence of fear. It's pressing on even when you're scared. And Sue exemplifies that quality every damn day. Sure, her anxiety is a part of her personality, but her tenacity is too.

After all, it takes a lot of pressure to make a diamond.

Her eyes cut to the kitchen, where it sits left of the entrance, and she shows no reaction as she studies the grocery bags sitting on the counter.

I'm not sure what I'm expecting to happen, but the way she's taking in her surroundings is concerning. It's *almost* like she was waiting for someone to attack.

When I came in to do a quick sweep of the property a few moments ago, I reset all the cameras, perimeter sensors, and alarms.

The cabin is secure — inside and out.

Breaking away from my side, Sue takes several steps into the center of the living room while I hang back to give her space. It's not a huge cabin — just two bedrooms, a bathroom, living room, and kitchen — so there isn't far to wander.

As the tension visibly leaves her shoulders, she seems to regain some comfort.

When I turn around from closing and locking the front door, I take in the way Sue's hands are resting on her curvy hips. I feel my dick twitch as my fingers ache to grab her by those hips. I shouldn't be thinking such things when she's upset... but her thick body just does things to me I can't always control.

"Huh," she harrumphs, shaking her head. "It doesn't make any sense."

"What doesn't make sense?"

Standing at the edge of the living room near the hallway, she shakes her head a few more times, then throws her hands up in defeat. "This doesn't look anything like the inside of the cabin from my dreams."

She sighs loudly, running her hand through her hair.

Leaving the groceries unpacked, I take a few steps in her direction. "Ready to talk?"

"I guess now that I'm done freaking the fuck out, I owe you an explanation."

She tosses a hint of a smile in my direction, and my heart squeezes at the sight. She's calming down — it's going to be all right.

"You don't owe me anything. But if you're ready to explain, then I'm ready to listen."

Her smile grows wider and more vibrant as her eyes meet mine for only the second time since we left the grocery store over a half hour ago. "Let's get the cold stuff put away, then I can try to explain."

"It can wait. You're more important than groceries."

She scoffs and says, "Nothing is more important than making sure this ice cream doesn't melt."

I follow her as she heads into the kitchen, where we start unloading in silence. She hands me the items one by one as I put them away.

While we work, I think back to how upset she was when we arrived. I've never seen her like that before.

Guarding her in the spring, I remember a few times when she got scared or her anxiety got out of hand. But it never was *that* bad, and I was always able to calm her down. Instinctively, I just knew how to handle the situation.

That's probably because I have a shitload of experience defusing tense situations — mostly from my fucked-up childhood.

Today's panic was on a whole other level. She must have had some intense dreams to cause panic like that. I'm dying to ask for an explanation, but I know she needs time to get her thoughts in order. That's something I've known about Sue since the day we met. Fortunately, I've got all the patience in the world when it comes to her.

We're shifting from putting away the cold stuff to the non-perishables when, out of nowhere, she starts rambling. "I'm sorry for flipping out on you when we got here. It was just quite a shock. I never expected to see this place in real life. Only now, I'm not entirely sure it's the same place I've seen in my recurring nightmare. Well, I'm sure the outside is the same, but the inside is different, which makes no sense. Then again, dreams rarely make sense."

Her volume is starting to increase, pace becoming frantic. "Nothing about this is logical. And now I have no clue what's happening. I don't like not knowing what's happening."

I reach out to touch her forearm, stilling her. "Slow down. Breathe."

I have no fucking clue how she's having nightmares about the exterior of my cabin. I've never taken her here. It's baffling.

But I do believe her.

Her shoulders slump forward, and she screws her lips to one side of her mouth. "Sorry."

"Stop apologizing. It's fine, angel. I just don't want you to get worked up again, and it sounded like you were heading in that direction."

She takes a deep breath. "You're right. Maybe we should sit down and talk."

"Good idea." I take her hand and lead her to the couch. With all the cold stuff put away, I can get the rest of the bags unpacked later.

Before we sit down, she clutches my hand with both of hers. "Leo, actually... can you give me a tour of the rest of the cabin first? Maybe it would help if I saw the whole thing. Just to be certain it's not the same as my nightmares."

"Sure. Whatever you need to be comfortable."

I want her to feel safe here, so if she needs a tour before we talk, I'll gladly oblige. Keeping hold of her hand, I lead her to the hallway.

"This is the bedroom," I say as I point out the only actual room that contains a bed. "You'll be sleeping in here."

She remains quiet as I show her the shared bathroom and second bedroom — which is set up like an office.

"This is where I'll stay." I nod to the small couch beside the desk and watch her gaze follow.

She frowns, and I can see an objection forming on her lips, so I keep talking in hopes of distracting her. "I'll also be able to monitor the security feeds from here. All my tech gadgets and gizmos run through this computer system."

Next, I open the closet and show her my mini-armory — a selection of rifles, handguns, ammo, and knives. She nods thoughtfully.

"And I assume you've got every possible home security system, right?" she asks with a shit-disturbing grin.

"For the most part," I answer slyly, drawing out the words. I'm waiting for whatever joke she's about to drop. I can sense one coming.

"Where do you feed and water the dogs?"

Confused, I ask, "The dogs?"

"Yeah, the home security dogs. Oh, wait. You probably upgraded to the cyborg robot dogs with laser eyes, didn't you? Or maybe you opted for the guard sharks and camera-assisted attack parrots?"

I start laughing, but she continues, clearly encouraged by my response. "It stands to reason you also have crows trained to carry machetes circling above and carrier pigeons that know to drop grenades on evildoers."

"Lots of bird references," I say between laughs.

"Well, you know what they say... bird is the word," she deadpans.

She cracks me up. I can't resist drawing her in for a hug while we laugh together. In the midst of all this stress, she still brings me joy. *Damn this woman.*

After we stop laughing, I continue with the tour.

"Behind this panel is a small panic room," I tell her while pointing to a hideaway door.

"As you can see, it looks like a shelf, but if you press here, the whole thing opens." I show her how to open the hidden door panel, and she peeks inside.

"You can fit two people in there along with a small amount of supplies. It's not a lot of space, so it's for worst-case scenarios. It locks from the inside too." She eyes me carefully as I demonstrate how to lock the bolt on the panel's interior.

My gut twists at the mere thought of shit going ass up to the extent she'd need to use this room, but I'd rather we have this option than not.

She eyes everything cautiously before looking up at me with a sheepish grin. "You're ready for the zombie apocalypse out here, huh?"

A soft chuckle escapes from my chest while I close the closet door. "This place has been used as a safe house, so it's good to be prepared. As you can see, I've got everything I need to protect you right here. That's why I picked this place."

"Redleg doesn't play around, huh?" she jokes.

I remain silent, not wanting to lie to her. This cabin has nothing to do with Redleg. It's mine, bought under an alias with cash. All utilities are in the name and social security number connected with the alias and are paid for with cash-based credit cards so they can't be traced back to me. It's functioned as a safe house for a handful of jobs, but it primarily exists for a different reason. Although, I don't think now is the time to get into that with her.

Some secrets are best kept closer to the vest.

"That's basically everything," I tell her as we exit the room.

While we walk down the hall, she says, "I know you said to stop apologizing, but I'm truly sorry for being such a freak. Not just for panicking but also for having nightmares about your lake cabin. It's a really nice place."

Her mood seems to have shifted from jovial to solemn. I glance over my shoulder at her, but she puts her head down and shields her face from me.

Oh, my sweet angel... that'll never do.

I stop moving and plant myself in front of her. "Look at me," I command softly while tugging on her chin with my thumb and forefinger.

Her gaze stays downcast, so I just hold my grip and patiently wait for her to make eye contact. I need her to see the sincerity written on my face when I tell her this.

Her sweet scent surrounds me since we're crowded in the narrow hallway. With her mouth open slightly, her tongue sweeps across her lips a few times. My dick swells, and I have to physically hold myself back from kissing her right now.

This is *not* the time.

She's just had a panic attack of some sort because apparently, she's seen a cabin like mine in her nightmares. And now she's apologizing for being upset and calling herself a freak.

Definitely not the right time.

Yet all I can think of is pressing my lips against hers to see if kissing her today is as good as I remember it being last night.

What the fuck is wrong with me?

Her lashes flutter, and she finally meets my eyes. I feel the side of my mouth lift in a victorious grin. I fucking love it when she looks into my eyes.

"Angel, you are *not* a freak. I don't want to hear you say that again. You're fucking amazing."

"It's okay, Leo. I know what I am. You don't have to try to protect me from the truth." She says the words in such a resigned manner — like it's a given fact. Why does she think that?

My spine stiffens with my disagreement. "But it's not the truth. Why would you think it is?"

"People have called me that all my life. Usually, it's freak — that's the most common one. But also... weirdo, spaz, or crazy. Someone once called me a highly anxious poodle of a human. Oh, and there are also those lowbrow insults like fat, ugly, and loser. And I get it. I don't have any friends, and I panic over the tiniest, inconsequential things. So with every meltdown, I know those words to be true. *I am a freak.*"

"No," I say quietly but with an unquestionable firmness. "No, you're not."

I grow angrier by the second — not at Sue, but at everyone who has ever disrespected her or mocked her. My fists clench at my sides, aching to punch each of those fuckers right in their lying mouths.

Rolling her eyes, she replies, "It's *swell* of you disagree, but look at the facts."

"Sue, you are *not* a freak."

"The numbers don't lie, Leo. You're only one person out of..." she trails off as she looks to the ceiling like she's counting.

"How many? How many people have called you those things?" Although my volume remains low and controlled, I'm positively seething with anger.

She puts her head down and mutters, "I don't know... dozens. Maybe a hundred."

Cupping her cheeks with both hands, I lift her face to meet mine and draw a step closer. I need to feel her body press flush against mine.

"Give me a number, and I'll tell you twice as many times exactly how wonderful and special you are. And I'm going to keep telling you until you believe me."

And I also want the number so I know how many asses I need to kick.

Her forehead pinches, and her eyes search mine like she doesn't believe me.

In response to her disbelief, I double down. "If I have to tell you a hundred times a day, every day, just how fucking perfect you are, then that's what I'll do. Because you are. And you deserve to hear those words over and over again to wash away all the times people told you lies."

"Leo." My name is a soft sigh on her lips.

I feel the tug again — that connection between us — like a cord drawing me closer to her. Yet with the way we're standing, toe to toe and chest to chest, there's only one way to be closer. Well, maybe two ways.

I'm not strong enough to resist the pull.

Once again, I press my lips to hers and claim her mouth.

Having her in this cabin — just the two of us inside my private escape — is firing up something primal in me. It's only been a few minutes since we arrived, but my desire for her is ramping up at an alarming speed. I'll never be able to make it through the night at this rate.

I catch her soft moan in my mouth as she opens for me and wraps her arms around my shoulders. Moving one hand from her cheek, I grab the back of her neck so I can angle her head to the side and deepen the kiss. Our lips caress and brush each other softly while my tongue dips in and out of her warm, welcoming mouth.

Although I know it's not possible, I wish I could kiss away every negative thought she's ever had about herself. I want to lick, nip, and worship her until she's able to see herself the way I do — like a priceless work of art. Just like her beautiful paintings and drawings, she's a multi-layered masterpiece to me. A beautiful soul with a loyal heart and intelligent mind.

And if her sweet kisses taste this good, I can't wait until I can taste the rest of her.

A sudden buzzing sound ruins the moment — which was quickly becoming more passionate than I intended. She jumps back and casts her eyes downward.

I grab the phone from my back pocket and cringe.

It's Big Al. He must have gotten another message from the tango. Otherwise, he'd probably just text.

Shit.

Every fucking time I take my eye off the ball and get lost in Sue's orbit, I'm pulled right back out and have to embrace the suck of my own reality.

"It's Leo," I answer.

"We have news," he says without preamble. "And it's not good."

Fuck.

Chapter Twenty-One

Grandma Leo's decorating service

Sue

Leo stiffens and takes a few steps away from me to talk to his boss. I overheard enough when he answered the call to know it was not going to be good news. I'm not exactly in a hurry to hear any more details right now, so it's no skin off my arse if he wants to have privacy. I trust him to protect me, and I know he'll tell me what I need to know in a way I can handle it.

That's the thing about Leo... he just knows how to treat me. Always respectful, never condescending or pitying... but also with enough patience and sensitivity that I don't get set off into a spiral of anxiety. He's so damn gentle with me, and it's exactly what I need. How does he do that? Who taught him how to be this way?

Part of me wishes I weren't the type of person that needs to be handled with care. But you know what they say about wishes. If you put them in your hands and fart...

Actually, I don't think that's the right saying, and it's gross, so I'm not going to finish the thought.

I decide to check out the bedroom where I'll be sleeping. It'll also give me a chance to collect my thoughts and cool my panties.

Damn, that man can kiss.

And the things he says to me could rival the greatest love stories. I just have no earthly idea why he thinks about me the way he does. Maybe he was dropped on his head as a baby or ate lead paint chips when he was a kid.

Kid.

Huh. He hasn't called me that in a while.

As I enter the bedroom, I'm hit with another reminder of how wrong I was about this place. I'm unsure of how my dreams could be so spot on with the cabin's exterior but completely wrong about the interior. It's nothing like the dark, dreary, stark space from my nightmares.

Leo's created a warm, inviting space here. It's sparsely decorated, but the warmth and coziness give it a woman's touch. It makes me wonder who decorated it for him or if he did it himself. Then again, nothing about Leo is as it appears on the surface. He looks so fierce and rough — like a big, burly bad boy — but he's really a teddy bear. Maybe he also decorates like an old southern woman. Who knows?

I run my hand along the smooth, polished wood of the dresser and stifle a chuckle when I see the white cloth doilies lining the top. The bedspread is off-white with delicate ivy vines. The pillow shams — yes, he has them — have the same pattern of lace on the edges as the doilies on the dresser. *Man!* I'm really starting to think his grandmother decorated for him.

Now I'm wondering if his grandmother is still alive. He doesn't talk about his family all that much. He seems to share the bare minimum about them. I wonder why that is.

I want to know all there is to know about Leo... every little thing.

The room smells subtly of clean linen, and I notice a dryer sheet on the bedside table. Probably to keep the room from smelling too stuffy since the cabin sits unoccupied so much.

After taking in the overwhelming comfort of the space, I feel completely at ease here and no longer want to run and hide. The sense of foreboding that caused my earlier meltdown is nearly gone. It's been replaced with a subtle excitement at being in such close proximity to the man I've been hung up on for so long, leaving the sensation of electricity running through my veins and a slight ache between my legs.

Being a little nosy, I open all the drawers, noting half of them have clothes in them. The top drawer has boxer shorts folded immaculately next to about a dozen socks — all of them paired, folded, and stacked together — resembling little sock soldiers. The next drawer contains T-shirts folded so tightly it warms my heart, and the bottom drawer has shorts in neat stacks that look color-coded.

I feel a tad more horny with each drawer I open. This level of detail and organization is like an aphrodisiac. If I go into his closet and it's equally tidy, I might orgasm on the spot.

Jokes aside, the way he's meticulously sorted everything speaks to something deep inside me. Like his inner neat freak is calling out to my inner neat freak.

Is he my soul mate?

Shaking off the insane thought, I decide to unpack — might as well make myself comfortable. Once I've carefully placed all my items in the empty drawers, I take my vanity bag to the bathroom.

As I exit, Leo ends his call. I head into the living room, where I see him sitting on the couch with his hands running through his dark-brown hair. It's a nice style for a guy — tight on the sides, but enough to tug on and play with on top. And he has that adorable little puff of hair in the front that spins into a curl.

When I'm done lusting over his hair and profile, I notice the phone sitting on the coffee table in front of him.

"Is everything okay?" I ask, then immediately cringe because it's obvious to anyone with a brain that things are not okay. This gentle giant of a man is radiating tension.

He raises his head and looks in my direction, his brows drawn together. "Not exactly, but it will be."

I walk slowly in his direction. "That was your boss, right?"

He nods and lifts his hand out to me with his palm open, beckoning me to his side. My feet comply instantly, and my hands itch to hold his. I don't deny them, eagerly taking his warm, calloused hand. He pulls me around and then gently tugs me downward, indicating he wants me to sit. I can tell this isn't going to be an easy conversation.

He drops my hand once I sit beside him. My thigh brushes against his, and his warmth seeps into my skin, comforting me.

Touching like this is a funny thing for me — the sensation can be uncomfortable at times. If it were anyone else, I would scoot over to the other side to put space between us — otherwise, I'm likely to hyper-fixate on the touching sensation and be unable to focus on anything else. But I don't want to be any farther away from Leo than this. It's the perfect distance. Instead of distracting me, his touch calms me, and I'm content to patiently wait for him to speak.

He finally does, shifting slightly to look in my direction. "Tell me about your nightmare first. Then I'll tell you about the call."

Oh, okay. Maybe he needs more time to process his conversation with Big Al. I certainly understand how that is — phone calls drain me.

"Well, I guess I can do that. Uh... um." I stutter a little as I try to decide where to begin.

"I started having them a few months ago. It always starts with me walking into a cabin — one that looks *exactly* like this one does on the outside. Even the bush beside the front steps is the same. In real life, it seems like it's grown a little more, but it's clearly the same bush — same cabin."

I catch a quiver in my voice, so I pause to steady myself.

Reaching over, Leo takes my hand again and pulls it into his lap. Instantly, my heart rate slows to normal levels.

"Take your time," he whispers.

"I'll be okay. I've talked about it a lot with Jaynie before, so I know I can tell you too."

"Who's Jaynie?"

"My therapist," I say without shame.

He knows I go to therapy, and I'm not the least bit embarrassed about it. I let go of that trifling feeling years ago. Nick used to joke that the only people who'd judge me negatively for being in therapy were the ones who probably needed it far more than I did.

Leo nods, encouraging me to continue, so I do. "Anyway, I never know why I'm going inside the cabin, but I always walk right in like I own the place. And the more I've dreamed it, the more fearful I become of the cabin — it's almost like I know what's going to happen. But I go in every single time like a dumbass. A lamb marching foolishly into the slaughterhouse. As soon as I get inside the cabin, I'm jumped from behind. Bam! No delay, no time to look around, no rhyme or reason. Someone is always waiting to get me."

Leo squeezes my hand tighter but stays silent.

"There's always a scuffle, and the dream sort of skips ahead in time. Next thing I know, I'm tied up with my hands bound behind me, and I'm lying on the floor."

I gulp, feeling the fear grip me like it does in my dream. I pause to take a cleansing breath. When I do, Leo lets go of my hand and wraps his arm around my shoulder, bringing me to his side.

With the safety of his bulky frame surrounding me, I snake my arm around his waist and squeeze. I smell the laundry detergent on his shirt, mixed with his own soothing scent. His abs are hard, with just enough cushion on them to be soothing and soft to the touch. Within seconds, I'm calm and grounded.

It's extraordinary how quickly it happens.

What usually takes several minutes of beach scene visualization takes only seconds in his embrace.

Somehow, I find a glorious sense of peace in this man's arms. It's almost as if Leo himself is the calm I've been seeking my entire life.

With a calmer voice, I continue telling him about my dream. "There is a dark figure standing over me, and I can feel the warm trickles of blood running down my cheek. Although I don't remember it happening, I somehow know I've been hit in the head. I'm lying there, totally powerless and at the mercy of this shadowy figure. It's absolutely terrifying. I usually wake up right about the time he leans forward to grab me."

I feel a little ashamed at the rest, but I finish the story because I want to tell him this — every detail — and I know he won't judge me. Plus, if we're staying here for a few days together, I'll likely have the dream at some point, and he needs to know what my reaction will be.

"Usually, I'm covered in sweat and scared as hell when I wake. It's the screaming that shakes me from sleep, I suspect. And then I have all this adrenaline running through me. My heart is pounding, and I end up crying like a baby. Falling back to sleep isn't usually an option, so I tend to get up and paint once I'm no longer a blubbering, shaking mess."

"And you're all alone when this happens?" he asks while running his hand through my hair.

"Well, yeah... it's the middle of the night. And I'm usually alone in general, so..." I trail off, feeling self-conscious about my life of solitude.

"How often do you have the dream?"

I shrug my shoulders as much as possible, considering his big arm is leaning on me. "It depends. A few times a month, at least once a week. Sometimes more if I'm having a bad week."

"Shit. That's terrible, angel." He places a kiss on the top of my head. I squeeze my arm around his waist even tighter.

After a moment of silence, he says, "You didn't have any when I was guarding you before, so when did it start?"

"Not long after that," I confess, feeling my eyes squint shut. I don't want to hurt him with the truth, but I won't lie either.

"*Right* after I left?"

"Yes," I admit.

Instantly, he shifts under me and adjusts our positioning. We're still seated but now facing each other. He holds me straight in front of him by placing his big hands on the outsides of my upper arms. I can't resist the pull to look into his eyes — which is still baffling to me. As much as I hate looking at everyone else dead in their eyes, it's all I want to do with him.

"You said you've spoken to Jaynie about it. What does she think is causing the dreams?" He tilts his head to the side, his gaze intensifying. "Be honest."

My eyes shift for a moment before landing back on his. "Well, she thinks it is my brain's way of processing the fear I felt when Millie's stalker threatened me."

"Why didn't it start right away then? Why did it start a few weeks later?"

I heave a sigh. I'm tempted to lie, but he'll know, so what's the point? I'm a terrible liar; he's told me as much dozens of times.

"She thinks it has to do with how much I was missing you." Twisting the knife the rest of the way into his chest, I say, "And that I felt abandoned by you."

I look away, but it's *not* because I'm uncomfortable with the eye contact. Seeing the pain my words cause him might break me, and I don't want to cry any more.

I'm so damn sick of crying.

He squeezes my upper arms. "Is that what you think? That I abandoned you?"

Nibbling on my lip, I nod but soften the confession by adding, "I only thought that at first."

"And after that?" he prods.

With my eyes closed, I tell him, "After that, I assumed I was just a job to you, and my feelings for you were completely one-sided. I thought I read the situation wrong — I was wrong about everything."

My painful admission is met with several seconds of tense silence. When my eyes finally open, I see his are downcast.

I take the opportunity to study his face. His lashes look thicker from this angle, and I can see the faint lines at the corner of his eyes. He has a few freckles across the bridge of his nose I don't usually see — after all, it's hard to have this view of him, considering he's about half a foot taller than me.

"Leo, it's okay." I try to shake him from his tortured silence.

He shakes his head. "No, it's not okay, Sue. It's not. All this time, you've been..." he trails off, then releases his hold on my arms before standing up and pacing. The wood floors creak under his heavy steps. Curling his hands into tight fists, he curses under his breath while repeating, "All this time," over and over.

I remain silent, unsure of what to say to ease his ache. I can only assume he's feeling guilty for hurting me. I can relate since I feel guilty for hurting him with my words.

And the magnitude of that hits me full force, physically knocking my back against the couch cushions.

I can *relate* to him.

I truly relate to him… relate to another person. I can feel what he's feeling, and it makes perfect sense to me.

For others, this probably doesn't mean much. But for me? It's everything.

No longer content to sit here and let him stew a few feet away, I rise and take three large strides until I'm standing in front of him. He stops pacing and looks at me, his head lowered and eyes sad. I have to ease this hurt for him. For both of us. If he's hurting, so am I.

"You feel bad for leaving and hurting me, right?" I ask because even though I *think* I know what he's feeling, this is all new territory for me. Empathy is *not* my strong suit.

"Yes, it's killing me, my sweet angel. I'm so damn sorry. You've been suffering all this time. Had months of nightmares because of me… and I had no idea."

"Well, how could you have known? It's not like we've kept in touch."

"No, but you wanted to. You asked me to, and I was stubborn enough to think if I left, you'd forget about me. Or I could forget about you. But I didn't. I never could. I've been a miserable asshole ever since I walked away. But my pain was nothing compared to what you've gone through. And it's all my fault."

I reach up and palm the side of his face to stop his rambling. He leans into my touch and closes his eyes. The scruff of his beard tickles my palm, but I soak in the feeling of him like this — something I've always wanted but never thought I'd have. The freedom to touch him. To feel his skin on mine.

"I'll forgive you as long as you tell me why you left. Why did you say those awful things that day?"

He steps forward and wraps himself around me like a tight blanket. My arms reflexively slide around him and clasp behind his back, resting at belt level.

"I left to save you… from me and from others. I have enemies, and I tend to be overprotective of people I love. I didn't want to smother you like that. And the thought of someone targeting you because of me was too much."

Oh, the irony.

"Talk about your ultimate backfires," I say flippantly, trying to lighten the mood.

He chuckles and shakes his head. His chest vibrates with his soft laughs. Making him smile again causes my heart to soar into the stratosphere.

"Yeah, I denied us… all this… whatever *this* might be and for absolutely no reason. You're still in danger, and I'm probably going to end up smothering the shit out of you because of it." He scoffs, complete with a dismissive head shake.

I shrug and beam at him, feeling so much joy at being with him like this. Regardless of the danger, I'm in Leo's arms, and it feels pretty damn good. "If the result is that we get to do this... then I'm okay with you smothering me some."

His expression shifts to sadness or concern — not sure which. "I don't want to snuff out your light."

"Then you won't."

"I'll try not to, but I don't know how successful I'll be." He pauses, looking like he's turning over his words. "I've had a lot of shit go wrong in my life, and I tend to get worried when I don't know for certain that someone I care for is safe. My sister..." he trails off, glancing at the ceiling before turning back down to face me. "Let's just say I struggle with protective boundaries."

"Okay. Thanks for telling me that."

I don't really know what else to say. Honestly, what he's expressing doesn't bother me.

Not one bit.

I've been smothered my entire life by virtually every member of my family — everyone who felt sorry for me or saw me as incapable. And it's a big fecking family! Six siblings and two parents. So that's eight times the smothering. And Leo is the least smothering person out of all of them. Sure, he has his moments — but from what I've seen now and six months ago, his *smothering moments* are all justified.

He leans down and presses his forehead to mine. I can feel his warm breath mingling with mine. "Once this danger is behind us... I want to..."

"To what?" I ask after he takes an achingly long pause. Did he forget what he was going to say? I do that sometimes. ADHD can be a bitch.

He squints and bites his lip. Oh hell, now I want to bite it too. Shit, I want to climb right up him and suck his lower lip into my mouth, then snag my teeth around it.

Am I turning into a cannibal?

Boy, that's a bizarre thought to have.

He captures my attention again when he says, "I want to take you on a date, I guess. That probably sounds weird given the timing... but yeah."

He swallows, seeming flummoxed with a creased forehead and adorably scrunched nose. "Sue, do you want to go out on a date with me?"

Oh my frick frack paddy whack.

I could die happy right now.

He's so adorable. My inner schoolgirl, who's been crushing on this big, tattooed hunk for more than six months, is squealing and jumping up and down. He wants to take me out on a date.

A date. Leo Mason and me. *On a date.*

I'm deceased.

Does he want to be my boyfriend too?

I've never had one of those, and if I could pick one, it would be him.

All day, every day.

Fecking hell!

I don't care that someone is out to get us, because this man is holding me, keeping me safe, and saying all the things I've always wanted to hear but never dreamed or even wished for.

Since I can't lie to him — or anyone, for that matter — I answer the only way I can.

Truthfully.

"Leo Mason, not only do I want to date you, but I want to do *all the things* with you."

Chapter Twenty-Two

After dinner bombshells

Leo

After our little *heart-to-heart* talk, we decided we were hungry. It's been a long, exhausting day.

Sue isn't exactly chomping at the bit to find out about Big Al's call, and I don't see the need to worry her. There's nothing we can do about it at this point anyhow. Redleg is handling things for now.

We make dinner together while we chat to catch up on things we've missed over the last half year. We share stories about our families and laugh about little things. Even after all these months apart, we pick up right where we left off.

When we're halfway through dinner — a simple shrimp pasta dish and salad — she finally asks the question I've been waiting to hear. "What did your boss say? I'm ready to hear it."

I put down my fork and take a drink of water. I meet her eyes as I say, "He got another text — two of them, actually. First one was some expletives about us giving him the slip, but he vowed to find us and claims he has endless resources at his disposal."

"And the second text?"

I hold up my hands, making finger quotes as I recite the text word for word. "You can't hide her forever. I'll get her back. You're going to pay for this."

Silently, Sue wipes her mouth, dabbing at the corners gently with her napkin. Her eyes are thoughtful and focused on her plate, but I can see her wheels turning.

"That makes no sense," she finally says.

"Which part?"

"He or she never *had* me. How can he get me back if he never had me to begin with?"

Good question.

"I asked Boss the same thing. He thinks it could be the perp wants you back where he can watch you. Maybe the guy was upset and just didn't choose his words properly."

"That doesn't sound right."

I agree. "What else could it be?" I'm purposely being a little vague because I'm interested in getting her take on the situation. She's extremely intelligent, and I'd be a fool not to consider her thoughts about this clusterfuck.

"This is stupid. Call him."

"Call him?"

"Yes. Enough with the cryptic texts. As much as it goes against every fiber of my being... make an actual phone call. Get him on the phone and find out exactly what he wants and why."

I feel like I've been hit in the face with a stupid stick for not trying that already.

"I'll call Big Al and Tomer with that suggestion. Maybe they can block him from tracking my location even if I call him from out here. I have an old signal scrambler here, but I'm not sure if it will do the job. Tech is always changing."

"Or have Big Al call him from Clearwater."

"That might work, unless he knows my voice."

"Only one way to find out."

Sue picks her fork up and continues eating. I take a few more bites to finish my meal, ball up my napkin, and push back from the table.

"After we do the dishes, I'll call Big Al."

She nods but then says, "Just call him now. I'll finish eating and start cleaning. Why wait?"

"You sure?"

"Leo, I assure you I can handle cleaning up two plates, two bowls, a pan, and some silverware. This is important."

"Thanks, angel. I'll handle breakfast."

Damn, it sounds good saying that. The thought of waking up with her, having breakfast, and planning our day — like we did once upon a time — feels like a little slice of chocolate pie.

Internally, I roll my eyes at what a smitten fool I've become in the last twenty-four hours.

But this is Sue... your angel, my conscience reminds me. Apparently, at some point, my mind, body, and soul all gave up the idea of resisting her.

But I need to keep that urge in check. I can't go all-in with Sue until she's safe.

Pressing up and away from the table, I grab the burner phone and make the call.

While Tomer and Big Al are discussing options, I pull up the security feeds on my tablet. Everything looks like it did the last time I checked, aside from some small wildlife detected around the property. If something goes off, I'll get an alert on my watch. But I like to watch the footage and manually check for issues frequently. I'll also need to go outside and walk the property soon.

After a few minutes, we decide that Tomer will route the call from my burner phone to Redleg's system so it looks like it's coming from there. When we finally make the call, the line rings and rings — no answer, and voicemail isn't set up.

Dammit.

We try three more times with the same result. We'll have to try again tomorrow. In the meantime, Big Al sends a text from my phone informing the tango we're ready to talk, and he needs to answer our call.

Back on the phone with only Big Al, he asks, "Everything else going okay out there?" He pauses, then adds, "With Sue? It's got to be... hard seeing her again. Just want to make sure you're okay and able to keep your focus where it should be. Protecting her and keeping yourself safe in the process."

He's in *caring friend mode* now, not *badass operative focusing on a mission mode.* His only goal at present is getting me to talk about my feelings like we're in a knitting circle or something. I suspect he wants to make sure I'm protecting my heart since he thinks Sue rejected me last time around. He likely assumes she'll push me away again after we take this asshole down and the job is done.

Should I tell him things are different now? Will he worry more? Will he think I can't protect her properly if I'm compromised — wrapped up in my feelings for her?

If I were a team leader, I wouldn't tolerate one of my crew protecting someone they have emotional entanglements with. It's too messy — too easy to get distracted. There are rules about that shit for a reason.

But Sue didn't hire Redleg. This is all me. Granted, the company is helping with the job from headquarters and providing additional guards for the other family members... but this is personal.

And I don't trust anyone to protect my angel except me.

Period.

I need to do the right thing and stop acting like this is a romantic retreat.

Stay focused on the mission, soldier.

"Everything is good. It was emotional seeing her again, but I'm focusing on protecting her. One hundred percent. Nothing to worry about."

The line is silent except for a heavy sigh on his end.

Finally, he responds, "I trust you to tell me if that changes. No questions asked. No judgment. I can protect her myself if you need to take a step back. I wouldn't blame you."

My throat tightens, thick with emotion that he'd do that for me. "Thanks, but I'm good."

"Offer stands."

"Copy that. Now, any word from the guys protecting my mom and Nick and Millie?"

"Routine. No news."

"Have Henderson let Mom know I asked about her, okay? I always check in each night, but I won't tonight since I don't want to risk any contact that could jeopardize our location. Her phone might not be secure."

"Will do. I'll make the call myself... how about that?" His voice has a teasing quality that ruffles my feathers a little.

"How about you don't hit on my mother, old man?"

"She started it," he jokes.

We end the conversation with a plan to check in tomorrow morning and try to call the tango again. He'll let me know if there's any news in the meantime.

After another check of the perimeter sensors and alarms shows no changes, I head to the kitchen to help Sue finish up. She's wiping a plate dry when I enter. The image is so domestic — so natural. But I'm not the type who likes being waited on hand and foot, so I sidle up next to her to help.

"There was a gray van. I keep forgetting to tell you about it," Sue says flatly, without any preamble.

My spine stiffens. "What do you mean? Where? When?"

She continues wiping the plate and carefully puts it away in the cupboard. She's acting like it's no big deal. I calm myself because she'd be acting a bit more jumpy if it were a new threat.

"Not today... not now. Calm down. This is old news, but it might be pertinent."

My shoulders roll back as I relax. "Okay, tell me about it."

We put the rest of the dishes away as she shares the details about a work van she kept seeing around town and on her street. Although it could be nothing, she was worried enough to discuss it with her therapist. I've learned the value of trusting your gut in situations like these. If Sue's gut says this might be related, it probably is.

"This could be the person who took pictures of you. It's probably the guy." My pulse jumps with a hint of excitement. This is a huge lead.

"Or gal," she teases with a wink.

Shaking my head, I excuse myself to call the guys at Redleg. They're both eager to start digging into it further.

Tomer's going to access the camera feeds at the gas station by Sue's house to see if they can get a plate number or a face shot of the van's driver. Starbucks and a half dozen other shops on the strip should also have security cameras if that fails. They're optimistic we can get somewhere with this tip.

"Finally! We have a lead I can follow," Tomer says with a shitload of excitement in his tone.

He lives for digging into data and camera footage, hacking shit he probably shouldn't be, and anything tech-related. It's been pissing him off that up until now, all we've had are a few untraceable text messages and pictures without trackable properties. Boss has been keeping him busy by researching the whereabouts of bad guys we've helped land behind bars over the years, but he's been itching to really dig into actionable intel.

"Leo, do you know anyone with a gray work van?" Boss asks.

"No one comes to mind, but I'll keep thinking of past perps and see if it rings any bells."

"Okay, we'll be in touch with any news," he says before adding, "Oh, and Madeline's good. All is well with Nick and Millie too."

It doesn't escape me that he just referred to my mother by her first name.

We disconnect the call, and I share the update with Sue while sitting together on the couch. Sick of the space between us, I reach over and pull her into my side. She instantly wraps her arm around my waist like she did earlier. My dick takes notice of her proximity.

Shit.

Didn't I just get done telling myself to keep my hands to myself?

"If you had to guess, who do you think is doing this?" she asks while stroking her hand across my stomach.

I resist shuddering under her soft teasing touch and instead focus on answering her question. "I wish I knew, angel. That would make things so much easier."

"No guesses at all?"

A list of potential creeps runs through my mind. "Well, a few of the bad guys we've put away since I've worked at Redleg are potential candidates, naturally. Tomer has been running down what he can on them — tracking which ones are no longer behind bars and what they've been up to — trying to find someone with motive or opportunity. He's doing what he can to track their locations, but he's turned up a lot of nothing so far on that front."

"That sucks."

I chuckle morosely.

"Anything else?"

"There are a few organizations that may have tracked me down because they want payback for my role in some of the covert ops my unit took part in back when I was enlisted. But the thing that makes it most difficult is the idea that I took something that belongs to this person. I haven't taken anything." I pause thoughtfully. "Well, nothing that I'm aware of."

"You've taken me," she teases.

Oh, sweet girl. I haven't taken you the way I want yet. I haven't buried myself inside you and heard you scream my name while your fingernails run up and down my back.

Fuck.

I don't know how much longer I can sit here with her — or even stay here in this cabin — without our connection becoming physical. I've never craved someone this much before.

I clear my thoughts and shake off my dirty fantasies. "I hadn't taken you when he sent the first text."

"That's true. Has anyone at Redleg done a profile on the bad guy?"

"You mean like an FBI profiler type of thing? *Criminal Minds* stuff?"

She lifts her head off my chest to smile up at me. "Yes, exactly." Her eyes flash wild, with excitement. My dick swells in response. I want to see her eyes widen with excitement like that because of what I'm doing to her body, not just from conversation.

"No, we don't have anyone like that at Redleg."

"Hmm. Maybe you should."

Not a bad idea. Considering how many threats we have to protect our clients from — known and unknown — having a glimpse into the perpetrator's psyche could be immensely helpful. Those of us who were in special ops have some experience in profiling. But having someone on the payroll whose sole focus is on diving into the mind of our enemies could be even more advantageous to our missions.

"Maybe this isn't a revenge thing," she says thoughtfully, her voice quiet and contemplative.

"What do you mean?"

"Well, you're focusing on someone who might be out to get back at you for something you did in the past."

"Right... but?" I prod.

"Maybe it's really as simple as it sounds."

"Meaning?"

"He says you took something that belongs to him. Consider for a moment that what he's saying is true, and you do have something that doesn't belong to you."

"But I don't have anything that doesn't belong to me. I haven't taken anything from anyone."

After a long pause, she says, "I know you think you haven't, but maybe you have. Then again, maybe you haven't..." She drags out the words slowly as her mind leads us toward some unknown point.

"Either way, what's important here is they *think* you have. Dare I say they truly *believe* you have. Which makes me wonder who could possibly think you're capable of stealing or harboring something from them? Who could be so certain that you'd double-cross them that they'd go to these extremes without physical proof? Who knows you well enough to not only make these assumptions but bet everything on them?"

A weight settles in my stomach with her words.

If this isn't someone out for revenge, but instead, merely someone who knows what I'm capable of... then we're looking in the entirely wrong direction.

My enemies don't know me that well. But a handful of others do — those closest to me.

Before I go through the very short list of people who know my capabilities, she continues with her thought-provoking analysis. "My next thought is this, Leo..."

"Yes?" My voice is barely a whisper as I start second-guessing everything I've done in the last twenty-four hours. Who I've confided in. Who I've relied on. Who's helping me. Who knows where we are.

"This mystery person is obviously very attached to this item, and therefore, the item is their weakness. If they're willing to threaten someone like you — with your contacts, experience, and resources — then they're probably desperate to get it back. It's valuable."

"Money, guns, drugs," I start listing items.

Sue interjects, "Those don't seem right. Call it a gut feeling, but I don't think that's it."

"What are you thinking?" I love to watch her mind work. I'm getting harder by the second.

"Information is also valuable, Leo. As are people."

"I haven't taken any of those things either," I restate my case as if I need to prove my innocence to us both.

"I know that, and you know that, but the bad guy *believes* you did, and they are desperate to get it back."

"Then why the hell don't they just tell me what the fuck it is so I can give it back?"

She sits up and twists to face me. Sensing she's about to say something important, I sit up straighter, mirroring her position.

"Leo, this person is a *true* narcissist, right down to their marrow. He or she assumes you already know what it is. They think they're the most important thing in the world — the world revolves around them — and as such, they don't feel the need to explain themselves, because you should already know."

I stay silent as my mind tries to catalog who might fit that description.

"There might also be a side of them that likes the *game*. They might enjoy making you paranoid. Maybe not telling you all the details is some sick type of fun for them. Someone like this probably hurt animals as a child or picks on people weaker than them — almost toying with them, like they're toying with you. And look at you — clearly, there aren't many people stronger than you physically. So they needed to make you weaker, and the only way they can do that is by withholding the information you'd likely need. They're putting you on the defense so they keep the upper hand."

My stomach starts to revolt at the idea of some puppet master pulling our strings like this. "A masterclass in manipulation. That's some sick shit you've come up with, angel."

She smiles and glances down to where my hands have landed on her legs. I *have* to touch her. "Some people are really fucked up. What can I say?"

When she says those words, an image pops into my mind of someone close to me... who knows exactly what I'm capable of... and is also the manipulative, narcissist type — and is seriously fucked up.

West.

My old army buddy who's used and abused our friendship over the years. The same guy who happened to call me the other night, right after the threats started coming in.

My pulse skyrockets as I chew on this possibility. Could my own friend really be out to hurt me? The profile matches, but as fucked up as West is... I can't believe he'd go this far.

Or would he? And if so, what does he think I took from him?

I shake off the dark thoughts and focus on Sue.

"Where did you come up with all this stuff, angel? How do you know all this?"

Suddenly, she looks uncomfortable. Like I've struck a nerve with my question. To reassure her, I take her hands, offering a gentle squeeze.

Her hands are safer — less tempting than her legs.

"What is it?" I ask when she doesn't respond after a few tense seconds.

I'm dying to know how she came up with this theory of hers.

"I've always been different. My entire life, I've known I'm not like my siblings. Not like other kids. I've always known this about myself, but what I didn't know was *why*. And as you know... I don't like not knowing things. I needed to know why."

She sighs, her chin wobbling. "So I did research — lots of research into the human mind — to find out what was wrong with me."

My teeth gnash together, and my jaw clenches.

I'm about to remind her of how amazing she is when she continues, "And I'm not saying that to make you disagree or feel sorry for me. It's a fact that I'm different from most. And now it's a medically diagnosed fact."

My head kicks back in confusion while my jaw falls open slightly. "Angel, what are you saying?"

When she looks up at me, unshed tears threaten to spill down her cheeks.

She inhales deeply before saying, "I haven't told anyone this, but I was recently diagnosed as being on the autism spectrum."

I try not to react outwardly to her words, but I feel my heart thump wildly in my chest. Thoughts and feelings pelt me from all sides.

She continues explaining, "But before I was diagnosed at the ripe old age of twenty-six, I did extensive research into the human mind. As you know, I don't forget things *easily*. I remember almost everything I read on the subject of psychological disorders. That's how I analyzed the person threatening us."

Us.

She said us.

Damn fucking right.

I don't give a damn about some diagnosis. I've always known who she is and what she means to me — it changes nothing. She's still *my angel.*

And she's told only me this news. Not her parents. Not her sister. Not her brothers.

Me.

She told me this news, which is obviously huge for her.

She trusts me with this news. She believes in me... *in us* and what we can become.

I want to give her everything. But there really can't be an *us* under these dangerous circumstances. I want her more than life itself, but I won't be able to give her what she deserves until this threat is buried behind us.

My angel deserves the best I can give her. Not half of me because I'm distracted or constantly worried about her safety, smothering her light.

Despite how much I want her in my bed and arms, I need to keep my focus on her safety.

Nothing else.

And I owe it to her to do that.

Unfortunately, that means keeping my hands, mouth, and dick to myself. Her faith and trust in me won't be misplaced. I'll deserve her. I'll earn that trust by being the best I can be for her.

Chapter Twenty-Three

Take what you want

Sue

"Good night, angel," he says from the bedroom doorway. "I'll be right next door in the office if you need anything." He flips the lights off and lingers a few seconds before slowly turning away.

Just like last night.

And the damn night before that.

We've been at the cabin for three days now. And ever since I told him about my autism diagnosis, things have felt stilted between us. *Different.*

It fecking sucks.

We have breakfast together each morning, then practice self-defense moves. After that, we studiously avoid each other. He spends a lot of time outside the cabin — saying he's patrolling the grounds.

Feels like he's trying to avoid me.

This is precisely why I didn't want to tell people. I knew they'd treat me differently.

I never expected it from Leo, though.

Shows what I know. I'm still a shitty judge of what's happening in anyone else's mind.

Before he gets more than a step away, I halt his retreat by asking, "Are you sure you don't want to take the bed for one night? I know you're uncomfortable on that damn couch. I really don't mind switching."

I've already asked him to share the bed with me, and I can't take *that* particular brand of rejection anymore. I feel gutted over how things have changed between us. No more kissing. No more cuddles on the couch. No more hand holding or forehead presses.

He's shut down all his affection for me. Flipped it off like that light switch he just hit on the wall.

Click.

"There's no way in hell I'd be okay with you taking the couch. My mama raised me better than that."

My head flops down onto the pillow in frustration. "Fine. Whatever. Good night."

Am I being a pissy bitch? Probably. Do I care? Nope.

I've been short with him all day today, and I refuse to feel bad about it. Not after the way things have drastically changed between us. Hell, I didn't do anything to deserve the cold shoulder from him. He can have my cold shoulder right back.

While he lingers in the doorway, I roll over so I don't have to see him anymore. Him and his stupid, sexy, handsome outline in the doorway.

After a few minutes, I hear his heavy footsteps grow quieter with each step he takes away from me.

Away from me — figuratively and literally.

My fist pounds the pillow twice as tears threaten to spill, but I hold them back.

I can't believe I fell for it again. Same shit as last time. It's like we're stuck in a loop. He shows up to save the day and protect me from a big, bad mystery man. In the process, he makes me feel special and seen. Tells me I'm capable, amazing, and worthy of love. Then he pulls back without warning, leaving me wondering what the hell I did wrong.

Shame on me at this point, I guess. He certainly fooled me twice.

After tossing and turning for at least two hours, sleep continues to evade me. In the back of my mind, I know if I fall asleep, the nightmare will come. I can feel it threatening me. It's a foreboding sense that makes me twitchy. Increased anxiety always triggers the dream, and the last few days have been stressful. It doesn't help that Leo's been a tense hulking figure around the cabin.

The pressure of trying to figure out what went wrong between us is making me spiral.

Maybe painting will help relax me. I haven't felt inspired to paint since we've been here, but maybe tonight will be different.

I've done some sketching each day and read a few books. Leo has a surprisingly good selection of paperbacks here — thrillers, cozy mysteries, and even some historical romance. But now that I'm here and can see the brown color of the cabin's exterior, the desire to paint hasn't been as strong.

I still have no clue how I knew the cabin existed.

It's bizarre as fuck.

At least my hyper-fixation on the cabin has subsided. My sketches are now of random things. Oddly, the compulsive need to paint the cabin faded quickly now that I know what it truly looks like.

Jaynie has been no help on that front either. We've spoken twice since I've been here. She's still searching for any link between autism and precognitive function, but there are surprisingly few studies on it. She thinks there's likely another reason I could visualize the exterior of this place — but she's not sure what it may be.

Who knows?

Maybe I'll never know. It doesn't seem as important as it did at first.

Instead, I'm more wrapped up in the complicated mess involving a six-foot-something giant who has mangled my heart over these last few days.

I rise from the bed, grabbing an old T-shirt and baggy shorts from the dresser. I try to stay quiet so I don't wake Leo. He needs his sleep — I know he's been getting by on far less sleep than I have. He's awake each morning before me and stays up after I retire each night.

When I peek into the spare bedroom, I see him sleeping soundly, but I cringe when I see how cramped he is on that couch.

Pigheaded man.

It's his own fault. I refuse to feel guilty about this a second longer.

My feet stomp a little harder than necessary as I move into the living room, dragging a metaphorical bag of emotions with me. Setting up my portable easel and supplies, I create a makeshift painting station on the kitchen table.

Before I begin, I close my eyes and count to ten. I try to force all thoughts out of my mind. Whatever refuses to leave my mind is what I'll paint.

Without thinking, I thrust my brush into the paint and go to work. Long strokes, short strokes, and little taps bring color to the white threads of the canvas. I use four different brushes to get the texture right. Browns, blues, and blacks collide with the peachy hue of flesh. I work frantically, like a woman possessed — painting faster than I ever have. The compulsion to create overcomes me, and I pour all my feelings directly onto the canvas.

Since I don't want to wake Leo with my blaring music, the only sound is my heavy breathing and the frantic taps and swipes against the canvas. It's almost like my brain is on autopilot — I'm in a zone unlike ever before.

This is why I love painting.

It's that euphoric moment when my entire being comes out through the brush. My brain can finally stop processing all the thoughts, worries, and swirling fears dancing in my mind. Everything is silenced, and my sense of self erupts out through my hands.

Art is magic for me.

When I pull back to see what I've painted and shake the fog of creation from my vision, I see the harsh lines of Leo's face reflected at me.

He looks cruel in this painting, so unlike the real man.

I've painted him before, of course. Back in the spring, he modeled for me. It was fun. We laughed afterward.

He wouldn't be laughing if he saw this painting, though.

It doesn't take a trained psychologist to see I'm dealing with some complicated feelings where Leo is concerned. Although I've never seen him look this angry in real life, I seem to have put all my anger and hurt onto the page. The result transformed him into a monster of sorts. His face is cold, eyes darkened, and brows drawn tight together. The downturn of his lips — which are pressed into a hard line — looks a little like what I've seen from him over the last three days.

"Couldn't sleep?" Leo's deep voice, heavy with drowsiness, comes from behind me.

Startled, I jump and spin around quickly. His eyes sweep up and down my body, lingering slightly on my chest where my braless nipples instantly harden at the sight of him. My body's stupid reaction to him is really annoying at times like this.

But damn. He's shirtless, wearing only black athletic shorts that hang low on his hips.

Whoa, mama.

I really can't blame my nipples for standing at attention in his presence. Leo Mason's presence commands attention. Especially standing there, in the middle of the night, *that* close to naked.

My nipples rightfully salute him.

I greedily soak in the heavenly image in front of me and commit it to memory. I want to paint him like this. In fact, I'd love to paint him in the nude. He's a work of art.

Speaking of art, the swirls and lines of his tattoos are beautiful. A mix of images, lines, and words. I want to know the story behind every drop of ink on his smooth skin.

He takes a few steps in my direction, stopping about two feet away. I know I'm not good at gauging people's motivations or intentions, but it almost looks like he's holding himself back from me. His hands are cast in fists at his side, and his defined abs are clenched tight. Even his breath seems strained.

Is that desire or disgust? I wish I could read him better.

"I was afraid of having the nightmare. I could feel it coming on... maybe another psychic moment or sort of like a sixth sense. I knew if I went to sleep, I'd have the dream," I confess. "So, I came out to paint. Sorry if I woke you."

I spin around and quickly remove the painting from the easel so he doesn't see what I've created. Hopefully, my body was blocking his view.

"Wait. Stop," he says while closing the distance. He places his hand on my forearm to halt my progress.

Busted.

"That's how you see me?" His voice is colder than normal.

I don't answer. I can't. Even if I'm mad at him, I don't want to hurt him.

Dammit. Why am I so weak? Why do I let him treat me however he wants? I hate this control he has over my emotions.

Fuck that.

"Sometimes," I finally admit, my shoulders rolling back, and my chin lifting. "You've been distant lately. It almost seems cruel."

He curses under his breath, then heaves a pained sigh. "I'm sorry if you think I've been cruel to you. That's not what I intended."

"Then what have you intended, Leo?" My voice comes out sarcastic and snippy, but I'm fucking pissed.

"I don't understand the hot and cold treatment. You show up and tell me how important I am to you. We seem to make peace with each other, and I forgive you for how you treated me in the past. Then you say you want to take me on a date. I share something very personal with you." My head cocks to the side in annoyance. "Do you know how hard that was for me? And look what happened. *Poof.* You turned into the iceman."

My blood is boiling. The more I talk, the angrier I get, and I refuse to keep it all canned up inside me. After setting down my paintbrush, I take a step closer to him and press my finger into his chest.

"I never thought you'd reject me because of my disability. I thought you'd still accept me, but you didn't. You don't. And so yes, Leo, this is how I see you."

He grabs my wrist and pulls it away from his chest, holding it between us. I close my eyes, cursing myself for enjoying the feel of his skin on mine.

"I'm not rejecting you. And I don't see you any differently. I still want you with every cell of my body."

Wait. *What?*

My cheeks warm. "That doesn't make any sense. You've barely spoken to me for the last two days. Aside from making sure I can defend myself, you seem like you couldn't care less about me. I don't understand."

"I had to distance myself from you."

"Why?"

Dropping my wrist, he opens and closes his fist between us in total frustration. "So I can protect you better," he growls. "Angel, I'm sorry if I'm giving you whiplash. But I was getting too wrapped up in you, and it scared me. I can't keep you safe if I'm consumed by your touch, your smell, the way you taste. Fuck, Sue... I want you so damn much. It's taking everything in me to keep my distance."

His words swirl in my mind. "You're only trying to protect me from getting hurt?"

"Yes. Everything I do is to keep you safe from harm."

"Can't you see that the distance you're putting between us is hurting me? Screw the distance. I need you close."

I step closer, pressing myself against him. The warmth of his chest soaks through the fibers of my cotton tee. It soothes me, and my voice softens.

"Leo, we're out here in the middle of nowhere. We have no reason to believe the bad guy knows where we are. You've taken every possible precaution. There are sensors, cameras, alarms, weapons, and a panic room, for shite's sake. This place is like Fort Knox. If I'm not safe here with you, then I'm not going to be safe anywhere. So, for the love of St. Paddy, stop trying to keep your distance."

Before I say anything else, I have to know if he is on the same page as me. "You feel it, don't you? That connection?"

Please tell me it's not just me feeling this invisible rope connecting us. I can't be wrong about this.

"Yes," he forces out through gritted teeth. "I feel it."

I knew it.

A smile tickles my lips. "It's like a tug, right?" I need his absolute confirmation before asking what I'm about to.

"Right here," he says with his fist against his chest.

"Leo, I'm aching for you. If you want me, take me. End this torture. I'm begging you."

"You don't have to beg, angel." He sucks his lower lip into his mouth while nodding repeatedly. "I'll ease your ache."

I rise on my tiptoes and wrap my arms around his shoulders. "And I can ease yours."

He slides one arm around my waist, and the other raises his hand to cup the back of my neck. After only a second more of anticipation, he claims my mouth. One gentle stroke of his tongue quickly turns into a feverish plundering of my mouth. His hold becomes impossibly tight around my waist, and my back arches in response.

I surrender to him completely — removing all traces of pretense. There is no resistance between us anymore. The walls between us come crumbling down with an explosive detonation of lust.

The feel of my breasts moving against his firm chest with each deep breath is pure ecstasy. He grunts as he shifts his erection against me. Pleasure floods my body, overwhelming all my senses as I envision what it would feel like to be filled with him.

He's devouring me, body and soul, and I've willingly offered myself up to him. My fingers trail across the smooth planes of his shoulders and neck, sending sparks of arousal from my fingertips straight to my clit. When he moves both hands down my back and squeezes my ass, he presses my lower body into his. His cock is so hard and thick and feels erotic grinding against me.

I break away from his mouth and toss my head back so he can place a trail of kisses, nips, and licks along my neck while I gasp for air. When he hits my collarbone and swirls his tongue along the sensitive skin there, a moan escapes me — I've become physically unable to control the sounds my body is emitting. I've never been this overwhelmed before. My senses focus on each place our bodies touch. It's like sparks lighting up all over my skin.

I'm not sure how it happened, but I find myself on the kitchen countertop. I must have been in a semi-blacked-out state, given how aroused I am. Perhaps a lack of blood flow to my brain. It's all heading to my core.

My thighs spread to accommodate his width. He squeezes his hands between my ass and the counter, pulling me forward until my center grinds against his shaft. It's like he was reading my mind — all I could think about was being closer to him, and he eagerly obliged. We rock back and forth against each other in a delicious rhythm as he returns his mouth to mine. The rush of climax builds quickly inside me, a tightness coiling deep in my belly. I'm so close with such little time or effort — only him rubbing his steel cock against me through our clothes.

Holy shit.

It's only been a few seconds... or maybe minutes. *Oh, fuck!* I'm not sure because time has no meaning when he's pressed against me like this.

My legs squeeze around his ass and hips, forcing him closer to my sweet spot. He responds, driving his cock against my clit even harder.

I bury my face in his thick neck as my fever builds to a crescendo.

"Oh shit, Leo," I rasp.

My breaths become shallow and frenzied, and I'm moaning louder and louder as I pant, "Yes, yes, oh my gosh, yes."

I feel a tinge of embarrassment at my volume, but I cannot stop praising him.

"Give it to me, my angel. I want to hear you come real sweet for me."

I feel my neck arch as my pussy contracts, aching to be filled as wave after wave of my orgasm washes over me. "Ah, Leo, yes, oh my God, I'm coming."

"That's it, angel." He continues pulsing against me as I ride out my pleasure.

As his thrusts slow, other sensations begin to return to my awareness. I know I shouldn't feel shame, but I can't help but cringe at how soaked my panties are with my juices. Idly, I wonder what Leo would think if he knew how wet I was right now. If romance novels are to be believed, men tend to like that. My curiosity gets the best of me, so I guide his hand under the waistband of my panties.

"Feel me," I order him.

"God damn, woman," he says with a deep growl as he runs his fingers through my wet folds. With his face buried in my neck, he begins leisurely stroking me, winding me up again.

While running my hands through his hair, I ask, "Is that good or bad? How wet I am. Do you like it or —"

He jerks his face back up to mine, cutting me off. "I fucking *love it*. Can I taste you now?"

"Do you *want* to do that?"

"Fuck yes, I want to eat your sweet pussy."

Wow. Leo is a deliciously dirty talker. I didn't ever think I would like that sort of thing, but I was wrong.

So wrong.

Hell, I'm getting even wetter with each filthy word that falls from his sultry mouth.

He pulls his hand from between my legs and draws his fingers to his lips, licking and sucking them one by one while staring into my eyes. "Mmm. I want more."

Yes, yes, and fuck yes.

"Okay, but no one has ever done that to me before."

I'm nervous but excited at the prospect of him feasting between my legs. I've read some naughty books and watched enough porn that I think I know what to expect. But I'll feel so exposed to him. I don't know if I'm ready for that.

"I kind of like the idea of being the first one to pleasure you that way." He pauses the trail he's kissing down my neck to my ear and pulls back to look at me, suddenly seeming alarmed. "Angel, have you ever had sex before?"

"Yes. One time."

"Only once?"

"A couple of years ago when I was going to college. My tutor. I was curious about sex and asked him if he wanted to have sex with me. He said yes, and we did it a few days later. It was... fine."

His forehead wrinkles as he scrunches his face. "Only fine?"

"Yeah... I mean, he wasn't especially attentive, I guess. He was an English tutor, not sexual — if that wasn't clear." Feeling flustered, I add, "But it was okay. It was fine. That's the only way I can describe it."

"Angel, I promise you this. When we make love, you'll feel much more than *fine*. So much more."

I nod my head a few times and widen my eyes. "I want that. Let's do that. Skip the other thing and go right to feeling more than fine."

He places a chaste kiss on my lips, and through a grin, he says, "Patience, my sweet. I need to bury my face between your legs first. That little taste wasn't enough. And I need to make sure you're able to take me. I'm a big guy everywhere, and if you've only had sex once a few years ago, I'll need to stretch you out so it doesn't hurt. Once I get inside you, I don't know how gentle I can be — I want you so fucking bad I'll probably start pounding away until we both see stars. You need to be ready for what I'm going to do to you."

Oh, I think I'm ready. I've got Niagara Falls happening between my legs right now.

Chapter Twenty-Four

Sexy times

Leo

I sure as fuck hope I don't regret this. But now that I have her pliant and willing in my arms, there's no way I can stop.

Well, that's not entirely true.

If she wanted me to stop, I would. But at this point, that's likely the only thing that could stop me from getting inside her and feeling her writhe underneath me. I've wanted her for so long, and these last few days have been brutal.

Fuck, it was agony staying away from her for six months, and that's when I thought she had probably forgotten about me. Now that she's right here where I can smell her and see her and fucking taste her — knowing how much she's burning for me — there's no reason worth holding back.

I'm done denying us what we both need desperately. I'll find a way to have her in my bed, my heart, and safe at the same time.

Somehow.

I can still taste her on my lips. She is fucking drenched for me, and I'm frantic for more.

Tugging her shorts down, I'm not even patient enough to move us to another room. She lifts her perfect thick ass off the counter to help me slide them off. Squatting down, I yank the shorts and panties completely off. When I rise back up, her perfect pink pussy catches my gaze, a dusting of trimmed brown curls sitting over the top of her mound.

She's exquisite — from the creamy white skin of her lower stomach to the wide expanse of her thighs.

Absolute feminine perfection.

I grab her hips roughly and relish the feeling of my fingers sinking deep into her soft flesh.

"Scoot to the edge of the counter for me, angel," I rasp.

She immediately complies. "Do you want me to stay like this?"

I grin at her curious tone of voice. "You can lean back if you'd be more comfortable, or you can sit up and watch me. Whatever you want. Just keep your legs open."

"Okay. Tell me if I do something wrong."

With a shake of my head, I rise and take her mouth for another branding kiss. She grabs my shoulders and sinks her fingertips into the back of my neck while pressing that sweet, hot pussy into my stomach.

As the kiss intensifies, her moans almost shake me from my plan to be the first to lick her to climax. Every sound she makes is practically my undoing, making me want to drive my cock into her raw and spill my liquid heat inside.

"You can't do anything wrong, angel. Just enjoy it. That's all you have to do."

"Okay," she whispers. Her fingers linger on my neck, sending little pulses of electricity down my spine.

She's so fucking innocent. It might make me a caveman, but the idea of being the *only one* to bring her this pleasure is making me harder than I've ever been. The head of my cock is testing the stretch capacity of my boxers. Reaching down, I adjust myself so I don't rip them.

I break the kiss and slide down her full body, nipping at her neck once more and giving her breasts a squeeze as I pass over them. She hasn't made a move to take her shirt off yet, and since this is the first time anyone has ever gone down on her, I figure she might need that layer of fabric to serve as some measure of security — something to stop her from being completely exposed to me. I'll have her completely bare soon enough.

Pulling away from her delicious body long enough to grab a chair from the kitchen table, I slide it over so I can sit down and place my head right between her thick, juicy thighs. It puts me at the perfect height to settle in and make myself comfortable. I'm going to feast on her until I've had my fill.

And I'm fucking starving.

My eyes travel up her soft frame until they come to rest on her bright blue eyes, looking down at me with wonder. "Are you ready, my angel?"

She nods three times before finally saying, "Yes. I'm ready."

The room is silent except for her heavy breaths and my racing heartbeat. I grin and wink.

She smiles, and I dive in with gusto, spreading her thighs wider and licking right up her seam. Her savory taste explodes on my tongue, and I feel my balls swell, becoming heavier. Focusing on the soft skin on both sides of her center, I nuzzle, lick, and suck to get her used to the sensation.

After placing gentle kisses along her swollen flesh, I use the pointed tip of my tongue to taste and explore between her folds until I find her opening.

She's soaked — fucking soaked — for me. After rimming her entrance a few times, I spear her pussy gently a few times and swirl around the sensitive hole.

"Oh, my heavens. That feels so good," she says quietly. Her voice is nearly quivering and filled with reverence.

Meeting her eyes, I give her an impish wink. "That's a good girl. I love it when you tell me what you like."

Diving back in tongue first, I pulse in and out of her a few times. Her arousal coats my mouth, and my cock throbs with need. She tastes so fucking good, and the noises she makes drive me mad with desire.

Replacing my tongue with my middle finger, I plunge it in and out in a deliberately slow rhythm, cricking it upward to her G-spot. Her hips start moving in time with my ministrations as she gains comfort. I love how she's starting to chase her pleasure. With my other hand, I spread her wide, then I swirl my tongue around her swollen clit.

She makes a keening sound, high-pitched and breathy.

"Do you like that?" I ask between gentle licks on both sides of her little nub.

"Uh-huh," she says, her voice barely intelligible.

When I look up, I see her eyes roll to the back of her head, and she bites down on her lower lip.

After leisurely dabbing a few more teasing strokes on each side, I flutter my tongue directly against her clit, and her back bows sharply. All the while, my finger keeps thrusting in and out of her in a steady rhythm, tapping at her special spot. Her silky walls squeeze and pulse around my thick digits. When I press the flat of my tongue on her swollen bud again, one of her hands shoots out and grabs the back of my head.

I nod, letting her know I like it.

I fucking love it.

"It's okay to hold you like this?" she asks, confirming she has my consent. *Sweet angel.*

Pulling off only long enough to reassure her, I respond, "Yes, angel. Touch me any way you want. Grind against my face, shove me right into this sweet pussy. Whatever feels good for you."

"It all feels good," she says on a soft groan as I draw her clit into my mouth and suck gently. "Oh my God. I'm gonna come again."

So soon? Damn, she's so responsive.

Her hips start rocking harder against my face as I coax her higher and higher. I add another finger to her tight pussy to stretch her even more while I continue sucking gently on her clit and twirling my tongue around it.

All too soon, she comes loudly while shaking, quivering, and moaning my name. The way her silky walls squeeze and contract around my fingers makes my erection throb and ache.

I need to be inside this woman.

Once her hips slow and her awareness seems to return, she has this adorable fucking smile on her face. I remove my fingers and stand tall, pressing the chair away with the back of my legs.

Still happily between her full thighs, I wrap my arms around her and bring her into my chest. "Have you ever tasted yourself?"

My normally gentle voice is thick and rough with arousal. My inner caveman has made his appearance. At first I worried my more dominant side would scare her, but the more demanding I got, the more her folds glistened for me.

She shakes her head. Her cheeks are blotchy with pink, and I absolutely *love* how sexy she looks right now.

Hell, I love how she looks all the time, but especially now with her rosy cheeks, heavy-lidded eyes, and swollen pink lips. She looks absolutely sated. The blue in her irises is more vibrant too. She's fucking enchanting me.

I press a kiss against her lips. She tries to shy away at first, but soon changes her mind and opens wide, surrendering to me. I sweep my tongue against hers, loving how I get the flavor of her mouth mixed with the taste of her salty arousal. I'd drink from her if I could.

I end the kiss as soon as my dick starts weeping, literally demanding attention.

"Is that what I taste like?" she asks, all innocent and wide-eyed.

I nod and tell her, "You're fucking delicious."

"Is that what yours tastes like too?"

"It's a little different. Saltier and thicker."

"I want to taste you."

Fuuuck.

Despite the illicit images flowing through my mind, I force myself to answer, "We can try that later. Right now, I want to take you into that bedroom, lay you down properly, and bury myself inside of you."

She doesn't respond with words, only with vigorous head nods that draw a chuckle out of me.

"You ready for my cock, angel?"

"*Very* ready."

"Wrap your legs around me," I order, sliding my hands under her ass and scooping her off the counter.

She lets out a startled squeal and tightens her hold around my shoulders. Her soaking wet pussy presses directly against my bare stomach, and I can't resist squeezing her luscious ass. Those motions make her thighs tighten around my waist even more.

Heaven.

Like a man on a mission, I move us quickly through the cabin, keeping her wrapped around me like a spider monkey. I catch a whiff of her shampoo when she throws her face against my neck — maybe it's strawberry. The heat of her breath against my skin makes my dick twitch. My legs carry us even faster.

Must fuck her. *Now.*

No. That's not right.

Not fuck.

One does not simply fuck a woman like this.

I'm going to make love to her — cherishing, worshipping, and caressing.

Laying her down gently on the bed, I guide her to right where I want her. She complies willingly with every nonverbal request — like she's inside my head.

"Wait here while I get a condom."

Running to the bathroom, I pull out my toiletries bag that's always with me. Rifling through it, I curse every second I'm away from her delectable body while simultaneously thanking my lucky stars I thought to throw a strip of condoms in it when I first guarded Sue several months ago. Must have been wishful thinking.

I return to the bedroom and toss the condoms on the bed.

Taking in her soft curves and feasting on every decadent inch of her ivory skin — minus what's hidden behind her T-shirt — I pull my shorts down, removing them and my boxers in one motion, then quickly toss them aside.

Sue studies my every move while her thighs press tightly together like she's craving friction there.

I know the feeling, so I give my aching shaft a few tugs, squeezing the tip and working the precum over the swollen head. Her cheeks redden into a deeper shade of crimson, and she bites her lower lip. Since it excites her, I give my cock a few more strokes. Idly, I wonder if she's ever watched a man do this but quickly shake the thought. I don't want to picture her with other guys. Much like I don't want to ever think about another woman. As far as I'm concerned, it's only ever been my angel and me.

After teasing us both as long as I can stand, I join her on the bed and crawl up her body. I place kisses along her legs and inner thighs while holding her gaze. She's quiet as she takes in everything I'm doing — and again, I get the feeling I'm being studied.

When I get to the apex of her thighs, I place another gentle kiss and lick along her seam, then spear my tongue into her folds until zeroing in on her swollen nub.

Fuck, she tastes so good.

I just pleasured her with my mouth, and yet, I can't resist one more sample — I'm insatiable for her delicious pussy. The longer I suckle her center, her moans and gasps become louder. The heavenly sounds she's making leave me feeling conflicted — do I make her come again like this first, or do I satisfy our desires by connecting with her in the most primal of ways?

She decides for me when she threads her fingers through my hair, presses me farther into her pussy, and starts rocking against my mouth.

My little angel is greedy for more.

Since this is new for her, and she was so quick to come on the counter, I think I'll delay my own gratification and give her another screaming orgasm.

My hips grind into the mattress by the time she's finished chanting my name and calling out to St. Paddy — which makes me smile against her pussy lips. My dick cannot wait any longer for relief and wants nothing but to hammer inside her.

Grabbing a condom, I unwrap it and sheathe myself while she floats back down from her momentary trip to heaven. I climb on top of her and wedge my hips between her legs. This feels so right.

My gaze travels up to her face as her eyelids flutter open and she locks her eyes with mine. My pulse increases the longer I stare into those turquoise pools.

Pulling me closer, she wraps her arms around my neck and runs her fingernails through my hair.

"You're fucking beautiful when you come," I tell her truthfully, my face inches from hers.

"I can't believe how loud I was. It's not like that when I'm alone." Her lashes flutter, and her eyes cast toward my chest like she's embarrassed.

Placing my hand under her chin, I lift her face and press my lips to hers. When I break the tender kiss, I tell her, "Angel, you don't ever have to hold back around me. Make all the noise you want. It only makes me want to fuck you even more — with my tongue, my fingers, and my cock."

"Damn, Leo. So dirty."

"Too dirty for you?"

Her eyes flash wild. "No, I like it. A lot."

"I like *you* a lot," I toss back through a smile.

She doesn't answer with anything more than a moan because I grab my cock and drag the head along her slit, coating the tip with her juices.

She presses her lips in a hard line and squints her eyes shut as I start to press in, and it makes me worry I'm hurting her.

Pausing with my tip barely nudging in her entrance — literally *just the tip* — I ask, "Are you okay, angel?"

Her eyes pop open, and she says, "Oh my gosh, yes. I'm a little nervous because you are fecking huge. But please, keep going. I *need* you inside me."

"Tell me if it hurts, and I'll stop."

Hurting her is the last thing I'd ever want to do.

She nods in agreement, so I nudge in about a half inch, and my fucking balls draw up — they're already primed, having waited so long for this woman.

Fuck she's tight, and it's heavenly torture. Fortunately, she's still soaking wet, so I glide in deeper, inch by silky inch. Once I'm halfway inside her velvety walls, I'm met with so much resistance it makes me wonder if she's a virgin — but I know she wouldn't lie about that. Unless she didn't know what real sex was.

No. That's a ludicrous thought.

"Angel, you okay?" I'm struggling with all my might to resist impaling my cock deep inside her with one long, hard stroke. It probably shows in the tension in my voice and the way I'm gritting my teeth.

"Give me a second."

Her eyes are pinched closed with wrinkles at each side, and her lips are mashed in a thin white line. Instinctively, my hips pull back so I don't hurt her, but she holds me tighter, squeezing my hips between her thighs, and firmly grips the head of my cock.

With her motherfucking pussy walls.

It's then I realize it wasn't some magical virginal barrier I was feeling, but she was clenching — hard.

"Don't pull out. Get in. Deeper, Leo. Now, please. I need you," she begs.

She punctuates her request by running her hands down my back and pressing my ass down so my dick starts sliding in again. This time, the resistance is less, and I can slip in a tinge easier.

"You feel like heaven," I hiss through clenched teeth.

Her channel is warm, soft, and so damn inviting that I can't help repeating the motion a few more times. Rearing back and pressing in a little farther each time, I draw out our pleasure. By the fifth stroke, I'm fully seated inside and finally feel my pelvis flush against her bottom. I pulse a few times, and we both moan, reveling in the sensation of being thoroughly joined.

Her hands are still planted firmly on my ass cheeks, squeezing occasionally and holding me in place. But I'm not mad about it. I know she needs some control in all measures of her life, and it's possible this is her way of getting that right now — even though I'm on top of her, and she's totally at my mercy.

"Fuck, Leo," she rasps. "You feel so good. I've never felt so full. It's... it's amazing."

"I know." A grin crests my lips as I look deep into her eyes — now beautiful turquoise rings surrounding huge black pupils, widened with arousal.

Like a cheeky bastard, I say, "Does this feel better than *fine*, angel?"

Her answering laughter causes her walls to contract around my throbbing cock, and it immediately removes the smiles from our faces, replacing them with parted lips and matching expressions of pure, unadulterated lust.

Suddenly desperate to kiss her, I take her mouth in a punishing kiss, but she gives it back to me just as furiously. Unable to hold back my primal need for her any longer, I plunge in and out of her tight heat. Over and over again, faster and faster, each thrust taking us higher.

She cries out in ecstasy as I open her thighs wider, shifting one up and over my hip to adjust the angle, taking her even deeper.

I wish she'd have taken the shirt off; I'd love to feel her breasts pushed up against my chest and be able to capture her nipples between my teeth, but something tells me she's kept that last bit of clothing on for a reason, and I'll deal with that another time. She's perfect to me, and I never want her to hide or cover her gorgeous body — not an inch should be hidden from my eyes.

I shake off my thoughts as her moans pitch higher and she writhes beneath me. I delve my tongue into her mouth, aching for more of her sweet kisses while my cock slams inside her hard and deep. My balls smack her ass a fraction of a second after each thrust.

"Holy shit," she wails. "Yes, Leo. Don't stop. Fuck! Fuck!"

Although my eyes are sealed shut with desire, they practically bulge out of my head at the unexpected words coming from this innocent beauty. She rarely cusses, and to hear her screaming like that — demanding I fuck her harder, faster, deeper — is almost enough to make me come.

"You feel so damn good. Love your sweet pussy," I growl in her ear as I continue pounding away.

A sheen of sweat coats my skin, and her hands slip across my shoulders. Fuck.

I glance down through the tight space between us to the spot where we're joined. "Look at us, babe. Watch how your body takes me inside yours. It's beautiful."

Her head shifts as she obeys my request. After looking along with her for a few strokes, I shift my focus to her face. She's staring with rapt attention as my thick cock thrusts slowly in and out. Her mouth falls open, and her breathing accelerates. She raises her hips in time with mine, increasing the friction and meeting me with each thrust. I feel like a voyeur as I watch her enjoy this, but I'm not on the outside. I'm right here, feeling whole for the first time in my life.

That gaping hole in my chest that I caused when I walked away has finally healed.

And each stroke of my cock soothes that ever-present ache to be close to her.

"Wow, that's so hot," she whispers, still focusing on where we meet.

I glance down and watch my cock fill her a few more times and revel in the feeling of Sue's lush body softening around me.

Our eyes meet again, and my heart constricts almost as much as my balls.

Wrapping her legs around my pistoning hips, she rises to meet each of my thrusts, chasing her pleasure. Feeling how she clings to me and hearing every sexy sound falling from her lips pushes me right up to the edge of that cliff. I planned for her to come again so we could finish together, but a man only has so much control. Slamming myself into her, I feel a tingle at the base of my spine, and it grows until lights flash behind my eyes. My shaft throbs as my release spills from me, and I climax with a roar.

I fuse my lips to hers as my hips slow and jerk a few more times as I ride out my orgasm.

Refusing to let it end like that, I reluctantly pull myself from her wet heat and slide quickly down her body — now slick with our combined perspiration. I shove two fingers, then three, inside her pussy and pump furiously while I suck on her swollen clit until she comes, keening away and arching her back.

I'm glad we don't have fucking neighbors out here, or they'd have called the cops. We were *that* fucking loud, but *fuck me.* That was unbelievable. Best sex I've ever had — without a doubt.

After she's ridden out her orgasm, I wipe my face off, deal with the condom, and return to the bed, pulling her on top of me. She molds herself to my prone form with the sounds of our huffing breaths echoing off the walls.

Without any more words, she falls fast asleep in my arms.

Right where she's going to be for the rest of her life.

Chapter Twenty-Five

Flick it good

Sue

"It's all in the wrist. You have to flick it harder." My frustrated moan is tinged with amusement.

"Angel, I promise you, I am flicking it plenty hard."

"Harder, Leo, harder. Here, watch me do it again."

He leans over to nuzzle my neck. "I like it when you tell me to do it harder."

"Pervert," I toss back playfully before batting him away.

If he keeps doing that, we'll be banging again in no time, and my lady land needs a minimum two-hour cooling off period. We've had sex four times in the last twenty-four hours.

And don't ask how many orgasms I've had — despite being quite good at math, I can't count that high.

Just kidding.

It's ten.

He's given me *ten* orgasms in the last twenty-four hours. It's insane. I went from having zero orgasms with another human to having ten in a fecking day.

It's probably my fault the tally is so high since each time we stop on an odd number, I quickly instigate another to even it out. Not sure why, but orgasms feel like things that should be balanced.

I'm weird like that, but Leo's not complaining.

And it turns out that sex with the right person can actually be more than just *fine*. Who knew?

I take another playing card from the top of the deck and pinch it between two fingers. Drawing it back, I press my fingers together to release the card while flicking my wrist at the precise speed to send the card flying straight into the empty cereal bowl.

Swish.

Shaking his head, he tries again. And once more, his card flails off to the side, sputters to the ground, and scoots under the couch.

"Pathetic," he whines.

I can't hold back my chuckle.

His head slumps backward and hits the wall behind us, a clear sign of his growing irritation. Meanwhile, I'm tickled fecking pink that I'm so much better at this than him. It's a novelty for me to dominate in anything even *remotely* athletic. Although card tossing isn't a sport by any means and certainly doesn't work up a sweat, it does require coordination of a somewhat physical nature. I'm usually terrible at anything *sport-ish*, so this feels damn good.

Yay me.

We've been sitting here on the floor with our backs against the wall for about a half hour, and I've been showing him some of my card tricks. He's not picking them up as quickly as I picked up the new self-defense moves he taught me this morning after we had sleepy wake-up sex. He leisurely took me from behind while we were both lying on our sides. I'd never done that position before, and I secretly hope he wakes me up like that again tomorrow.

To be fair, though, I'd never done anything but missionary before Leo. Now, I can add side-by-side to my ever-growing sexual positions list, along with doggy style, which we tried last night. I wasn't sure about putting my big ass right up in front of him like that, but he seemed to like it, so I went with it. I came twice that way, so no regrets.

He tries to toss the card into the bowl and misses yet again. I wonder if he's playing dumb or is this bad at card tossing. It just doesn't seem plausible that Leo's *this bad* at anything. I know he's good with his hands.

Very good.

"I bet you can flick coins using the tips of your fingers too," he says while giving me some choice side-eye.

"I don't know. I've never tried," I admit softly, then toss another card directly into the bowl.

He reaches into his jeans pockets one at a time. "I think it's a similar movement. I bet you can." He comes up with empty hands. "Dammit. No coins on me. We haven't exactly been to a store lately for me to break bills."

"Speaking of which, do you think we can make a run to the grocery store soon?"

We've only got enough food left for maybe three meals, unless we're going to live on peanut butter and jelly sandwiches. I'd survive that, but he wouldn't.

Poor man.

"Yeah, we'll probably need to hit the store tomorrow." A pained look crosses his face.

"What's the matter?"

"I hate exposing you like that. Every time we leave the cabin, you're at risk. But I also don't think we can get food delivery out here, and I wouldn't want to chance that either. The fewer people who know where we are, the better. And leaving you alone while I run to get something doesn't sit well with me either." He runs his big hands across his face and heaves a groan.

"What did Big Al say this morning when you spoke? Any news?"

"He told me my old army buddy West was trying pretty hard to get a hold of me."

"Oh? Is that related to the threats?"

"No. Not really. I'm just trying to delay telling you the bad news."

I frown. "That's not funny."

"It was worth a try." He tosses a flirty smile and a wink my way, and my heart and pussy both clench — which I think is their version of swooning.

He finally starts spilling the beans. "They were able to get video footage of the guy in the gray van and run the tags, which were registered to an old dead guy from Sarasota. So, it's obviously a fake plate or stolen. That lead was a dead end."

He pinches his lips together in a tight line and looks thoughtfully at the wall.

"And the photo of the guy... did it resemble anyone you know?"

"It was a pretty grainy photo, but I took a hard look. Unfortunately, I didn't recognize him. Could be anyone. Tomer is running it through his facial recognition software, but it takes time."

I nod, taking it in as disappointment floods my veins and a sick feeling stirs in my belly. "I know the bad guy hasn't answered your calls, but has he responded to any of the texts?"

"Big Al says he's gotten a few new texts from him, but it's just more of the same bullshit."

"So we still don't know what he wants," I restate the obvious, then grind my teeth. I hate that we aren't making any progress. "We're just stuck."

"I'm so sorry, angel."

He leans into me and reaches over, running his thumb across my lower lip in an intimate gesture. I kiss the pad of his thumb as it passes. A frown mars his handsome face, and I long to soothe his worries. I only wish I knew how.

"It's not your fault," I tell him, injecting as much emotion as I can into those simple words.

I want him to feel how much I truly believe what I'm telling him. Although, I know he doesn't feel the same way. He's determined to blame himself.

A sad grin lifts at one side of his face.

We stare into each other's eyes for a moment. The intensity of his gaze makes it feel like a rabble of butterflies has taken flight inside my tummy. Freaking eye contact. What used to cause all kinds of unease is now bringing me the sweetest comfort.

I am falling so damn hard for this man.

He's gentle, compassionate, and kind with an overwhelmingly powerful presence. Yet when I'm with him — despite being in hiding — I feel so calm.

My typical anxiety triggers are practically non-existent out here. I suspect another potential reason for that is not so much Leo's presence, but because we're so far away from my old nemesis. *People.*

Cringe.

Leo cricks his head to the side. "From what Boss says, they're thinking the *thing* I allegedly took..." He puts up air quotes around the word *thing*. "... is not a thing, but a person. Most likely a woman." His eyes are pained, and he's wringing his hands.

"Get *her* back," I recite the words from the previous text threat — words that stood out as odd to me at the time and still do. I feel like there's something in that phrase, no matter how quickly everyone else seemed to write it off as nothing. I don't think he was talking about me.

Leo nods in agreement but remains silent. His gaze is fixed on nothing — he's seemingly lost in thought.

"Did you ever help rescue any women? Remove them from abusive partners or take them out of bad situations?"

His eyes widen, and he nods quickly. "Several. In Nigeria, we saved a group of young women from a trafficking ring. Same thing in Ghana. And in Iraq, we removed dozens upon dozens of women from horrible situations — usually completely off the books."

"Do you get the feeling this is a foreign threat?" That doesn't sound right to me.

"No, not really. The texts have been in plain English, with no spelling errors, and sometimes contain texting slang common here. Not what you'd expect from someone who's not a native speaker of English."

"Right, and why would he target *you* instead of the others in your unit who were part of those missions?"

"Agreed. It doesn't add up."

"What about the profile we were discussing the other night? Instead of past revenge, maybe someone closer to you? Something personal? Has that led anywhere?"

He grimaces. "I have a few suspicions, and I relayed them to Big Al. He and Tomer are investigating those too."

The distinct sound of grinding teeth draws my eyes to Leo's tense jaw. As I look at his profile, I get a strange feeling there's something he's not telling me. I'm half-tempted to press but equally inclined to let it lie. If he's holding back, he's probably got his reasons.

Then again, maybe I can help him solve it while also easing my curiosity.

"What else? I feel like you're hiding something."

He gives me a sidelong glance and flips another card toward the bowl, missing it altogether.

"Sue, do you ever worry that if you speak something out loud, you're bringing it into existence? If I tell you what I'm thinking, maybe I'll jinx us."

With a tight grin, he shakes his head and closes his eyes, looking like he's laughing at himself.

"Well, that sounds like the law of attraction and manifesting thoughts into your physical reality."

His eyes go wide at my quick reply. I'd wager he wasn't expecting such a robust response from me.

Sheepishly, I reply, "Yeah... I guess you can say I *do* think about it sometimes."

We share a chuckle, then I continue, "As you know, I'm a big fan of logic and science. That doesn't always mesh with this concept you're referring to. Now, there is the psychological side of the coin with self-fulfilling prophecies. But I think you're talking about *like attracting like,* and if you speak the words, the universe sends you the things you spoke. It's as if you're attracting them into being. Right?"

His eyes sparkle and flash as he nods, leaning closer to me.

"Even though this concept is reverse logic — which, aside from peanut butter, is my best friend — I still think there might be something to all those mystical coincidences and psychic moments people experience. Maybe there is more to life than what we can see, feel, smell, taste, and hear." I chuckle softly to myself, amused at the turn this conversation has taken. "Plus, you're looking at someone who was compulsively painting this cabin for six months before she ever saw it. So, who the hell knows what's real anymore? Maybe science and logic aren't everything, and magic is real."

He sets the card he was about to throw down and looks at me. "You never told me you painted the cabin."

"I sketched it too." I groan, then add, "Like a lot."

Leaning forward, he asks, "Really? How?"

"I have no idea, but I've been doing it for six months. Almost all my art has been of this cabin, and I have no idea why. It's been a frequent topic at my therapy sessions."

Leo looks truly shaken — exactly how I feel every time I think about what a bizarre turn of events this cabin has been. What started as a place straight from my nightmares is where Leo and I are starting something wonderful... *together*.

"Let me get this straight. Not only were you dreaming it, but you were painting and sketching it? That's insane."

I jerk my head back, feeling offended.

He notices my reaction right away. "I don't mean you're insane, angel. It's just crazy how this could happen. The situation is insane."

"Oh, I see, and I agree. It's bizarre as fuck." I press my hands into the floor and bring myself to a stand, shaking my legs out once I'm fully upright. "Hang on a second," I tell him.

Scurrying off to the bedroom, I pull my sketchbook out of the dresser and bring it back out to him. He's risen from the floor and meets me in the middle of the room.

"What is it?"

"Take a look." I hand it to him, and he begins flipping pages. His jaw falls lower and lower to his chest with each page he turns.

"First off, these are amazing. The attention to detail is beautiful."

"Thank you."

I put my head down and flap my hands a few times while nibbling my lip. I'm unaccustomed to having my art critiqued. It's a squishy feeling — awkward, humbling, and satisfying all at once.

"Second, this is unreal. It's definitely my cabin."

"I know it is."

"But how is this possible? I've never taken you here or described it to you. This doesn't seem possible. It just doesn't."

"And yet, here it is."

His head shakes back and forth as he continues looking through the book.

Excusing myself, I head to the kitchen for a glass of water. I feel like I've swallowed a cotton ball, and my pulse is ratcheting up. It's probably my body responding to the reminder of how I felt these last months — creating the same image from a memory that doesn't exist. It's been a nagging worry producing more anxiety than all the *peopling* I've had to do in the last decade.

He must notice the shift in my demeanor because he sets the book down and comes over to the kitchen.

With his head angled down at me and a gentle voice, he asks, "What's the matter, angel?"

After chugging a few gulps of water, I heave a rough sigh. "When I think about it, I feel the old panic rising."

"Think about what, specifically?"

My eyes search the ceiling. "I don't know. All of it, I guess."

My troubled gaze finds his calming one. "Like how I managed to dream this place? And how did I know what it looks like so well that I could create those images?"

I point to the table where he set the sketch book. "How is any of it possible, Leo?"

He wraps his arms around me, settling them on my lower back and pulling me against him.

His skin is soothingly warm, and I can't resist the urge to place my palms against his hard chest, then trail them upward until I lace my fingers together around the back of his neck. My gaze travels the path my hands took, soaking in every inch of his chiseled physique that's straining to escape the tight white tank he's wearing.

When I look up at him, his gaze is probing and pensive. Leaning forward, he places a chaste kiss on my lips. I sigh softly as he pulls back and places his forehead against mine.

The gesture is sweet and comforting.

Just like Leo himself.

"I don't know, but I'm sure we're going to find a logical explanation."

"I asked my therapist if there was a connection between autism and clairvoyance."

He raises his brows skeptically. "And?"

"When we spoke yesterday afternoon, she said she couldn't find anything reliable yet. She wonders if maybe I saw a picture of the cabin at some point, and my mind filled in the interior details, which could explain why I knew what the front looks like, but not the inside."

"I don't think I have any pictures of this place. I like to keep it private for a reason. Taking pictures would defeat the purpose."

"Well, then I guess I'm magic," I say with heavy sarcasm. I add an eye roll to ensure he gets my meaning.

He snickers, then kisses me — deeper this time. I open for him, letting his velvety tongue ravage me.

Before I know it, I'm completely lost in him — happily tumbling headfirst into a metaphorical puddle of my arousal on the kitchen floor.

Chapter Twenty-Six

Rearranging furniture and my insides

Sue

A few minutes later, we've quickly become wrapped up in one another, and the rest of the world falls away.

Hands are groping and wild, and tongues are madly exploring each other's mouths. He palms my breast through my shirt, flicking his thumb over the nipple. It hardens instantly into a tight little bud. He captures my answering moan in his mouth and pulls me closer.

Feeling emboldened by his affection for me, I stick my hand down his pants and give his hardening cock a few firm strokes. I mimic the action I've seen him use on himself. He groans, and I smile against his lips, enjoying how I affect him with only my touch.

I haven't had time to admire his penis yet. Normally when we start fooling around, he focuses on my pleasure, distracting me with his amazing mouth and hands. The next thing I know, he's buried inside me.

I'm not complaining, but I want to inspect his manhood closer while I have the chance.

With my first and only prior lover, I didn't touch or look at it much either. Curiosity is really killing me here. Watching porn has taught me a lot about sex, but you can't feel an erection through a screen.

Sadly.

Leo's cock feels like the smoothest velvet over granite, and I swear I could touch it all day. The soothing sensation of fisting him rivals all the sensory-stimulating surfaces my hands have ever touched. And the head is a whole other level of sensory overload for my needy hands — but in a good way.

Desperate for a closer look while I fondle him, I break the kiss and quickly drop to my knees. Suddenly, my mouth aches to run over his delicate flesh. My lips are always so much more sensitive to touch — as a kid, I sucked my thumb much longer than I should have, but it was because I loved the feeling of my thumb against my lips. And I just know feeling his cock plunging into my mouth would give me an equal or greater amount of satisfaction.

He helps remove his erection from his pants, and I stare wide-eyed at the most magnificent sight of my life.

Leo's dick.

It's an artistic display of masculine perfection as it juts from his body, defying gravity and bobbing inches from my face.

"It's beautiful," I rasp as I take it in my hands again, watching in rapt fascination as the skin folds and bunches with each stroke up and down the shaft.

He chuckles. "Not sure it's been called *that* before."

I meet his eyes from under my lashes and smile. "It should have been. It's amazing. The head is so soft and squishy too. Oh, I love it so much. Can I lick it?" I feel giddy with excitement at the prospect of giving my first blow job.

He starts out chuckling, which makes his erection twitch in my hand.

Suddenly, he hisses when I squeeze a bit harder. "Fuck!" His voice is raspy and full of breath.

I dial back the pressure, not wanting to hurt him. I'm kind of winging it here, so I think I'm going to need to pay attention to his reaction if I'm going to make this good for him. And I want it to be good for him.

He runs his hands through my hair and tucks a strand behind my ear. "Yes, you can lick it, beautiful."

"Okay, I've never done this before. You'll need to tell me if I do something wrong."

"Mmm. Another first." He looks positively gleeful at this news. After biting his lower lip, he says, "Just watch the teeth, and you'll do fine. There really isn't a wrong way to suck a cock."

My eyes travel down his body until landing on his thick shaft where it sticks out proudly from a small patch of dark hair. I lift it with one hand, angling it toward my mouth. When I do, I get my first up close look at a ball sack — kind of gross-looking — but I also see the underside of his dick has a thick, rope-like vein. *Oh, me likey that!*

My mouth waters, and my tongue twitches, so I make a beeline for the bulging vessel. Using the flat of my tongue like he did on my clit last night, I start at the base of his cock and run slowly up the vein until I reach the tip.

In response, he growls and pulses his hips forward. That seems like a good reaction, so I repeat the motion while keeping my eyes on his face to gauge his reaction.

His eyes roll back, and his jaw hangs slack, telling me that's definitely a good move, so I'll come back to it. Let's see what else I can do to get an even better reaction from him.

I rub the pad of my thumb across the opening on his thick, bulbous head — which is turning purple the more I handle it — and notice a few drops of clear liquid escape the hole.

"What is..." I trail off and narrow my eyes, wondering if he's just come already. That doesn't seem possible. And it looks like so much more in porn.

"It's precum, angel. Means I like what you're doing."

"Oh, okay."

I can't hold back a proud grin as I return to my task, rubbing my thumb around the tip and squeezing the soft tissue there a few more times. The sensation of his skin on mine is hypnotic.

He runs his hands through my hair and glances down at me with a fixed, wide-eyed gaze. His expression is undecipherable at first glance, but I'm too distracted by this magnificent peen to focus on it right now.

I fumble around to find the best grip and how to angle my head for efficiency, but soon enough, I've found other ways to lick and tease him that work for us both. He seems to like it when I flick the point of my tongue right at the underside of his tip where there's a tight little piece of flesh, so I repeat it a half dozen times before I decide to go all-in and take him in my mouth. His cock is long and girthy, and I'm not sure how much will fit. I give it my best effort, though, stretching my mouth wide and sheathing my teeth behind my lips.

"Jesus, baby. Fuck, that feels good."

It's natural to try to respond audibly, but since I have his dick in my mouth, my answer comes out like a garbled moan sounding something like, "argh mmm kah."

He moans again, which makes me think that the vibrations from my voice felt good to him too. I'm glad he likes that because I fucking loved the tingling feeling of my vocal vibrations dancing along the flat underside of my lips and his steely flesh.

I'm definitely doing that again — maybe a nice, long actual moan instead of trying to speak next time, though.

I draw him deeper into my mouth, feeling the stiff bit of flesh under his head as it runs along my tongue while plunging him closer to the entrance of my throat. Remembering he was sensitive there, I try to hit it each time I pull him back. I add a moan, and he cusses under his breath.

That's a keeper too.

Pardon the pun, but I'm easily getting sucked up into what I'm doing to his cock. This is as heavenly for me as it seems to be for him.

Suspicion confirmed: They knew what they were doing when they coined the term *oral fixation*.

After a few more minutes of gentle exploration and testing theories, I've decided I'm most definitely doing this again. And often.

For one, it's a heady feeling to bring him this kind of pleasure and hear him calling out my name. I feel like the queen of blow jobs. And two, the feel of this velvety delight in my mouth is something I can see myself craving for the sheer physical sensation alone.

All too soon, he's reaching down and grabbing me under my arms.

He hauls me to my feet as he says, "That's enough for now. I want to come inside your sweet pussy."

Before I can protest and ask for my penis popsicle back, he smashes his lips to mine, kissing me deeply. His hands sink down and squeeze the globes of my ass so hard I wonder if I'll have delicious bruises tomorrow.

As soon as he breaks the toe-curling kiss, he yanks my shorts down and bends me over the kitchen table by pressing his hand on my spine.

As he feeds his cock into me from behind, he grunts out, "You're fucking magic, all right, Angelica Sue O'Malley. This pussy is filled with magic, and you're a fucking blow job enchantress."

Despite using my detested given name, I moan in ecstasy while he forges deeper and deeper into my soaking wet core. He's much less gentle this time, but I like it.

Somehow I manage to say, "I'm glad you liked it because I can't wait to do it again."

"Fuck, you're still so tight. And hot and wet. You feel so damn good, angel. It's like you were made to take my cock."

"Maybe I was," I hiss out through gritted teeth.

Yet again, I wonder if soul mates are real. And if so, could Leo be mine?

The stinging pain of his intrusion quickly turns to utter pleasure once he's fully seated and my body relaxes to accommodate his girth. He pistons in and out of me at a furious pace. I have to brace myself on the table, which starts scratching across the kitchen floor with each thrust.

Undeterred by the furniture moving, Leo keeps going — in fact, I think he likes pushing me and the table across the room because his tempo increases.

He's pounding into me with an animalistic ferociousness, and I can feel his balls slapping against my clit with each forward thrust. A keening sound escapes my throat as I hurtle rapidly toward my first orgasm.

My body is alive with sensation awareness. I feel his every move and touch like my body is covered in sensors.

His fingertips dig deep into the flesh around my hips to the point of near pain. But I don't want him to let go, so I inch one hand back to cover his, holding it in place. He lifts two of his fingers to lace them with mine without missing a single stroke. The intimacy of the gesture — no matter how small it may seem — sends me right over the edge.

Even when he's fucking me with abandon like this, he does little things to show me how much he cares. It's my undoing every damn time.

"That's it. Come for me, angel. I know you're close. Take me with you."

With my cheek pressed against the cool tabletop, I glance back at him for a glimpse of ecstasy on his face. His lids are heavy, his eyes are glazed, and his lips are pinched between his teeth. I suspect my face mirrors his.

As the tingle of my orgasm blossoms into a burst of sensation, my lips curl, and I yell out unintelligibly, "I'm coming, Leo. I'm coming. Oh my fuck!"

Grunting and groaning, he thrusts into me a few more times as my clenching walls do just as he demanded, and we come together with fireworks dancing behind my eyes.

Fecking hell, we're getting good at this.

Each time is better than the last. I can almost feel warm jets of his essence pour into me, pulse after scorching pulse. It feels so fucking good. And so wet.

Wait. Why is it so wet? Did the condom break?

Instant panic replaces my post-sex glow as he pulls out slowly, and I feel warm droplets leaking from deep inside me.

Oh fuck. What did we just do?

Chapter Twenty-Seven

This is the perfect time to panic

Leo

Shit. Shit. Shit.

Wincing, I pull out and instantly realize what I've done. Her eyes, which were glazed in bliss a moment ago, are wide in horror.

"Shit, angel. I'm sorry. I'm... oh, fucking hell."

A rock settles heavy in my gut. How could I have been so stupid and reckless?

"Is that what I think it is... *leaking* out of me?" she asks while still bent over the table, looking like she's afraid to move.

"Yes, baby. I'm sorry. I forgot to put a condom on."

"You forgot?"

"Yes," I whisper, shame coating my words.

I brace myself for her rage — I know I deserve it.

"You mean *we* forgot," she corrects me, craning her neck to look me in the eye.

My heart squeezes at her words.

Quickly scuffling over to the counter — the best I can with my pants around my ankles — I grab the box of tissues and penguin walk back to my angel's side.

Arching her back, she presses up from the table slowly. If I weren't so torn up about what I just did, I'd take a moment to admire her naked ass, the way she's moving so gingerly, and how her skin is all flush from our exertions. Not to mention the sight of my release dripping out of her pussy. That alone almost makes me hard again, even if I know it's wrong — it's still fucking hot.

I remove several tissues and start to clean her up, but she hastily grabs at them and cleans herself. I can't tell how angry she is. Her words were soft and understanding, but she looks annoyed as hell right now. Fuck.

I dry myself up, tuck my troublemaking dick into my pants, and bend down to get Sue's discarded shorts and underwear. Wordlessly, she places her hand softly on my shoulder while she steps one foot at a time into her bottoms. When I rise and meet her eyes, I shove down the fear of what I'll find written on her face. A worst-case scenario flies through my mind. One where she'll be so angry that she'll decide she's done with me.

It's then I realize how much power she has over me — her response could make or break me so easily. She holds my happiness in her hands.

Studying my face, she asks, "Are you okay?"

Raising one hand, she cups my cheeks sweetly. I place my hand on top of hers.

"Sue, I'm so sorry. I got carried away and lost my head. But if we just..." I gulp, momentarily unsure how to form the words.

"Made a baby," she finishes for me, completely unfazed and logical.

Her lack of visible emotion over this is becoming worrisome.

"Yes... *that*. If we did that, then you won't need to worry. I would never abandon you or shirk my responsibilities."

Despite the way my mind is whirling, I almost like the idea of her carrying my child. I've never spent a lot of time thinking of becoming a father. When you have a childhood like mine, there's always the fear that the cycle of violence will repeat — although I know without a doubt, I could never do what my father did to us. But with the possibility of having a child looming in the air, I'm quickly coming to terms with the concept.

While I wait for her response, I notice my mouth has suddenly become dry.

She smiles sweetly. "Leo, darling..." She draws out what she's about to say, almost like she's enjoying building the suspense.

She fucking *finally* administers her sentence as judge, jury, and executioner. "I've got an IUD."

My head lolls back, and my shoulders drop. Surrounding her face in my palms, I kiss her deeply. After breaking the kiss, I shake my head, and we grin at each other. Although I'm relieved I didn't just get her pregnant, I'd be lying if I said there wasn't a trace of disappointment too.

"You should have seen your face," she says between snickers, doubled over and slapping her knees.

"That's not funny," I pout.

She holds up her thumb and forefinger about an inch apart. "It was a little funny."

This woman.

She distracts me from my fake sulking with a beaming smile.

Rubbing my hands up and down her arms, I tell her, "Let's get showered, then make dinner together. I'm getting hungry."

"Me too. Sex gives me the munchies like a mofo. I'm glad it burns so many calories, though. Maybe I'll actually lose a few pounds while we're in hiding since we have nothing better to do than bang."

My face shifts into a frown, and I grip her tighter. "Selfishly, I hope you don't lose too much. I love your body exactly how it is."

She scoffs, shakes her head at me, and pushes lightly at my chest, but I maintain my hold on her.

"I mean it, angel. And after dinner, when I've restored my energy and my fluids, I'm going to show you precisely how much I love your body."

"Oh, that sounds promising," she says, waggling her twinkling eyes. "I can hardly wait."

Even though I just had her, I want her again.

"Me either."

Don't hide from me

We take separate showers despite my request for her to join me. She didn't even consider my bullshit excuse of conserving water. It's like she doesn't care for our planet at all.

Kidding.

Despite all the sex we've had, I haven't had more than a few grasps and tweaks of her nipples over the clothes and only a partial view of her top half. Well, aside from that first night in her house when she forgot I was there and nearly stripped in front of me. I guess I could say she's never willingly bared herself to me.

I'm going to rectify that tonight, come hell or high water.

Hell, I want so badly to pay homage to her breasts and lavish them with all my attention. She still seems shy when it comes to nudity, hiding her body. I've let her hide so far because I know she needs time to get used to new experiences. But I want her naked the next time I bring her to orgasm. I need to lay my eyes on every delectable inch of her and watch her skin flush with pleasure. And I want her to ride me too.

After she gets dressed, she joins me in the kitchen to prepare our meal together.

Spending all this time with her this week has helped me understand why I was so hung up on her during our time apart. Sue and I fit together, plain and simple.

It's not only the tug of connection and deep-seated desire to be inside her — that's the tip of the iceberg. It's everything from our tastes in food, enjoyment of similar leisure activities — mainly art and reading — our matching homebody nature, and our senses of humor.

We *mesh*.

That's how it was all those months ago when I guarded her the first time around. We clicked instantly, and I wanted to be by her side as much as possible. When I factor in the overwhelming urge to make her happy and keep her safe, I know I've found my other half... age difference be damned.

Sue is meant to be mine, and I am meant to be hers.

After playing footsie throughout our pleasant dinner of grilled ham and cheese sandwiches with tomato soup — pickings are really getting slim around here — she wants to do some painting, saying she feels inspired tonight. And I want nothing more than to watch her enjoying her craft. It's one of the many things I've missed during our time apart.

When Sue paints, she gets so wrapped up in her creation she might as well be part of the canvas.

It's mesmerizing.

After helping her set up the painting supplies in the living room, I take a seat on the couch with a book on my lap. Not sure who I think I'm kidding with the book — I know I'll be watching her work. She probably knows it too, but the book makes me feel like less of a creeper. And it can sit in my lap to hide the hard-on I'll inevitably get from watching her.

Tonight, she starts with a pencil, sketching lines and measuring spaces across the canvas.

I watch with unwavering attention when she starts mixing colors and humming along to the music she put on — some ethereal-sounding Irish folk music. I force myself to stop staring at her when I get an alert on the security tablet, which monitors the sensors around the property. Checking the camera feeds, I see two bucks having a territorial dispute have triggered the system. Everything else seems fine.

Sue must notice my movements out of the side of her eye because she pauses with her paintbrush hovering right over the canvas. "Everything okay outside?"

"Yeah, it's just a few deer that tripped a sensor," I tell her with a soft smile. I pick up my book and make a show of flipping pages, attempting to reinforce that I'm not worried.

"Okay," she says flatly and returns to her painting.

After several minutes have passed, I ask, "Have you ever thought of selling your art?"

Her head whips over, and she nibbles her lower lip. "Yes, I have."

"And?"

"I don't think it's something I'm comfortable with at this time. Maybe one day."

"Why not?"

She scratches her neck while looking thoughtfully at the ceiling. My eye catches on the reddening skin under her nails, and my dick twitches. It reminds me of how she looks when her skin is blotchy and flushed from our lovemaking.

Fuck. How long has it been since I've had her? Is it possible I need to have her again so soon? I'm insatiable for this vixen.

"I honestly don't need the money, so I don't see a reason to sell them. Plus, I wouldn't know how to go about it. Maybe eBay? Etsy? I don't know. It doesn't matter."

My nose wrinkles. "Everyone can use extra money. Don't tell me Nick pays you that well for running Naughty Dogs. You're cut out for more than that."

"He pays me well enough. And I might want to do something else one day, but it's fine for now. And I don't have to deal with people, which is an added perk."

"Does the job make you happy?"

Not sure why I'm asking all these questions, but I feel compelled to make sure she's fulfilled in all aspects of her life. If she wants more than Naughty Dogs, I want to help her get it. If she doesn't, that's fine too. I suspect she's not as happy there as she lets on.

She sets the paintbrush down on the color pallet, then wipes her hands on the old T-shirt I gave her to cover up her clothes. Sauntering in my direction, she scrutinizes me closely. It's like she's trying to see through me — reveal my motivations for asking, perhaps.

"Why do you ask?"

"I honestly have no reason, other than I think you're talented, and I'm sure there are plenty of people who'd love to have an Angelica O'Malley hanging in their living room."

Fire flashes in her eyes, and she inhales sharply, placing a hand on her chest mockingly. "Please never call me that again. I don't want any elementary school flashbacks," she says playfully as she places her hands on my knees and leans in for a kiss.

When she tries to back away, I tug her onto my lap. She huffs and lets out a soft giggle. I place a few kisses on her warm, supple neck, and her giggling turns into an all-out laugh. The sound is music to my ears and a shot of arousal to my cock.

"You never did tell me why you hate your name so much. I think it's beautiful."

She looks at me like I've got a second head.

"What?" I ask behind a smile.

Her shoulders fall after a second, and she tilts her head as some type of understanding dawns. "You might be too old to know this, but Angelica was a character on a popular children's show called *Rugrats*. She was a horrible character, and the name was forever tarnished. By the time I got to elementary school, kids were constantly asking where my Cynthia doll was and if I'd tortured any dumb babies lately. It was horrible." She vibrates her body like she's trying to shake the memory away.

I can't help but kiss her pouty lips.

"By the time I went into third grade, I had all but banished that name from existence and insisted everyone refer to me by my middle name. My family started the Susie Q nickname not too long after that, if memory serves."

"I see," I say with a nod.

"You don't remember that show, do you, old man?" She softens her dig with a sexy wink.

Our age difference seemed like a much bigger deal before this week. It doesn't bother me anymore. I've learned patience in my three and a half decades on this planet, and with Sue's condition and anxiety, she probably needs more patience than many other women would. I'm happy to give that to her. In fact, it's an honor.

"Well... do you?" she prompts, pulling me back to the Rugrats topic.

A memory of this show tugs at the back of my mind, but the entire time frame is hazy with dark memories of fists, black eyes, and busted lips.

"Nickelodeon, right?"

She nods, then quirks her head to the side, eying me closely. "What's wrong?"

"Nothing. Why do you ask?"

I shift her weight to hold her closer to my chest and start kissing her neck, hoping to make her forget this line of questioning.

In addition to attempting to distract her, I'm trying to use her body to help me chase away the demons from my childhood, which are clawing to get out of the box buried deep in the corners of my mind.

"Leo, look at me."

Ignoring her, I slip my hand under her shirt while drawing a bit of her fleshy neck between my lips, sucking gently.

"Stop," she says, then shifts her body to straddle me and braces herself on my chest.

I have zero complaints about this position either. But since she asked me to stop, I respect her wishes, withdrawing my hands and preparing to face the music.

"What?" I try to play dumb, making one last feeble attempt to dissuade her from pushing me to talk about the haunted thoughts she saw behind my eyes.

"Your face paled all of a sudden, and your eyes went dark. Do you hate that show as much as I do?"

She raises one brow while she awaits my answer, and I know I'm going to cave.

Dammit.

"I don't hate the show, Sue. I barely remember it."

"Then why the sad face?"

Fuck. She's like a dog with a bone. My muscles tense, and my stomach sours as I prepare to share some of my darkest memories with her.

"My childhood wasn't good, angel. When I started shifting through my memories to find the show, other memories surfaced instead."

With barely a whisper, she asks, "What kind of memories?"

She moves her palms up my chest until they rest on my shoulders.

My voice sounds shaky when I finally attempt to speak. "Really bad ones, Sue. Depressing ones. I don't want to burden you with them."

She squeezes the hard planes of my shoulders, then shifts herself closer so there is less space between us. Reaching up, she cups my face and looks deep into my eyes. I'm stricken with how brilliant the blue and silver flecks in her irises are tonight. They sparkle like matching turquoise pools at sunset in the Caribbean.

"Leo, while you certainly don't have to tell me about it, I want you to. You made me tell you about my nightmares and autism diagnosis. And I want to reciprocate. I don't want you hiding anything from me — the good or the bad. I want to know you the same way you know me. You don't always have to protect me. I'm tougher than you think."

Ouch.

That was a one-two punch to the gut, calling me out for always trying to protect everyone around me and for demanding from her what I, myself, am unwilling to give.

Both of those points strike true.

"You're right, angel. I'm sorry. Believe me, I know you're strong."

She doesn't respond, just looks at me — her eyes roaming over my face and landing on my eyes. I break, deciding to go all in here. She's right. It's not fair to demand her truth, then hold my own from her. I want this relationship to work — more than anything — and to do that, I need to be open with her.

"My father was abusive to my mom, brother, and sister."

"And to you?"

"Yes," I admit, feeling my throat tighten instantly with the confession almost to the point of it choking off my airflow.

"Oh, Leo, I'm so sorry." Her voice softens with compassion.

"He was fine when he was sober, but he drank a lot, and the alcohol turned him into a monster. He'd start in with my mom while I tried to keep my brother and sister hidden upstairs. As the oldest, I felt like it was my duty to protect them."

Her chin quivers, and I'm tempted to stop the story there. But she needs to know who I am before I give her all of my heart. Just like I don't want those layers of cotton to come between us when we're making love, I can't let my secrets be a barrier to my heart.

I close my eyes, swallow, and continue, "Once he grew tired of knocking my mom around, he'd come stomping up the stairs."

My cheeks heat, and my heart pounds as those memories come to life through my words.

"I'd take all the anger from him that I could, but it wasn't always enough. I couldn't protect them all the time. I hate that I failed them — wasn't strong enough to take it all. He always had more to give than my body could take."

Memories of blow after blow raining down on my chest, stomach, and back assault me, pulling me right back into my painful youth.

Once I was down, he'd start kicking, never letting up until I begged for mercy. I knew once he stopped with me, Sammy and Drew would be next if he still had more anger left in his blackened soul.

So I learned to never yield.

Even now, my instincts warn me to fold my body in on itself to protect my midsection. He knew better than to leave marks where teachers could see them, so my center mass was at the most risk. My mom didn't have that same luxury, though, and she still has the scars on her face to prove it.

I fight the instinct to curl into a ball by telling myself *I'm safe*, over and over again in my head.

When I open my eyes, Sue's tear-stained cheeks are blurry, hidden behind a curtain of my own tears. She leans forward and presses her wet, salty lips to mine, whispering, "He can't hurt you anymore."

Nodding wordlessly, I kiss her back, soaking in the love and comfort she gives so freely.

With every swipe of her lips across mine, my soul lightens.

With each breath we take together, blackened memories fade to gray.

And with every lick of her tongue against mine, another layer of my burden is lifted. She's healing me with her body, heart, and soul.

"Thank you for telling me," she says quietly when I finally pull my lips off hers.

"Angel, I want to take you to bed and get lost in your body."

Chapter Twenty-Eight

What is love? (Baby, don't hurt me)

Leo

With a sniffle, she nods and presses her lips to mine once more for a kiss as light as air. I rise from the chair, carrying her to the room slowly. She keeps her legs wrapped tight around my waist.

With a soft smile, she says, "It still amazes me how you manage to carry me."

There she goes again, putting down her size. Time to nip that shit in the bud.

Having always liked curvy women, I've been with some who were self-conscious before. Some of them seemed far more shame-filled than Sue does. She's not over the top with negative talk, but I've noticed enough self-deprecating comments these last days that I'm making it my mission to banish any negative thought she might have from her mind.

"Woman, you're mine. I'd carry you all around the world if I thought you'd let me."

She groans when I put my nose into the crease between her chin and neck and inhale deeply. "You smell delicious, angel."

"You always know how to make my skin sing with need."

I gently place her on the bed, leaving her sitting near the edge. After removing my shirt, I kneel between her slightly parted legs and spread them wide. My palms run up and down her thighs as I feel my cock stiffen.

She places her hands atop mine to slow their movements, then leans forward to offer me her mouth. Kissing her eagerly, I suck her lips between mine and swipe at them with my tongue. She opens for me right away, gasping delicately when I delve inside to taste her.

As the kiss deepens, I feel her hands tighten on top of mine while she scoots to the edge of the bed to get closer. I hold her in place, keeping her right where I want her. If she starts rubbing her hot core against me, I'll end up in a mad rush to bury myself inside her depths. I want to go slow and unwrap her like a present.

She breaks the kiss with a bewildered look on her sweet, heart-shaped face.

"Stay right there, my angel. I want to take my time with you tonight."

A shy grin lifts the corners of her mouth, and my dick strains behind the fabric of my shorts. I'm ravenous for her, tempted to move faster. But tonight, I'm not settling for less than every inch of her skin bare before me.

I trail my hands from her thighs to the hem of her shirts — she's wearing two since she used my old tee as a cover. As I start to lift them over her head, she reaches down to hold the bottom shirt close to her stomach. Once I've removed one shirt from her frame, I toss it behind me. Narrowing my eyes at her, I tug at the cotton, making my intention clear.

"Arms up," I command softly.

Her eyes dart to the lamp on the bedside table, and I know what she's thinking. Not a fucking chance. "The light stays on, angel. I need to see every inch of you."

Her eyes pinch as a worried expression mars the smooth planes of her face. "I don't know... I'm not —"

I cut her off with a firm, "You are. You're everything. Everything I want and everything I need. You're mine, and I want to worship every last bit of you tonight. Don't hide from me, my love."

With a whimpering sound that's almost a pout, she complies, raising her arms over her head. "It's not fair to throw my words back at me," she says, sullen and positively adorable.

Before removing her top, I lean in and kiss her once more. "I never said I play fair, angel."

Without giving her a chance to reconsider, I swiftly pull the shirt over her head and am blessed with the sight of her smooth ivory skin. Two full breasts are spilling out of a utilitarian beige bra. My mouth waters as I take in her beauty. The last time I saw her like this, I wasn't allowed to look, but now I can have my fill.

It was worth the fucking wait.

"Beautiful," I say with complete honesty, then place a line of soft kisses along her collarbone and the top of her chest. I skim my hands over the top of her mounds and watch as her skin pebbles under my touch.

Slowly, I trail my hand to the waistband of her shorts. "Now, the bottoms."

This time, she doesn't hesitate to help me remove the remaining articles from her body. Once she's completely naked, I help her lie down, pushing her farther up the bed. Standing at the foot of the bed, I drink her in, letting my gaze travel from her head to toe.

My tongue dabs at my lips as I remove my pants. Taking my cock in my fist, I give it a firm stroke, rubbing my thumb across the weeping head.

"Angel, I wish you could see the view from up here. It's breathtaking."

Her chin wobbles and tears fill her eyes, drawing me to her side to comfort her. I didn't expect this tender moment to affect her this much, and she needs my reassurance. Moving swiftly, I join her on the bed and travel up her body. I place a few gentle kisses along her legs, hips, stomach, and neck as I move over her. I'll get back to her lush breasts in a minute once I know she's okay.

I brace my arms on each side of her head and settle my hips between her inviting thighs. I place a feather-light kiss on her lips and tell her in earnest, "You're absolutely perfect."

"You make me feel so beautiful, Leo."

"Because you are."

A tear spills down her face, and I wipe it away, then place a kiss on her damp skin.

"What does love feel like?" she asks suddenly, making my eyes go comically wide in surprise.

This.

It feels like this.

Her cheeks flame red, and she starts rambling. "Oh my fecking hell. I'm sorry for asking that. Never mind. Forget I asked that. Just erase that from your memory. Where is the *Men In Black* flashy thing when a girl needs it, huh?" She laughs awkwardly and palms her forehead.

A deep chuckle causes my shoulders to shake, and my head swirls with adoration for her.

For all of her.

I'm so damn in love with this woman.

I love everything about her. Her awkwardness and quirks. Her honesty and lack of artifice. Her rambling moments when she's flushed with embarrassment. The way her filter doesn't always work. I can't imagine anyone else asking that at a time like this.

But it's perfectly Sue. Perfectly us.

"Angel, to be clear, I'm not laughing at you. I'm laughing *with* you."

Her cheeks pull tight with a self-deprecating smile. "Sure, sure. That's an important distinction. Whatever. Just another day in the life of Sue O'Malley — the awkward gal next door."

Leaning in, I claim her mouth. It's the only way I can think to reassure her and stop myself from chuckling. My cock is still throbbing, reminding me of how I need to be inside her more than I need air.

As our kiss turns passionate, her hands roam over my shoulders, and she pulls me tight against her body. My erection starts prodding around her entrance like it has a mind of its own — keep your jokes about man-brain syndrome to yourself, please.

"Since you're on birth control, can we forgo condoms? I'm clean, and I know you are since I was the first one to take you bare."

A ripple of pride swells inside me at being the only one who's had her like that.

And I'll be the only one who ever does, I think smugly.

"Yes," she answers simply. But it's when she adds on, "I trust you," that I lose it and start pressing inside her silky channel.

I press my hips forward, then withdraw. Repeating the motion again and again, I work my way inside her body slowly, drawing out the pleasure of our joining. We're not as frantic as we were when I took her earlier in the kitchen, and now I can focus on the sweet feel of her pussy welcoming me one inch at a time without any barriers.

When I bottom out, she throws her head back and moans. I'm barely able to hold back a growl when I feel her clench and unclench her walls around me. With each shallow thrust of my hips, I press another kiss on her face while whispering the sweetest words I can think of — anything to tell her how I feel about her.

You're beautiful.

You feel so good.

You make me want forever.

I'll never let anyone hurt you.

You're mine.

I adore you, my sweet angel.

She doesn't answer with poetic words, but I can still see how my proclamations affect her. It's how she looks intensely into my eyes and how reverently she whispers my name as I bury myself inside her. And when her first orgasm overtakes her, I kiss her deeply, capturing her cries of ecstasy.

I'm not sure how I manage it, but I don't let her climax take me with her. I just keep making love to her, driving her right on through her first orgasm and letting her build to the second. We move together at a languid pace, grinding and touching each other like we can never get enough.

The world's disappeared — it's only Sue and me.

Reveling in feeling her hardened nipples scraping against my chest reminds me that I need to worship those beautiful breasts. I reduce my tempo and prepare for a change in position. I want her on top so I can stare at her luscious body and suck on her breasts when she comes again.

"You on top," I say in between staccato breaths before rolling over to my back. She comes along willingly, but my cock slips out in the process.

Looks like we'll need to practice that move, which means more sex — what a crying shame.

Her hands lift to cover her breasts, but I grab them and place them on my abs. "We don't hide from each other, remember?"

Gulping audibly, she nods. "I've never done this," she says, sounding breathy and flustered.

"Grab my cock and put it back inside."

She does as I order without delay, making my dick throb. Once I'm notched back at her entrance, I thrust upward slightly, and gravity does the rest. She's already stretched to accommodate me and slick with arousal, so I'm met with only the smoothest of resistance.

For the umpteenth time in the last few days, I wonder if I'll ever grow tired of how it feels to be inside her.

Doubtful.

"Now what? Do I stay up here?"

"You can, or you can bend down and lean close. Try it both ways to see what you like."

I guide her movements by grabbing her hips and help her find the rhythm with gentle, leisurely upward strokes.

"Oh, damn. It's deeper like this." Her mouth falls open, and her eyes roll back in her head.

I groan as her walls grip me. "Fuck, baby. I can feel you clenching."

"You like that?" she asks, then pulses two more times.

"Ahhh, fuck. You could make me come doing that."

"Good to know for another time," she replies, getting comfortable and regaining confidence in her voice. "But right now, I need to figure out how to ride my man."

She's studying her positioning, looking around my body and hers like she's cramming for a test.

"That's right, angel. Ride your man. Make yourself come on my cock." My head sinks back deeper into the pillow as her tempo increases.

My eyes take in the glorious rise and fall of her tits while she moves erotically on top of me. I curl my lower back, bowing up my pelvis with each of her downward thrusts to grind into her clit. She responds by thrashing her hips faster, really getting the movement down pat. I slip and slide out of her with ease, nearly bottoming out each time.

My angel is a quick study in riding dick.

With one hand braced on my stomach, the other creeps higher onto my chest. Grabbing a fistful of chest hair, she works her hips back and forth furiously.

Our breathing gets louder, filling the air with rasps and moans. By the time she nears her climax, her gasps are short and frenzied, and the prick of pain from where she's grabbing at my chest unlocks a kink I didn't realize I had. Maybe we can explore that pain-pleasure barrier of mine another time.

Right now, my girl is about to get her first cowgirl orgasm, and I'm beaming like a loon for selfishly claiming so many of her firsts.

In a way, I wish I could claim all her firsts, but then again, I'm glad she wasn't a virgin when we first made love. This way, she'll know without a doubt how fucking good we are together.

"You're so close, baby. Let me have it. Come for me," I tell her while holding off my own pressing release.

She bends forward as that coil of pleasure tightens in both of us, her mouth hanging open and unintelligible gibberish falling from her lips. I lift my head from the pillow to meet her halfway so I can take one of her breasts into my mouth, swirling my tongue around her nipple, then hollowing my cheeks to suck it in deep.

That's all it takes. She comes beautifully around me — screaming my name and cursing six ways 'til Sunday. I join her, this time succumbing to the pleasure and letting her fluttering pussy milk me dry. I empty my release deep inside her and thrust a few more times as we ride out the aftershocks.

She collapses on me, laughing and gasping for breath.

"Fuck, that was amazing," she says.

"Bet your sweet ass it was."

Reaching around, I grab a handful of her thick ass and thrust up once more. She hisses a moan of approval.

A few minutes later, we're cleaned off, and I'm spooning her from behind. She's quiet while I try to position myself around her, but I can sense her smiling. I'm not entirely sure where to rest my hand, shifting it higher and lower on her body, trying to find the right spot. When I move it a third time, she grabs my hand and cups it over her breast.

I squeeze it happily.

"There. You happy now?"

A sharp breath exits my mouth, fluttering her hair. Through a smile, I sigh, "Very."

Chapter Twenty-Nine

If you can dodge a wrench

Sue

When I rise with the sun, Leo's wrapped around me like a hairy, naked blanket and sound asleep. The streaks of sunlight coming through the blinds glare across his lightly bronzed skin and inky tattoos. I take advantage of the blissful moment to study the hard and soft lines of his face and the thickening beard in need of a trim. He sighs gently as I run my knuckles over his cheek. Even in his sleep, he leans in to my touch.

My heart squeezes.

It's not like him to sleep later than me, and it gives me a smug feeling that I wore him out with my sexual prowess.

Ha!

I'm still such a noob, but I think he likes teaching me all the sexy things. I'm sure as hell enjoying the learning.

I can't believe he got me fully naked last night, and even more, he didn't instantly lose his boner at the sight of my stretch marks. What twenty-six-year-old without kids has stretch marks across her belly?

This one.

I'm not especially ashamed of my body. It's the best I can do without giving up all the food I love — I'm looking at you, peanut butter. But I admit I wasn't keen on showing him my stretch marks.

Yet he didn't shy away from them. In fact, he seemed to grow harder and longer the more he studied my entirely bared body. It made me love him even more.

And yeah, I think I'm totally in love with him.

Not that I have much to compare my feelings to except for the love I have for my family. But if given the choice between losing my family or Leo... I'm ashamed to say it would be an extremely difficult decision.

That tells me all I need to know.

When my bladder demands attention, I regretfully extricate myself from his large frame and pad to the bathroom. Once I've used the facilities and freshened up, I throw on a baggy tee and some comfy shorts, then bend to place a kiss on his forehead. He murmurs something I can't decipher. With a sleepy smile, I thank my stars for sending me this gentle giant.

Once I'm in the kitchen, I decide to start the coffee. I don't care that it's not a Saturday. This morning calls for java.

Looking over the mess we left in the living room, I remember everything Leo shared with me last night about his childhood. I've never wanted to hunt someone down and kill them before — but if I knew where his fecking father was, I might consider it.

As hard as my childhood was with undiagnosed autism and being the youngest of seven kids, it was nothing compared to Leo's. And yet he came out as one of the kindest and most loving men I've ever known.

Leo wakes and joins me in the kitchen a few minutes later. He looks mouthwatering in baggy sweats that hang low on his hips, showing off his happy trail and defined ab muscles.

With my back to the kitchen counter, he snakes his arms around my waist and presses a chaste kiss on my lips. He smells and tastes of minty fresh toothpaste.

My nipples pebble, and my vagina contracts.

Fucking hell. Again, ladies? Settle down.

I'm a little sore from all the sex we had last night — and the last few days — and my body needs a little break.

"Good morning," I say to his chest while I pepper some kisses in his soft chest hair.

"Did you sleep well?" he asks.

"Like the dead."

He cringes and pulls back with an alarmed look on his face.

"Is that not a good analogy?" I ask through a wide smile.

He shakes his head emphatically. "Just makes me visualize sleeping with a corpse."

He pulls me against his warm chest, and I love the feel of his laughter vibrating and his chest hair tickling my cheek.

Damn, this feels good.

Having a lazy morning together, sharing all these tender moments. It's like I've never been lonely a day in my life — he's wiped all those years away. I didn't know I was waiting for him, but I know it now.

A buzzing sound distracts us, and he takes his phone out of his pocket.

And by the way, that's utter gobshite. It's completely unfair that all men's clothing comes with pockets. Sexism in fashion is total bullshit. We all need pockets. Give us the pockets, fashion industry!

Anyway.

With a grin on his face, he swipes his thumb across the screen and sends a reply. When he sees the curious look on my face, he shows me the text.

Big Al: Good morning. I know you're going to ask, so I already checked on your mother today. She's fine. Nick and Millie are good, too, so don't fucking ask about them either. No news on the investigation. Stay vigilant. My gut tells me something is coming.

Leo: Thanks, Boss. 10-4.

"Nice." I nod. "Thank you."

I like that he's being so open with me. He didn't even try to hide the ominous warning at the end of the text. We really got somewhere good in our relationship last night.

No more walls between us.

"Pancakes again?" he asks. "It's pretty much all we have left."

"Can I have peanut butter on mine?"

He wrinkles his nose and cringes. "Gross."

I pat his chest. "Shut your mouth, Leo Mason. How dare you? Peanut butter is a versatile food and cut out for so much more than just sandwiches."

He shakes his head at me, making a tsking sound. "Whatever humps your camel, princess. Just don't plan on kissing me afterward."

"I'll brush my teeth and mouthwash all the little allergens away. I promise."

The other day we learned that lesson the hard way. His lips got bright red and swollen. Fortunately, he had Benadryl in the cabinet, and he was better in a few hours. He's lucky his peanut allergy is mild. I've heard horror stories about people who have trouble breathing from the smell of peanut butter alone.

What tragic lives they must lead.

He smiles and kisses me, soft and gentle. When we break the kiss, I release my hold on him, and he instantly spins around to grab the peanut butter from the cabinet. He shoots me a sexy smirk over his shoulder.

Pleased with the outcome, I lift my shoulders and shimmy my breasts against him. "Yay! Thanks, my sweet giant."

He groans and pushes me away. "Stop that, or we'll never eat... well, we won't eat food." He waggles his brows at me.

Together, we make breakfast, using up the remaining pancake mix. After getting dressed, we embark on what's quickly becoming our morning routine of taking a short hike around the property looking for wildlife. When we're done with that, we follow it up with an hour of self-defense training.

I don't want to be a helpless victim, and even though Leo's determined to keep me far from any danger, I'd rather be safe than sorry. He can't always be with me, and heaven forbid something happens to him. I need to know I can defend myself to some extent.

Once we're back at the cabin, we rest together on the couch while downing water to restore the fluids we've been expending. In more ways than one.

"Leo, one of the things you mentioned outside was how everyday objects can be used as weapons."

I've asked him a few times about weapons training, and he's still warming to the idea. He said he'd rather not risk an accident. He followed that up with a boring lecture about how accidents can happen when someone lacks confidence in handling a gun.

Whatever.

I feel a tad petulant about the topic but not enough to fight him on it. He's probably right because he knows his weapons — far more than me.

"Yeah?" he asks, prompting me to continue.

"Well, what types of things did you mean? I'm having trouble visualizing it."

He looks around the room and leans forward to pick up the deck of cards off the coffee table.

"Take these, for example."

I reach out to grab them, and his shoulders shake with silent laughter.

I frown.

Through a tight grin, he says, "I didn't mean for you to actually take them."

"Say what you mean, Leo. I'm a literal person." I cross my arms and pout.

"Sorry. My bad. But since you're able to use sarcasm and metaphors so freely, I often forget how literal you are."

"Fair enough. In fact, I always wondered why I could grasp it so much in my own thoughts and in what I say but struggle to understand it from others. Now that I know I'm on the spectrum, it makes sense."

"People with autism are often very black and white, huh?" Leo asks. I nod.

"Then how can you wield sarcasm so well?"

"Jaynie thinks it's because of my family and upbringing. The O'Malleys are all kinds of sarcastic with each other. If I couldn't speak at least a modicum of sarcasm, I wouldn't have understood anything in my household growing up."

A grin lifts half his face.

I angle my head in the direction of the cards he's holding, prompting him to continue with his impromptu lesson on using playing cards as a weapon

"Right, so if you were to wrap your hand around them like this and get a good solid grip on the deck, you can jab the edge into a soft spot on your opponent's body and cause quite a bit of pain."

A hissing sound escapes me.

Ouch. That seems insanely painful.

"Like this."

He demonstrates using a solid grip and slowly jabs the deck of cards toward my neck in a back-handed motion, applying only the slightest pressure on my trachea.

Next, he moves the deck to the corner of my face and twists it so the pointy edge gets close to my eye — but not touching. "You could take an eye out." He shifts to my temple. "Or even pop here to take someone down."

My pulse ratchets up with excitement. Knowing these things, it's almost like I'm learning something most people don't. It feels forbidden or naughty and perhaps a little titillating.

"Oh, that's interesting. What else?" I tuck my knees under my bottom, shifting on the couch to face him.

He chuckles, and I think it's because he likes when I'm this animated.

"A cell phone can be used in much the same way."

Grabbing his phone, he demonstrates a few other ways to strike, careful not to cause me any discomfort. He then scans the room to see what else is lying around. "You could also use keys. They're great weapons."

Wrapping his thick fingers around my thinner ones, he teaches me to tuck them between my fingers and slash at vulnerable spots on the inner arm, torso, and neck, explaining step by step. He also points out a few places where I can jab the keys into the body to pierce the skin and make a puncture wound.

"For such a nice guy, you're dangerous," I say when he's done with his thorough explanation.

The lines around his eyes are crinkled with amusement. "You know what this whole thing reminds me of?"

"What?" I ask, tilting my head to the side and trying not to get lost in those beautiful blue eyes of his.

He drops his chin and lowers his voice even deeper than his usual timbre. "If you can dodge a wrench, you can dodge a ball."

"*Dodgeball!*" I squeal. "I fecking loved that movie."

Leo's method of teaching me to fight with everything *except* weapons is ironically similar to the coach in that film teaching the team to dodge everything but dodgeballs.

While we laugh together, he laces his fingers in mine and pulls me onto his lap. Somehow we end up kissing and half naked on the couch — shocking, I know — and he makes me ride him in the middle of the living room.

We've had sex in every room except the bathroom.

A few minutes later, he finally convinces me to shower with him. He lovingly lathers up every inch of my skin with sudsy bubbles and rinses me squeaky clean.

Breaking news: By the time the water runs cold, we've officially had sex in *every* room in the cabin.

Chapter Thirty

Do you want eggrolls with that?

Leo

After our incredibly satisfying shower, we're getting ready to leave. Sue's brushing her hair at the edge of the bed and studying my moves closely as I attach my gun holsters to my belt before sliding on my cargo pants. After filling a pocket with extra ammo, I secure two Smith & Wesson pistols to my holsters — one on each hip.

Mockingly, she fans her face. Her shoulders fall, and her head tilts to one side adorably.

"Can ya tell me why watchin' ya strap on a gun is so feckin' sexy despite the fact that guns don't overly enthuse me?" Her muddled attempt at an Irish accent is cute as hell.

"I've never pretended to understand what goes on in a woman's mind." I flash a wink.

She chuckles and returns to leisurely brushing her damp hair.

Placing my foot on the edge of the bed, I lift my pant leg to strap a sheathed knife to my leg before rolling the fabric down.

From the corner of my eye, I notice her bite her lip and shake her head while emitting a groan.

With all my weapons secured, I put on a long button-down shirt, leaving it untucked to conceal the weapons.

"If I had known you'd get this hot by watching me handle weapons, things might have ended up differently six months ago."

Her mouth drops at the corners, and her eyes fall to the floor.

Dammit.

I want to throat punch myself for bringing up the heartbreak I caused her — caused us both — by leaving the way I did. I deserve a buttstock to the head for that shit.

"I'm sorry for mentioning that, and even sorrier for hurting you." Rising, she meets my gaze, and I wrap my arms around her waist.

While looking up at me, she tilts her head to the side, exposing a column of smooth peach flesh peppered with fading flush marks from the heat of our shower. I place a gentle kiss on her warm skin and inhale the fruity scent of her body wash mixed with her freshly shampooed hair.

She tosses her hairbrush down on the bed behind her and spins to face me again. Her arms surround my neck, tugging me down until our noses touch.

"Stop apologizing for that. I've forgiven you, and even though I disagree with your reasons for leaving, I do understand them."

"But you'll never forget. I hate how I hurt you. As long as you remember that pain and I see it reflected on your perfect face, I'll keep apologizing."

"Oh, Leo," she scoffs. "My face is *not* perfect." Her playful tone lightens the mood.

"It's perfect to me."

"When's the last time you had your vision checked? They say vision is one of the first senses to go when you age. How many fingers am I holding up?"

She puts up her middle finger in front of my face, essentially flipping me off. I gently bite down on it.

Her laugh draws me in, and I press a kiss against her smiling lips. It brings some of our typical lightness back.

After a quick squeeze of her ass, I tell her, "I'm going to put my shoes on. Tie your hair up. I want you to tuck it in a hat when we leave."

She rolls her eyes but nods.

Her silent agreement reminds me of something I've wanted to tell her.

I touch her chin, bringing her gaze back to mine. "Thanks for not fighting me on safety shit. You've always done everything I've asked of you. And it means a lot to know you trust me and that I can trust you to follow my instructions."

She smiles and bats her dark lashes at me, grabbing my hand at the wrist. "Well, I've read a lot of romantic suspense novels, and it always pisses me off when the main character does something totally daft, like ignoring the big, strong bodyguard's orders. Obviously, the bodyguard is intending to keep her safe. So..." She licks her lips, shrugs, then adds, "You're welcome."

I want to kiss her again, and since there's no reason to hold back, I claim her mouth.

Repeatedly.

What starts as sweet and doting quickly turns passionate as hell.

I'm beginning to wonder if I'll ever get enough of her. I've already had her twice today. I swear, I've never been this achingly desperate for a woman before. It's like I can't get enough of making her come, hearing her scream my name, and feeling her dig her nails into my skin.

She ends up sitting on the dresser with her legs spread, one thigh on each side of my hips. One hand is holding the small of her back, and the other is dipped into her panties, my fingertips furiously working over her clit. She sucks on my earlobe while panting shallow and sultry breaths in my ear. Her hips buck against my hand. As her climax overtakes her, she arches her back and yells my name while pressing her tits into my chest.

Perfection.

With her cheeks rosy, she tries to reach into my pants to repay the favor, but I cut her off at the wrist and jerk away from her grasp.

"Don't you need me to..." she trails off, raising her eyebrows in question.

"No, darling. Not right now. You can owe me one."

I honestly don't know if I can go again right now. We've had a lot of sex. Not complaining in the slightest — but I think delaying the gratification might be in order. I'm thirty-five, not eighteen, and a man can only expel so many fluids in a given period.

A half hour later, we're pulling into a parking lot at the Publix grocery store in town. There's a Chinese food restaurant next door — just like there is at every self-respecting grocery store plaza in Florida. We decide to pop in to order takeout to pick up after our shopping is done.

As much as I'd like to take her out for a nice dinner instead, we can't risk that much exposure. This needs to be a quick trip. Something just feels *off* today, and I've learned to trust my gut. Big Al's text warning hangs ominously too.

We make quick work of the grocery shopping, hurriedly throwing items into the shopping cart and checking out all within fifteen minutes. We even manage to avoid brawling in the checkout lane.

After loading the groceries into the back of the SUV, we head to the restaurant to grab our takeout order. When we're waiting for our number to be called, my phone starts chiming one rapid-fire blast after another.

My hackles rise instantly — I knew something was wrong.

Without delay, I push Sue to the side of the restaurant where I can block her from the door with my body. My hand goes to my gun as my instincts take over. I scan the area for threats, eyes sharp and head on a swivel.

Everything seems to be calm around us, minus the clatter of dishes and the hiss of the fryers and woks from the partially open kitchen to my left.

"What's the matter?" Sue asks, panic in her tone. Her arms reach out and squeeze my biceps.

With everything seemingly safe around us, I pull out my phone and quickly scan through the text messages while keeping one hand on my sidearm. I've got a long text from Big Al followed by several images from Klein — another one of my Redleg counterparts.

Big Al: Threat level increasing to yellow — initiate lockdown. We show a signal 30 at your residence. I called 911 and sent Klein to investigate since he was in the area. Definite signal 21 B&E - damage pics incoming from Klein. Looks like the tango was searching for something. Sending Shep to you for extra protection.

Big Al: I'm sorry, man. We're handling your place on this end but take extra precautions out there. Confirm status req.

Fuck.

Dammit. It seems this fucker stepped up his game, breaking into my home.

All Redleg personnel's homes are outfitted with home security systems monitored by Redleg — a proprietary program designed by Tomer and Klein. Real high-end shit that is tough as hell to bypass, even for experienced hackers and criminals.

If I don't confirm we're okay like Boss requested, he'll start calling or perhaps even send local law enforcement to my location — which I know he can track with the GPS tracker in the SUV.

Me: 10-4. We are in town but heading to cabin now. Will call when secure.

After a few swipes of my thumb, I pocket my phone — not looking at the photos. That can wait until we're safely back at the cabin in lockdown.

Right as I'm about to whisk Sue out of here — leaving our takeout behind — our number is called. Sue looks to me for instruction. I nod, and we move together as a unit to the counter to get the food.

"We need to leave quickly. Do you mind getting those? Normally I'd carry those for us, angel, but I want my hands free while I get us to the car."

She nods and grabs the food. It's only two bags, and she's a capable woman, but the chivalrous side of me still feels like an ass as we hustle to the car with her hands full and mine empty.

Once we're safely in the car and leaving the parking lot, she breaks the tense silence. "What did the text say? What's going on?"

Raising my finger to indicate I need a moment to think, I check the rearview and side mirrors to start mentally cataloging the cars behind us.

Red Toyota, black Jeep, silver Cadillac, yellow VW Bug, blue Chevy S10.

I turn at the first stoplight to see who follows. She waits patiently, but out of the corner of my eye, I can see her fingertips tapping against her thumb in the pattern she does when she's upset.

"It's okay, angel. Let me make sure we aren't being followed, and then I can explain."

I'm trying to reassure her without giving a false sense of safety. Reaching over, I pull her hand over to my lap so I can offer her the smallest measure of comfort.

Red Toyota, black Jeep, blue Chevy S10.

Her other hand resumes the fingertip tapping, and she takes a few calming breaths. "Okay," she whispers.

I make a quick series of turns to return us to our original route, feeling confident that we aren't being followed.

My pulse slowly returns to normal, and my teeth unclench, but I remain hypervigilant.

"All right. No one is trailing us. We're in the clear."

She heaves a shaky sigh. "Okay. Good. So, what happened?"

"Big Al texted with a signal thirty." I catch myself using codes, shake my head, and adjust fire to speak in layman's terms. "An alarm was set off at my house. They sent Klein to investigate, and he confirmed my house had been ransacked. He sent pics of the scene, but I haven't looked at them yet. Boss wants us to get back to the cabin and lock it down. I'll look at the pics once we're secure."

"Jaysus!" Her jaw falls slack, and she sinks deep into her seat, almost like she's trying to hide.

"Yeah, looks like shit's getting real. But we got this. You're going to be fine. I'm not going to let anyone hurt you. Ever."

"I know you won't. Leo, I... I..." she trails off with a quick shake of her head.

I imagine she's got a lot of things racing through her mind right now, and it's not the time to push her to talk.

A few minutes later, and seemingly out of the blue, she asks, "Leo, the other day when we were talking, I felt like you were hiding something. Remember when you said you were afraid to speak it and put it out into the universe?"

"Yes." A lump forms in my throat at her reminder.

"This wasn't it, was it? Because if that happened, then maybe all that shit about speaking words into existence and my paranormal dreams are coming true. And in that case, I'm going to insist we leave the cabin so I don't end up tied on the floor and bleeding from my head like in my nightmares."

I offer a tight smile and a shake of my head. "No, angel. It was something else."

She shifts in her seat and lays her left cheek on the headrest, looking at me straight on. "Can you tell me what it was?"

I nod, then swallow down the discomfort choking me. "When I spoke with Big Al earlier in the day, he said something that made me think he's holding back intel from me. Like there's more going on than he's telling me."

"Like what?"

"I can't be sure, and it's just a hunch." Shrugging, I hope she drops it.

I don't want to explore these feelings and worries anymore. But they sit heavy in my heart and prick at the back of my mind.

"What makes you think that?"

I feel my face pinch, muscles tightening in my hand where it grips the steering wheel. "I had asked him to send Sawyer to us with groceries and supplies since I knew we were running low and didn't want to risk leaving. Big Al and Sawyer are the only people at Redleg who know my cabin's location. Boss said he sent Sawyer to look into something else, so he wasn't available for the food run."

"That could be anything, though," she offers.

"Yeah, but it was the way he said it, sweetheart." My face contorts to the side. "It felt like he was debating whether to give more details." My voice comes out soft and reticent.

"You think Sawyer is looking into something related to the case, but Big Al doesn't want you to know? Why would he hide something from you?"

"The only reason Big Al would lie to me or conceal the truth is to protect me. I suspect he's sending Sawyer to get all the facts before they tell me about it."

Or about *whom*, if not *it*. And that's the kicker for me.

There are only a handful of people Big Al might need to hide bad news about. One of them is with me in this car, and the others are my family — Redleg family and my blood family.

Despite my hesitancy to share my theory, I can admit it feels better to get it off my chest. The load has been lightened, and even my spine feels straighter.

We ride the rest of the way in silence, her hand tightly grasping mine while I stroke my thumb across her soft skin. We're both deep in thought.

Adrenaline shoots through my veins, ratcheting up my alertness level as we turn down the long driveway.

"Shepherd is coming to help guard you since the threat has escalated, but he probably won't be here for another hour. Let's get you inside and secure. Leave the groceries for now and stay right by my side."

I don't like the fact that someone else will learn the location of my cabin — especially with my suspicion that the culprit is someone close to me. But I have to trust Big Al's judgment. I have no reason to suspect Shep is involved in this clusterfuck. But still — the more people who know where we are, the more danger.

Sue nods in agreement with my instructions, showing more of that unquestionable faith she has in my ability to protect her. Every time I look at her, another wave of adoration hits me. She's so damn brave, even if she might want to crawl into a ball and hide from the world. And I love her for it.

My chest constricts as I realize now more than ever how *much* I fucking love this woman. And I'll do everything I can to protect her.

Chapter Thirty-One

Status report: All the feels

Sue

"When we get inside, I need you to stay right behind me while I do a quick sweep." Leo's tone is all business. Sexy as fuck too.

Not the time, hormones.

"But the alarms? Wouldn't you know if someone was inside the cabin?"

"In theory, yes. But I'm not taking any chances. No technology is infallible. Let's move."

Leo swiftly escorts me into the cabin, locking the door behind us. Somewhere along the line, he took out his gun. My throat tightens as I stare at it. I'm doing my best to hold it together, but I'd be a liar if I said I wasn't scared.

Together, we move quickly, going from room to room in the small cabin. He opens all the closets and looks under the bed and behind every door.

"All clear," he says as he puts the gun back in its holster.

My head lolls backward with relief. He takes me by the shoulders and smooths his hands up and down on the outside of my arms, comforting me.

"You okay, angel?"

My only response is a terse nod.

"We should bring in the groceries before everything spoils in the heat."

Again, all I can do is nod. If I speak, my voice will reveal how scared I am. As if sensing my worries, he wraps me in a firm embrace, surrounding me with his calming love.

"I've got you, babe."

"I know you do."

My fear recedes.

A few minutes later, he has me open and close the front door behind him while he deftly carries in the groceries and the Chinese food, grabbing it all in two trips. Impressive. Without speaking, we put everything away.

His phone rings a few minutes into our tense silence. He glances at the screen before answering.

"We're secure at the cabin. What's the status?"

He listens intently for a few minutes before speaking again. "Can you text me the photos? Maybe I'll recognize him."

I swallow around a newly formed lump in my throat. Somehow they got pictures of this dick-nosed prick.

"And the plates were the same too?" he asks, then quickly curses under his breath while running a hand through his hair.

He grows silent, and I continue piecing together what might be happening. But only hearing one side of the conversation makes it difficult.

His replies come in a clipped tone. "Send me the picture of the gray van too. I want to show Sue."

A few seconds pass by. Leo's eyes search the ceiling.

"No, nothing comes to mind that ties to the cabin."

He runs his free hand over his face.

"You trust Shep fully, right? You know how protective I am of this location."

He nods wordlessly, and I almost chuckle since I know Big Al can't see his nonverbal response.

"And what about my mom?"

Leo spins around and braces one strong arm on the counter. From my vantage point, I can see the tension set along the side of his face.

Oh, shit ass. I hope nothing happened to his mother. She's already had a rough life and sounds like such a sweet woman. She'd have to be to raise someone as loving and gentle as Leo.

"Any change on the whereabouts of my dad?" he asks, his voice suddenly taking on a steely quality.

Chills break out along my arms. His father is still alive? The way Leo referred to him, I assumed he was dead. But apparently, that isn't the case.

What if his dad is behind this? Did Leo take something away from him?

Leo's mother, maybe? Could she be the *thing* the perp wants back?

My heart speeds up as my mind recalls the profile I came up with about the person making these threats.

A narcissist who enjoys taunting those weaker than him to make himself feel more important.

Someone who knows Leo inside and out, believing without proof that Leo took this person or thing he covets so deeply.

An abusive father could certainly meet the criteria.

"All right. Talk soon."

He ends the call, then places the phone on the counter. Stretching out both arms taut on the counter, he hangs his head — either deep in thought or pain.

Leo always comforts me when my world goes to shit. Maybe I can do the same to him.

Inching up behind his large frame, I place the flat of my palm on his spine. My hand looks so small compared to the wide expanse of his shoulders and upper back. I rub my hand up and down his spine, feeling him lean back into my touch ever so slightly. That tiny gesture is all the encouragement I need.

Moving in close, I press my front to his back and wrap my arms around his middle. With my cheek leaning against his back, I hold him close and whisper comforting words — just like he would do to me.

"It's going to be okay, Leo."

With a shaky breath, he lifts his hands from the counter and places them on top of mine, where they rest around his waist. He laces his fingers through mine, and I try to infuse my fragile strength into my touch.

"Big Al is going to send me some pictures from my home surveillance system of the person who broke in."

"Okay. What else can you tell me?"

I don't want to assume he's going to tell me everything. As curious as I am, there are some things I might not want to know.

Leo turns in my arms until he's facing me. Placing his palms on my cheeks, he bends down to give me a gentle kiss. When he pulls back, he's wearing a face of disbelief.

"What?"

"You," he answers plainly, as if that one word explains anything.

"Me? Me what?"

"You're so fucking amazing. All this is happening to you and around you, and still... you've never once demanded I tell you everything or second-guessed my judgment." He shakes his head repeatedly, still cupping my cheeks between his warm, large hands. "I don't know what I did to deserve you, Sue. But I'm going to work every day to be the man you deserve. I love you so damn much."

Oh, my heart. This man.

I feel my chin quivering as tears prick the back of my eyes. "Leo, I love you too. So much."

"You do? Even after I hurt you?"

Unable to say anything else, I simply nod my response.

With a tight pinch in his eyes and a furrowed brow, he looks pensive, shaking his head at me.

I can understand the doubt he seems to be feeling. At one point, I didn't think I'd be able to forgive him either. Even after he apologized, explained, and made a promise to never do it again, I was still leery about trusting him with my heart.

What made me believe him, more than the sound logic of his explanation, were his actions. Leo made himself vulnerable in front of me, not only telling me how he felt, but by showing it. By sharing about his childhood, he showed how much he values me. He cherishes me — not just my body, but my mind and soul too. He treats me like a partner, not a child. He doesn't merely understand my quirks and eccentricities, he celebrates them. I've never felt more beautiful and more whole than I do with him. I can drop my mask and be my true self — something I can't even do around my closest family members.

I know he hurt me once, but I absolutely believe him when he says he'll never do it again.

I believe him, and it's truly as simple as that.

He kisses me again, this time long and deep. It's the toe-curling kind of kiss. The type of kiss people write love songs and poetry about.

When we come up for air, he gently lays my head on the wide plane of his chest and pats my hair down. I bask in the warmth of the moment, despite the circumstances surrounding his proclamation of love and the looming threat hanging over our heads.

Damn you, broccoli

With no immediate danger at our door, we take a break from the drama to eat. While we dine on lukewarm chow mein, Leo looks over the photos he received. He transferred them to his tablet so he can have a better view with higher resolution images.

He slides the tablet over to me. "Is this the same van you saw following you last week?"

Narrowing my eyes, I quickly nod. "Absolutely."

Apparently, I never forget a name, face, *or* gray van.

"That's what I figured. The asshole who broke into my place was driving this van. At least we've been looking in the right place trying to find out who he is."

He taps the screen and brings up another series of images. "This is the man who broke in and ransacked everything. Do you recognize him?"

"No, I don't. Not that we get a good view with the pullover and hat."

"Yeah, he didn't leave any prints behind either. Here... see the gloves." He points to a spot on the screen where you can see the bad guy's hands covered in black fabric.

"I guess we can call Millie and let her know the bad guy is indeed a bad *guy*," I toss out with a smirk, trying to bring a smile to his stoic face.

He cracks a minuscule grin, but it doesn't reach his eyes.

Tapping the screen, he brings up the next picture.

"Here he is again. It's a little better view, but he knew to keep his head down from the camera. He must have known where they were."

Shaking my head, I reply, "No. Still nothing. You?"

"It's not my father, that's for sure."

I nearly choke on a piece of broccoli with those words.

"You okay?" He pats my back as I sputter and gasp for air.

In my mad quest to suck in oxygen — a chemical element necessary to the survival of our species — I inhale the cursed vegetable instead, and it lodges solidly in my throat sideways, cutting off my airway.

Dropping my fork, I wrap my hands around my neck, making the international sign for choking.

Oh my hell. I'm going to die. And what a shit-tastic way to go.

I knew vegetables would kill me one day. Peanut butter would *never* do this to me.

Without missing a beat, Leo springs into action. He's behind me in the blink of an eye and lifting me from my chair. All the while, I'm frozen in panic — I don't think I've ever been this scared.

He raises my arms and braces his arms around my midsection, pressing one hand between my navel and sternum and cupping it with his other hand, getting us both into the familiar Heimlich maneuver position. He makes a short series of quick upward thrusting motions, but the damn death vegetable doesn't budge.

Unfortunately, something else in me does start to move, thanks to his ministrations.

My lower intestines.

After three more short thrusts under my ribcage, my stomach and bowels decide it's the perfect time to release gases. *Loudly.*

Why did I think a can of black beans was a good side dish to have with dinner last night?

With each additional press he makes into my upper abdomen, another wave of flatulence expels from my lower body. *Toot, toot, rooty toot, toot.* My ass sings its joyful chorus of humiliation.

Have you ever tried to clench your butt cheeks while you're choking? It's not as easy as one would think.

I think I'd rather die than have him continue to save me. If the broccoli doesn't kill me, embarrassment will surely take over to finish the job.

Eventually, Leo defeats the homicidal cruciferous killer, and it goes hurtling out of my mouth, knocking over my glass of water as it goes. It's like it wanted one last parting shot at me. Might as well have been waving its little broccoli middle finger on the way out of my body.

I inhale so fast and deep that the air stings my battered windpipe. With a few more deep surges of oxygen, my senses finally return.

Leo loosens his hold on me, and I collapse onto my chair.

"Baby, are you all right?"

I guess I'm not an angel anymore. Babies fart, but angels probably don't.

"Sue?" he asks again, shaking my shoulder lightly.

I nod but refuse to make eye contact. In fact, I may never open my eyes again.

While I focus on long, deep breaths, Leo proceeds to clean up the spilled water. He pours me another glass from the gallon-sized bottle of chilled drinking water in the fridge and sets it down in front of me.

"Thank you," I say.

Once he dries off his tablet and sits down opposite me, I decide it's best to be grateful I didn't shit myself. I'll just pretend it never happened.

"So the picture isn't your dad, huh?" I ask, my voice flat and monotone, like the last five minutes never happened.

He busts out laughing, his face immediately flashing bright red.

And to be clear, we aren't talking a girly giggle or a subtle snicker.

Oh no.

Leo's suffering from deep guffaws interspersed with silent, stabbing hysterics. He even adds a few smacks on the table while gasping for breath.

Did I say I love him? I was wrong. Turns out, I hate him.

His laughter must be infectious — someone alert the CDC — because the next thing you know, I've joined him, and we spend the next several minutes doubled over.

When he's finally able to speak, he says, "Angel, you have the cutest little farts."

"Oh, go fuck yourself," I toss back, but with no venom in my tone.

"Hey, is that any way to talk to the man who just saved your life?"

I put the back of my hand to my forehead and mockingly sigh, "My hero!"

Chapter Thirty-Two

We have a guest

Leo

After recovering from Sue's near-death experience, we finish our meal. Neither of us eats any more broccoli, though. Something tells me it will be years before she tries the stuff again.

As for me? I'll never *not* smile when I see it. Of course, that's not because it tried to kill her. It's forever branded into my mind because of the gut-busting few minutes following the incident. Pun intended.

We're rinsing off our dishes and silverware in the sink when she acknowledges the elephant that's been hanging out in the corner of the room. "Anything else you can share from your call with Big Al?"

Deep breath. Here we go. I sure as hell hope this doesn't upset her.

"Well, with your confirmation of the gray van, along with Tomer's photo comparison, we can safely assume it was the same guy who followed you, and we already ran those plates. No help there."

My shoulders rise as I try to remember what she already knows and what she doesn't so I can get her up to speed without overwhelming her with a data dump.

"As I was about to say before the broccoli attacked you." I pause for a quick smirk. "I was starting to suspect it might be my father."

"And your mother was the *she* he wanted back?"

"That was my working theory."

"Why?" she asks, handing me the dish towel.

I wipe them dry, then drape it over the edge of the sink. "Your psychological profile was partially the reason, but also a few other things were making me think that."

"Such as?" She mirrors my position, placing her back against the countertop, crossing her arms at her chest and legs at the ankles.

"You remember how I felt like Big Al was hiding something from me?" She nods, and I continue, "One of the few things he might hide from me would be news regarding my family — especially my dad. He knows about my childhood. And my mother is the only other female I could think of being the *thing*." I curl my fingers into air quotes around the word thing.

"And you're sure it wasn't him in the photos from your home surveillance?"

"Not unless he's gotten a few inches shorter and lost a ton of weight."

"I guess that rules him out," she surmises.

"Not entirely. There's always the chance he's hired someone to do his dirty work, although it doesn't seem like his style. Plus, Redleg hasn't been able to turn up anything we didn't already know about him. He's not on the move or anything. And Mom's not exactly in hiding — I couldn't get her a new identity or anything."

I did consider it, but I knew she wouldn't have gone for it. She didn't want to live a life in hiding, hence this cabin sitting empty most of the time.

"The way you spoke about your dad, I assumed he'd already shuffled off his mortal coil."

My lip quirks at her phrasing. "No, we aren't that lucky," I joke humorlessly. "He's very much still *of this earth* and living it up in Maine."

"Maine?"

"Yeah, that's where my family is from — we lived on the coast. I've always been near the ocean. I moved my mother down here to get her away from my father after my..."

I swallow the words, not wanting to bring up Sammy's death, then quickly shift topics before she can press me to explain. "My brother

Andrew and his wife stayed behind, and they see Dad around town on occasion. I know Dad's still up there."

"All right, so we don't think it's your father. Any other ideas?"

"Remember the other day when I mentioned my old Army buddy was trying to get a hold of me?" I scratch absently at my scruffy chin.

Her eyes go wide.

When I realize she's not going to answer, I continue, "The pictures weren't entirely clear, but it's possible..." I shift my weight, and my boots make a scuffing sound against the kitchen floor. My heart feels heavy to even think of my friend as a possible suspect. "Let's say the guy had a similar build to West."

She moves to stand in front of me and reaches her hand out to grab mine. With compassion thickening her voice, she asks, "Babe, do you really think it could be him? Your own friend?"

I shake my head, the thought making me queasy. "I don't think so, but let's face the facts here. It's probably someone I know. That doesn't leave that many people."

"Do you have anything of his?"

"Not that I know of, but he meets all the other criteria, with a side of addiction issues to boot. He's very manipulative and mentally unstable. He was pretty fucked up over things we did in Iraq and Afghanistan. Hasn't been the same since."

"Who else could it be? Maybe there's someone else? Let's talk it out."

"Angel, my life is pretty simple. There's West, my Redleg family, and my blood family. And now you. That's it."

"And yet you don't seem thrilled to have Shep coming out here. Isn't he part of your Redleg family?"

She's so fucking smart.

I lean forward to press a kiss on her forehead, wrapping her in my arms. Her warmth seeps through my clothes and thaws the frost around my heart as I think about who could be gunning for me.

"Shep is Redleg family, and he's fine. I just have trouble trusting people with this place."

"What's so special about it?" she asks. "Don't get me wrong, I love it here, but I heard you question whether Big Al trusted Shep to come here. Am I missing something?"

She's putting the pieces together quickly with only the bare bones of information — her mind is truly a marvel.

"This place is meant to stay hidden." I hesitate to tell her more but add, "I had the cabin outfitted like this for my mother. I wanted her to have a safe place to live where Dad couldn't find her if he came after her."

"Oh, Leo." She runs her hands up my arms. "Is that why you put a panic room in the closet? For your mother?"

"Yeah."

Fuck, getting this off my chest is rough, but I can feel more of that burden lifting. And as I search Sue's face for any signs of stress or panic, I find none.

"Aside from you and my mother, only Sawyer and Big Al know about this place. The two clients I hid here previously don't know where it is. That was part of the deal when I agreed to let them stay here."

After a brief cringe, she jokes, "I'm so glad you let me into your circle of trust."

"On the phone earlier, Big Al told me he made Shep sign a blood oath that he'd take this secret to the grave." I chuckle, mostly to myself. "It's funny because I said the same thing to..."

Oh, fuck!

No, no, no.

My muscles tighten as a memory hits me from out of nowhere. West and I were sitting on the front porch of the cabin. He was smoking those god-awful cigarettes. I'd just finished nursing him through a week-long detox.

"Said the same thing to whom?" Sue asks, pulling away from my chest and looking at me with worry etched in the laugh lines around her eyes.

"West. I brought him here to help him detox once. I forgot he knows about this place. Fuck."

How could I forget that?

Pressing myself fully upright, I start pacing while I run my hands through my hair, pulling it at the roots.

"Hey, Leo, listen to me." She sticks her arm out to stop me on my second pass. "We don't know it's West. You said you don't have anything of his. There isn't any reason to believe it's him."

"What about your profile?"

"Fuck my profile. I'm not a professional profiler. I was mostly talking out of my ass. It's probably not even someone you know."

I can tell she doesn't believe those words, but she's trying to calm me down and assuage my guilt. If I've put her in more danger by bringing her here instead of hiding out in Redleg or hunkering down somewhere else, I'll never forgive myself.

A shrill sound pierces the air, making us both jump. The perimeter alarm sounds from the tablet.

"We've got company," I tell her. "Let's hide you in the closet."

My phone rings at the same time as I start guiding her down the hallway. I answer while we move, holding the phone with one hand and keeping Sue's arm in my other.

"What?" I snap.

"Leo, it's Shep. I'm in your driveway. Don't shoot."

Pausing where we are in the office, I let my shoulders go slack with relief.

"It's Shep. He's here. That's what the alarm was," I tell Sue.

"Oh, thank St. Paddy!" she says, then promptly collapses on the couch in my office. The highs and lows of today are probably catching up to her. I feel exhausted too.

"Stay here, and I'll bring Shep in."

A few moments later, Shep and I are in the living room when Sue joins us.

"Hey, kiddo," he says to her.

She offers a shy wave. "Hey, Shep. How have you been?"

"Oh, I can't complain. You?"

"Fine." She comes to a rest at my side, planting herself ever so subtly behind me.

It's almost unnoticeable, but she did the same thing in the grocery store and Chinese food place. She's so comfortable around me that I'd almost forgotten how shy she gets around other people.

"Here's the latest," Shep says, capturing my attention. "Kri's en route to Sue's place in case the tango tries to hit there next. She'll stay hidden once she arrives, hoping to catch him off guard. Maybe he'll think whatever you took was stashed there."

Sue looks up at me, tugging on my shirt sleeve. "Is that safe? Leo, she could be in danger."

"Kri will be fine, angel. She's a highly trained operative and can defend herself." As long as her smart mouth doesn't get her in trouble first.

"If the bad guy is your *Army* buddy, I certainly hope she has more than a deck of playing cards and a cell phone to protect herself."

"What?" Shep asks, his brows drawn tight.

I laugh and ignore his question, responding to Sue while wrapping my arm over her shoulder. "She's carrying a weapon — perhaps even more than one — and will be fine. It's sweet how concerned you are, but you don't need to worry, angel."

Shep looks between Sue and me, eying the intimate way I'm holding her close to my side. "*Angel,* huh? Something going on here I need to know about?"

"Leo and I are in a sexual and emotional relationship," Sue answers flatly. Her filter is obviously malfunctioning.

"No shit?" Shep looks up at me with mouth agape, seemingly impressed.

I shrug but keep my mouth closed. At least she added the emotional tag to the description. I guess that about sums it up.

He shakes his head. "Okay then. Anyway... Big Al wants to know if you looked at the pictures Klein sent from your place yet."

"Oh, no. Not yet. I looked at the other ones from the security footage, but not the damage shots Klein sent. However, I transferred them to my tablet already. Let me get it."

I head to the kitchen to grab the tablet, returning in short order. A few taps, and I'm looking through the damage.

"Fuck," I hiss, surveying the damage.

"Oh, man. Leo, I'm so sorry," Sue says, looking on at my side. "Your house is trashed."

My lips draw tight as I scan through.

"It's only stuff. It can be replaced for the most part."

I meet Shep's gaze. "Why did Big Al need me to see this shit?"

"He wants to know if you see anything missing. He's also hoping you might see something there in the photos that could jog your memory. Remind you of anything we might have missed. There's got to be a reason the perp hit your place the way he did."

"Makes sense," I concede and walk over to the couch to sit. I'm going to study these photos as closely as possible. This could take some time.

"Shep, would you like something to eat or drink?" Sue offers.

"Water would be good," he responds.

Sue heads to the kitchen, but Shep sits down on the coffee table. He watches me as I flip through the images, occasionally stopping to zoom in on something that catches my eye.

Sue returns and hands him a glass of water, which he takes silently.

Like the true older brother I am, I swat him across the back of his head. "Manners, asshole!"

"Sorry," he says to me, then faces Sue. "Thanks for the water. That was very kind of you, ma'am." He cocks his brows high as he cuts his glance back at me. "That better?"

"Yes." I nod, then return to the photos.

Sue curls up beside me and looks on with me.

After a few minutes, she says, "Hang on. Leo, can I see that for a second?"

I hand the tablet to her, and she zooms in on something. Turning to Shep, I figure I can use the opportunity to pump him for info about whatever Big Al might be hiding.

"Anything going on with my mom?"

"Other than the call she got, everything has been fine. Henderson is there all the time and won't shut up about how sweet she's being to him. Spoiling him rotten."

He rambles on, but I put my hand out to stop him. "What call did my mom get?"

His face goes ashen, and his eyes flit from one side of the room to the other, avoiding my intense gaze.

"Shep, talk. What call did my mom get?"

"You didn't hear this from me," he starts.

I roll my eyes, then flick my hand in between us, urging him to cut the shit.

"Your mom got a call a few days ago. No one talking on the end of the line, just breathing."

"Breathing?" I ask.

"Yeah, but not like perverted deep breathing — just someone on the other end of the line afraid to talk."

"What happened next?"

"Henderson took the phone from her and demanded to know who was calling. A woman's voice was on the other end. Said something like, 'Who's this?' to which Henderson replied something like, 'Right back atcha.' There was some back and forth. The woman ended up hanging up without identifying herself or saying what she wanted. Tomer traced the call to an arcade down by the pier."

"The pier in Clearwater?"

"Yeah."

"And I assume they've pulled video footage?"

"We aren't rookies here, Lionheart." His northern accent comes out when he adds, "Of course they pulled the fucking video footage from the arcade. But I haven't heard what came of it yet. That's all I know."

"I knew Boss was hiding something from me. That fucker!"

Making a fist, I press it into my thigh and rise off the couch. I have to pace some of this anger out before it boils over.

As I'm marching back and forth, Sue silently keeps her gaze trained on the tablet. Shep comes over to stop me, putting a hand on my chest. I glance from his hand to him and back again. He lifts it immediately, catching my meaning.

Backing away with his hands raised, he tells me, "Listen, you know how Boss is. If he's hiding something from you, then you can bet your ass he has a damned good reason for it."

"Not helping, Shep."

"Well, that's all I got. You guys got any stuff to make a sandwich? I'm starving."

"Sue just offered you food a minute ago," I tell him, shaking my head at his antics.

"Well, it took a minute for my stomach to tell me what was up. Anyway... do you?"

I point him toward the kitchen. "Help yourself. I'm going to call Big Al."

"Leo, wait," Sue's worried voice stops me in my tracks, my thumb hovering right above the call button.

"I figured out where I've seen your cabin before, and you're not going to like it."

Chapter Thirty-Three

The unraveling

Sue

"Talk to me, angel," Leo says after taking two giant steps to join me on the couch.

My breaths start coming shallow and fast, and my heart rate spikes sharply. With my vision going hazy, I raise my right hand to stroke my neck while the fingertips of my left hand start tapping at the pad of my thumb in a sequential pattern.

Try to hold it together, Sue. You can do this. Leo's here. You're safe.

I steel myself and face Leo. "Picture," I manage to choke out, but it sounds a little garbled, like I'm choking on my tongue.

He pulls my hand from my throat and threads his fingers with mine. "What about the picture? Angel, I need you to calm down and talk to me. Tell me about the picture."

We're not safe here.

We need to leave.

He's going to find us.

We're not safe.
Must leave now.
He has the picture.
He's going to know where we are.

I can't seem to get the words out, though. They just swirl around my head in a flurry.

My stomach wretches violently as the growing sense of panic rises, probably even more so due to my inability to tell Leo what he needs to know to keep us all safe. My vocal cords aren't fecking working!

"Breathe, angel. Listen to the sound of my voice." Leo's tone is calming, like a balm to my soul, and luckily, I'm able to follow his directives. "That's it, angel. I'm right here. You're safe. Just breathe."

I muster my courage with all my strength, heap it in with everything I've learned from Jaynie, and channel it all into forcing myself to ground, clearing my head. With Leo beside me, whispering those reassuring words, my vision clears, and my breathing slows enough that I can speak.

I put the tablet in Leo's free hand and jab my finger at the screen. "Look at this picture. Here."

He studies the photo silently while I focus on steadying my breathing. *In one, two, three. Out one, two, three.* My shoulders roll back with a tinge of pride at how quickly I was able to pull my shit together and get this out.

"I'm not seeing it. Tell me what I'm missing, angel."

With a shaky voice, I force out a better explanation. "See here? There's a space on the wall with a dust outline around it where a framed picture was hanging. You can even see the hole in the wall from the hanging screw."

His lips form a hard line. "I keep a lot of framed photos on my walls, angel. I'm not sure which one was in that spot. Could be me with my Ranger unit. Graduating from Ranger school, maybe? There's a few with Big Al and my Redleg team. One from when we opened up the new Redleg Headquarters. Some of my family. My brother's wedding photos. I don't know. I have a lot of pictures."

Yanking the tablet from him, I deftly swipe a few more photos ahead in the reel. I zoom in on an empty frame lying on the floor of his room in a pile of Leo's trashed belongings. "It was this one, wasn't it?"

"It might be," he answers. "I'm not sure."

"Well, I *am* sure. Autistic brain, remember?" My voice grows stronger and more confident with each word.

He raises his brows at me, and the corner of his mouth quivers like he's holding back a grin. I probably shouldn't be joking at a time like this, but if we can't laugh at ourselves, we're no better than the animals.

"How do you even know that, Sue?"

"You brought me to your house back in the spring when you were guarding me and wouldn't let anyone else come on shift. One evening, we stopped by to get a change of clothing for you, and I lingered in the hallway while you puttered around your house. I remember looking at the photos on the wall. *This* wall."

My finger points at the empty wall in the first photo, then swipes back to the other shot containing the discarded picture frame. "And this frame right here held a picture of you and another man standing out in front of this cabin. He had brown hair and was about a foot shorter than you. A wiry, thin frame."

"Angel..." he trails off, staring at the picture as if he's trying to validate what I'm saying.

Finally, he concedes. "Dammit. You're right. It was West and me that time I brought him out here to detox. He wanted a picture of himself clean and sober before we left. He used the timer setting on his phone to take the camera after placing it on the hood of my car so we could both be in the picture."

"Don't you see, Leo? That's why I associated this place with you. It's just like Jaynie said! My nightmares weren't a premonition after all, and the constant painting of the cabin was just a way for my mind to cope with missing you and process all the fear I had due to Millie's stalker. It all makes sense now. I must have blocked out my memory of this photo until now, but my damn subconscious gripped onto it and held on for dear life."

The relief I feel at this revelation is enough to make me lighter than air. I'm surprised I don't levitate right off this couch like a helium-filled *Sue balloon.*

I can tell the instant Leo catches the implication. His facial muscles tighten, and his eyes pinch tight.

"Shit. And now the fucker has this picture. The frame is empty because he took it. He must have figured out where we're hiding."

"Exactly. Why would someone take that picture unless he needed to use it to find this place?"

Shep breaks in, interrupting my back and forth with Leo. "This is really cool and all, but would either of you like to tell me what this means in terms of your safety? Do we need to leave or take up arms?"

Leo grabs his cell phone and calls Big Al, putting it on speakerphone so Shep can hear the conversation. Me too, I suppose. Looks like he's done hiding things from me since I've proven I can handle it. Another shot of pride fills my joy well.

Big Al's deep voice comes through after two short rings. "Status."

Leo sets the phone on the coffee table. "Safe and secure for now.

Shep is here with us. You're on speaker. Listen, we looked at the pictures you guys sent, and Sue made an interesting discovery."

He explains the connection between the empty frame and the photo of the cabin with West, making it clear that the perp might be aware of our location, or at a minimum, has a picture he can run against public records or reverse image search to find us.

"Did you guys get a twenty on West yet?" Leo asks.

I've watched enough cop shows to know that twenty means location. Leo's asking if they've found West. The request makes it sound like he's missing, but didn't Leo say West was trying to get a hold of him the other day?

"No, but I'll bump him up to the top of our suspect list. Did you ever bug his phone or put any trackers on his person or vehicle?"

Leo and Shep meet eyes, both of them shaking their heads.

"No, Boss," Leo says, sounding sarcastic. "I don't make a point of tracking my friends' locations." Under his breath, he mutters, "Sick fuck."

I'm taken aback at how he'd refer to Big Al. He's always speaking so highly of the man. But the grin on his face and the twinkle in Shep's eye leads me to believe he means it in jest.

I think.

People are so fecking weird.

"It's getting pretty late, so I don't think it's safe for you guys to move tonight. There's a lot of woods out there and windy fucking roads where shit could go haywire. Hunker down for the night, taking shifts to guard. Leave at first light. I'll find another safe house for you to hole up. In the meantime, I'll put all my resources into tracking down West since you think it's him. Although, I'm still not entirely convinced."

Leo mashes his lips into a tight line but doesn't reply. He probably wants to leave now, knowing him. I'm with him on *team-let's-fucking-leave-right-now*. He's also probably gutted over his friend being a prime suspect. My poor, sweet, gentle giant.

"Any news from Kri?" Shep asks Big Al.

"She's on her way to Sue's. I expect a report any minute," he responds, all business in his tone.

"What's this shit about a call my mom got the other day that Henderson intercepted?" Leo asks while giving Shep a seriously scorching glare.

Oh, baby. That glare is hot.

Not now, hormones.

"Shep, your ass is grass, and I'm a weed whacker," Big Al says with a coltish lilt to his voice.

"Sorry, Boss. He tortured it out of me. He knew you were hiding something, and Lionheart is a big fucker." Despite the heaviness of the words coming from his mouth, his smile is pure sarcasm, and the glint in his eye screams cheeky bastard — and I should know. I have five male siblings just like him.

A haggard exhale reverberates from the speaker. I've only seen Big Al a few times, but I can almost picture the handsome older man looking flustered, having been caught hiding something from Leo.

"We're still looking into that lead. I sent Sawyer to investigate."

"How long does it take to get to the damn pier and follow a lead like that?" Leo's fists clench and release where they rest on his meaty thighs. I place my hand on his to offer some support.

"He's run into a complication or two."

"Explain, Boss," Leo demands.

"Hang on a second. My other line is ringing."

And he's gone.

Leo grabs the phone off the coffee table to confirm. "Fuck! He hung up." Leo drops the phone to the coffee table, and it clatters before falling to the floor. I pick it up and gently set it back.

"You don't know anything else about my mom's call or what Sawyer's found?" Leo asks Shep.

"Big Al has kept it very close to his vest. Whatever it is, it seems big."

"That doesn't fucking help, Shep." Leo rarely yells, so his booming voice makes me flinch. He squeezes my hand immediately, which I interpret as a nonverbal apology.

Shep has a sheepish grin on his face as he shrugs his shoulders. "Sorry." He reminds me of my trouble-making brother Callum right now. "So, if we're not leaving, then how about that sandwich?"

Leo pulls a pillow off the couch and slaps it across Shep's face.

I rise to make him a sandwich to shut him up but turn to face the men before leaving the room. "Play nice, you two. Don't make me separate you."

"Yes, ma'am," Shep answers with a joking salute. "I like her for you," I hear him tell Leo while I saunter off.

A smile spreads slowly across my face at getting the vote of approval from one of Leo's Redleg family members.

I wonder what my family will say about Leo for me. Nick and Millie will be all for it, I'm sure. Fiona too. The other brothers are more of a toss-up. Time will tell how that plays out.

A few minutes later, I return to the living room with a ham and cheese sandwich on a paper plate — nothing but the best for our sarcastic guest.

"Thank you," he says as he takes the plate from me, then raises his brows at Leo pointedly. I read the expression as him saying: *I remembered to use manners this time like a good boy.*

As I sit down beside Leo, I ask, "What happens now?"

"Boss thinks we should stay, but I'm not so sure. Why don't you pack your bag, angel? If we need to leave, I want to be able to do it quickly."

No objection here. So I head to the bedroom to throw my crap in my bag. I decide to leave my paint supplies here — it's too much to bother with right now. We can always return for them after this drama is over. My medication, toiletries, and remaining clean clothes will have to do for a quick departure. I'm done packing in three minutes flat.

When I return, both men are standing, wearing tense expressions and body posture. Shep's half-eaten sandwich is on the coffee table. Leo's face is pained, his hair messed from pulling at the roots, and he seems to be dealing with some inner turmoil I'm not privy to.

"What's wrong now?" I ask, my hands flopping to my sides.

I fucking give up. This night — and I say this respectfully — can kiss my fat white ass. First, the lukewarm Chinese food that tried to kill me, the ill-timed gas attack, and now all this crap. D-O-N-E. I'm done!

"Big Al heard back from Kri," Shep says.

Leo steps closer to me, grabbing me by the arms like he's about to deliver some bad news. *Great.*

"And?" I ask.

"Angel, your house was hit too."

My eye starts to twitch. Not with sadness or tears but with irritation. My cup of fucks has officially been depleted.

Without any vocal inflection, I ask, "Do we know if he was there before or after he hit your house?"

Leo eyes me carefully. He's probably either afraid I'm going to snap or wondering why I haven't yet.

"We don't know yet. No alarm on your property, so we don't know the time of the break-in. Why?"

"It might not matter, but it could," I reply, my jumbled thoughts quickly falling into place.

"How so?" Shep asks, stepping closer to us.

My eyes shift from his to Leo's. "When he got to my house, he'd have seen the cabin again. So it could reinforce his assumption that we're here."

Leo's head tilts to the side in apparent confusion, so I explain. "Babe, I've been painting this cabin for six months. My art studio is *filled* with painted canvases and sketches of this place. There's even a mural of it spanning an entire wall. If he saw it there — which I'm sure he did — then went to your house..."

Leo finishes my sentence, "Then the framed picture on the wall at my house would have confirmed his suspicion that this place was important to us. If it's West, he'll be here any minute. If it's not him, then as soon as the perp finds a picture of the cabin on the Property Appraiser's website or any of another dozen online sources, he'll have our location."

"Yep," I say, popping the p sound and still feeling unnaturally chill.

Leo looks from me to Shep and announces matter-of-factly, "We're leaving now. I want to be on the road in two minutes."

Chapter Thirty-Four

The secrets we keep

Leo

I hang up the cell phone and slide it into my pocket. Facing Shep and Sue, I relay what Big Al said.

"Boss ordered us to stay put. Says he and Sawyer are on the way here to provide backup."

Shep voices my own inner confusion. "Boss is leaving headquarters? What the actual fuck?"

"Is that a big deal or something?" Sue asks.

"He rarely — and I mean *rarely* — goes out in the field anymore. He's got a huge operation to oversee out of Redleg HQ. It was shocking enough that he helped us leave Nick and Millie's. Going on a protection detail is even more unheard of."

Sue's eyes flash wide. "Wow. Okay, I think it's safe to assume this is pretty damn serious." She turns to me. "Babe, what do you need me to do?"

My eyes blink a few times, a little shocked at how calm she's acting right now. I expected her to be in full-on hysterics when I told her about her place being broken into. But she's oddly chill about it.

"Nothing much we can do but wait," I tell her. "Keep your sneakers on, though. I want us to be ready to go at the drop of a hat."

"We're not wearing hats," she says flatly, missing my meaning.

Shep chuckles, and I want to punch him. I cut him a glare, which he notices and stops his mocking instantly.

Sue swats my arm playfully. "Gotcha!" she says. "I know the expression, Leo."

Her eye roll is what does me in, and a deep laugh erupts from my chest. It feels good to have a tension release, however fleeting it may be.

While we wait, Sue sits down with her sketch pad on the couch, and I give Shep a tour of the cabin — including my weapons selection and panic room.

"Maybe I should set up some of these heat sensors outside for us," he suggests when we're looking over my gear. I hadn't gone to that extreme yet, but I think maybe I should have.

"The problem with them is the wildlife out here. They go off all the damn time," I tell him.

"You can adjust the sensitivity, though."

"No shit, Sherlock. But there's a lot of fucking bears and deer out here. Even when only looking for large masses, they still go off constantly."

He chews on the inside of his cheek. "I still think it's worth it."

"Well, once the guys get here, you can knock yourself out."

We're seated back in the living room, and I'm laying out a mini-arsenal of weapons and ammo on the table. Shep and I start loading our tactical vests with ammo and supplies.

Shep checks his phone and relays the gist of a text he received from Henderson. "He wants me to tell you that your adorable Mom is fine and to stop worrying."

"He knows me so well," I say flippantly.

I've been worried sick about her these past few days. If someone wanted to hurt me — which they clearly do — it's odd they haven't gone after her. And yet again, I find myself regretting not bringing her out here to hide out with us.

But if I had, Sue and I wouldn't be at the place we are in our relationship. As I give her a sidelong glance, I can't regret how things have unfolded. Mom is safe, and my angel is safe. And she's mine — as she should be — and I'm hers.

Minutes later, out of the blue, Shep asks me, "Have you checked in on your brother lately?"

My heart pinches with a twinge of guilt. Andrew and I aren't on the best terms over how things went down after Sammy died. He blames me and rightly so.

"Boss told me he's checked with him a few times this week to get a twenty on my father. All seems fine up there."

"Is there any reason to think that he..." Shep trails off, eyes downcast. He doesn't want to finish that sentence.

"Andrew isn't capable of something like this, and there isn't a damn thing I have that he wants."

"Is anyone watching your sister?" Sue asks.

Shep cuts a hard glare at her, and my hackles rise in her defense. It's not her fault she doesn't know.

When she notices my prolonged silence and the reproachful look Shep is giving her, she goes on the defense. "What? You guys keep talking about his brother and mother, but what about his sister? Why isn't anyone checking on her? Is she safe?"

"You didn't tell her about Sammy?" Shep asks me.

"Tell me what?" Sue's voice grows unsure as she turns to me, placing a hand on my arm to still my movements. I drop the knife I was about to sheathe. "Leo, please tell me. What don't I know about your sister?"

The pinch I felt in my heart when Shep asked about my brother turns into an all-out stabbing pain when I think about Sammy.

"I think I'll go do a quick perimeter sweep while you guys talk," Shep quietly says before making his exit.

Sue sets her sketch pad on the table and adjusts on the couch to face me, placing her hands in her lap. "Whenever you're ready."

A sad smile lifts a corner of my mouth. She's so damn sweet.

"I don't talk about this often, and I probably should have told you already."

"It's okay. You can tell me now." She reaches out to take my hand, entwining our fingers. Her warm, soft skin soothes me.

With a somber voice, I speak the words no one ever wants to say. Ever.

"My sister committed suicide a few years ago."

Sue's free hand lifts to cover her mouth as a gasp escapes her lips.

"You know how they say children of abusive parents often grow up and find partners who are a lot like their abusers?"

"Yes," she answers meekly.

"Well, Sammy went out and found the biggest fucking dirtbag she possibly could. He was a monster, but she hid the abuse from Mom, Drew, and me."

I swallow a tight lump, then continue, "This all happened a year or so after I got out of the Army. When I got back to Maine, I wanted to catch up with her and Drew, so we spent a lot of time together. At first, things seemed fine. She was glad to hang out with Drew and me — family dinners, going to the movies, and stuff like that. But then her behavior changed drastically when she started dating him. Craig Banks. Some douche executive she met at the software company where she worked. Next thing you know, she's withdrawing from the family, not taking our calls, blowing off plans, and shit like that. Classic signs of being in a controlling relationship."

"Then what happened?"

"I confronted her about it as soon as I recognized the pattern of behavior. She denied everything, accused me of projecting our childhood trauma on her and Craig. After that, I started getting extremely protective of her, and I can admit I went overboard with my hovering. It made her resist even more — she really dug in her heels, stubborn as hell and determined to convince me that Craig was nothing like our father. But I knew from the first time I met him he wasn't on the up and up. It was how he looked at her, some of the shit he said, and how she acted around him. She quickly became a shell of her normal self."

It still hurts to recall how she changed in such a short amount of time.

"We'd all spent so much time trying to crawl out from our shared trauma — healing and finding strength in our bond as siblings. Then, Craig fucking Banks came along and destroyed all the progress she'd made."

"That's awful," Sue says, giving my hand a reassuring squeeze.

"They moved in together and started talking about getting married. I was getting ready to relocate with Mom to Clearwater and work with Big Al. At that point, Mom had left Dad, but he was hounding her. I wanted to get her far away from him. One day, I showed up unexpectedly at Sammy and Craig's place. I was planning on convincing her to move down here with us. She wouldn't let me inside and only talked to me through a crack in the front door with her face partially hidden. I shoved my way inside, and she had a huge black eye."

Sue puts her chin down, shaking her head softly.

"The shitbag wasn't home, or else I probably would've killed him right then and there. Consequences be damned."

"No one would blame you."

"Sammy would have. She's the only reason I didn't go after him. She begged me and told me she'd leave him if I just let her do it on her terms. I didn't believe her since I'd heard that from my mother my entire life. We had it out, and I said some shit I shouldn't have — telling Sammy she was acting just like Mom when she'd defend our father and make excuses... always promising to leave him soon."

Sue scoots close and puts her arm around me, running her hand up and down my spine. "Oh, babe. It's not your fault."

"Her note..." I choke on my words, my vision blurring with my pooling tears. "It said I'd smothered her too much, made her feel like a failure, and drove her to it. She never wanted to see the look in my eyes she saw that day. It sickened her, making her feel like she wasn't worth the air in her lungs."

I hear Sue gasp. The pain I felt back then stings as much as a fresh burn. As my tears fall freely, her grip on me tightens.

Fuck, I miss my sister so damn much.

"Leo, it wasn't your fault," Sue says in a feeble attempt to release me from my guilt. "She was angry and hurt from a lifetime of abuse. Instead of blaming her abusers, she turned it on you, but it was *not* your fault. I hope you fecking know that."

I pull her onto my lap and bury my face in her neck, inhaling her soft strawberry scent. She peppers kisses on the side of my face and head, holding me close to her with all her might.

We stay wrapped up in each other for so long I lose track of time. It's a different experience for Sue to be the one providing the comfort. It gives me even more faith in my future with her. I feel safe enough with her to be vulnerable and let down my guard. It's freeing to love someone this much.

My tears subside, and she brings her head back to look at me, right in my eyes.

I cover her hands with my own, where they rest, cupping my cheeks. She brings her lips to mine and seals our mouths in a healing kiss. Relief overwhelms me. I didn't realize it, but I was scared Sue would see me differently. That's why I held this part back from her. But the look of pure love and affection in her eyes is as true now as it ever was.

"I love you so much, Leo. You have such a big heart — which makes sense considering the size of your body." She cracks a quick grin, then sobers her expression. "I don't blame you for what you did, and I hope one day you can forgive yourself. I'm sure Sammy wouldn't want you to live with that guilt for the rest of your life."

"Thank you, angel. I love you too."

After a few more minutes, she asks, "What ever happened to Craig? Did you —"

"As much as I wanted to, I didn't kill him. In fact, I couldn't find him. He disappeared shortly after her death."

"He was probably ashamed to show his face or scared of you."

I nod solemnly, recalling the last time I saw him. "I still can't believe that fucker had the nerve to show up at her funeral. Mom told me if I went after him there and caused a scene, she'd never make banana bread again."

I can't stop the grin that tugs at my mouth at the memory. She'd never be able to disown me or threaten anything too severe like that — we're too close — but she knew she could withhold the banana bread.

"And so you stayed away from him that day?"

"Yeah, but I'm pretty sure he knew from the looks I was shooting in his direction if I ever saw him again, he was as good as dead."

"Good riddance."

Chapter Thirty-Five

Darkness

Sue

"Shep's been gone a while," I tell Leo a few minutes after the dust settled from his bombshell about his sister.

He gets up from the couch and peeks out the front window, scanning the darkness of the forest surrounding the cabin.

"He knew we needed time to talk. He's probably waiting for me to tell him it's safe to come back inside."

Sliding his phone from his pocket, he taps the screen, then puts it up to his ear. With two fingers spearing the vertical blinds open a crack, he keeps peering out to spot Shep.

My heart aches for this mountain of a man and all he's been through. This protective, kind, gentle man only wanted to protect his siblings and mother from the abuse they suffered for so long, even taking on extra beatings to protect his family. And then to lose his sister by her own hand — blaming himself, no less, because of words written in anger — has got to weigh unbearably heavily on his broad shoulders. No wonder

I sometimes notice a haunted look in his eyes when it comes to my safety. It also explains why he stepped up to guard me around the clock when we first met all those months ago, refusing to let anyone else cover for him.

I'm convinced that Leo and I are soul mates or share some mystical bond that science has yet to explain. And he knew it back then, which is why his protective instincts were always so overwhelmingly strong around me. He's been trying to atone for what happened with Sammy by protecting me with his own life.

I'll never know what I did to deserve this man, but I'm going to hold on to him with all I've got.

"Shep, you can come back in now."

A few seconds pass, and his voice raises slightly as he demands, "How many of them?" Another short pause before he snaps, "Double time it back here."

His solemn eyes meet mine. "You might need to try out that panic room, angel. You think you can do that? Are you scared of the dark?"

I rise from the couch while replying, "It's not my favorite thing, but I'll be fine." He cricks his finger at me, beckoning me to follow him.

"Shep is on his way back in. He said someone's tampered with my sensors."

My heart jumps into my throat. "Wouldn't your alarms have signaled if someone got close enough to mess with them?"

"I told you all technology is vulnerable to a hack, and West was our tech specialist in the Rangers — he used to disable enemy surveillance systems for us. Fuck! I can't believe he'd do this to me."

I don't have any words of wisdom for him, but I hate how all signs are pointing to his friend. I don't want to believe someone Leo trusted would try to hurt him like this.

And what does West want?

"I'm honestly not sure who we're dealing with or how many of them there are, but they must be here since the sensors were working when Shep got here earlier, and now they're smashed. They obviously have some skills." He's mostly muttering to himself at this point.

When we get to the closet in the office, my mouth goes dry at the thought of being shoved in that little cubby. I'm not *entirely* claustrophobic, but I'm also not terribly keen on small spaces.

"I'm going to need you to stay in here until Shep or I come for you, okay?"

I nod wordlessly, too stunned to speak.

He pops open the panic room door and ushers me inside. "Do you have your phone on you?"

Thankfully, I wore jean shorts today, and I have a pocket to hold my phone for a change, so I've had it on me all day. Reaching into my back pocket, I pull out the phone and show it to him.

"How much charge is left?"

"Plenty," I respond after checking the screen. Sixty-five percent battery remains.

"I hate that I have to hide you in here. I'm so sorry, angel."

"I'll be fine, but please be careful. I can't lose you."

He tucks a lock of hair behind my ear while looking at me with sad eyes. "You'll need to stay quiet in here; it's not soundproof. I want you to call 911 if you hear gunshots or have reason to believe we've been overpowered. You'll need to do it quietly, though, on the off chance they get inside the cabin. But you're totally safe in here. No one knows about this panic room except you, Shep, and my mom. Al and Sawyer don't even know about it."

"Does West?"

"No. I had no reason to show him."

The tension in my shoulders relaxes slightly with that news. "Thank St. Paddy!"

"Hold the phone and sit tight. Got it?"

Once again, a nod is all I can manage.

"I'm going to close you in here, and I want you to shine the light from your phone around so I can check to see if it's visible from the other side of the door."

He starts to close the door, but I put my hand out to stop it. "Don't leave me yet, okay?"

While nodding, he replies, "Let's test the light first. I won't leave your side yet. But we need to hurry."

With shaking hands, I fumble the phone around until I find the flashlight app and click it on as Leo pushes the door closed. Like I was instructed, I wave around the light in all directions.

"Are you shining the light?" he asks through the wall.

"Yes," I reply.

The door opens, and he's got a half smile on his face. "All clear out here. I couldn't see a thing. So you'll be fine to use it to keep some light in here if you need it."

I try to force a smile for his sake. He needs to be focused when he's out there playing GI Joe, not worried about me.

"I love you," he tells me, his voice barely a whisper.

Bending down, he presses a brief kiss on my trembling lips. All too soon, he's pulling back and shutting the door on me.

"I love you too," I tell the wall after he's gone, and I finally find my voice again.

I hear Leo and Shep talking, so that must mean he got back safely.
Thank goodness.
A few seconds later, a door closes — sounds like the front door.
And then it's only me with my darkness and silence.
Alone again.

Chapter Thirty-Six

Lights out

Leo

Shep returns with his hands full of smashed sensors he found on his perimeter walk.

Fuck my life.

The sensor monitoring software on my tablet never showed so much as a blip, and even now, it's not reporting any disturbance — it's obviously been tampered with.

I toggle over to my surveillance camera app and quickly scan the exterior cameras. It's time to upgrade these to better night vision lenses — the imagery isn't as clear as I'd like, and I can't see much of anything.

"With Sue safe, we need to go on the offensive instead of waiting to be smoked out," I tell him.

He nods in agreement. We quickly don our bulletproof vests, and I strap another knife to my leg. Shep adds some extra ammo to his belt. We each take a few smoke grenades and flashbangs in case we need to cause a distraction.

"Infrared goggles?" He takes them from me, a seemingly impressed look on his face.

"Yep."

He slides them on his head, and I do the same.

"Nice," he mutters with a hint of amusement in his tone.

"Big Al know you've got all this out here?"

"Are you complaining?" I ask, avoiding his question entirely.

"Not at all, Lionheart." He's got an impish grin — like always. "Let's take this fucker down!"

With our strategy decided, we're ready to roll. But like all the best-laid plans of mice and men, it's probably going to go tits up at some point, and we'll have to revert to the Army way — adapt, improvise, and overcome. It hasn't failed me yet.

After exiting the cabin from the front door, I immediately turn and lock the door behind me. If someone's determined to get in, they'll blow the locks — but the extra time it would take to do so could make all the difference in the world.

Shep and I stay low and move stealthily, sticking together like stink on shit. He's watching my six while I bound ahead.

When we aren't jumped as soon as we get outside — it's always a possibility — we take cover on the side of my SUV to regroup. Shep and I work in tandem like old pros — probably because we've been on hundreds of jobs together. None hit quite so close to home before, though.

Shep inches under the SUV to scan for the tango's heat signature on the other side of the vehicle. He's taking the north side of the property since there's no fucking way my big ass would fit under the vehicle. Meanwhile, I use my infrared goggles to search over the south side of the property.

After the preliminary scan of the property turns up nothing bigger than a squirrel and a boar, we meet back in position by the SUV. He gives me the hand signal for splitting up — him to the left and me to the right so we can circle the cabin and meet back here.

I'd prefer not to split up, but if we don't, it's easier for the combatant to evade us. For all we know, he could be wearing an infrared-blocking suit — a fabric that's been metallized to reduce the thermal imaging a camera or goggles like ours can detect. The holes around his eyes and mouth would look like nothing but small animals to us. Hell, it's what I'd be wearing for a job like this if I were him.

I hold up four fingers, lowering them one at a time until I get to one. Like ninjas in the night, we split up and sneak to opposite corners of the cabin. Standing on the northeast corner of the cabin with my back to the side of the front porch, I wait for him to take his position on the other side.

Once he's mirroring my pose, I hold up one hand and bend it to signal our advance. I poke my head around the corner of the cabin so I can check for anyone who might be lying in wait. I repeat the move a second time and feel confident enough to proceed.

Moving on the balls of my feet, I shuffle silently like a fucking gazelle. It's something I had to master over a long period of time, especially since I've got a body mass closer to a rhino than a gazelle.

It's a mixed bag of luck on my end — no one is shooting at me, but there are also no heat signatures of a trespasser. Approaching the back of the cabin, I prepare to stop on the corner to repeat the same process before advancing around the blind corner. My gut is heavy with dread, and my heart is pounding as adrenaline heats my veins, sharpening my senses.

When my feet come to a stop at the northwest corner of the cabin, I hear the unmistakable sound of gunfire. Twin pops in quick succession, followed by the grunt of someone in pain. Either Shep got hit or did the hitting.

Fuck.

The lake caused the gunshots to echo so much I'm unable to determine the source of the gunfire. My feet move swiftly toward Shep's position. When I turn the southwest corner of the cabin, Shep's on the ground, writhing in pain.

As I drop to my knees at his side, I scan the area for signs of the shooter but see nothing except darkness through the green tint of my lenses.

"Leo, watch your six," Shep chokes out, then sputters and coughs on the blood from his wound — looks like he got hit in the side of his neck. I glance behind me again, and there's still no sign of anyone.

I tear a large chunk of material from the bottom of Shep's shirt, wad it up, and press it to the side of his neck to help slow the bleeding. I take his hand and place it on the shirt. "Hold pressure here, buddy. You're going to be okay."

Not sure I believe my own words, but I say them anyway.

"Behind you," he says with wide eyes.

Before I can turn around, a thick arm comes around my neck and cuts off my airflow. One hand lifts to pry him off me while I stand, hoping he's not tall enough to maintain his grip. But he must be anticipating the move. He kicks the back of my knee, causing me to buckle, and shoves me back into the ground.

When I hit the dirt, his grip loosens enough for me to shake him off for the briefest of moments. I spin around with my fists blocking my face. He lands on top of me and has a black wool cap covering his face. He moves to choke me, but I land a punch on his nose, knocking him back for the briefest of seconds. When he pops back up like one of those inflatable clown punching bags I had as a kid, I grab his mask and yank it off.

My eyes bug wide, and I'm momentarily stunned.

What? How? Why?

He capitalizes on my shock. The last thing I see is the butt of a gun coming toward the side of my head. Stabbing pain shoots from my temple.

Then it's lights out.

Chapter Thirty-Seven

A woman's work is never done

Sue

"Nine-one-one. Is the nature of your emergency police, medical, or fire?"

"I don't know. There were gunshots outside, and my boyfriend is out there trying to protect me. He might have been shot," I whisper into the cell phone, heeding Leo's warning to be as quiet as possible. "We were in hiding out here because of some threats. He's a bodyguard with Redleg Security." I'm probably giving far too many details, but I can't seem to stop my mouth from flapping.

"What is your location?"

"I... I don't know. I'm hiding in a closet. We're at a cabin in the woods at Ocala National Forest. By Half Moon lake."

"What's your name?"

"Angelica Sue O'Malley, but everyone calls me Sue."

Ugh. Again with the oversharing.

"Sue, that's a very large lake. I'm going to need more details so we can find you. Do you have any other details about your location? A street? House number? Landmarks?"

"No, it's a lake and trees. That's about it. We took a long winding dirt road to get here. It's about twenty-five minutes from a Publix with a China Wok restaurant in the plaza."

She groans in annoyance, and I honestly can't blame her. I'm as useless as stormtrooper bullets right now.

"Is there any mail lying around that might have the address on it?"

"I'm not supposed to leave the closet. He told me to stay here until he comes back."

"Please hold while I try to get your location another way," the disembodied voice tells me, then the line goes silent.

Leo, please be okay. Please be okay. Please be okay.

There are no sounds while I wait except my shaky breaths and the loud thumps of my heartbeat. I keep praying Leo will come marching into the cabin any minute now and open the door with a big smile on his handsome face. But the more time goes by, the more my hopes plummet to the floor.

He would've already come for me if he was able, having expected that I'd heard the gunshots — he wouldn't want me to worry needlessly. Perhaps he or Shep was shot. And there were two gunshots. What if they were both hurt?

I close my eyes, tapping my toes and the fingertips of my free hand in a synchronous rhythmic pattern. Tears pool at the thought of Leo lying there, bleeding from a gunshot wound.

"Ma'am, the phone you're calling from doesn't seem to have GPS enabled. Can you go to your phone's settings and turn it on so we can try to pinpoint your location?"

"It's a special phone so we couldn't be tracked, but I can try."

The tears overflow and drip on my shirt one by one as the situation feels more and more hopeless. Wiping my eyes, I look at the screen of my cell, but more tears replace them as quickly as I dry them.

Maybe I can leave the panic room and find something to identify the address and come back before anyone gets inside. I haven't heard either door open yet. And there are no footsteps throughout the cabin.

After a few calming breaths, I wipe my eyes again. It's enough to see the settings and enable GPS.

"It's on now," I tell her.

"Good job, Sue. You're doing great. I'll try to track you the best I can, but cell reception out there isn't the best. If you have any way to get your location without putting yourself in more danger, please do it."

"All right."

After another achingly long few minutes go by, she's still unable to get closer than a quarter of a mile radius. Not only have my hopes been tossed on the floor now, they've been set on fire, and the ashes were thrown out to sea.

No one is coming to save me this time.

I'm going to have to do this myself.

"I'm going to look for something with the address on it," I tell her.

"If you think that's safe, go ahead. Keep the phone with you, though."

I place my ear to the back side of the hidden door, listening for any signs that someone is in the cabin. There are none.

Mustering every last ounce of courage, I unlock the door and slowly press open the door. All is clear in the office, so I quietly step out into the room. Leo must have turned the lights off in here when he left because it's pitch black. With the cell phone as my only light, I search frantically around the desk for any mail or paperwork that might have the address.

Finding a file, I quickly open it, unsure of what I'm looking for but hoping Leo had some type of important document with the address.

I'm out of places to look in the office, and I turn to eye the door leading to the hallway. I remember a fire safe box in the closet in the bedroom. That's got to have something important in it — maybe the deed to the cabin or something.

Fuck, I hope so.

"Anything yet?" I ask the operator with a voice barely audible.

"Nothing better, but I'll stay on the line with you. I've got a few patrol cars in the general vicinity. I'll have them blare sirens, and if you hear them approach, let me know so we can get them to you."

"Okay."

My ears are wide open, listening for even the slightest sound inside or outside the house. I'm too scared to peek out of the window in the office to see if anything is visible outside the cabin.

Right when I'm brave enough to leave the office to find the box in the bedroom closet, a loud banging sound comes from the living room. It sounds like someone attempting to kick down the door. Before I can react, two gunshots fire, blasting the door open.

"Honey, I'm home," a loud, deep voice roars.

My eyes slam shut on instinct, and I hunch down with my back to the wall.

A memory of the weapons closet fills my mind, and I force open my eyelids to see if Leo left the cabinet open. My gaze travels to the cabinet as I remember seeing a key inside — I bet it opens the weapons cabinet.

But can I get to the key, open the cabinet, get a weapon, and be ready to fight off this man without him noticing?

Not likely.

I mentally curse myself for not grabbing a weapon as soon as I got out of the panic room. Then again, Leo never taught me how to use a gun, so not a whole helluva lot of good it would have done to take one.

All I can do is hope the police find us, Leo is still alive and can fight, or some other miracle happens.

I'm waiting silently with my back to the wall when I hear a chilling voice calling out from the front room. "Where are you, honey? Come on out."

His voice reminds me of that creepy guy from a movie called *The Shining* that my brothers watched when I was a kid. They told me I couldn't watch it, but that made me want to see it even more. So I hid in the hallway, looking on without their knowledge. And now the scary scenes live rent free in my mind. I should've listened to them and stayed in my room.

Once again, fuck you, hindsight.

Chills run down my spine when the haunting voice yells again. "Babe, where are you? Now that I've found you, I'm here to take you home. You know how much it pisses me off when you hide. Don't make it harder on yourself than it has to be."

That's definitely *not* Leo, Shep, Big Al, or anyone else I want to see.

Whoever it is, he's obviously gotten past my gentle giant and his sarcastic sidekick.

Tears fill my eyes again, but I'm not going down without a fight. Although Leo didn't teach me how to use a gun, we spent hours preparing for a similar situation.

I can do this.

I'm not fucking going down without a fight.

Footsteps come down the hallway, getting closer to me. I force a few deep breaths as a plan takes shape in my mind's eye. My tears cease, and my mind clears like I'm channeling some inner Zen I didn't know I could. My hands are still trembling, and my pulse is going a million miles an hour, but I can't worry about that right now.

I slide the cell phone into my back pocket, rise to my feet, and put my hands up in surrender. Taking a nervous step into the hallway, I yell, "I'm here! I'm coming out. Don't shoot!"

The hallway light flips on, illuminating the tall, lean Caucasian man I've never seen before in my life. I don't forget faces — and I know without a doubt this is not Leo's friend from the picture.

I have no idea who this man is.

He's got a gun pointed in my direction, which he lowers halfway to the floor when he sees I'm coming out unarmed as promised.

"Hello there, Angelica Sue O'Malley." He cricks his head and adds,

"It's nice to finally meet you in person. While not the person I was hoping to see coming out, you'll do for now. Come here and keep your hands where I can see them."

My feet move slowly, like I've got cement bricks for shoes. This man screams danger. He's wearing dark clothes that look like some type of military tactical gear, dark black from head to toe. He's got the bulging dark eyes of a sociopath or a junkie, with dark circles under them. His skin is ashy and dirty, his dark hair greasy and shaggy. As I get about three feet from him, his foul stench wafts in my direction, and it's clearly been a while since he's seen a shower or a bar of soap. My lip curls, and my nose scrunches in disgust. Blood drips from his nose, which looks crooked, like it's broken.

Good. I hope Leo got a punch in.

Leo.

"Where's Leo? What did you do?"

A slimy smile plays at his lips. "He's going to be tied up for a while."

"Did you hurt him?"

My chest tightens, and my legs lock in place with an almost paralyzing fear.

My sweet Leo. Please be okay. Please be okay.

"Shut up, turn around, and put your hands behind your back," he orders.

I comply, not wanting to anger him.

With my hands at my back, he slips thick-feeling plastic around my wrists. I hear the familiar zip of a tightening zip tie, and I have to force myself to conceal my grin. He's just made a tactical mistake, and he has no idea.

Once he's got my hands tight at my rump, he spins me around and gets right in my face. He's shorter than Leo by a few inches, but he's still a large man. I remind myself of the hundreds of times I broke free from Leo's hold in practice.

I hope he wasn't taking it easy on me.

The adrenaline pumping through my veins gives me a laser-like focus. I know when the time comes, I'm throwing everything I've got at this guy.

"Where is she?" he seethes, sending drops of spit at my face.

Yuck.

I long to wipe my face, but without the use of my hands, I have to settle for twisting my head down to rub on the shoulder of my T-shirt.

Not wanting to see the crazed look in his eye, I stare at his chest while asking, "Who?"

"Don't play dumb with me, you fat bitch."

"I have no idea who you are or what you want. There's no one else here but me."

I notice one hand balling into a fist at his side while the other aims the gun at me.

"I know your dumb ape of a boyfriend has her. No one else could have gotten her away from me. Now talk."

Tears fill my eyes as terror overwhelms me. I can't break loose from the zip ties with him watching me, and I don't have the answers he wants.

"Oh, good. Fucking cry. Just like a woman. You're all the same. Here, I'll give you a reason to cry."

Without warning, he backhands me across the cheek. It stings, but I don't go down. He didn't put much into that one, clearly trying to make more of a point or scare me into giving him the info he's seeking.

"I don't know who you're talking about. If I did, I would tell you."

"Oh, we'll see about that."

He wraps his clammy hand around my upper arm, squeezing enough to leave a bruise, and drags me quickly down the hall and out the front door. When we go down the front steps, I almost trip, thanks to the concrete shoes I'm apparently still wearing. He pulls and manhandles me around to the side of the cabin.

When I see Leo and Shep lying deathly still, side by side with their hands bound at their backs, my heart splits in two.

A sob racks my chest. "Nooo!" I wail into the trees surrounded by inky night.

My feet ground to a halt. I'm terrified to move any closer for fear of seeing the love of my life lying in a pool of his own blood, or worse yet... dead.

Chapter Thirty-Eight

I see dead people

Sue

"Stay right there! That's close enough!" the man screams at me, then releases my arm while shoving me to the ground.

I fall to my knees, almost teetering over onto my face since I can't use my hands to break the fall.

This guy is such a fuck nugget.

He stomps a few more feet and hovers over Leo's prone form, a sight that will surely be front and center in my nightmares for years to come.

My voice is shaky, but I yell out, "Please, leave him alone. I'm begging you. Tell me who you're looking for, and I'll help you find her. Is it his mother? Someone else? Please, don't hurt him anymore."

"Leave her alone," Shep's frail voice rings out from where he lies on the ground.

Oh, thank goodness.

If Shep's still alive, then maybe Leo is too.

When I take a closer look at Shep, I can see he's bleeding from a neck wound. Probably one of the gunshots I heard. It's a miracle he's survived.

The man grabs Shep roughly by the back of the head, hefting him to his knees by the hair. Shep grunts in pain.

"This is what happens to people who lie to me and try to keep me from what's rightfully mine," he spits, then looks back at me.

"No one knows what you want, man," Shep tries, clearly in unspeakable pain.

"I promise, we have no idea who you're looking for. We've taken no one. There's been some mistake," I plead, but my words only seem to anger him.

"I want my fucking wife," he says with a voice thick with malice.

"Who the fuck is your wife, asshole?" Shep asks.

"Don't you dare fucking talk to me like that!" the man yells, then roughly shoves Shep into the ground by the head, practically folding him over in the process.

Since the fuck nugget isn't looking at me, I seize what might be my only opportunity to break free.

Leaning forward from the waist, I put myself in the position you'd use if you were about to throw up. I remember Leo using that visual to describe it for me. With one smooth motion, I raise my joined wrists toward the sky as far as my shoulders will allow, then slam them down with all my might, landing them on the upper part of my ass. It takes two quick thrusts, but the ties snap cleanly, freeing my hands.

Without wasting a second, I grab the cell phone from my back pocket and run full speed at our attacker. With a death grip on the cell phone, just like Leo showed me, I swing my arm and jab the phone into the side of his throat.

Clearly not expecting me, he falls to the side from the force of my attack, dropping his gun in the process. I kick it away, unsure of what to do next. For all my bluster and big plans, I didn't really think this through.

He coughs and sputters on the ground with his hands to his neck. I think I got the side of his Adam's apple, and I can only imagine that hurts like a bitch.

Leo's breathing but unconscious. Shep is still lucid, so I squat down beside him.

"Run, Sue. Get out of here. Get in the car and drive."

"I hate driving at night," I answer in an almost nonsensical fashion while I search in Shep's pockets for a knife to free his hands and legs.

A quick glance over my shoulder shows our assailant climbing up to his knees and still coughing, gasping for air.

"Where's your knife?"

"He took our weapons. Just run. *Now*. While you have the chance."

"I won't leave you guys," I say through my tears.

"Get his gun," Shep suggests.

He sounds weak. Probably the blood loss.

On my hands and knees, I scurry around the ground to find the gun I so foolishly kicked away. A hand grabs my foot, yanking me back.

Dammit. I had him. I fucking had him, and I blew it.

I try to kick him, but freeze in place when I hear the sharp, metallic click of his gun as a round enters the chamber.

"Don't fucking move, you bitch!"

Conceding defeat, I spin around with my hands up. He grabs me by the wrists, yanks me to my knees, and points the gun at me.

A deep voice comes out of nowhere. "If you fire that weapon or harm a hair on her head, there won't be a place on Earth you can hide from me."

Leo.

I don't even have time to send up a silent thanks to St. Paddy that Leo's alive before the sound of roaring engines, screeching tires, and the crunch of gravel breaks the silence following Leo's icy threat. Beaming headlights illuminate the darkness enveloping us.

The man moves behind me, grabbing me and wrapping his forearm tight around my neck. He points the gun at my temple while using me as a human shield. My chin lowers like Leo taught me, and instinctively, I try to pry myself free from his chokehold.

"Craig! Stop! I'm here!" a meek, feminine voice calls from somewhere around the front of the house.

Craig? Why is that name familiar? The lack of air from his tight grip on my neck is making it hard to think.

"Sammy? Is that you?" he yells, not paying any mind to how close his mouth is to my eardrum.

Rude.

And hold up.

Did he just say... Sammy? As in Leo's sister Sammy? How is that possible?

"Yes. I'm here. And I'll go with you right now as long as you leave them alone. They had nothing to do with this. I left on my own."

"Sammy?" Leo's voice cracks from somewhere behind me. I ache to turn around to see him, but I can't because I'm being choked by this asshole.

"No tricks?" the fuck nugget — who is apparently Craig, the abusive boyfriend — asks Leo's sister, who's very much still alive and standing ten feet away, inching closer by the second.

"No tricks," she replies.

"And it'll go back to how it was? Just you and me?" Craig asks her, a hint of hysteria in his tone.

Now that she's moved closer, I can make out the silhouette of her small, dainty frame, narrow waist, and medium-length hair, thanks to the blinding headlights behind her.

"I promise. We can leave right now. I have a car waiting to drive us to the airport. Let her go and come to me." She raises her hand toward him with her palm open.

"Sammy?" Leo asks again.

Along with Leo's pained voice, I hear the rustle of leaves against the ground behind me. He's probably struggling to get up.

Sammy's close enough now that I can see the tears in her eyes as she stares at her brother. Eyes that look so much like his that my heart aches even more.

"I'm so sorry, Leo," she says. Her voice is filled with so much sorrow I can feel it down to my core.

This poor woman. What has life done to her?

"You're alive?"

The sadness and disbelief in Leo's voice nearly break me. I need to go to him, comfort him and support him, like he'd do for me. But I can't because this fucking shit stain of a human still has a gun to my head.

"Yes, I'm alive. I'm so sorry for lying to you. I had to. And I have to do this too."

The rustling sounds grow louder as Leo's struggle to get upright likely increases.

Leo's sister comes to a stop in front of Craig and me, putting her hand on his arm. He complies with her request to release me. The gun lowers, and I collapse at their feet.

"Come on now. It's time to go," she tells him. Her voice is soft and gentle, reminding me of Leo, but also resembling someone trying to talk a jumper off a ledge.

I crawl to Leo's side and pull his head onto my lap as if I can offer some type of comfort or protection in case shit goes wrong. He's bleeding from the side of his forehead, and a large knot is swelling.

"Are you okay?" I ask him quietly, trying not to distract from whatever fucked-up reunion is happening between Craig and Sammy.

"She's alive," Leo tells me wistfully, tears pooling in his eyes.

"It looks like it," I answer with a sad smile.

My head turns to watch them walk toward the headlights. Sammy has Craig by the hand, leading him away.

Leo clears his throat and cranes his neck so he can watch her go. "She's sacrificing herself to save us."

"She's very brave, just like her brother."

We can't do anything but watch them leave. Two car doors slam closed, and the car drives away. When the taillights have disappeared, Shep's coughing distracts us from our sorrow.

"Oh my gosh. I need to cut you guys free and get you to a hospital."

"We'll take it from here, Sue," Big Al's booming voice comes out from behind us.

He comes over and uses a knife to cut the ties around Leo and Shep's wrists and ankles. A woman I've never seen before is beside Big Al. She sets a first aid kit on her knee and immediately goes to work on Shep's neck.

Damn. They're two minutes too late.

Chapter Thirty-Nine

'Tis but a scratch

Leo

The throbbing pain in my head must be making me hallucinate. Sammy couldn't possibly have been alive after all this time.

And why the fuck did Big Al and Kri just saunter up from behind us like they were watching the whole thing from the front row? Why didn't they intervene and take him out when they had the chance?

"We have to go after them, Boss. Give me your gun," I demand as soon as I'm on my feet.

My vision flashes in and out from the quick position change, but I shake off the haze and focus my eyes on my boss.

Must leave. Now. Must stop them.

Big Al narrows his eyes and *tsks* at me. "Lionheart, give me a fucking break. You know I don't give anyone my weapon — not even you. And sit back down already so we can check your head. I didn't bring my damn step ladder, and you might need stitches."

"Fuck the stitches!" I shout. "He's got Sammy. She's alive, and we need to stop them before they get to the airport. I'm not going to lose her again, dammit!"

He cocks his head at me and hits me with a look that has me seriously questioning my sanity. He must have seen what I did. Right? I couldn't have imagined this whole thing. How hard did Craig hit my head?

Fucking Craig Banks.

Must stop them. Must leave now.

After a few silent shakes of his smug face, Boss finally explains why he's not freaking the fuck out like me. "Leo, have you ever known me not to have a plan? And further... for my plan not to have a backup plan and then a secondary backup plan? Give me some fucking credit. Now, let's check that head."

"All I know is we're wasting time." Feeling my rage spike like never before, I do something I've never done.

I put my hands on Big Al in anger.

With my fists in his shirt, I lift him a few inches off the ground. "What the fuck is wrong with you?"

He doesn't even bat an eye or try to fight me. Just stares at me with a blank look on his face. "Are you done yet, Lionheart?"

Boiling with frustration, I set him down and spin on my heels. I double-time it toward the front of my cabin. With the fog of my concussion and the shock at seeing Sammy fading, I remember we're at my cabin, and I still have a few more weapons inside.

He halts my retreat when he announces, "Sawyer is hiding in the back seat of that car, armed to the teeth. He's probably already disarmed that cocksucker and taken control of the vehicle."

My feet plant, and I turn around to face him. He cricks his head to one side and gives me the biggest *I-told-you-so* grin I've ever seen.

Relief at knowing Sawyer is with Sammy helps calm my nerves marginally, but I won't be able to relax until she's back here with me.

Safe and sound.

And fucking *alive.*

"Leo?" Sue's shaky voice shakes my attention from my boss.

"Oh, angel... are you okay?" I open my arms, and she rams into me, knocking me back a step.

"*Oof,*" I grunt at the sudden contact.

Pulling back, I study her face. Her cheek is red, but otherwise, she looks unharmed. *Thank fuck.*

"Your girl can fight, Leo," Shep tosses over Kri's shoulder where she's irrigating his neck wound.

My head snaps back to my angel, who has a sheepish look on her face.

My lip quirks. "She can, huh? What did I miss while I was unconscious?"

"When I heard the gunshots, I called 911 like you told me to do. But I didn't know the address, and they couldn't track me close enough. I had to leave the panic room to find something with the address on it. And when I got out, fuck nugget — I mean Craig — came into the house with guns blazing. I slid the cell phone in my pocket and surrendered to him. He put zip ties on my wrists and brought me out here. When he wasn't looking, I broke loose, charged at him, and jabbed the cell phone into his throat. He fell down and dropped his gun."

Shep interjects, "If she's an angel, she must be from the south side of heaven, that's for damn sure. She took homeboy down!"

I let loose a tension-breaking chuckle.

Sue's face sobers. "But that's when I blew it."

"What do you mean?"

"Instead of grabbing the gun and holding him hostage or whatever, I kicked it away and tried to free you and Shepherd. But you didn't have any knives on you."

"He probably took them when he tied us up," I tell her.

At the same time, Shep says, "I told you, he took that shit off us."

Sue rolls her eyes at him, then aims those turquoise pools at me. "I'm sorry I didn't stop him from taking your sister. Do you think Sawyer will be able to stop Craig?"

Big Al laughs from over my shoulder — he knows how capable Sawyer is on a mission like that.

I do too, but it's *my* sister.

Nodding, I place a kiss on Sue's head and stroke her hair. "You really kicked some ass tonight, huh?"

"I tried to." She shrugs.

"I'm so damn proud of you, angel. So proud."

She leans up and presses her lips to mine for a quick kiss.

Big Al clears his throat, breaking the moment. "Sawyer and your sister will be back in about two minutes." He flashes his phone at me, open to a text screen showing a message from Sawyer.

"That was fast," Sue chimes in.

"Sawyer is an expert at close range, hand-to-hand shit. He's also one of the stealthiest guys I've ever had the pleasure to work with."

"Well, I'm glad he's on our side then."

Shep curses at Kri. "Dammit, woman. Are you trying to kill me?"

I look over my shoulder and see she's trying to stitch up a wound in his neck.

"Hold still if you don't want to be stabbed," Kri sasses him.

"Right here in the fucking dirt, Kri?" I ask with my hands out to the sides. "We have a whole cabin with a sink and lighting and everything."

"'Tis but a scratch," Shep balks in a shitty English accent.

Big Al joins in, trying out his own Monty Python impression. "Yeah, Leo. It's just a flesh wound."

With Sawyer in control of the fuck nugget and Sammy on her way back, I can laugh at the absurdity of these two morons — even with the night we've had. Perhaps partially *because* of the night we've had. The more morbid the jokes, the better. You can ask any veteran, and they'll tell you that if you can't laugh at your own mortality, then the bad guys have won.

"Old people are so weird," Kri scoffs under her breath.

"Hear, hear!" Sue agrees.

The trill of my phone's ring tone — from my personal cell phone, not the burner — distracts the *young* ladies from their old man shaming. Big Al pulls it out of his pocket, glances at it, and looks at me under lifted brows.

"Who is it?" I ask him.

"Unknown number."

I nod while reaching my hand out for the phone. "This is Leo," I answer.

"Are you all right, Leo?"

"West, is that you?"

"Yeah, man. It's me, and fuck! I'm so sorry. I didn't want to do it, man. I'll never forgive myself if you got hurt. He tortured me and said he would kill me if I didn't help him find your cabin and take down your sensors. Are you okay?"

My pulse accelerates again with another shot of adrenaline. It's a damn good thing I do a lot of cardio. If I didn't, my heart would probably be ready to throw in the towel right about now from all this panic.

"Damn, man. I'm okay. We're all safe. My team is here with me. Calm down," I soothe while wondering how the hell he was involved.

"You're at the cabin, right? Did you guys take that fucker down?"

"Yes and yes. Are you okay? Where are you now?"

He sighs heavily, the sound crackling the speaker. When he speaks again, his voice is less frantic. "I'm fine — just a little banged up and some deep cuts that'll need stitches. Once I could finally escape, I made it about a mile down the road where a concerned motorist stopped to offer assistance. He's letting me use his phone and taking me to the hospital now."

"How did you end up mixed up in this?"

I can guess it has something to do with the picture taken from my house.

"I got jumped just before sunset — fucker came out of nowhere. Knocked me out, tied me up, and drove me out to the middle of nowhere. When I woke up, he showed me the picture of us at your cabin and demanded I take him there and help him get to you. When I told him to go fuck himself, he beat me up pretty bad and started carving me up like a honey ham until I started talking."

Of course a shitbag like Craig would beat up and torture a bound, unarmed man.

That sick fuck.

"Shit, West. I'm... I'm sorry you got sucked into this mess. It had nothing to do with you. But I understand why you caved."

The line goes silent except for the sound of his shaky breaths. "I'm sorry, man. I was just too weak. After everything you've done for me, I'll never be able to make this up to you."

"It's okay, man. I'm just glad everyone came through this okay. Take care of yourself. Call me after you get to the hospital and the doctor treats you."

"I'll be all right, man. I'm so fucking glad you took him down."

My eyes cut to my spunky angel, who fights like she's from the south side of heaven, at the faces of my Redleg team, and then glance to the driveway where Sawyer and Sammy should be returning any minute now.

"It was a team effort. But yeah... we got him. Get better, and I'll talk to you soon."

"I owe you, man. You're like family."

"And family doesn't keep tallies on debts. We're good, West."

We end the call right as Sammy and Sawyer pull into the driveway. She's out of the vehicle and sprinting into my widespread arms.

Damn. I can't believe this is actually happening.

My sister. After all this time.

I've got my angel... and my sister back. My heart is well and truly whole now.

Chapter Forty

My boulder

Sue

"Sammy, I'd like you to officially meet my angel. This is Sue O'Malley."

"It's lovely to meet you, Sammy," I say proudly as we grasp hands.

I just shook the hand of a dead woman.

Well, you know what I mean.

Leo and his sister hugged for twenty-two minutes straight when she got back with Sawyer.

Side note: Although it's a nice even number, it is an exaggeration. I was too swept up in emotion to count the minutes, but it felt like a long time.

And now, we're all awkwardly standing around in the cabin waiting for the authorities to show up. Or maybe I'm the only awkward one.

Oh well. *What's new, amiright?*

Big Al called an ambulance for Shep and a squad car for Craig. At least someone was finally able to provide emergency services with a proper address. As it turns out, Redleg's specialized software caused our burner phones to ping false GPS locations. Badass shit if you're trying to hide from a bad guy, but much less helpful if you need 911 to find you.

Once the cops show up, they'll be hauling Craig off to jail, where he'll hopefully rot like the garbage he is. Sawyer has him hog-tied, gagged, and lying on the front porch. Sawyer's standing in the open doorway where he can keep an eye on him but also be part of our conversation inside.

Occasionally we can hear him groan and whimper, and the looks everyone gives each other when he whines are especially amusing.

Craig certainly looks a little worse for wear and is sporting some cuts and bruises — more than the ones Leo gave him during their earlier scuffle. A beam of pride shoots up my spine when I see a large bruise near his trachea — that was my handiwork.

With that thought, I fight the urge to dust imaginary lint off my shoulder.

Interestingly enough, there doesn't appear to be a scratch on Sawyer. I guess he really is as good as they claimed.

"Henderson just called. He and Madeline will be here in about ninety minutes," Big Al announces to the group before pocketing his phone and grinning widely.

Oh, wow. I'm going to meet Leo's mom.

Am I ready for a *meet-the-parents* moment? Leo's my first boyfriend slash lover, so obviously, this is my first time being introduced to a mom like this.

And she's a "people." People aren't my thing.

Breathe, Sue. She raised Leo — the man you love — she can't be that bad.

I head to the kitchen, grab some frozen peas from the freezer, and make Leo hold them to his forehead on that nasty-looking lump.

He's still handsome as hell, though.

The bag keeps falling down, and he doesn't want to let me or his sister go long enough to hold it, so I go and grab his ball cap and loosen it, then put it on him, tucking the peas under the brim.

Problem solved.

When I'm done fussing over him, he kisses me unabashedly, despite our mixed company. My toes curl in my cross-trainers.

"Now that everyone is here and *alive,* can we talk about what the hell happened?" Leo asks no one in particular once we all take seats around the living room — except Sawyer, who is standing sentry over the fuck nugget with arms crossed over his wide chest.

Leo takes my hand once we're seated and grasps Sammy's hand on the other side. He's wearing the most blindingly beautiful smile I've ever seen. His sister is beaming, too, and staying locked in tight to his side since she got back. The sight warms my heart.

Shep is kicked back in the recliner, with color coming back to his cheeks. The sooner we get him to the hospital, the better. He lost a lot of blood, but it hasn't stopped him from being a jokester.

In addition to the three of us on the couch and Shep in the chair, we have quite the campfire circle going on here. Kri and Big Al have brought in kitchen chairs and are tucked in around us on both sides of the coffee table.

Perhaps we should all hold hands, sing, and make s'mores?

Giggling emoji.

"Before we talk about how you found my sister..." Leo pauses to glance at Sammy again. Both sets of their eyes are sparkling with unshed tears. He continues, "... why the hell didn't you guys just take out Craig while he was waving his gun around on the side of the cabin?"

Big Al answers, "That was the original plan, but the way he was manhandling Sue, we couldn't get a clean shot. As soon as he let her go, he was wrapped around your sister tight, and I didn't want to risk hitting her. I made the call to have Sawyer take him out instead."

Leo tilts his head toward his boss. "Sawyer was your backup plan, then?"

A diabolical grin spreads across Big Al's face. "He was the second backup plan, actually. Things changed rapidly all afternoon, but we ended up in a good place."

"Now tell me how you found Sammy. I assume she's the news you've been hiding from me these last few days."

Sawyer responds this time. "It was Sammy who called your mom's phone the other day. Once I saw the footage from the arcade where she placed the call, I recognized her immediately. From there, we were able to run Tomer's facial recognition software against all the security camera footage from nearby businesses to track her to a local motel. That was time-consuming — hence the last few days where we were reluctant to talk to you all that much." He pauses and locks Leo's gaze. "Lionheart, we would have told you, but we didn't want to give you false hope until we were sure."

Leo swallows audibly, and I squeeze his hand, offering my silent support.

"I can understand. If it hadn't been her..." Leo trails off, then puts his head down.

Sammy cuts in, pulling Leo's attention away from the downward spiral of what-ifs. "Anyway, when I left Craig, I came to Florida to find you and Mom. But once I got here, I was scared to contact you."

"Why were you scared?" Leo asks, then purses his lips.

Her eyes cut to the fuck nugget on the front porch, who's yelling through his gag. No clue what he's saying, but if I had to guess, I'd say he's upset about the leaving Craig comment Sammy made.

She leans in closer to Leo and speaks quietly, probably because she doesn't want Craig to hear her.

"I knew Craig would be following me. I couldn't bear it if you or Mom got hurt because of me... well, hurt any more than I've already hurt you both."

She looks down, fiddling with the hem of her shirt. "When I got down to Florida about three weeks ago, I hid out in a motel until I figured out my next move. After these last few horrible years living with a..." she pauses and shoots a glare in Craig's direction before continuing, "... a *monster*, I wanted to hear a loving voice so badly. It's been ages since anyone was kind to me, and I wanted my *mommy*."

She wipes a tear with her free hand, and my emotions lodge in my throat.

I can't even imagine what she's gone through these last few years. It doesn't seem like she left of her own free will. This poor woman.

Sammy eyes her brother from under her lashes. "To be this close and not be with you or Mom was even more torture than the last few years I've suffered at Craig's hands."

A sad smile lifts one side of her mouth. "I was lucky Mom kept the same phone number since it was the only one I had memorized. And I *had* to hear her voice, so I made the call."

With tears flowing down her cheeks in rivulets, she chokes out a sob. Leo pulls her into his side, then places a kiss on her head.

"And we're so damn glad you did, Sammy," Sawyer says, looking at her with fondness and warmth in his gaze.

I wonder if they knew each other before all this. It would seem so if Sawyer recognized her from the arcade security camera images.

No less than a dozen questions are racing through my mind, but I'm forcing myself to be quiet, letting them have their moment.

But it's *fecking killing me* not to interrupt and demand answers.

Leo looks over at Sawyer, then Big Al, and asks, "Then what happened? How did you guys come up with the plan? Did you know Craig was coming here?" He practically hisses the name.

"You mean the fuck nugget," I emphatically correct, getting a laugh from everyone. My cheeks grow warm.

Another grunting sound comes from the front porch — the fuck nugget in question probably objecting behind his gag at the use of the anti-Craig slur.

Tough shite, fuck nugget.

Big Al explains, "Once we brought Sammy into Redleg headquarters and told her about the threats, we figured out PDQ it was Craig. She helped us get pictures of him, and we were able to find him and the gray van on the security cameras outside the bar where he jumped West earlier today."

Leo breaks in to connect the remaining dots. "And you figured since West knew where the cabin was, he'd be coming here immediately."

"Exactly," Sawyer says, looking thoroughly pleased with himself.

He's pretty smug.

I like it.

Being with these Redleg guys feels like being at home with my siblings. That's probably why I'm not panicking around all these people. There's a built-in comfort level.

Also the fact that I overcame some scary shit today, and we all came out fine on the other side — minus Shep's neck, Leo's goose-egg forehead, and my stinging cheek. All in all, not that bad.

While absently scratching his face, Big Al says, "Then we loaded up to come and save the day. You know... as we do."

"*Red... leg!*" Shep yells with his voice deep and melodic, drawing out each letter and setting it to some type of rhythm. It's like a chant or cheer or something.

The other guys and Kri join in, returning his call.

Yep, it's definitely some kind of cheer.

A huge smile plays across Leo's handsome face, and a few deep chuckles bounce around the room.

Once the ruckus ceases, Leo shakes his head. "I still can't believe that asshat got the drop on West earlier, and then me and Shep. Three former Rangers? That's virtually impossible for a civilian."

"Well, he did train to be Delta Force," Sammy offers.

All heads in the room whip toward her.

"What?"

"Excuse me?"

"The hell?"

The questions fly so fast I can't keep track of who asks what.

Sammy draws into herself, and her eyes shift to the floor as she explains, "Well, he was in the Army and went through all the Delta Force training, but he got discharged at the end of the program. Something about not passing some evaluation. He said his peers had it out for him and sabotaged him."

"You mean he peered out. Figures. Psycho like him." Kri shakes her head dismissively.

The rest of the Redleg guys seem to agree, judging by the head nods.

Sammy angles her head to one side and narrows her eyes at Kri. "What's that mean?"

Kri leans back in her chair, crossing her legs. "When you finish Delta training, there is a peer review process where the soldiers you trained with and your superiors have to evaluate and rate you. If they don't think you're up to the job, you don't pass the peer review, and you can't become a Delta. Those guys have to be able to trust each other with their lives on the most dangerous ops, and not everyone can cut it."

"They must have figured out he was too dangerous. The sick bastard," Sammy mutters.

Fuck nugget groans again, evidentially getting more pissed off by the moment.

"Excuse me for a minute," Leo says before stalking over to the front porch.

Curiosity gets the best of me, so I follow him to eavesdrop.

Leo squats down and removes the gag. Craig spits and sputters, then unleashes a long series of derogatory words that don't bear repeating. He's just not worth my brain space.

With a pleased grin on his face, Leo asks him, "You done?"

"Fuck you!" Craig seethes.

"Tell me how you knew to target Sue," Leo demands.

"Fuck off! I'm not telling you anything!"

Leo shakes his head, then pinches the flesh just above fuck nugget's elbow. It must be a trigger point or something because Craig thrashes around to get out of the hold, but Leo is relentless.

"Stop it! I'll tell you!"

That was easy — like tapping the Staples easy button.

"I followed you for a few weeks."

"And?" Leo asks, pinching him again. I guess that wasn't enough of an answer for him.

"Fine! Fuck!" Craig groans. "It was all those *message in a bottle* notes you threw into the ocean for Sammy, you dumbass. Waxing all sad about how much you wanted Sue but couldn't have her. Pathetic fuck!"

Leo intensifies the pressure on his arm as he asks, "How did you get them?"

"You're so dumb you didn't even see me twenty feet behind you. As soon as you'd leave, I'd run into the surf and get them before they sank. After I collected enough of them, I was able to piece together who the magical Sue was."

"Shit," Leo mutters under his breath.

He shoves the gag back into fuck nugget's ugly mouth and gets up, meeting my eyes.

"You were writing about me?"

He shrugs his shoulders, looking a little shy.

"Oh, my sweet giant. You really did miss me all that time."

"Every day. Every minute."

He wraps me in his arms and kisses me deeply, and the last segment of my broken heart stitches closed.

When you love someone, you can't hurt without them hurting too. Somehow, knowing he was in pain at the same time I was makes our connection that much stronger.

As we walk back to the living room to join the others, he looks over at his boss.

"Do you think we need a psychological profiler at Redleg?" he asks.

Big Al tilts his head, contemplating the suggestion. I know he and Leo talked about my amateur profile; it *did* influence their efforts.

"It certainly can't hurt. Now that we know who the perp was, did Sue's profile hit the mark?"

"One hundred percent on the money," Leo says proudly, then casts a glance at me. "Not only that, but she cracked the case wide open on our end when she spotted the missing picture and connected all the dots. She's brilliant."

My cheeks burn with embarrassment and something else. Pride maybe?

I've always seen my autism as a disability — something that was wrong with me. But Leo has never viewed it as something needing to be fixed. And it turns out my unique brain has been more of an asset than I ever would have thought possible.

Through it all, Leo helped me find strength in what I thought was a weakness.

My heart swells, threatening to break out of my chest. I never thought I'd find love — let alone love *this* powerful.

Big Al catches my gaze. "Sue, can Redleg call upon you in the future should the need arise? Maybe we can hire you for jobs on a consulting basis."

"You don't have to answer right now, angel," Leo says quietly.

I adore how he knows I need time to process Big Al's question.

Perhaps there's a future for me at Redleg. Of course, I'd need to do more work and look into further education or certifications before committing. And I'd still want to work with Nick at Naughty Dogs. But yeah... this might be a good path for me. Hmm.

Weirder things have happened.

My shoulders roll back, and my chin lifts. Yep. It's definitely pride I'm feeling. Not only am I comfortable around the Redleg guys, I'm proud of what I did and how I contributed to the team.

This day has been an absolute roller coaster — which I normally hate. Not today, though.

About an hour later, after the cops have taken Craig the fuck nugget off to jail and the paramedics have taken Shep to the hospital, I have to give my statement to an officer.

That was an *interesting* experience.

The officer was very impressed with my ability to recall so many details. Leo held my hand the entire time, giving me all the confidence I needed to get through the chaos.

He's my steadiness.

My calm.

My rock.

Or maybe I should say my *boulder*. You know? Because he's so big.

A little while later, the reunion between Sammy and her mother has everyone wiping tears from their eyes, even all the big tough men of Redleg.

Madeline's knees hit the floor when she sees her daughter. Sammy joins her, and they stay embraced and crying for a long time. I don't even count the minutes — too wrapped up in the emotion.

When they finally break apart, Leo is there to help them both stand. He brings his mother into a warm embrace and wipes away her tears. I'm not the least bit surprised to see him being so gentle with her.

He helps them both to the couch, and I excuse myself to make some hot tea. Despite it being Florida in August, this seems like a moment for hot tea.

And I can't explain why, so please don't ask.

When I return with the tea, Leo pulls me onto his lap. We've taken over the recliner Shep vacated when he left for the hospital.

"Is that my ring?" Sammy asks her brother, staring at his hand, which is resting on my leg.

Leo grins, then reaches to take off his pinky ring. The same ring he's often twirling and tapping when he's deep in thought.

"I guess you can have this back now."

He hands the ring to her, and she takes it with a sad smile on her dusty rose lips.

"You've been wearing my thumb ring *all* this time?" Sammy asks as she takes the ring and slides it on her thumb.

"Well, you left it for me, didn't you?"

She nods silently, her lips drawn in a tight line. A lone tear treks down her cheek and falls onto her chest.

Leo leans over and whispers in my ear, "The ring was sitting on top of her suicide note."

Sammy sniffles before saying, "I wanted to leave something behind for you — give you something to remember me by. I felt so bad for what he was making me write. It was the only thing I could think of to ease the ache."

"Why *did* you write those awful things? And why did you leave with that horrible man?" Madeline asks Sammy through free-falling tears. She wrings her hands in her lap.

For some reason, I find myself mimicking the motion until Leo puts his palm over them, calming me instantly.

Big Al comes over and hands Leo's mother a box of tissues, and they share a look.

That was a definite *look*. Like the kind you give someone you care about.

What the hell?

Sammy's shaky voice distracts me from the heat being tossed between Leo's mother and boss.

"I was really messed up. He had beaten me down inside far worse than he did on the outside." She pauses, and her throat bobs with a tight swallow. "He told me he would kill you if I didn't go with him, Mom. I was so scared of him, and I believed him."

"You should have told me that, Sammy," Leo says with a tight-set jaw. "I would have ended him."

"I was scared. Please forgive me."

"I'll try," Leo whispers, his voice shaky.

The two share a look, so much emotion running across their features I can't even begin to decipher it all. Even though I've improved, I'm not always the best at reading faces.

Clearing my throat, I finally speak up. "I'm sorry, but I can't hold back my questions any longer. Can I ask a few things? I have a list."

Madeline looks at me for the first time. Not that I blame her for only now noticing the other people in the room. Her eyes scan me briefly, gaze lingering where Leo's hands rest on my waist.

She smiles at me, then looks at her son. "Leo, who's your friend?" Her voice is pleasant, with a teasing quality.

Some of the guys chuckle. Leo taps my thigh, and we rise together. He guides me over to his mother, and as she stands, she sticks out her hand for a shake.

"Mom, this is Sue O'Malley. She's my..." He looks down at me and smiles. "She's my everything."

I hear Kri *awwing* from the side of the room, but my gaze stays locked on the captivating blue eyes of my love.

My heart.

My future.

My man.

After shaking my hand, Madeline squeals, "What a day! It's like all my dreams are coming true at once!"

I couldn't have said it better myself.

"So about those questions," I ask, attempting to get us back on track. Enough with the social pleasantries already. *I need answers.*

"Fire away!" Sammy responds.

Oh, thank St. Paddy.

I hope she's ready because I'm absolutely heading into a Q&A lightning round.

"Thank you. Question one. Did you fake your death and run away with the fuck nugget, or were you abducted?"

"Uh. Maybe both."

I crook my head to the side, raising a brow at her.

She clarifies, "I mean, I did leave voluntarily, but only because he forced me. It's..." she trails off.

"Complicated?" I ask.

"Yes, it's complicated."

"Okay, fine. Question two. How long were you gone?"

"Three years."

"Wow. That's a long time. Question three. Did you want to escape the entire time?"

"Yes, but I didn't feel strong enough to try until recently."

"Interesting. Question four. Did you ever try to contact your family during the three years?"

"I wanted to, but I was too scared."

"Okay. Question five. How did you manage to escape? Did you tell him you were leaving him and then go? Or was it more like an escape under the cover of night type of thing?"

She looks flustered, and it's entirely possible I should ease up on the intense questioning. But I have so many more questions.

Sammy starts to reply, opening her mouth, but Leo interrupts. "Tonight has been hard for everyone. Why don't we take a break? We'll have plenty of time to get all our questions answered over the next few days."

Pinching my eyes shut, I accept the inevitability of, yet again, being too much for people to handle.

I look up at my man and plead, "Can I ask you one quick question?"

Please say yes. Please say yes. I'm *dying* to know this one. If I had known there was a limit to the number of questions I could ask, I would've started with this one.

Fuck you, hindsight.

"Sure, angel."

Yes! I *love* this man.

"Thank you, babe. When you said she committed suicide, I assumed there was a body. And you told me there was a funeral. What did you bury? Was there a fake dead body? Because I saw this episode of *CSI: Miami* once where —"

He smiles and puts his finger across my lip to silence me. My brows raise expectantly while I await his response.

"Mom, Drew, and I each picked something to put in the mostly empty casket. We buried personal effects like family pictures, her sports trophies, key chains, and knickknacks. Anything we could part with. It helped us to get some closure."

"So no body?" I ask around his finger.

He shakes his head and removes the ineffective silencing digit.

"In Sammy's note, she said she was taking her sailboat out to sea, never to be found. Not to bother looking because she'd make sure her body couldn't be recovered."

My hands go to my head as if they're going to stop my brain from exploding.

"And you believed her?" I don't think I've ever felt this much disbelief in my entire existence.

"You know me better than that, babe." He grins somberly, then adds, "We had the Coast Guard, local fisherman, and anybody with a boat out there looking for her. For four days and nights, I searched the ocean without taking a break. I didn't even sleep. When one ship captain needed to rest, I got another one to take me to the next area."

His shoulders drop, and he looks at his sister with tears filling his eyes again. "We finally found her capsized sailboat near Bass Island in Cape Porpoise Harbor. All the lifejackets were accounted for, and there was no sign of her. A few days later, her shredded shirt washed up on the island. That's when they called off the search, assuming sharks had gotten her body."

"That was Craig's plan." Sammy's voice yanks me from the haunted look in Leo's eyes. "He knew you'd keep looking for me unless you truly believed I was dead."

"Wow," I whisper, more to myself than anyone else.

Despite how tired I feel, I doubt I'll be able to sleep while my mind unpacks all that's happened. There's a lot for me to process.

Hell, there's a lot for *everyone* to process.

"I'm sorry, Leo. I'll never be able to make up for what I've done to you." Sammy rises from the couch, walks over to her brother, and wraps her arms around his middle.

He doesn't let me go from his side while holding her with his other arm. Madeline rises, joining us, and now it's a great big group hug. I try to back away, letting them have their family moment. But Leo holds me tight, refusing to let me escape.

My heart pounds, and my breathing accelerates. It's a lot of feelings. Also, a lot of smells, sounds, and touching.

If I'm honest, it's almost too much touching.

But I take it all in and stand firm beside Leo and his family. I can tell he needs me right now.

By his side. Silently supporting him.

And so I stay there beside him. Just like he's been there for me when I've needed him.

Because that's what you do when you love someone.

And I love this man with my whole sense of being.

Chapter Forty-One

She's my cherry pie

A few weeks later

Leo

"Are you ready for this, angel?"

Turning off the ignition, I face her, waiting for her response. She's staring out the windshield, wringing her hands, and nibbling on her lower lip.

I regret not taking my bike. I'd bet the purr of the engine beneath us would have helped calm her nerves.

Since we returned from the cabin in Ocala, we've taken several motorcycle rides, and she loves it more each time. When I suggested buying her a bike of her own one day, she laughed in my face and told me there was no way in hell she'd ever even consider getting on a bike without me driving.

My ego approves. I mean, I want her to be independent, but I secretly love being the only one she's pressing that luscious body against.

Damn. Why didn't we take the bike?

Oh yeah.

Because she's wearing a dress. It was so fucking cute how she wanted to dress up for tonight.

Finally looking at me from the corner of her eye, she asks, "Are you sure this is necessary?"

"I'd never force you to do anything you don't want to do. But..."

She cracks a grin. "All right. Let's go inside."

"I'm proud of you, babe."

Her eyes roll as she shakes her head and groans. She reaches for the door handle, but I stop her with my hand on the creamy skin of her exposed thigh. I can't help myself, and I squeeze her flesh.

Whipping her head over, she chastises me. "Leo, not here. My gosh. You're insatiable."

I was only stopping her so I could come around and open the door for her, but now that she mentions fooling around...

"Me?" I feign outrage. "What about you and your four orgasms a day keeps the doctor away?"

"Four is a balanced number, Leo. We've discussed this."

While we banter, our upper bodies inch closer to each other until we end up kissing. She grabs my collar, pulling me closer, and my hand starts to trail up one creamy thigh, sneaking under the hem of her dress until it comes to rest against her core. Cupping her mound over her panties, I elicit a moan from those sweet lips, capturing it in my mouth.

Deepening the kiss, I snake my fingers around the edge of her panties and brush them against her slit. Like a clit-seeking missile, my fingers zero in on the little nub and start teasing it. After a few flicks, I travel lower and plunge into her pussy a few times to gather up some wetness, then return to circle her clit.

She breaks the kiss and says, "My brothers are probably watching from the front windows." She says it like she wants me to stop, but her hips are rocking and thrusting into my hand.

Glancing over, I see that there are at least three people looking out the bay windows on the front of her parents' house.

Busted.

My hand pulls back, and she tilts her head back against the headrest while letting out a moan of frustration.

"Looks like Fiona. And is that Millie?"

Sue looks over and chuckles. "Yeah, it is. You can tell because of how short she is. Unless it's Sydney. You remember Fiona's daughter, right?"

"I'm going to do you a favor *by not* telling Millie you compared her height to that of a seven-year-old."

Sue's hand covers her giggling mouth.

"Let's go," I tell her, tapping her on the thigh twice.

"Hold on." Rifling through her bag, she pulls out a pack of hand wipes and thrusts it at me.

"Am I dirty?" I tease.

"You can't go into my parents' house and shake my father's hand with my female juices on your fingers."

Instead of taking the wipes, I slowly move my hand toward my face and open my mouth, holding eye contact the entire time.

With a shaky breath, she knocks my hand away one second before I'm able to suck her arousal off my fingers.

"Hey, that's not nice," I pout.

After removing a wet wipe from the package, she wipes my hand clean while muttering under her breath.

I can't hold back my chuckle. "Don't act like you don't like it when I taste you."

"Yeah, that's precisely the problem. I like it too damn much. And I can't get all revved up when my family is watching."

Two minutes later, we walk into the O'Malley home and are greeted eagerly by a room full of friendly faces — young and old.

Sue is wrapped in hugs, one after the other, and looks increasingly uncomfortable as they continue. I know she loves her family. We talk about them all the time. But I also know she's easily overwhelmed by loud noises and big groups, which is exactly how I'd describe this house full of people.

"Good to see ya, Leo," Mrs. O'Malley says, sticking her head out of the kitchen and waving a dish towel in my direction. "Sue, c'mere and give us a kiss."

Sue heads off to the kitchen, leaving me to face the firing squad.

"Leo. It's right grand to see ya again." Mr. O'Malley has a hell of a grip, especially considering his age. "After dinner, we should take a walk and have a stogey. We can spin a yarn and get better acquainted. Do ya smoke, boyo?"

"No, sir. I don't."

"Well, nobody is perfect," he teases, drawing a chuckle from me. With a pat on my back, he ushers me to a seat beside him at the head of the table.

A few minutes later, everyone is seated around an immense table that spills from the dining room into the living room with the extra leaves added on to accommodate such a large gathering. Sixteen of us in total.

Sue requested the entire family be present tonight, so all six siblings are here in addition to her parents. Millie has joined Nick, and Finn's wife is here too. Fiona's husband is noticeably absent, but her two kids are happily enjoying the attention of their aunts and uncles.

Dishes are passed around, and plates are filled amidst hearty chatter. The scene is familiar to the last time I was a guest here but different in a few key ways. In the spring, I strong-armed my way into an O'Malley family meal when I was guarding Sue. I passed off my presence by pretending to be her friend.

This time, we're not pretending. And we're a whole lot more than friends.

When we returned from the cabin, we stayed at Nick and Millie's for a week until we could clean up my ransacked house. Since then, Sue has stayed with me every night. We've slowly moved her stuff into my place over the last few weeks, and for all intents and purposes, we live together.

If I have my way, I'll never spend another night without her body curled up beside me and her head resting on my chest.

Setting down her glass of water, Sue clears her throat to get everyone's attention.

"I have something I need to tell everyone," she announces, a tremble in her voice.

Her knee bobs up and down under the table, and I place my palm against it to lend her my support. After a moment, she calms.

"What's the news, Susie Q?" Nick asks while cutting his eyes to me, brows raised.

My only response is a tight smile.

"I have autism," she blurts out.

The room is silent for a solid fifteen seconds.

Millie finally breaks the silence. "And?"

There's a rustle under the table. Millie looks over at Nick and says, "Ouch! What was that for?"

Nick bends his head toward his wife and widens his eyes, silently telling her to shut up.

The thing is, no one tells Millie to shut up without some type of clapback.

And here it comes.

Millie raises her pointer finger to Nick's face and looks sternly at him. "That's enough of that shit, Lucky Charms." Then she tweaks his nose and says, "Honk!"

The room breaks out in laughter, lifting the tension from Sue's shocking announcement.

Once the laughter dies down, serious faces reemerge on Sue's family members. I put my arm over the back of her chair to make it easier for me to wrap her up if need be.

"Darlin', how do ya know ya have the autism?" Mrs. O'Malley asks, straightening her glasses. "Ya might be a little anxious, but yer a smart girl."

At the same time, her father leans back in his chair, crossing his arms over his chest. The wrinkles of his face are furrowed and drawn downward.

"Ya ain't autistic any more than I'm a goat. What are ya goin' on about, Angelica Sue?" He sounds irritated, and it raises my hackles.

Sue and I prepared for this type of reaction.

Jaynie told us there might be doubt, disbelief, and even some outright denial to work through. Sue's parents are bound to be defensive. After all, shouldn't they have known if their little girl had this disorder her entire life? Even if it's not true — since autism is very hard to spot in women who are as good as Sue is at masking their behavior — that's likely how her parents will feel.

I squeeze Sue's shoulder, and it seems to be enough to get her going.

With her gaze fixed on the table, she replies, "I got the diagnosis from a neuro-psychologist. My psychiatrist confirmed it, and my therapist also agrees." She pivots her head to face her mother. "Autistic people are usually very smart, Mom. Just because I'm autistic doesn't mean I'm stupid."

Mrs. O'Malley looks contrite and puts her hand on her chest. "I'm sorry. I should nigh have said that. I'm just shocked, love."

"Autism is a very broad *spectrum* disorder. There are many facets of this condition. No two people with autism are the same. And women especially are often misdiagnosed with other conditions like anxiety and bipolar disorder because we're so good at masking our disability. But I promise you, I have autism. I don't need to defend it to you. You need to accept it as I have done."

As I scan the table, I notice the O'Malley siblings looking at their parents. It seems they are either taking their cues from their parents or waiting to see how they react before speaking. Feeling irritated at the lack of support they're showing, I roll my head and tug at my collar.

I promised Sue I'd let her handle this. My job is only to support her and be by her side. That's all she wants from me.

It's killing me not to swoop in and save her, but I know she's perfectly capable of doing anything she sets her mind to. This is not a moment when she needs a hero. She only needs my loving presence

"How long have you known about this?" Fiona asks.

"I've known for..." Sue looks over at me. I nod, giving her more of my silent support. "I've known I was different my entire life. But I was diagnosed thirteen months ago." She puts her head down and mutters, "Terrible number."

"Well, what can we do to help you, sis?" Callum asks.

"Yeah, whatever you need, we've got ya, lass," Finn adds.

Finally.

Sue's lips tug upward as she looks at the loving faces of her siblings, now starting to rally their support.

"I don't need anything from you," she tells them. "It was important for me to tell you. I've been masking my true self all my life, and I didn't want to hide this too. Enough is enough. I'm not ashamed. It's part of who I am."

Her spine straightens, and her shoulders roll back as she juts her chin.

So brave and strong.

Unable to hold back, I lean in and press a kiss to her temple. She gives me a sheepish grin as I pull away.

Her sister audibly sighs, and when I look in her direction, I see a very dopey-looking Fiona with her hands pressed together over her heart in the physical embodiment of a swoon. Her eyes practically have stars and hearts shining from them.

Nick rises and walks around the table to Sue's side, forcing me to drop my arm and release my hold of her.

"Come here, Susie Q," he requests quietly with his arms open wide.

She rises from the chair, and he wraps her in a tight embrace. Her frame lifts and falls as she sobs silently into his chest. A lump lodges in my throat.

"I love you, Susie. I'm sorry I didn't see this sooner. I would've done more. Should've done more," he mutters over her head while patting her hair down in a loving gesture. His typically dormant Irish accent has made an appearance, betraying how emotional he is right now.

Sue pulls back and looks up at her brother with a morose smile. "You are the greatest brother a girl could have."

"Hey! We're sitting right here!" Callum hollers jokingly.

"Yeah, ouch, Susie," Finn piles on.

At the same time, Connor throws his hands to the side with his jaw to his chest, feigning shock.

"You all noticed she said *brother* and not *sibling*, right?" Fiona snickers.

"Unbelievable," Shane mutters, then grins for the first time since I've known him.

"You guys know what I mean!" Sue defends, then looks back up at Nick. "I thought we already decided it wasn't your job to raise me, Nicky."

"Yeah, but I should've known."

She shakes her head at him, refuting his assertion. "No, you shouldn't have. Unless you're a trained psychologist, you are not to blame for not knowing about my diagnosis."

Mr. O'Malley rises from his seat and takes Nick's place, holding Sue. When Nick backs away, Millie is there, ready to offer her husband some compassion.

"Did we fail ya, baby girl?" Sue's dad asks after a few seconds.

Sue pushes away from him, breaking out of his hold. "No," she says emphatically, but with a practiced kindness. "It wasn't anybody's fault."

Turning to the rest of the room, she eyes them individually while speaking. "This is precisely why I didn't tell you guys sooner. I knew you'd all blame yourselves. But it's nobody's fault. There is nothing wrong. No fault. No blame. There is nothing wrong with me."

"Damn right!" Millie says, giving Sue a thumbs-up.

"Mama, can we say damn?" Sydney asks her mother in a whisper.

Fiona looks over at Millie and huffs. "Will you please try a little harder to stop your potty mouth from flushing in the presence of my kids?"

"My bad!" Millie replies. She turns to Sydney and says, "Aunt Millie is not the kind of role model you want. At least not until you're menstruating."

"What's menstradatiting?" Sydney mumbles to a panic-stricken Fiona.

Millie's lips take on a sadistic grin. "It's the red tide, the crimson killer, the blooming of the fire lily, the —"

Fiona cuts off Millie's rant. "It's nothing. Aunt Millie is just being silly."

Sydney looks at her mother with a half-terrified, half-confused expression.

Millie winks at Sydney and says, "Don't worry, kid. There's a whole ritual for when the time comes. Aunt Millie's got you covered."

Laughter erupts around the table.

Sue's mom speaks up, redirecting us back to what Sue shared. "Of course, there's nothin' wrong with ya, my lovely girl. But if we'd known sooner, we would have... done somethin' different. Gotten you help."

"We can't change the past, Ma. You loved me and raised me the best you could — all of you did your best. I know I wasn't an easy child, but I never felt unloved. That's all any child can ever ask for. There isn't any sense in worrying about what could have been. Please, stop with the guilt already."

"Susie Q, you know our parents, right? Irish Catholic guilt is what they made for dessert," Finn jokes, garnering a few chuckles.

"Well, I hereby forgive you. You're all absolved of your sins!" Sue says loudly, then lets loose a nervous giggle.

"Actually, it's cherry pie!" Mrs. O'Malley says. "Who's ready for dessert?"

Everyone sits back down, and conversation begins flowing naturally over a delicious homemade cherry pie. After a few minutes, Millie gets Sue's attention from across the table.

"Sue, my nephew Miles is on the spectrum. You definitely present differently than he does. But now that I know about your diagnosis, I see some similarities. He's doing great with his therapy and all, and I'm sure we can ask my sister Cara if we can get you guys together. You know... if you want to talk to him or anything. Or to my sister. I don't know." Millie shrugs and sinks back into her chair, and I wonder if she's suddenly regretting her offer.

"Thank you, Millie. I think I'd like that. I don't know any other autistic people. It might be nice to commiserate, even if he is a teenager."

"He's an awesome kid," Nick adds. "I'm sure you'll like him."

A smile lights up Millie's face as she meets Sue's eye and nods. My own heart swells in response to how quickly her family processed her news. I realize the emotions are still flowing, but there was no anger, and other than the initial denial, everyone seemed to accept it.

Time will tell what other emotions come up among the family members. No single dinner can accomplish everything. Regardless, Sue did what she needed to do tonight. And with her secret out in the open, she and her family can work toward real understanding and acceptance.

Tonight was a huge first step.

A few times during dessert, I catch Sue looking up at me, smiling. She's proud of herself, as she should be.

Leaning over into her ear, I whisper, "You're fucking amazing, angel. I'm so proud of you. And when we get home, I'm going to show you how much I love you. With my tongue."

She drops her fork, and it clatters across her pie plate.

"Everythin' okay, love?" her dad asks with a knowing smile.

"Uh-huh," she replies quickly without meeting his eyes.

"When's the weddin'?" her mom asks me out of nowhere, mischief swirling in her deep blue eyes — so much like Sue's.

A chorus of *oohs* and *ahhs* comes from the other end of the table, led primarily by Millie and Callum.

"Ah ah ah. Nope. First, he has to ask me," Mr. O'Malley says to his wife.

"Oh my gosh! Kill me now!" Sue groans, dramatically putting her head in her hands.

After a quick chuckle, her parents share a sweet look before he leans in to kiss her. It's not a full-on make-out kiss, but it's enough to make me slightly uncomfortable. My eyes flit down the table until I see Fiona making that swoony face again. She's quite a sap for romance, I see.

Taking my last bite of pie, I think about what Sue's parents just said.

Am I going to ask Sue to marry me?

Absolutely.

But she's going to need time to get used to the idea. I don't want to spook her, and it hasn't been long enough yet.

However, there's nothing wrong with asking Mr. O'Malley for his daughter's hand when we go out on our little walk after dinner tonight. Right? It'll be like getting the old-fashioned technicality he expects out of the way ahead of time.

Nah. Nothing wrong with that at all.

It's just good planning.

A strategy starts forming in my mind.

I'll start dropping hints about marriage. Talk to her about having kids. Ask where she sees herself in the future. Let her pick out new bedsheets and a comforter for us. Ask her if she'd like to change the paint color in our bedroom to something of her choosing. Maybe I can build an art studio at my house.

Things like that.

Knowing what I know about Sue, she's going to need time to prepare herself. And I've got all the patience in the world when it comes to her.

We've got forever.

Epilogue

Two years later

Sue

"Nothing else you need to address today? We still have fifteen minutes left."

That's a decent number of minutes to end the session on.

Beaming at Jaynie, I shake my head. "I don't think so. Honestly, I think I'm doing all right. No other issues this week. And I'm not even nervous about attending the graduation ceremony. Even with all the people."

"Excellent. That's simply outstanding. You've done amazing."

"I couldn't have done it without you," I offer.

Blushing, she tucks her pen behind her ear and sets down her notepad. "No, you did the hard work. Going back to college full-time, navigating your first serious relationship, and holding down *two* part-time jobs is no easy task. Most neuro-typical people would have caved under that kind of pressure."

My chest swells with pride.

"Well, I have a great support system with you, Leo, and my family."

"That you do," she agrees, nodding.

This weekend I'm graduating with my second bachelor's degree. This one is in forensic psychology. Now the work I do with Redleg as a profiler will feel more legit, and hopefully, lessen my impostor syndrome.

Big Al has put me to work on several cases on a trial basis, and I've enjoyed it immensely. It's so fulfilling to assist the men and women of Redleg in doing their jobs and help make them safer.

Boss — I call him that now too — even gave me my very own office right down the hall from Chuck No Fun Fuck. I mean Tomer.

Giggle emoji.

He's become a good friend. As people who are often misunderstood, Tomer and I had an instant kinship.

When I'm not working with Redleg or studying, I'm still helping Nick run Naughty Dogs. I've even trained a few more dogs — entirely on my own.

Shockingly, I'm still not a fan of the people part of the job, but I'm getting by. The dogs are worth it.

"Before you go, I have something for you."

Jaynie rises and hobbles over to her purse, hanging on the back of the office door. Reaching in without looking, she pulls out something and hands it to me.

It's a thick linen envelope with tiny gold flecks woven into it.

While trailing a finger over my name, which is written in script on the front, I ask, "What's this?"

"Just a little something from Sandra and me. The note inside is from me, though."

Feeling sheepish, I tuck my neck in and open the card. That was sweet of Jaynie and her wife to get me a graduation gift. The envelope has an embellished rose gold foil lining.

It's gorgeous.

Retrieving the card from inside, I open it, and a Starbucks gift card falls onto my lap.

She knows me so well.

Before I pick up the gift card, I read the inside of the card. It's says *Congratulations* across the top in a beautiful rose gold font and has a personalized inscription.

My Dearest Sue,

I've always thought life could be boiled down to a series of tests. Some we pass, and some we fail. Of those we fail, very few are we able to retake. And when we do, it's our chance to show how much we've learned from our past failures. It's the moment of truth when we either repeat our mistakes or rise above them.

Not everyone is brave enough to retake some of life's tests, though. And for a time, I didn't know if you were going to be strong enough to give love another chance.

Having been unable to love openly for a large part of my life, I cherish the ability to be in an openly loving relationship. The thought of you denying yourself love or feeling unworthy was one of my greatest fears for you.

I'll never be able to express how happy I am that those fears were unfounded.

Over these last few years, I've had the pleasure of watching you study tirelessly for every one of life's tests. It's been my privilege and honor to be part of your support team.

Because I'm married to a woman and come from a different era, I didn't have the luxury of having a child. But if I did, I'd want her to be exactly like you in every way.

While you may not have passed every test, there were many you aced with flying colors.

When you felt broken, you glued your pieces back together.

When you felt defeated, you brushed yourself off and fought harder.

When you felt scared, you found strength deep inside.

When no one was there to save you, you saved yourself, becoming your own hero in the process.

And when love came around a second time, you chose to trust and let it back inside your heart.

You're braver than your fears. You're smarter than you know. And you love deeper than most. What makes you different also makes you a beautifully complex, perfectly imperfect soul.

Congratulations on all you've accomplished, and thank you for letting me help you prepare for some of life's tests.

With you, life never has to grade on a curve.

Love always,
Jaynie

"It's beautiful," I tell her, wiping a tear from my cheek.

"And I meant every word of it. I'm incredibly proud of you."

She hands me a box of tissues, and I take one.

While I try to collect myself, she adds, "I hope you'll forgive the cheesy education puns. It seemed fitting with the graduation and all."

"It was perfect, Jaynie." I offer a wide smile that I feel deep in my soul.

When I stand, she brings me in for an embrace. It lasts for three seconds. Although that isn't a great number, it's good enough for a short hug. She knows I'm not a fan of long hugs.

"Thank you so much for the gift card as well. Does this mean I have your permission to have more caffeine?"

"I'll leave that for you to decide." Her smile is bright and genuine.

We say our goodbyes, and I tell her I'll see her in two weeks for our next appointment. It's a relief to have this much time in between sessions. If I have a setback in the future, I can always increase the frequency. But I'm optimistic things will continue on this favorable track.

As I'm leaving, my phone rings. It's Nick.

"Hey. What's going on? And more importantly, why aren't you telling me about it over a text?"

Grrr.

"Susie Q, I've got good news, and I'm driving, so it was easier to call."

"Whatever. Likely story, old man."

"Just for that, I'm going to call you more often. How about every day for a month?"

"I apologize. Please, don't do that."

The thought of daily phone calls makes me twitchy. Maybe I should turn around and use some of those remaining minutes with Jaynie to talk about my phone aversion.

"Do you want the good news or not?"

I roll my eyes since he can't see it and hold it against me. "Go ahead, Nicky."

"I just saw Pete from Clearwater PD, and he got approval for you to shadow their detectives. Six weeks' worth, if you're still interested."

"Yes. Oh my gosh. That's awesome."

Big Al had suggested that more exposure to real-life criminal investigations might increase my confidence.

Nick's been incredibly supportive of me consulting for Redleg. He even said he'd understand if I needed to leave Naughty Dogs altogether to pursue profiling full-time. He just wants me happy.

But working with my brother *does* make me happy. I like how things are, splitting my time between Redleg and Naughty Dogs. And now that school is over, I'll have more time for Leo and my art, which has taken a back seat to all the schoolwork.

I honestly couldn't ask for anything else in life.

Except Leo has mentioned getting me a shiny ring a few times, so I'm starting to look forward to that. He also suggested looking for bigger houses with more rooms, just in case we want to have kids one day.

At first, the idea was horrendous. Me as a mom? That sounds like a terrible idea.

But after some time marinating on it, I've warmed to the idea. Leo would make the most loving, caring father any child could ask for. And I know with him beside me, I'm strong enough to weather any storm.

After thanking Nick profusely for talking to Pete on my behalf, I end the call. As I exit the medical office building, I bump into Sammy in the parking lot.

"Hey, Sue. Did you just leave therapy?" Her eyes are swollen and red-rimmed.

"Yes. Are you on your way in?"

She nods in response and tries to walk around me. But I stop her with a hand on her forearm. "Are you okay?

"I'm not sure. I mean, yes, I'm okay. But it's just one of those days. You know?"

"I've had plenty of those days. At least you're going to the right place. I'm glad you took my advice about seeing Jaynie. She's been a lifesaver for me."

"She's very kind. Thanks again for the recommendation."

Her chin quivers, and tears fill her eyes. She's obviously struggling to keep her composure.

Sammy's always been an affectionate person. As much as I hate to offer... here goes.

Try not to cringe. Try not to cringe.

"Would you like a hug?"

Without answering, she throws herself around me. Forcing myself not to count the seconds, I whisper soothing words like Leo does for me when I'm upset.

"Hey, you're going to be fine, Sammy. It's okay. You're safe now. He can't hurt you."

Her tears dampen my shoulder.

When she pulls back, a sad smile mars her pretty face, and her eyes are downcast.

Out of instinct, my eyes shoot to the ground too.

And now we're just standing here at the edge of the parking lot, staring at the ground.

Awkward. Party of two. Your table is ready.

She heaves a deep breath and catches my eyes. "Well, I guess I'll see you tonight."

My head cricks to the side. "I'm seeing you tonight?"

Her face blanches, and her eyes widen. Sucking in her lips, she looks from left to right.

"Uhh. Never mind. I was confused. Anyway, gotta run. Bye, Sue."

She scurries around me, and I stand flat-footed, wondering what the hell that was all about.

I know peculiar behavior. I've written the book on it. And that was essentially a *Sue O'Malley level of awkward* right there.

Shrugging it off, I head to my car and drive home.

Twenty minutes later, I walk through the door to Leo's house.

Well, it's my house too. I don't own it, but I do live here. It *feels* like home. If I'm being honest, it feels more like my home than any other house I've ever lived in except my parents' home. Maybe even that one too.

But it's not the walls, roof, or tile flooring.

It's the man who lives here with me.

Wherever he is... that's my home.

He arrives home twenty-six minutes after me. That's a great number since it's the age I was when I realized I was in love with him.

After setting down his motorcycle helmet, he marches right over to me in the kitchen.

"Hi, angel. How was your day?"

"Great. Dinner is almost ready. How was your day?"

Wrapping his arms around my midsection, he lifts me off the ground and peppers kisses along my neck, cheek, and side of my mouth. I hold on to his shoulders and laugh at his overzealous greeting.

"It's much better now that I'm home with you," he mutters into my neck, then inhales deeply. His beard tickles my skin, making me giggle even more.

Twenty-eight years old, and I'm giddy like a teenager at this behemoth of a man.

When he's done kissing the daylights out of me, he sets me down on unsteady feet. We stare at each other like lovesick fools, just happy to be in each other's presence.

Like me, he's come so far these last few years. Getting Sammy back wasn't all sunshine and roses, and they had a lot to work through to get back to a loving relationship. His brother Andrew was a whole other story, but thankfully, the Mason family is whole again.

"Therapy go okay?" he asks while straightening my hair that he mussed with his antics.

"Yes. And Jaynie gave me the most beautiful card and free coffee money as a graduation present." I shimmy my shoulders, and the movement causes my breasts to rub against his chest.

Growling, he turns off the stove's burners and scoops me back up. "Dinner can wait. I need to be inside you."

He whisks me down the hall to the bedroom and tosses me on the bed like I weigh nothing.

"Get naked," he orders as he frantically unbuttons his shirt, removes his gun, and sets it on the dresser, then goes to work on his pants.

"What if I don't want to get naked?"

He pauses with his pants at his knees and searches my face. I can't keep a serious facade for more than two seconds, and he pounces on me the moment I release a snicker.

"Just kidding. Of course I want to get naked with you," I bark out through deep guffaws due to his relentless tickling.

A playful Leo is a beautiful thing.

We're both joyously naked a few moments later, and he's easing between my spread thighs. As he makes his way up my body, he pauses to place kisses along the pink lines across my stomach, then inches upward. He takes one of my breasts in his hand and draws the nipple into his mouth, laving it with the flat of his tongue. It sends a jolt of electricity straight to my core, making my clit ache with need.

My head lolls back in ecstasy as he mercilessly teases and sucks at my breasts.

I nibble so hard on my lower lip that I feel a twinge of pain. I'm desperate to get him inside me. Without him filling me, I'm empty and needy.

After running my fingers through his hair, I give his head a slight tug to get him on top of me.

"Leo," I beg. "I need you."

Removing his lips from my breast, he meets my eyes through his lidded gaze. "I'm right here, angel."

"Yeah, but I want your cock. Inside me. Now."

His mouth quirks into a devious grin, then he crawls farther up my body. As he takes my mouth in a searing kiss, I feel his cock's thick head prodding and poking through my soaking wet folds, brushing up against my clit with each forward thrust. The slip and slide of his shaft against my core are almost as heavenly as when he fills me. But I want more.

I *need* all of him to connect with me. It's the only way he ever feels close enough.

Tilting my hips upward, I'm able to get him lined up with my pussy's weeping entrance.

"That's it, angel. Tell me what you want," he says between positively sinful kisses.

With my legs spread wide, I bend my knee and use my heel to shove his ass forward, and he impales me with his delicious cock in one hard thrust.

"Uh," I gasp in ecstasy. "Oh, damn, Leo. You feel so fecking good."

He moans his approval.

Our mouths join as he unleashes his desire on me. Each time he withdraws, he pulls almost entirely out and pauses before ramming into me again, prolonging the delicious feel of our initial joining. His moves are slow and deliberate as he grinds against my clit with his pelvis, driving me toward my climax while chasing his own pleasure.

"I love you so damn much," he grunts between hard but leisurely thrusts.

Our hands roam, tongues entangle, and bodies move in unison.

We've fucked plenty of times before. But this is profound, sensual lovemaking. So much kissing and touching, and his thrusts are long, deep, and carnal.

It's almost too much.

When I open my eyes, I find his locked on mine. I can't hold back a whimper from the overwhelming emotion his expression brings me. My chest swells with love, and I feel my chin wobble.

His movements slow and grow gentler when my vision goes blurry with unshed tears.

"What's wrong, angel?" he asks before wiping the tears as they escape.

"I love you so damn much. I'm so happy." I cough a little on the emotion clogging my throat. "I never thought I'd find someone like you. I thought I'd be alone forever. But you're here, and you're so amazing. I love you more than anything. But it's too much for me to handle sometimes. Too many feelings."

The words falling from my mouth make me cringe a little because they seem simplistic. As much as I'd love to articulate my love for him, words will never do it justice.

Stilling inside me, he brushes my hair out of my face and kisses away my tears. With a thickness in his voice, he tells me, "Angel, I feel the same damn way. I'm never letting you go. I feel like the luckiest man in the world to get to call you mine. I love you."

He kisses me again, and this time, I taste my salty tears. When I pulse my pussy walls around him, he hisses and languidly drives in and out of me.

Our bodies grow slick with perspiration as our lovemaking grows faster and more desperate. With our hot breaths mingling and the slight squeaking of the bed, everything else falls away.

It's just Leo and me.

His tempo increases, and I know he's getting close because of the way his eyes pinch at the corners and his teeth grind. Reaching between us, he flicks my clit so I can join him in euphoric ecstasy.

As his cock thickens and swells with his pending release, he brings me over the edge with him.

Lights flash behind my eyes, and my body stiffens as my orgasm overtakes me. Leo bucks into me a few more times as jets of his liquid warmth fill me, and we ride out our climaxes together.

When he finally slows to a stop, he kisses me once more, then hits me with those captivating blue eyes, making my heart squeeze with love.

"Marry me," he says.

I feel my eyebrows shoot upward, but a grin also spreads across my face.

He squints and shakes his head slowly. "I'm sorry. I didn't mean to do it like this. I had this whole evening planned. We were going to ride my bike down by the beach for a short drive to relax you, and then we'd head back here. I asked Sammy to set up a surprise picnic on the back porch while we were driving. And then I was going to look deeply into your eyes, grab your hand, and get down on one knee. I was going to promise to be the kind of man who'll make you proud to be my wife and ask you to be mine forever."

My eyes refill with tears as I nod frantically.

"That's a yes? Are you saying yes?" he asks.

"If you're asking me to marry you, the answer is yes. I don't need a big, fancy proposal. As wonderful as it sounds, I like this one better. You don't need to plan anything special to make me say yes to you. I want to marry you, Leo Mason. I want it with my whole heart."

"I love you, angel. I'm going to work hard every day to be the husband you deserve."

Raising off the pillow, I press my lips to his.

"Aww, babe. Me too."

My eyes spring wide, and my cheeks warm when I realize what I implied. "No, wait. I didn't mean it like that. I'm not going to be the husband. You'll be the husband. I'll be the *wife* you deserve. I'm going to... you know what? Forget it. I love you, and we're getting married. The end."

After we're done laughing at my awkwardness, he kisses me and whispers, "Oh no, angel. This isn't the end. It's only the beginning."

Thanks for reading Sue and Leo's story.

Continue the Redleg Security with "Forbidden Hero" now on Amazon.

Want a bonus scene to see how what happens when Sue meets Leo's brother Drew and his kids for the first time? Scan this code with your phone for access.

From the Author

Dear Reader,

I'd like to talk to you about Sue's character to explain how and why I wrote her the way that I did.

First, I hope you love her as much as I do. She's so special to me.

Autism Spectrum Disorder (ASD) is a very complex and broad disorder. That's why they call it a *spectrum*. No two people with autism will present the same. What is true for one person on the spectrum might be completely at odds with someone else on the spectrum. This makes writing a character with autism (as well as ADHD, anxiety, and depression) a unique challenge.

Over the years, as a mom to a child on the spectrum, I've done extensive research and talked to many professionals, as well as adults and children with ASD in an attempt to help my son live the best life possible. During these conversations, I've learned so much and am still learning every day. I'll never know everything about this disorder, and I don't claim to be an expert on the subject. In addition, ASD research is constantly evolving. For example, they used to have a separate diagnosis for those with high-functioning autism that was formerly called Asperger's Syndrome. That term is no longer used, and even in the last few years, they are getting away from labeling people as high or low functioning autism. For this reason, I chose not to give too many details about Sue's particular "level" on the spectrum.

As an author, I aim to make stories as enjoyable as possible for my readers. It's also a goal to keep things as real and relatable as possible for a wide variety of readers who come from many walks of life. With that in mind, I acknowledge some of Sue's behaviors, thoughts, or mannerisms might not ring true with what you know about autism. Some of that is intentional for storytelling and character relatability purposes. Some of it is because of my own personal experiences and research might differ with your own. I hope that when you were reading, you took it with a grain of salt and simply enjoyed the story.

I did my best to represent Sue's character in a positive light, while still showing some of the struggles faced by adult females on the spectrum. Females on the spectrum, in particular, are often extraordinarily skilled at masking their behaviors. This does — as in Sue's case — lead to misdiagnosis or delayed diagnosis. Females also present differently than males on the spectrum. Much work is still needed to help all people with ASD and their families get early diagnosis and better access to research-based services.

If you'd like to learn more about autism, I encourage you to explore the wealth of resources on the web including some of the following:

- National Institute of Neurological Disorders and Stroke (NIH)

- Autism Speaks

- The Autism Society of America (and local chapters)

With love,

Jackie

Acknowledgements

Thanks for reading Sue and Leo's love story. When did you figure out who the bad guy was? Did I stump you?

Late last year, when I finished writing my debut series, it felt like I'd been hit by a margarita truck. I was exhausted, had trouble focusing, and felt a sense of loss each day that I couldn't quite pinpoint. After a while, I realized I was grieving the loss of my first book family: the Amos siblings. After writing five full length books featuring the Amos-holes over the course of a single year, it was a shock to my system to not "be with them" in my mind each day. They were a huge part of my world for more than 365 days. And then they were just gone.

Poof!

Now what? Start the spinoff series, of course.

With the grief of losing the Amos-holes so prominent (and unexpected) in my psyche, the process for writing *Heartbreak Hero* started out slow. But then once it got going... bam! It was like I awoke from a coma. Trees were greener, birds sang louder, and everything was clearer.

And then I fell hopelessly in love with Sue and Leo.

As you probably saw in my *Dear Reader note* on the prior page, my son has autism. It's a condition I've had lots of exposure to and know the struggles *and joys* all too well. When the character of Sue O'Malley came to mind as a side character in my last Amos-holes' book, I had an inkling that she'd make a great neurodivergent heroine *one day*. I didn't realize it would be so soon. When she and Leo met toward the end of Nick and Millie's book, I saw fireworks, and I couldn't wait to bring their story to the world.

One of the best parts of this story was that I got to throw in some Millie and Nick cameos, and even threw in a glimpse of Cara Amos-Hale and baby Jace, as well as Archer Bliss and his big ass truck! Did you catch those Easter eggs? I have more eggs to hide in future Redleg and O'Malley books in the future. I can't wait!

Sue is a complex character, much like my son in so many ways. I'm sure Sue's family worried that she'd never find someone who could tolerate her eccentricities and quirks. They probably wondered if she'd be alone forever. Like many other parents to ASD kiddos, I have those same worries about my son. So I wrote this book as a way to process some of my feelings on what I want for my son's future. I hope with all my heart and soul that he finds a gentle, patient, kind partner to care for him and love him the way that Leo loves Sue. In a way, this book is my wish for my son, Casey (minus the death threats and bad guy chasing him, of course).

I'm so glad I didn't let the grief over my first series swallow me whole. Because I am so in love with the guards of Redleg and the O'Malley siblings. There is so much more to come! I'm planning on pressing on with more Redleg Security stories that have a similar suspense/romcom vibe as this book right away, and then I'll pivot to an O'Malley traditional romcom series next. I already have tons of ideas for the next two stories, and I can't wait to begin. I hope you join me on that journey.

Be sure to subscribe to my newsletter and follow me on social media and/or join the Jackie's Junkies FB group so you don't miss out on future book news.

A special thanks goes out to my editor, Mindy, (and all around best bitch) for tirelessly working through her vacation to ensure we met our deadlines. We did it, Thundercunt! Another shout-out to the amazing proofreading queen, Beth, for such a speedy turnaround. In addition, Megan, Annette, Debbie, and Kelsey all stepped up in different ways to give me a hand when needed — like the amazing unicorns they are. My cover designer, Kim, is an priceless gem, and if she ever decides to stop doing covers, I can't be held responsible for my actions. I deeply appreciate my beta and ARC reader teams, as well as my VIP reader group: Jackie's Junkies. You all bring me so much love and support all year round, and I adore you! THANK YOU for being part of my story.

One more special shout-out goes to Mike, Joey, and Jhean for representing the menfolk in Jackie's Junkies. You guys are rock stars, and I love you madly!

Love,

Jackie

ALSO BY JACKIE WALKER

Redleg Security Series:

- **Heartbreak Hero** – Age gap, second chance, forced proximity with a neurodivergent/plus-size heroine and the gentle giant protector who loves her.
- **Forbidden Hero** – A brother's best friend, secret relationship romance with action, adventure, healing, heart, and so much spice.
- **Comeback Hero** – A coworkers, forced proximity romance with a ton of spice and a soft-dom who will have you swooning and sweating.
- **Rival Hero** – A one night stand turned office rivals to lovers with a former CIA intel specialist and a cinnamon roll Dom.
- **Unexpected Hero, & Bossy Hero** – coming soon!

Curious to learn more about Millie and Nick? Their story (Love & Other Accidents) is the last book in my debut series of steamy romantic comedies called: **Love and Laughs.** The books in the series follow the Amos siblings, aka: the Amos-holes. Each book features its own couple and HEA. They are all stand-alone novels.

If you prefer to read in order, here you go!

- **Love & Other Chaos** – Sarcastic hotmess Cara Amos falls for her autistic son's favorite teacher, Brody "Mr. Hottie" Hale, in my debut novel.

- **Love & Other Mistakes** - Opposites attract in this one-night stand, accidental pregnancy love story featuring laid-back surfer, Hudson, who wants nothing more than to crack the outer shell of this uptight redhead, Chloe, who wants nothing to do with him.

- **Love & Other Lies** - A fake-marriage unexpectedly turns into a fake-honeymoon across Europe, throwing Cort and Amber together in this steamy love story.

- **Love & Other Trouble** - A growly single-dad named Archer Bliss meets a ray of sunshine, CJ Amos, and the unlikely pair team up to take down their cheating exes after a steamy rage kiss and lo mein is sent flying.

- **Love & Other Accidents** - Feisty and sarcastic Millie Amos smashes (literally) into a sexy dog trainer when her pup is up to no good. But she's got trouble following her, and now is not the time for romantic entanglements. Especially with someone who gets under her skin like Nick O'Malley does.

ABOUT THE AUTHOR

Jackie is a new face on the romance scene destined to shake things up with her signature blend of light-hearted comedy, over-the-top characters and romantic heartwarming moments. A voracious romance reader herself, Jackie writes stories featuring the four Ss: Snark, Swoons, Steam and Sarcasm. Her heroines are badass, and her heroes are easy on the eyes and heavy on the charm.

When she is not writing funny stories about swoony heroes and the women who get to play with them, she is reading all types of romance novels or taking care of her army of cats and her teenage son (who also speaks fluent sarcasm).

Connect with Jackie

Website & Newsletter Sign-up: www.authorjackiewalker.com

Facebook Reader Group: Jackie's Junkies

Facebook: @AuthorJackieWalker

Instagram: @AuthorJackieWalker

Goodreads: JackieWalker

TikTok: @AuthorJackieWalker

Made in the USA
Las Vegas, NV
14 September 2024

95299418R00204